Praise for George P. Pelecanos's

HELL TO PAY

"Pelecanos is 'the Seurat of Washington, D.C.,' because like the great pointillist painter he piles on tiny details of ordinary working lives until they glow with an inner light. . . . But all around these commonplace details — and largely because of them — shines that unmistakable light of true art." — Dick Adler, *Chicago Tribune*

"It's high time that cult favorite George P. Pelecanos received the popular acclaim he so richly deserves. . . . The characters in *Hell to Pay* are exquisitely drawn, the storyline fast-paced and compelling, the action brutal and immediate. But the heart of any Pelecanos book is in the details: the appreciation of Washington, D.C., neighborhoods and culture, the music, the slang, the street life, the cars, the urban vibe." — Bruce Tierney, *BookPage*

"Sure enough, there's hell to pay, and as in Pelecanos's previous outings, the fast-moving, mournful tale is full of action, tough talk, and hard men. The story itself is about consequences, however, and with Pelecanos's deft touch for music, it resonates like a soul medley — full of love, loss, heartache, and somewhere, in a lost time, 'that blue sky stuff.'" — Jesse Sublett, *Austin Chronicle*

"*Hell to Pay* is a thoughtful crime novel, with heroes more human than heroic. They are trying to do what they can to make it through each day while making their world just a little bit better. But while their best, taken alone, is not enough to miraculously fix their world, they are able to hold a candle or two against the darkness. Part of the beauty of Pelecanos's work is that he, too, is doing his best to hold up a candle, honor those who are bringing light, and inspire others to take on a part." — Robin Vidimos, *Denver Post*

"What sets Pelecanos apart from much of the crime mainstream today is an uncommon decency. These are flesh-and-blood characters who love, hope, worry, and give a damn, not just about the arc of their lives, but about the life of their community, and, yes, even the bad guys." — Jay MacDonald, *Fort Myers News-Press*

"A superb piece of crime fiction."
— Oline H. Cogdill, *Newark Star-Ledger*

"It's all wrapped in such rich detail, so carefully laid out and so full of multidimensional characters that readers who don't require a lot of bloodletting will have trouble putting it down. And more trouble not shoving it in friends' faces and telling them 'You gotta read this.'" — Jim Knippenberg, *Cincinnati Enquirer*

"Pelecanos has a knack for drawing detailed characters. Even the minor walk-ons are memorable, but the most intriguing of them is the setting: non-tourist Washington, D.C. Predominantly black, poor, and violent, it's a rough place in which Pelecanos's people struggle to do the right thing — or give in to the bad. Put Pelecanos in the same group as Michael Connelly, James Hall, and Dennis Lehane and call them the best thriller writers at work today." — *Rocky Mountain News*

"Once readers find their way to George P. Pelecanos, they'll want to read every book he's written, and then they'll want him to pick up the pace and give us more."
— John B. Clutterbuck, *Houston Chronicle*

"Themes like human frailty and honor — plus good old-fashioned action — are more crucial to Pelecanos's storytelling here, and he handles them with an elegance rare to the genre."
— Paul Fontana, *Seattle Weekly*

"At once more powerful and more agile than its predecessor. . . . The prose is telegraphic: a scaffolding of nouns and verbs, a few load-bearing adverbs, and a near-absence of adjectival frippery. Within three sentences, we have the car, the gun, and the cigar wrapper used for rolling paper: the paragraph has the feel of a police report. And though it's the kind of mentholated prose you might expect to wear out its welcome, it holds up well over the course of the story."   — Ben Greenman, *The New Yorker*

"Pelecanos has pared down his narrative style to such a clean, hard edge that you're afraid it might cut you if you get too close."
                                                    — Gene Seymour, *Newsday*

"In a book that is devoid of gratuitous violence, Mr. Pelecanos is tough and savvy enough to make sure that justice is done. . . . Without sounding preachy, he manages to pack a lot of moral accountability into a suspenseful, unusually cinematic thriller."
                                                    — Janet Maslin, *New York Times*

"He's right in there with the best of them, a kind of fiction-writing Hunter Thompson, unafraid, spirited, and profoundly entertaining."   — Craig Nova, *Washington Post Book World*

"With its breakneck speed, simmering tensions, and flawed but charming protagonists, *Hell To Pay* shows Pelecanos at the top of his craft, and will leave readers begging for the next hardboiled episode of this thrilling series."
                                                    — Mark Luce, *San Francisco Chronicle*

HELL TO PAY

A Novel

GEORGE P. PELECANOS

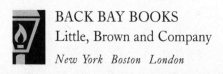

BACK BAY BOOKS
Little, Brown and Company
New York Boston London

Copyright © 2002 by George P. Pelecanos
Reading group guide copyright © 2011 by George P. Pelecanos and Little, Brown and Company
Excerpt from *Soul Circus* copyright © 2003 by George P. Pelecanos

Back Bay Books / Little, Brown and Company
Hachette Book Group
237 Park Avenue, New York, NY 10017
littlebrown.com

Originally published in hardcover by Little, Brown and Company, February 2002
First Back Bay paperback edition, February 2011

Back Bay Books is an imprint of Little, Brown and Company. The Back Bay Books name and logo are trademarks of Hachette Book Group, Inc.

The publisher is not responsible for websites (or their content) that are not owned by the publisher.

Library of Congress Cataloging-in-Publication Data
Pelecanos, George P.
    Hell to pay : a novel / by George P. Pelecanos. — 1st ed.
        p. cm.
    ISBN 978-0-316-69506-0 (hc) / 978-0-316-09935-6 (pb)
        1. Private investigators — Washington (D.C.) — Fiction. 2. Teenage prostitution — Fiction.
    3. Runaway teenagers — Fiction. 4. Washington (D.C.) — Fiction. I. Title.
PS3566.E354 H45 2002
813'.54 — dc21   2001038111

10 9 8 7 6 5 4 3 2

RRD-C

Book design by Bernard Klein
Printed in the United States of America

To Dennis K. Ashton Jr., seven years old,
shot to death on June 27, 1997,
by a criminal with a handgun in Washington, D.C.

"Don't Look down
On a man . . .
Unless you gonna
Pick him up."

*Written on a mural outside Taylor's Funeral Home, on the corner of
Randolph Place and North Capitol Street, NW, Washington, D.C.*

HELL
TO
PAY

1

GARFIELD Potter sat low behind the wheel of an idling Caprice, his thumb stroking the rubber grip of the Colt revolver loosely fitted between his legs. On the bench beside him, leaning against the passenger window, sat Carlton Little. Little filled an empty White Owl wrapper with marijuana and tamped the herb with his thumb. Potter and Little were waiting on Charles White, who was in the backyard of his grandmother's place, getting his dog out of a cage.

"It don't look like much, does it?" said Potter, looking down at his own lap.

Little grinned lazily. "That's what the girls must say when you pull that thing out."

"Like Brianna, you mean? *Your* girl? She ain't *had* no chance to look at it, 'cause I was waxin' her from behind. She *felt* it, though. Made her forget all about you, too. I mean, when I was done hittin' it she couldn't even remember your name."

"She couldn't remember hers either, drunk as she had to be to fuck a sad motherfucker like you." Little laughed some as he struck a match and held it to the end of the cigar.

"I'm talkin' about this gun, fool." Potter held up the Colt so Little, firing up the blunt, could see it.

"Yeah, okay. Where'd you get it at, man?"

"Traded it to this boy for half an OZ. Was one of those project guns, hadn't even been fired but once or twice. Short barrel, only two inches long, you'd think it couldn't do shit. But this here is a three fifty-seven. They call it a carry revolver, 'cause you can carry this shit without no one knowin' you strapped. I don't need no long barrel, anyway. I like to work close in."

"I'll stick with my nine. You don't even know if that shits works."

"It works. Yours jams, don't be askin' me for mines."

Potter was tall, light skinned, flat of stomach and chest, with thin, ropy forearms and biceps. He kept his hair shaved close to the scalp, with a small slash mark by way of a part. His irises were dark brown and filled his eyes; his nose was a white boy's nose, thin and aquiline. He was quick to smile. It was a smile that could be engaging when he wanted it to be, but more often than not it inspired fear.

Little was not so tall. He was bulked in the shoulders and arms, but twiggish in the legs. A set of weights had given him the show muscles upstairs, but his legs, which he never worked on, betrayed the skinny, malnourished boy he used to be. He wore his hair braided in cornrows and kept a careless, weedy thatch of hair on his chin.

Both wore carpenter jeans and button-down, short-sleeve plaid Nautica shirts over wife-beater Ts. Potter's shoes were whatever was newest in the window of the Foot Locker up at City Place; he had a pair of blue-and-black Air Maxes on now. On Little's feet were wheat-colored Timberland work boots, loosely laced and untied.

Little held a long draw in his lungs and looked ahead, exhaling a cloud of smoke that crashed at the windshield. "Here comes Coon. Lookit how he's all chest out and shit. Proud about that dog."

Charles White was walking his pit bull, Trooper, past a dying oak tree, its leaves nearly stripped bare. A tire hung on a chain from one of the branches. When he was a puppy, Trooper had swung on the tire for hours, holding it fast, strengthening his jaws.

"That ain't no game dog," said Potter. "Coon ain't no dog man, neither."

White had Trooper, brown with a white mask and golden-pink eyes, on a short leash attached to a heavy-ringed, wide leather collar. Trooper's ears were game-cropped at the skull. White, of average size and dressed similarly to his friends, moved toward the car, opened the back door, and let the dog in before getting inside himself.

"S'up, fellas," said White.

"Coon," said Little, looking over the bench at his friend. Others thought White's street name had something to do with his color, dark as he was. But Little knew where the name had come from. He'd been knowing Coon since they were both kids in the Section Eights, back in the early nineties, when White used to wear a coonskin hat, trying to look like that fool rapper from Digital Underground, that group that was popular then. There was the other thing, too: White had a nose on him, big and long like some cartoon animal. And he walked kind of pitched forward, with his bony fingers spread kind of like claws, the way a critter in the woods would do.

"Gimme some of that hydro, Dirty."

Dirty was Little's street name, so given because of his fondness for discussing women's privates. Men's, too. Also, he loved to eat all that greasy fast food. Little passed the blunt back to White. White hit it deep.

"Your champion ready?" said Potter.

"What?" said White.

It was hard to hear in the car. Potter had the music, the new DMX joint on PGC, turned up loud.

"I said, is that dumb animal gonna win us some *money* today?" said Potter, raising his voice.

White didn't answer right away. He held the smoke down in his lungs and let it out slow.

"He gonna win us *mad* money, D," said White. He reached over and massaged the dense muscles bunched around Trooper's jaw. Trooper's mouth opened in pleasure and his eyes shifted over to his master's. "Right, boy?"

"Sure he's strong enough?"

"Shoot, he was strong enough to drag a log down the block yesterday mornin'."

"I ain't ask you can he do circus tricks. Can he hold his shit in a fight?"

"He will."

"Well, he ain't showed me nothin' yet."

"What about that snatch we did with that boy's dog over on Crittenden?"

Potter looked in the rearview at White. "That dog at Crittenden wasn't nothin' but a cur. Trooper a cur, too."

"The hell he is. You're gonna see today."

"We *better* see. 'Cause I ain't wastin' my time or my green paper on no pussy-ass animal." Potter slid the Colt under the waistband of his jeans.

"I said, you're gonna see."

"C'mon, D," said Little. "Let's get a roll on, man."

Garfield Potter's street name was Death. He didn't care for it much since this girl he wanted to fuck told him it scared her some. Never did get that girl's drawers down, either. So he felt the name was bad luck, worse still to go and change it. His friends now called him D.

Potter turned the key in the ignition. It made an awful grinding sound. Little clapped his hands together and doubled over with laughter.

"Ho, shit!" said Little, clapping his hands one more time. "Car's already started, man, you don't need to be startin' it *again!* Maybe if you turned that music down some you'd know."

"Noisy as this whip is, too," said White.

"Fuck you, Coon," said Potter, "talkin' mad shit about this car, when you're cruisin' around town in that piece-of-shit Toyota, lookin' like a Spanish Cadillac and shit."

"All this money we got," said Little, "and we're drivin' around in a hooptie."

"We'll be gettin' rid of it soon," said Potter. "And anyway, it ain't all that funny as y'all are makin' it out to be."

"Yeah, you right. It just hit me funny, is all." Little took the blunt that White handed to him over the front seat and stared at it stupidly. "I ain't lyin', boy, this chronic right here just laid my ass out."

❐

THE dogfights were held in a large garage backing to an alley behind a house on Ogelthorpe, in Manor Park in Northwest. The fights went down once a week for several hours during the day, when most of the neighbors were off at work. Those neighbors who were at home were afraid of the young men who came to the fights, and did not complain to the police.

Potter parked the Chevy in the alley. He and the others got out of the car, White heeling Trooper to his side. They went down the alley, nodding but not smiling at some young men they knew to be members of the Delafield Mob. Others were standing around, holding their animals, getting high, and drinking from the lips of bottles peeking through the tops of brown paper bags. Little and Wright followed Potter into the garage.

Ten to twenty young men were scattered about the perimeter of the garage. A group was shooting craps in the corner. Others were passing around joints. Someone had put on *Dr. Dre 2001*, with Snoop, Eminem, and all them, and it was coming loud from a box.

In the middle of the garage was a fighting area of industrial carpet, penned off from the rest of the interior by a low chain-link fence, gated in two corners. Inside one corner of the pen, a man held a link leash taut on a black pit bull spotted brown over its belly and chest. The dog's name was Diesel. Its ears were gnarled and its neck showed raised scars like pink worms.

Potter studied a man, old for this group, maybe thirty or so, who stood alone in a corner, putting fire to a cigarette.

"I'll be back in a few," said Potter to Little.

" 'Bout ready to show the dogs," said Little.

"Got a mind to put money on that black dog. But go ahead and bet Trooper, hear?"

"Three hunrid?"

"Three's good."

Potter made his way over to the cigarette smoker, short and dumpy, a raggedy-ass dude on the way down, and stood before him.

"*I* know you."

The smoker looked up with lazy eyes, trying to hold on to his shit. "Yeah?"

"You run with Lorenze Wilder, right?"

"I seen him around. Don't mean we run together or nothin' like that." But now the smoker recognized Potter and he lost his will to keep his pride. His eyes dropped to the concrete floor.

"Outside," said Potter.

The older man followed Potter into the daylight, not too fast but without protest. Potter led him around the garage's outer wall, which faced the neighboring yards to the west.

"What's your name?"

"Edward Diggs."

"Call you Digger Dog, right?"

"Some do."

"Lorenze called you that when we sold him that hydro a few weeks back. You were standing right next to him. Remember me now?"

Diggs said nothing, and Potter moved forward so that he was looking down on Diggs and just a few inches from his face. Diggs's back touched the garage wall.

"So where your boy Lorenze at?"

"I don't know. He stays in his mother's old house —"

"Over off North Dakota. I know where that is, and he ain't been there awhile. Leastways, I ain't caught him in. He got a woman he cribs with on the side?"

Diggs avoided Potter's stare. "Not that I know."

"What about other kin?"

Diggs took a long final drag off his cigarette and dropped it to the ground, crushing it beneath his sneaker. He looked to his right, out in the alley, but there was no one there. Everyone had gone inside the garage. Potter spread one tail on his shirt and draped it back behind the butt of the Colt, so that Diggs could see.

Diggs shifted his eyes again and lowered his voice. He had to give this boy something, just so he'd go away. "Lorenze got a sister. She be livin' down in Park Morton with her little boy."

"Maybe I'll drop by. What's her name?"

"I wouldn't . . . What I'm sayin' is, you want my advice —"

Potter open-handed Diggs across the face. He used his left hand to bunch Diggs's shirt at the collar, then yanked Diggs forward and slapped him again.

Diggs said nothing, his body limp. Potter held him fast.

"What's the sister's name?"

Diggs's eyes had teared up. He hated himself for that. All

he meant to do was advise this boy, tell him, don't fuck with Lorenze's sister or her kid. But it was too late for all that now.

"I don't know her name," said Diggs. "And anyway, Lorenze, he don't never go by the way or nothin'. He don't talk to his sister much, way I understand it. Sometimes he watches her kid play football; boy's on this tackle team. But that's as close as he gets to her."

"Where the kid play at?"

"Lorenze said the kid practices in the evenings at some high school."

"Which school?"

"He live in Park Morton, so it must be Roosevelt. It ain't but a few blocks up the street there —"

"I ain't asked you for directions, did I? I *live* up on Warder Street my own self, so you don't need to be drawin' me a map."

"It ain't too far from there, is all I was sayin'."

Potter's eyes softened. He smiled and released his grip on Diggs. "I didn't hurt you none, did I? 'Cause, look, I didn't *mean* nothin', hear?"

Diggs straightened his collar. "I'm all right."

"Let me get one of those cigarettes from you, black."

Diggs reached into his breast pocket and retrieved his pack of Kools. A cigarette slid out into his palm. He handed the cigarette to Potter.

Potter snapped the cigarette in half and bounced the halves off Diggs's chest. Potter's laugh was like a bark. He turned and walked away.

Diggs straightened his shirt and stepped quickly down the alley. He looked over his shoulder and saw that Potter had turned the corner. Diggs reached into his pocket and shook another cigarette out from a hole he had torn in the bottom of the pack.

Diggs's boy Lorenze was staying with this girl he knew over in Northeast. Lorenze had kind of laughed it off, said he'd crib with that girl until Potter forgot about the debt. Didn't look to Diggs that Potter was the type to forget. But he was proud he hadn't given Lorenze up. Most folks he knew didn't credit him for being so strong.

Diggs struck a match. He noticed that his hand was shaking some as he fired up his cigarette.

❐

BACK in the garage, Potter sidled up next to Little. The owner of the garage, also the house bookie, stood nearby, holding the cash and taking late bets.

In one corner of the pen, Charles White finished sponging Trooper down with warm, soapy water. Diesel's owner, in the opposite corner, did the same. Many dogs were treated with chemicals that could disorient the opponent. The rule in this arena was that both dogs had to be washed prior to a fight.

White scratched the top of Trooper's head, bent in, and uttered random words into his ear with a soothing tone. The referee, an obese young man, stepped into the ring after a nod from the owner of the garage.

"Both corners ready?" said the referee. "Cornermen out of the pit."

White moved behind his dog into the space of the open gate, still holding Trooper back.

"Face your dogs," said the referee. They did this, and quickly the referee said, "Let go!"

The dogs shot into the center of the pit. Both of them got up on their hind legs, attacking the head of the other with their jaws. They snapped at each other's ears and sought purchase in the area of the neck. In the fury of their battle, the dogs did not make a sound. The garage echoed with the shouts and laughter of the spectators crowding the ring.

For a moment the dogs seemed to reach a stalemate. Suddenly

their motions accelerated. Their bodies meshed in a blur of brown and black, and the bright pink of exposed gums. Droplets of blood arced up in the center of the ring.

Diesel got a neck-hold and Trooper was taken down. Trooper, adrenalized, his eyes bright and wild, scrambled up and out of the hold. One of his ears had been partially torn away, and blood had leaked onto the dog's white mask. Diesel went in, back to the neck. And now Trooper was down again, in the jaws of Diesel, squirming beneath the black dog.

"Stop it!" shouted White.

Potter nudged Little, who nodded by way of reply.

"That's it," said the referee, waving his arms.

White went into the ring and grabbed Trooper's hind legs, pulling back. Diesel's owner did the same. Diesel relaxed his jaws, releasing Trooper to his man. The spectators moved away from the pen, laughing, giving one another skin, already trying out stories on one another that exaggerated the details of the fight.

"You were right," said Little. "That dog was a cur."

"What I tell you?" said Potter. "Dog's personality only as strong as the man who owns it."

White arrived with Trooper, back on his leash. "I need to fix him up some," said White, not looking into his friends' eyes.

"We'll do it now," said Potter. "Let's go."

◗

A COUPLE of blocks away, near Fort Slocum Park, Potter pulled the Chevy into an alley where there seemed to be no activity. He cut the engine and looked over the backseat at White; Trooper sat panting, his hip resting against his owner's.

"Dog needs to pee," said Potter.

"He went," said White. "Let's just take him to the vet place."

"He already bleedin' all over the backseat. He pees back there, too, I ain't gonna be too happy. Gimme the leash, man, I'll walk him."

"*I'll* walk him," said White. His lip quivered when he spoke.

"Let D walk him if he wants to, Coon," said Little. "Dog needs to pee, don't make no difference who be holdin' the leash."

Potter got out of the car and went around to White's side. He opened the door and took hold of the leash. The dog looked over at White and then jumped his lap and was out of the car.

Potter walked Trooper down the alley until they were behind a high wooden privacy fence. Potter looked around briefly, saw no one in the neighboring yards or in the windows of the houses, and commanded the dog to sit.

When Trooper sat, Potter pulled the .357 Colt from his waistband, pointed it close to the dog's right eye, and squeezed the trigger. Trooper's muzzle and most of his face exploded out into the alley in a haze of bone and blood. The dog toppled over onto its side and its legs straightened in a shudder. Potter stepped back and shot the dog in the ribcage one more time. Trooper's carcass lifted an inch or two off the ground and came to rest.

Potter went back to the car and got behind the wheel. Little was holding a match to the half of the White Owl blunt he had not yet smoked.

"Gun works," said Potter.

Little nodded. "Loud, too."

Potter put the trans in gear, draped his arm over the bench seat, and turned his head to look out the rear window as he reversed the car out of the alley. White was staring out the window, his face dirty from tears he had tried to wipe away.

"Go on and get it out you," said Potter. "Someone you know see you cryin' over some dumb animal, they gonna mistake you for a bitch. And I ain't ridin' with none of that."

❐

POTTER, Little, and White bought a kilo of marijuana from their dealer in Columbia Heights, dimed out half of it back at their place, and delivered the dimes to their runners so they could get started on the evening rush. Then the three of them drove north up Georgia Avenue and over to Roosevelt High. They went into the parking lot at Iowa Avenue and parked the Chevy beside a black Cadillac Brougham. There were several other cars in the lot.

Potter looked in the rearview at White, staring ahead. "We straight, Coon?"

"Just a dumb animal, like you said. Don't mean nothin' to me."

Potter didn't like the tone in White's voice. But White was just showing a little pride. That was good, but he'd never act on his anger for real. Like his weak-ass dog, he wasn't game.

"I'll check it out," said Potter to Little.

He walked across the parking lot and stood at the fence that bordered the stadium down below. After a while he came back to the car.

"You see him?" said Little as Potter got back behind the wheel.

"Nah," said Potter. "Just some kids playin' football. Some old-time motherfuckers, coaches and shit."

"We can come back."

"We will. I'm gonna smoke that motherfucker when I see him, too."

"Wilder don't owe you but a hundred dollars, D."

"Thinks he can ignore his debt. Tryin' to take me for bad; you *know* I can't just let that go."

"Ain't like you need the money today or nothin' like that."

"It ain't the money," said Potter. "And I can wait."

2

D E R E K Strange was coming out of a massage parlor when he felt his beeper vibrate against his hip. He checked the number printed out across the horizontal screen and walked through Chinatown over to the MLK library on 9th, where a bank of pay phones was set outside the facility. Strange owned a cell, but he still used street phones whenever he could.

"Janine," said Strange.

"Derek."

"You rang?"

"Those women been calling you again. The two investigators from out in Montgomery County?"

"I called them back, didn't I?"

"You mean *I* did. They been trying to get an appointment with you for a week now."

"So they're still trying."

"They're being a little bit more aggressive than that. They're heading into town right now, want to meet you for lunch. Said they'd pick up the tab."

Strange tugged his jeans away from his crotch where they had stuck.

"It's a money job, Derek."

"Hold up, Janine." Strange put the receiver against his chest as a man who was passing by stopped to shake his hand.

"Tommy, how you been?"

"Doin' real good, Derek," said Tommy. "Say, you got any spare love you can lay on me till I see you next time?"

Strange looked at the black baggage beneath Tommy's eyes, the way his pants rode low on his bony hips. Strange had come up with Tommy's older brother, Scott, who was gone ten years now from the cancer that took his shell. Scott wouldn't want Strange to give his baby brother any money, not for what Tommy had in mind.

"Not today," said Strange.

"All right, then," said Tommy, shamed, but not enough. He slowly walked away.

Strange spoke into the receiver. "Janine, where they want to meet?"

"Frosso's."

"Call 'em up and tell 'em I'll be there. 'Bout twenty minutes."

"Am I going to see you tonight?"

"Maybe after practice."

"I marinated a chuck roast, gonna grill it on the Weber. Lionel will be at practice, won't he? You're going to drop him off at our house anyway, aren't you?"

"Yeah."

"We can talk about it when you come back by the office. You got a two o'clock with George Hastings."

"I remember. Okay, we'll talk about it then."

"I love you, Derek."

Strange lowered his voice. "I love you, too, baby."

Strange hung up the phone. He did love her. And her voice, more than her words, had brought him some guilt for what he'd just done. But there was love and sex on one side and just sex on the other. To Strange, the two were entirely different things.

❏

STRANGE drove east in his white-over-black '89 Caprice, singing along softly to "Wake Up Everybody" coming from the deck. That first verse, where Teddy's purring those call-to-arms words against the Gamble and Huff production, telling the listener to open his eyes, look around, get involved and into the uplift side of things, there wasn't a whole lot of American music more beautiful than that.

His Rand McNally street atlas lay on the seat beside him. He had a Leatherman tool-in-one looped through his belt, touching a Buck knife, sheathed and attached the same way on his right hip. His beeper he wore on his left. The rest of his equipment was in a double-locked glove box and in the trunk. It was true that most modern investigative work was done in an office and on the Internet. Strange thought of himself as having two offices, though, his base office in Petworth and the one in his car, right here. His preference was to work the street.

It was early September. The city was still hot during the day, though the nights had cooled some. It would be that way in the District for another month or so.

"'The world won't get no better,'" sang Strange, "'if we just let it be. . . .'"

Soon the colors would change in Rock Creek Park. And then would come those weeks near Thanksgiving when the weather turned for real and the leaves were still coming down off the trees. Strange had his own name for it: deep fall. It was his favorite time of year in D.C.

❐

FROSSO'S, a stand-alone structure with a green thatched roof, sat on a west-side corner of 13th and L, Northwest, like a pimple on the ass of a beautiful girl. The Mediterranean who owned the business owned the real estate and had refused to sell, even as the offers came in, even as new office buildings went in around him. Frosso's was a burger-and-lunch counter, also a happy-hour bar and hangout for those remaining workers who still drank and smoked or didn't mind the smell of smoke on their clothes. Beer gardens in this part of downtown were few and far between.

Strange made his way through a noisy dining area to a four-top back by the pay phone and head, where two women sat. He recognized the investigators, a salt-and-pepper team, from an article he'd read on them in *City Paper* a few months back. They worked cases retrieving young runaways gone to hooking. The two of them were aligned with some do-goodnik, pro-prosti organization that operated on grants inside D.C.

"Derek Strange," he said, shaking the black woman's hand and then the white woman's before he took a seat.

"I'm Karen Bagley. This is Sue Tracy."

Strange slid his business card across the table. Bagley gave him one in turn, Strange scanning it for the name of their business: Bagley and Tracy Investigative Services, and below the name, in smaller letters, "Specializing in Locating and Retrieving Minors." A plain card, without any artwork, Strange thinking, They could use a logo, give their card a signature, something to make the customers remember them by.

Bagley was medium-skinned and wide of nose. Her eyes were large and deep brown, the lashes accentuated by makeup. Freckles like coarse pepper buckshotted her face. Sue Tracy was a shag-cut blonde, green-eyed, still tanned from the last of summer, with smaller shoulders than Bagley's. They were serious-faced, handsome, youngish women, hard boned and, Strange guessed —

he couldn't see the business end of their bodies, seated at the table — strong of thigh. They looked like the ex-cops that the newspaper article had described them to be. Better looking, in fact, than most of the female officers Strange had known.

Tracy pointed a finger at the mug in front of her. Bagley's hand was wrapped around a mug as well. "You want a beer?"

"Too early for me. I'll get a burger, though. Medium, with some blue cheese crumbled on top. And a ginger ale from the bottle, not the gun."

Tracy called the waitress over, addressed her by name, got a burger working for Strange. The waitress said, "Got it, Sue," tearing the top sheet off a green-lined pad before turning back toward the lunch counter.

"You're a hard man to get ahold of," said Bagley.

"I been busy out here," said Strange.

"A big caseload, huh?"

"Always somethin'." A glass was placed before Strange. He examined a smudge on its lip. "This place clean?"

"Like a dog's tongue," said Tracy.

"Some say that about a dog's hindparts, too," said Strange. "But I wouldn't put my mouth to one."

"Maybe they ought to put that on the sign out front," said Tracy, without a trace of a smile. "Good food, and clean, too, like the asshole on a dog."

"Might bring in some new customers," said Strange. "You never know."

"They don't need any new customers," said Bagley. "The regulars float this place."

"I take it you two are numbered with the regulars."

"We used to come here plenty for information," said Tracy. "Here and the all-night CVS below Logan Circle."

"Information," said Strange. "From prostitutes, you mean."

Bagley nodded. "The girls would be in the CVS at all hours, buying stockings, tampons, you name it."

"Them and the heroin lovers," said Strange. "They do crave their chocolate in the middle of the night. I remember seein' them in there, grabbing the Hershey bars off the racks with their eyelids lowered to half-mast."

"You hung out there, too?" said Bagley.

"Back when it was People's Drug, which must be over ten years back now, huh? Used to stop in for my own essentials when everything else was closed. I was a bit of a night bird then myself."

"The demographics have shifted some the last couple of years," said Tracy. "A lot of the action's moved east, into the hotel cluster of the new downtown."

"But this here tavern was a known hangout for prostis, wasn't it?"

"More like a safe haven," said Bagley. "Nobody bothered them in here. It was a place to have a beer and a smoke. A moment of quiet."

"No more, huh?"

Bagley shrugged. "There's been an initiative to get the girls out of public establishments."

Tracy moved her mug in a small circle on the table. "The powers that be would rather have them shivering in some doorway in December than warm in a place like this."

"I guess y'all think they ought to just go ahead and legalize prostitution, right? Since it's one of those victimless crimes, I mean."

"Wrong," said Tracy. "In fact, it's the only crime I know of where the perp *is* the victim."

Strange didn't know what to say to that one, so he let it ride.

"What about you?" asked Bagley. "What do *you* think about it?"

Strange's eyes darted from Bagley's and went to nowhere past her shoulder. "I haven't thought on it all that much, tell you the truth."

Bagley and Tracy stared at Strange. Strange turned his head, looked toward the grill area. Where was that burger? All right, thought Strange, I'll have my lunch, listen to these Earnest Ernestines say their piece, and get on out of here.

"You come recommended," said Bagley, forcing Strange to return his attention to them. "A couple of the lawyers we've worked with down at Superior Court say they've used you and they've been pleased."

"Most likely they used my operative, Ron Lattimer. He's been doing casework for the CJA attorneys. Ron's a smart young man, but let's just say he doesn't like to break too much of a sweat. So he likes those jobs, 'cause when you're working with the courts you automatically got that federal power of subpoena. You can subpoena the phone company, the housing authority, anything. It makes your job a whole lot easier."

"You've done some of that," said Bagley.

"Sure, but I prefer working in the fresh air to working behind a computer, understand what I'm saying? I just like to be out there. And my business is a neighborhood business. Over twenty-five years now in the same spot. So it's good for me to have a presence out there, the way —"

"Cops do," said Tracy.

"Yeah. I'm an ex-cop, like you two. Been thirty-some-odd years since I wore the uniform, though."

"No such thing as an ex-cop," said Bagley.

"Like there's no such thing as a former alcoholic," said Tracy, "or an ex-Marine."

"You got that right," said Strange. He liked these two women a touch more now than when he'd walked in.

Strange turned the glass of ginger ale so that the smudge was away from him and took a sip. He replaced the glass on the table and leaned forward. "All right, then, now we had our first kiss and got that over with. What do you young ladies have on your minds?"

Bagley glanced briefly over at Tracy, who was in the process of putting fire to a cigarette.

"We've been working with a group called APIP," said Bagley. "Do you know it?"

"I read about it in that article they did on you two. Something about helping out prostitutes, right?"

"Aiding Prostitutes in Peril," said Tracy, blowing a jet of smoke across the table at Strange.

"Some punk-rock kids started it, right?"

"The people behind it were a part of the local punk movement twenty years ago," said Tracy, "as I was. They're not kids anymore. They're older than me and Karen."

"What do they do, exactly?"

"A number of things, from simply providing condoms to reporting violent johns. Also, they serve as an information clearinghouse. They have an eight-hundred number and a Web site that takes in e-mails from parents and prostitutes alike."

"That's where you two come in. You find runaways who're hookin'. Right?"

"That's a part of what we do," said Bagley. "And we're getting too busy to handle all the work ourselves. The county business alone keeps us up to our ears in it. We could use a little help in the District."

"You need me to find a girl."

"Not exactly," said Bagley. "We thought we'd test the waters with you on something simpler, see if you're interested."

"Keep talking."

"There's a girl who works the street between L and Mass, on Seventh," said Tracy.

"Down there by the site for the new convention center," said Strange.

"Right," said Tracy. "The last two weeks or so a guy's been hassling her. Pulling up in his car, trying to get her to date him."

"Ain't that the object of the game?"

"Sure," said Bagley. "But there's something off about this

guy. He's been asking her, Do you like it rough? Telling her she's gonna dig it, he can *tell* she's gonna dig it, right?"

Strange shifted in his seat. "So? Girl doesn't have to be a working girl to come up against that kind of creep. She can hear it in a bar."

"These working women get a sense for this kind of thing," said Bagley. "She says there's something not right, we got to believe her. And he doesn't want to pay. Says he doesn't *have* to pay, understand? She's scared. Can't go to the cops, right? And her pimp would beat her ass blue if he knew she was turning down a trick."

"Even a no-money trick?"

Strange stared hard at Tracy. Her eyes did not move away from his.

Tracy said, "This is the information we have. Either you're interested or you're not."

"I hear you," said Strange, "but I'm not sure what you want me to do. You're lookin' for me to shake some cat down, you got the wrong guy."

"You own a camera, right?" said Tracy.

"Still and video alike," said Strange.

"Get some shots for us," said Bagley, "or a tape. We'll run the plates and contact this gentleman ourselves. Trust me, we can be pretty convincing. This guy's probably got a wife. Even better, he has kids. We'll make sure he never hassles this girl again."

"Damn," said Strange with a low chuckle, "you ladies are *serious*."

The waitress came to the table and set Strange's burger down before him. He thanked her, cut into it, and inspected the center. He took a large bite and closed his eyes as he chewed.

"They cooked it the way I asked," said Strange, after he had swallowed. "I'll say that for them."

"The burgers here are tight," said Bagley, smiling just a little for the first time.

Strange wiped some juice off his lips. "I get thirty-five an hour, by the way."

Tracy dragged on her smoke, this time blowing the exhale away from Strange. "According to our attorney friend, he remembers paying you thirty."

"He remembers, huh?" said Strange. "Well, I can remember when movies were fifty cents, too."

"You can?" said Tracy.

"I'm old," said Strange with a shrug.

"Not too old," said Bagley.

"Thank you," said Strange.

"You'll do it, then," said Tracy.

"I assume she works nights."

"Every night this week," said Tracy.

"I coach a kids' football team early in the evenings."

"She'll be out there, like, ten to twelve," said Tracy. "Black, mid-twenties, with a face on the worn side. She'll be wearing a red leather skirt tonight."

"She say what kind of car this guy drives?"

"Black sedan," said Bagley. "Late-model Chevy."

"Caprice, somethin' like that?"

"Late-model Chevy is what she said." Tracy stubbed out her cigarette. "Here's something else for you to look at." She reached into the leather case on the floor at her feet and pulled out a yellow-gold sheet of paper. She pushed it across the table to Strange.

The headline across the top of the flyer read, IN PERIL. Below the head was a photo of a young white girl, unclear from generations of copying. The girl's arms were skinny and her hands were folded in front of her, a yearbook-style photo. She was smiling, showing braces on her teeth. He read her name and her statistics, printed below the photograph, noticing from the DOB that she was fourteen years old.

"We'll talk about that some other time," said Bagley, "you want to. Just wanted you to get an idea of what we do."

Strange nodded, folded the flyer neatly, and put it in the back pocket of his jeans. Then he focused on finishing his lunch. Bagley and Tracy drank their beers and let him do it.

When he was done, he signaled the waitress. "I see on the specials board you got a steak today."

"You're still hungry?"

"Uh-uh, baby, I'm satisfied. But I was wondering, you guys got any bones back there in the kitchen?"

"I suppose we do."

"Wrap up a few for me, will you?"

"I'll see what I can do."

The waitress drifted. Strange said to the women, "I got a dog at home, a boxer, goes by the name of Greco. Got to take care of him, too."

Later, Bagley and Tracy watched Strange exit the dining room, his paper bag of steak bones in hand. Bagley studied his squared-up walk, the way his muscled shoulders filled out the back of his shirt, the gray salted nicely into his close-cropped hair.

"How old you figure he is?" said Bagley.

"Early fifties," said Tracy. "I liked him."

"I liked him, too."

"I noticed," said Tracy.

"Like to see a man who enjoys his food, is all it is," said Bagley. "Think we should've told him more?"

"He knew there was more. He wanted to find out what it was for himself."

"The curious type."

"Exactly," said Tracy, draining her beer and placing the mug flat on the table. "I got a feeling he's gonna work out fine."

c h a p t e r

3

STRANGE turned down 9th, between Kansas and Upshur, one short hop east of Georgia. He saw a spot outside Marshall's funeral home, steered the car into the spot, and locked the Chevy down. He walked past a combination lunch counter and butcher shop, the place just said "Meat" in the window, and nodded to a cutter named Rodel, who was leaning in the doorway of Hawk's Barbers, dragging hard on a Newport.

"What's goin on, big man?"

"It's all good," said Strange. "How about you?"

"Same old soup, just reheated."

"Bennett workin' today?"

"I don't know about workin'. But he's in there."

"Tell him I'll be by in forty-five or so. Need a touch-up."

"I'll let him know."

Strange looked up at the yellow sign mounted above the door to his agency. The sign read "Strange Investigations," half the letters bigger than the rest on account of the picture of the magnifying glass laid over the words. Strange really liked that logo; he'd made it up himself. He made a mental note that there were smudges on the light box of the sign.

Strange stood outside the windowed door of his offices and rapped on the glass. Janine buzzed him in, a bell over the door chiming as he entered. George "Trip Three" Hastings, his hands resting in his lap, sat in a waiting area to the right of the door.

"George."

"Derek."

"I'll be with you in a minute, soon as I get settled."

Hastings nodded. Strange turned to Ron Lattimer, seated behind his desk. Lattimer wore an off-the-rack designer suit with a hand-painted tie draped over the shirt, had one of those Peter Pan–looking collars, the kind Pat Riley favored. A little too pretty for Strange's taste, though he had to admit the young man kept himself cleaner than the White House lawn. And he made the office his home as well; Lattimer sat in an orthopedically correct chair and had one of those Bose compact units, always playing some kind of jazz-inflected hip-hop, set back behind his desk.

"What're you workin' on, Ron?"

"Faxing a subpoena right now," said Lattimer.

"You still on that Thirty-five Hundred Crew thing?"

"Many billable hours, boss."

"Shame, clean as you look, can't nobody see you in here. I mean, you go to all that trouble to be so perfect, how's anybody gonna know?"

"*I* know."

"Let me ask you somethin'. You ever walk by a mirror you forgot to look into?"

"SUVs are pretty good, too," said Lattimer, his eyes on the screen of his Mac. "The windows they got in those things, they're just the right height."

Strange passed a desk topped with loose papers and gum wrappers and stood in front of Janine Baker. He picked up the three or four pink message slips she had pushed to her desk's edge and looked them over.

"How was lunch?" said Janine.

"Nice women," said Strange. "C'mon in the back for a second, okay?"

She followed him back to his office. Lamar Williams, a gangly neighborhood boy of seventeen, was emptying Strange's wastebasket into a large garbage bag. Lamar took classes at Roosevelt High in the mornings and worked for Strange most afternoons.

"Lamar," said Strange, "need some privacy for a few. Why don't you get yourself the ladder and Windex the sign out front, okay?"

"Aiight."

"You comin' to practice tonight?"

"Can't tonight."

"You got somethin' more important?"

"Watchin' my baby sister for my moms."

"All right, then. Close the door behind you on your way out."

The door closed, leaving Strange and Janine alone. She came into his arms and he kissed her on the lips.

"Good day?"

"Now it is," said Strange.

"How about dinner tonight?"

"If we can eat right after practice. I got a job from those women and I'm gonna try and knock it out late."

"Sounds good to me."

Strange kissed her again and went behind his desk. He had a seat and noticed the PayDay bar set beside his phone.

"That's you," said Janine, her liquid eyes looking him over. "Thought you'd like to cleanse your palate after that lunch."

"Thank you, baby. Go on and send George in."

He watched her walk to the door in her brightly colored outfit. She was the best office manager he'd ever had. Hell, she ran
the damn place, he wasn't afraid to admit it. And, praise God, the
woman had an ass on her, too. It moved like a wave beneath the
fabric of her skirt. All these years, and it still stirred Strange to
look at her. The way she was put together, some people who knew
something about it might say it was poetry. He'd never been into
poems himself. The best way he could describe it, looking at
Janine, it reminded him of peace.

❐

GEORGE Hastings and Strange had known each other since the
early sixties, when both had played football for Roosevelt in the
Interhigh. In those days he ran with George and Virgil Aaron,
now deceased, and Lydell Blue, also a football player, a back who
was the most talented of the four. Strange and Blue had gone into
law enforcement, and Hastings had taken a government job with
the Bureau of Engraving.

"Thanks for seeing me, Derek," said Hastings.

"Ain't no thing, George. *You* know that."

Strange still called Hastings George, though most around
town now called him Trip or Trip Three. Back in the early seventies, Hastings had played the unlikely combination of 3-3-3 and
hit it for thirty-five grand. It was a fortune for that time, and it
was especially significant from where they'd come from, but, with
the exception of the new Deuce and a Quarter he'd purchased,
Hastings had been smart and invested the money wisely. He'd
bought stock in AT&T and IBM, and he had let it ride. By
neighborhood standards, Strange knew, Hastings had become a
wealthy man.

He also knew that Hastings liked to hear Strange call him by
his given name. George was a name out of fashion with the
younger generation of blacks. It had been a generic name used by
plantation owners to refer to their male slaves, for one. And in the

modern world it had become a slang name to refer to a boyfriend, as in, "Hey, baby, you got yourself a George?" So young black people didn't care much for the name and they rarely considered it as a name for their own babies. But George Hastings's mother, a good old girl whom Strange had regarded with nearly as much affection as his own, had thought it was just fine, and that made it all good for Hastings and for Strange.

Hastings leaned over and flicked the spring-mounted head of the plaster Redskins figure that sat on Strange's desk. The head swayed from side to side.

"The old uniform. That goes back, what, thirty-some-odd years?"

"Forty," said Strange.

"Who painted his face brown like that? I know they weren't sellin' 'em like that back then."

"Janine's son, Lionel."

"How's he doin'?"

"Finishing up at Coolidge. Just applied to Maryland. He's a good boy. A knucklehead sometimes, like all boys tend to be. But he's doing all right."

"You see Westbrook the other night?"

"Boy made some catches."

"Uh-huh. Still makin' that first-down sign when they move the sticks. That drives the defenders crazy. He is cocky."

"He's got a right to be," said Strange. "Some call it cocky; I call it confidence. Westbrook's ready to have the season of his career, George. Gonna bust loose like Chuck Brown and all the Soul Searchers put together."

"He ain't no Bobby Mitchell," said Hastings. "And he sure ain't no Charley Taylor."

Strange smiled a little. "No one is to you, George."

"Anyway," said Hastings. He reached inside his lightweight sport jacket. Strange figured from the material that the jacket went for five, six hundred. Quiet, with a subtle pattern in there. Good quality, and understated, like all George's possessions. Like the high-line, two-year-old Volvo he drove, and his Tudor-style house up in Shepherd Park.

Hastings dropped a folded sheet of paper on Strange's desk. Strange picked it up, unfolded it, and looked it over.

"I got what you asked for," said Hastings.

Strange read the full name of the subject: Calhoun Tucker. Hastings had provided the tag number for the Audi S4 that Tucker owned or leased. Mimeographed onto the sheet of paper was a credit card receipt from a nightspot that Strange recognized. It was located on U Street, east of 14th. Hastings had scribbled a paragraph of other incidental character details: where Tucker said he'd lived last, where he'd last worked, like that.

"How'd you get the credit card receipt?" said Strange.

"Looked through my little girl's purse. They went to dinner, he must have said, Hold on to this for me, will you? Didn't like going through her personal belongings, but I did. Alisha's getting ready to step off a cliff. I mean, young people, they decide to get married, they never do know what it means, for real."

"I heard that."

"My Linda, God love her, she'd be doing the same thing, she was still with us. She was harder on Alisha's boyfriends than I ever was, matter of fact. And here this boy just rolls into town six months ago — he's not even a Washington boy, Derek — and I'm supposed to just sit on my hands while everybody's world gets rocked? I mean, I don't even know one thing about his family."

Strange dropped the paper on the desk. "George, you don't have to justify this to me. I do this kind of background check all the time. It's no reflection on your daughter, and as of yet it's no reflection on this young man. And it damn sure is no reflection on you. You're her father, man, you're *supposed* to be concerned."

"I'd do this even if I thought the boy was right."

"But you don't think he's right."

Hastings ran a finger down his cheek. "Somethin' off about this Tucker boy."

"You sure the off thing's not just that some young man's getting ready to take away your little girl?"

"Sure, that's a part of it; I can't lie to you, man. But it's somethin' else, too. Don't ask me what exactly. You live long enough, you get so you know."

"Forget about exactly, then."

"Well, he's drivin' a luxury German automobile, for one. Always dressed clean, too, real sharp, with the gadgets that go with it: cells, pagers, all that. And I can't figure out what he does to get it."

"That might have meant somethin' once. Used to be, you had to be rich or a drug dealer to have those things. But look, any fool who can sign his name to a lease can be drivin' a Benz these days. Twelve-year-old *kid* can get his own credit card."

"Okay, but ain't no twelve-year-old kid gonna march my baby girl down to the altar. This here is a twenty-nine-year-old man, and he's got no visible means of support. Says he's some kind of talent agent, a manager. Puts on shows at the clubs around town. He's got this business card, says 'Calhoun Enterprises.' Anytime I see 'Enterprises' on a business card, way I look at it, might as well print the word 'Unfocused' next to it, or 'Doesn't Want No Real Job,' or just plain 'Bullshit,' you know what I'm sayin'?"

Strange chuckled. "Okay, George. Anything else?"

"I just don't like him, Derek. I plain do not like the man. That's somethin', isn't it?"

Strange nodded. "Let me ask you a question. You think he's into somethin' on the criminal side?"

"Can't say that. All I know is —"

"You don't like him. Okay, George. Let me handle it from here."

Hastings shifted in his seat. "You still gettin' thirty an hour?"

"Thirty-five," said Strange.

"You went up."

"Gas did, too. Been to a bar lately? Bottle of beer cost you five dollars."

"That include the two dollars you be stuffin' in their G-strings?"

"Funny."

"How long you think this is gonna take?"

"Don't worry, this won't take more than a few hours of my time. Most of it we do from right here, on computers. I'll have you happy and stroking checks for that wedding in a couple of days."

"That's another thing. This reception is gonna cost me a fortune."

"If you can't spend it on Alisha, what you gonna do with it? You got yourself a beautiful girl there, George. Lovely on the outside, and in her heart, too. So let's you and me make sure she's making the right decision."

Hastings exhaled slowly as he sat back in his chair. "Thank you, Derek."

"Strictly routine," said Strange.

4

STRANGE dropped the paper Hastings had given him on Janine's desk.

"You get time, run this information through Westlaw and see what kind of preliminary information you can come up with."

"Background check on a . . ." Janine's eyes scanned the page. ". . . Calhoun Tucker."

"Right. George's future son-in-law. I'll pick up Lionel and swing him back with me after practice."

"Okay."

"And, oh yeah. Call Terry; he's workin' up at the bookstore today. Remind him he's coaching tonight."

"I will."

Lattimer looked up as Strange passed by his desk. "Half day today, boss?"

"Need a haircut."

"Next door? You ever wonder why they got the butcher and the barber so close together on this block?"

"Never made that connection. One thing I don't need is to be spending forty dollars on a haircut like you."

"Well, you better get on over there. 'Cause you're startin' to look like Tito Jackson."

Strange turned and looked into a cracked mirror hanging from a nail driven into a column in the middle of the office. "Damn, boy, you're right." He patted the side of his head. "I need to get my shit correct."

❐

STRANGE dropped a couple of the kids off at their homes after practice. Then he and Lionel drove up Georgia toward Brightwood in Strange's '91 black-over-black Cadillac Brougham, a V-8 with a chromed-up grille. This was his second car. Strange had an old tape, *Al Green Gets Next to You*, in the deck, and he was trying hard not to sing along.

"Sounds like gospel music," said Lionel. "But he's singing it to some girl, isn't he?"

"'God Is Standing By,'" said Strange. "An old Johnny Taylor tune, and you're right. This here was back when Al was struggling between the secular and the spiritual, if you know what I'm sayin'."

"You mean, like, he loves Jesus but he loves to hit the pussy, too."

"I wasn't quite gonna put it like that, young man."

"Whateva."

Strange looked across the bench. "You got studies tonight, right?"

"I guess so."

"Don't want you to let up now, just 'cause you already applied to college. You need to keep on those books."

"You want me to stay in my room tonight, just say it."

"I didn't mean that."

Lionel just smiled in that way that drove Strange around the bend.

Janine Baker's residence was on Quintana Place, between 7th and 9th, just east of the Fourth District police station. Quintana was a short, narrow street of old colonials fronted with porches. The houses were covered in siding and painted in an array of earth tones and bright colors, including turquoise and neon green. The Baker residence was a pale lavender affair down near the 7th Street end of the block.

In the dining room they ate a grilled chuck roast, black on the outside and pink in the center, along with mashed potatoes and gravy and some spiced greens, washed down with ice-cold Heinekens for Strange and Janine. Lionel went upstairs to his bedroom as soon as he finished his meal. Strange had a quick cup of coffee and wiped his mouth when he was done.

"That was beautiful, baby."

"Glad you enjoyed it."

"You want me to come back after I'm done working?"

"I'd like that. And I've foil-wrapped the bone from the chuck for Greco, so bring him back, too."

"Between you and me we're gonna spoil that dog to death." Strange came around the table, bent down, and kissed Janine on the cheek. "I'll be back before midnight, hear?"

❒

STRANGE returned to his row house on Buchanan Street and hit the heavy bag in his basement for a while, trying to work off some of the fat he'd taken in from his meat consumption that day. He broke a sweat that smelled like alcohol when he was done, then showered and changed clothes up on the second floor, which held his bedroom and home office. In the office, Greco played with a spiked rubber ball while Strange checked his stock portfolio and read a stock-related message board, listening to Ennio

Morricone's "The Return of Ringo" from the Yamaha speakers of
his computer.

Strange checked his wristwatch, a Swiss Army model with a
black leather band, and looked at his dog.

"Gotta go to work, old buddy. I'll be back to pick you up in a
little bit."

Greco's nub of tail made a double twitch. He looked up at
Strange and showed him the whites of his eyes.

❑

STRANGE drove down Georgia in his Chevy, through Petworth
and into Park View. The street was up, Friday night, kids mostly,
some hanging out, some doing business as well. Down around
Morton a line had formed outside the Capitol City Pavilion, called
the Black Hole by locals and law enforcement types alike. D.C.
veteran go-go band Back Yard had their name on the marquee, as
they did most weekends. In a few hours, Fourth District squad
cars would be blocking Georgia, rerouting traffic. Beefs born
inside the club often came to their inevitable, violent resolution at
closing time, when the patrons spilled out onto the street.

Strange saw Lamar Williams, wearing pressed khakis and
wheat-colored Timbies, standing in the line outside the club.
Strange drove on. Between Kenyon and Harvard, kids sold marijuana in an open-air market set up on the street.

Georgia became 7th. Soon Strange was nearing the convention center site, a huge hole that took up several of D.C.'s letter
blocks, on his right. On his left ran a commercial strip. His
hooker, wearing a red leather skirt, was standing in the doorway of
a closed restaurant, her hard, masculine face illuminated by the
embers of her cigarette as she gave it a deep draw. Strange did not
slow the car. He went west for a couple of blocks, then north, then
east again, circling back to a spot on the east side of the future center, where he parked the Chevy on 9th, alongside a construction

fence. He slipped a notepad into his breast pocket and clipped a pen there before exiting the car.

Strange opened the trunk of his Chevy. He pushed aside his live-case file, his football file, and his toolbox, and found his video camera, which was fitted in a separate box alongside his 500mm-lens Canon AE-1. He checked the tape and replaced it in its slot. Strange liked this camera, his latest acquisition. It was an 8mm Sony with the NightShot feature and the 360X digital zoom. Perfect for what he needed, perfect for this job right here. He'd gotten the camera in a trade for a debt owed him by a client; the camera was hotter than Jennifer Lopez in July.

Strange went over to a place by the fence at 7th and L, just north of the hooker's position, where there was an open driveway entrance breaking the continuity of the construction fence. He situated himself behind the fence in a position that would render him unseen by the passengers or drivers of any southbound cars. He stood there for a while, setting up the camera the way he wanted it and shooting some tape for a test. He watched the hooker talk to a potential john who had pulled up his Honda Accord beside her, and he watched the john drive off. The hooker smoked another cigarette. Strange's stomach rumbled, as he thought about AV, his favorite sit-down Italian restaurant, just around the corner on Mass. Hungry as usual, and having just eaten, too.

A black late-model Chevy rolled down 7th, slowed, and came to a stop near where the hooker stood. Strange leaned against the corner of the fence, brought the zoom in so the car was framed and clear, and shot some tape. Cigarette smoke came out of the driver's side of the car as the john rolled his window down. The hooker rested her forearms on the lip of the open window. She shook her head, and Strange could hear male laughter before the car drove off. The car wore D.C. plates. It was an Impala, the new body style that Strange didn't care for.

He waited. The Impala came out of the north once again,

having circled the block. The driver stopped the vehicle in the same spot he had minutes earlier. The hooker hesitated, looked around, walked over to the driver's side but this time did not lean into the car. She seemed to be listening for a while, her face going from passivity to agitation and then to something like fear. Strange heard the laughter again. Then the driver laid some rubber on the street and took off. The hooker flipped him off, but only after the car had turned the corner and was gone from sight.

Strange wrote down the Impala's license plate number on the notepad he had placed in the breast pocket of his shirt. He didn't need to record it, not really; he had memorized the number at first sight, a talent that he had always possessed and that had served him well when he had worn the uniform on the street.

Anyway, the two letters that preceded the numbers on the plate had told him everything he needed to know. Bagley and Tracy must have known it, too. They had put him onto this, he reasoned, as some kind of test. He wasn't angry. It was just a job.

The letters on the plate read GT. Plainclothes, undercover, whatever you wanted to call it. The abusive john was a cop.

5

"HOLD on a second, Derek," said Karen Bagley. "I'm going to conference you in with Sue."

Strange held the phone away from his ear and sat back in the chair behind his desk. He watched Lamar Williams climb a stepladder to feather-dust Strange's blinds.

"You coming with me to practice tonight, Lamar?"

"You want me to, I will."

"I was just wonderin' on if you could make it. If you had to sit your baby sister again, I mean."

"Nah, uh-uh."

"'Cause I saw you outside the Black Hole Friday night."

Lamar lowered the duster. "Yeah, I was there. After I did what I told you I had to do."

"Kind of a rough place, isn't it?"

"It's a place in the neighborhood I can listen to some go-go, maybe talk to a girl. I don't eye-contact no one I shouldn't; I ain't lookin' to step *to* nobody or beef nobody. Just lookin' to have a little fun. That's okay with you, isn't it, boss?"

"Just tellin' you I saw you, is all."

Strange heard voices on the phone. He put the receiver back to his ear.

"Okay," said Strange.

"We all here?" said Bagley.

"I can hear you," said Tracy. "Derek?"

"I got what you needed," said Strange. "It's all on video-tape."

"That was quick," said Bagley.

"Did it Friday night. I thought I'd let the weekend pass, didn't want to disturb your-all's beauty sleeps."

"What'd you get?" said Tracy.

"Your bad john is a cop. Unmarked. But you two knew that, I expect. The flag went up for me when you said he was talkin' about 'I don't have to pay.' Question is, why didn't you just tell me what you suspected?"

"We wanted to find out if we could trust you," said Tracy.

Direct, thought Strange. That was cool.

"I'm going to give the tape and the information to a lieu-tenant friend of mine in the MPD. I been knowin' him my whole life. He'll turn it over to Internal and they'll take care of it."

"You've got a videotape of his car," said Bagley, "right? Did you get his face?"

"No, not really. But it's his car and it's a clear solicitation. He might say he was gathering information or some bullshit like that, but it's enough to throw a shadow over him. The IAD people will talk to him, and I suspect it'll scare him. He won't be botherin' that girl again. That's what you wanted, isn't it?"

"Yes," said Bagley. "Good work."

"Good? It was half good, I'd say. You two ever see that movie *The Magnificent Seven*?"

Bagley and Tracy took a moment before uttering a "yes" and an "uh-huh." Strange figured they were wondering where he was going with this.

"One of my favorites," said Strange. "There's that scene where Coburn, he plays the knife-carryin' Texican, pistol-shoots this cat off a horse from, like, I don't know, a couple hundred yards away. And this hero-worship kid, German actor or something, but they got him playin' a Mexican, he says something like, 'That was the greatest shot I ever saw.' And Coburn says, 'It was the worst. I was aiming for his horse.'"

"And your point is what?" said Bagley.

"I wish I could've delivered more to you. More evidence, I mean. But what I did get, it might just be enough. Anyway, hopefully y'all will *trust* me now."

"Like I said," said Tracy, "there's no such thing as an ex-cop. Cops are usually hesitant to turn in one of their own."

"There's two professions," said Strange, "teaching and policing, that do the most good for the least pay and recognition. But you want to be a teacher or a cop, you accept that goin' in. Most cops and most teachers are better than good. But there's always gonna be the teacher likes to play with a kid's privates, and there's always gonna be a cop out there, uses his power and position in the wrong way. In both cases, to me, it's the worst kind of betrayal. So I got no problem with turnin' a cat like that in. Only . . ."

"What?" said Tracy.

"Don't keep nothin' from me again, hear? Okay, you did it once, but you don't get to do it again. It happens, it'll be the last time we work together."

"We were wrong," said Bagley. "Can you forget it?"

"Forget what?"

"What about the other thing?" said Tracy. "The flyer we gave you."

"I've got a guy I use named Terry Quinn. Former D.C. cop. He's a licensed investigator in the District now. I'm gonna give it to him."

"Why not you?" said Bagley.

"Too busy."

"How can we reach him?" said Tracy.

"He's not in the office much. He works part-time in a used-book store in downtown Silver Spring. He can take calls there, and he's got a cell. I'm gonna see him this evening; I'll make sure he gets the flyer."

Strange gave them both numbers.

"Thank you, Derek."

"You'll get my bill straightaway." Strange hung up the phone and looked over at Lamar. "You ready, boy?

"Sure."

"Let's roll."

❑

STRANGE retrieved the videotape of the cop and the hooker, wedged in the football file box, and shut the trunk's lid.

"This here is you," said Strange, handing the tape over to Lydell Blue.

"The thing you called me about?"

"Yeah. I wrote up a little background on it, what I was told by the investigators who put me on it, what I heard at the scene, like that. I signed my name to it, Internal wants to get in touch with me."

Blue stroked his thick gray mustache. "I'll take care of it."

They walked across the parking lot toward the fence that surrounded the stadium, passing Quinn's hopped-up blue Chevelle and Dennis Arrington's black Infiniti I30 along the way.

Strange knew Roosevelt's football coach — he had done a simple background check for him once and he had not charged him a dime — and they had worked it out so that Strange's team could practice on Roosevelt's field when the high school team wasn't using it. In return, Strange turned the coach on to some up-and-coming players and tried to keep those kids who were headed for Roosevelt in a straight line as well.

"You and Dennis want the Midgets tonight?"

"Tonight? Yeah, okay."

"Me and Terry'll work with the Pee Wees, then."

"Derek, that's the way you got it set up damn near every night."

"I like the young kids, is what it is," said Strange. "Me and Terry will just stick with them, you don't mind."

"Fine."

Midgets in this league — a loosely connected set of neighborhood teams throughout the area — went ten to twelve years old and between eighty-five and one hundred and five pounds. Pee Wees were ages eight to eleven, with a minimum of sixty pounds and a max of eighty-five. There was also an intermediate and junior division in the league, but the Petworth club could not attract enough boys in those age groups, the early-to-mid-teen years, to form a squad. Many of these boys had by then become too distracted by other interests, like girls, or necessities, like part-time jobs. Others had already been lost to the streets.

Strange followed Blue through a break in the fence and down to the field. About fifty boys were down there in uniforms and full pads, tackling one another, cracking wise, kicking footballs, and horsing around. Lamar Williams was with them, giving them some tips, also acting the clown. A few mothers were down there, and a couple of fathers, too, talking among themselves.

The field was surrounded by a lined track painted a nice sky blue. A set of aluminum bleachers on concrete steps faced the field. Weed trees grew up through the concrete.

Dennis Arrington, a computer programmer and deacon, was

throwing the ball back and forth with the Midgets' quarterback in one of the end zones. Nearby, Terry Quinn showed Joe Wilder, a Pee Wee, the ideal place on the body to make a hit. Quinn had to get down low to do it. Wilder was the runt of the litter, short but with defined muscles and a six-pack of abs, though he had only just turned eight years old. At sixty-two pounds, Wilder was also the lightest member of the squad.

Strange blew a whistle that hung on a cord around his neck. "Everybody line up over there." He motioned to a line that had been painted across the track. They knew where it was.

"Hustle," said Blue.

"Four times around," said Strange, "and don't be complaining, either; that ain't nothin' but a mile." He blew the whistle again over the boys' inevitable moans and protests.

"Any one of you walks," yelled Arrington, as they jogged off the line, "and you *all* are gonna do four more."

The men stood together in the end zone and watched the sea of faded green uniforms move slowly around the track.

"Got a call from Jerome Moore's mother today," said Blue. "Jerome got suspended from Clark today for pulling a knife on a teacher."

"Clark *Elementary?*" said Quinn.

"Uh-huh. His mother said we won't be seein' him at practice for the next week or so."

"Call her back," said Strange, "and tell her he's not welcome back. He's off the team. Didn't like him around the rest of the kids anyway. Doggin' it, trash-talking, always starting fights."

"Moore's nine years old," said Quinn. "I thought those were the kind of at-risk kids we were trying to help."

"They're *all* at risk down here, Terry. I'll let go of one to keep the rest of the well from getting poisoned. It'll school them on something, too. That we're tryin' to teach them somethin' more than football here. Also, that we're not gonna put up with that kind of behavior."

"Way I see it," said Quinn, "it's the giving up on these kids that makes them go wrong."

"I'm not giving up on him or anyone else. He straightens himself out, he can play for us next season. But for this season here, uh-uh. He blew it his own self. You agree with me, Dennis?"

Dennis Arrington looked down at the football that he spun in his thick hands. He was Quinn's height, not so tall, built like a fullback. "Absolutely, Derek."

Arrington gave Quinn a short look. Quinn knew that Arrington wouldn't agree with him on this or anything else. Arrington was quick with a smile, a handshake, and a back pat for most any black man who came down to this field. And Quinn did like him as a man. But he felt that Arrington didn't like *him*, or show him respect. And he felt that this was because he, Quinn, was white. Quinn had gotten that from some of the kids when he'd first started here as well. The kids, most of them, anyway, had gotten past it.

Strange turned to Quinn. Quinn's hair was cropped short. He had a wide mouth, a pronounced jaw, and green eyes. Among friends his eyes were gentle, but around strangers, or when he was simply in thought, his eyes tended to be flat and hard. In full winter dress he looked like a man of average height, maybe less, with a flat stomach and an ordinary build, but out here in sweatpants and a white T-shirt, his veins standing on his forearms and snaking up his biceps, his physical strength was evident.

"Before I forget it, some women might be callin' you, Terry. I gave them your number —"

"They already called me. Got me on my cell while I was driving over here."

"Yeah, they do work quick. I brought you the information, if you're interested."

"Do you want me to take it?"

"It's a money job for both of us."

"It would mean more jack for you if you just took it yourself."

"I'm busy," said Strange.

The boys came back in, sweating and short of breath.

"Form a circle," said Blue. He called out the names of the two captains who would lead the calisthenics.

The captains stood in the middle of the large circle. They commanded their teammates to run in place.

"How ya'll feel?" shouted the captains.

"Fired up!" responded the team.

"How y'all feel?"

"Fired up!"

"Breakdown."

"Whoo!"

"Breakdown."

"Whoo!"

"Breakdown."

"Whoo!"

With each command the boys went into their breakdown stance and shouted, *"Whoo!"* This running in place and vocal psych-out lasted for a few more minutes. Then they moved into other calisthenics: stretches, knuckle push-ups, and six inches, where they were instructed to lie on their backs, lift their legs a half foot off the ground, keep their legs straight, and hold the position, playing their bellies like a tom-tom until they were told they could relax. When they were done, their jerseys were dark with sweat and their faces were beaded with it.

"Now you're gonna run some steps," said Strange.

"Aw!" said Rico, the Pee Wee starting halfback. Rico was a quick, low-to-the-ground runner who could jook. He had the most natural talent of any of the players. He was also the first to complain.

"Move, Reek," said Dante Morris, the tall, skinny quarterback who rarely spoke, only when he was asked to or to motivate his teammates. "Let's get it done."

"C'mon Panthers!" shouted Joe Wilder, sweeping his arm in the direction of the bleachers.

"Little man gonna lead the charge," said Blue.

"They're *following* him, too," said Strange.

A few more mothers had arrived and stood on the sidelines. Joe Wilder's uncle had shown up, too. He was leaning against the fence that ran between the track and the bleachers, his hand dipped into a white paper bag stained with grease.

"Humid tonight," said Blue.

"Don't make 'em run those steps too long," said Strange. "Look, I gotta run back up to my car for a second. Wanted to give you the Midget roster, since you'll be takin' them permanent. Be right back."

Strange crossed the field, passing Wilder's uncle, not looking his way. But the uncle said, "Coach," and Strange had to stop.

"How's it goin?" said Strange.

"It's all right. Name's Lorenze. Most call me Lo. I'm Joe Wilder's uncle."

"Derek Strange. I've seen you around."

Now Strange had to shake his hand. Lorenze rubbed his right hand, greasy from the french fries in the bag, off on his jeans before he reached out and tried to give Strange the standard soul shake: thumb lock, finger lock, break. Strange executed it without enthusiasm.

"Y'all nearly through?"

"We'll be quittin' near dark."

"I just got up *in* this motherfucker, so I didn't know how long you been out here."

Lorenze smiled. Strange shifted his feet impatiently. Lorenze, a man over thirty years old, wore a T-shirt with a photograph of a dreadlocked dude smoking a fat spliff, and a pair of Jordans, laces untied, on his feet. Strange didn't know one thing for certain about this man. But he knew this man's type.

Blue called the boys off the bleachers. Exhausted, they began to walk back toward the center of the field.

"I'll be takin' Joe with me after practice," said Lorenze. "I ain't got my car tonight, but I can walk him back to his place."

"I told his mother I'd drop him at home. Same as always."

"We just gonna walk around some. Boy needs to get to know his uncle."

"I'm responsible for him," said Strange, keeping his tone light. "If his mother had told me you'd be comin', that would be one thing . . ."

"You don't have to worry. I'm *kin*, brother."

"I'm taking him home," said Strange, and now he forced himself to smile. "Like I say, I told his mother, right? You got to understand this."

"I ain't *got*ta do nothin' but be black and die," said Lorenze, grinning at his clever reply.

Strange didn't comment. He'd been hearing young and not-so-young black men use that expression around town for years now. It never did settle right on his ears.

They both heard a human whistle and looked up past the bleachers to the fence that bordered the parking lot. A tall young man was leaning against the fence, smiling and staring down at them. Then he turned, walked away, and was out of sight.

"Look," said Strange, "I gotta get something from my car. I'll see you around, hear?"

Lorenze nodded absently.

Strange walked up to the parking lot. The young man who had stood at the fence was now sitting behind the wheel of an idling car with D.C. plates. The car was a beige Caprice, about ten years old, with a brown vinyl roof and chrome-reverse wheels, parked nose out about four spaces down from Strange's own Chevy. Rust had begun to cancer the rear quarter panel on the driver's side. The pipe coughed white exhaust, which hovered in the lot. The exhaust mingled with the marijuana smoke that was coming from the open windows of the car.

Another young man sat in the shotgun seat and a third sat in the back. Strange saw tightly braided hair on the front-seat passenger, little else.

Strange had slowed his steps and was studying the car. He was letting them see him study it. His face was impassive and his body language unthreatening as he moved along.

Now Strange walked to his own car and popped the trunk. He heard them laughing as he opened his toolbox and looked inside of it for . . . for *what?* Strange didn't own a gun. If they were strapped and they were going to use a gun on him, he couldn't do a damn thing about it anyway. But he was letting his imagination get ahead of him now. These were just some hard-looking kids, sitting in a parking lot, getting high.

Strange found a pencil in his toolbox and wrote something down on the outside of the Pee Wees' manila file. Then he found the Midget file that he had come to get for Blue. He closed the trunk's lid.

He walked back across the lot. The driver poked his head out the window of the Caprice and said, "Yo, Fred Sanford! Fred!"

That drew more laughter, and he heard one of them say, "Where Lamont at and shit?"

Now they were laughing and saying other things, and Strange heard the words "old-time" and felt his face grew hot, but he kept walking. He just wanted them gone, off the school grounds, away from his kids. And as he heard the squeal of their tires he relaxed, knowing that this was so.

He looked down toward the field and noticed that Lorenze, Joe Wilder's uncle, had gone.

Strange was glad Terry Quinn hadn't been with him just now, because Quinn would have started some shit. When someone stepped to him, Quinn only knew how to respond one way.

You couldn't answer each slight, or return each hard look with an equally hard look, because moments like this went down out here every day. It would just be too tiring. You'd end up in a constant battle, with no time to breathe, just live.

Strange told himself this, trying to let his anger subside, as he walked back onto the field.

6

T H E Pee Wee offense said "Break" in the huddle and went to the line. Strange saw that several of the players had lined up too far apart.

"Do your splits," said Strange, and the offensive linemen moved closer together, placing their hands on one another's shoulder pads. Now they were properly spaced.

"Down!" said Dante Morris, his hands between the center's legs. The offense hit their thigh pads in unison.

"Set!" The offense clapped their hands one time and got down in a three-point stance.

"Go! Go!"

On two, Rico took the handoff from Dante Morris, bobbling it a little, not really having possession of the ball as he hesitated and was cut down by two defenders behind the line.

"Hold up," said Quinn.

"What was that, Rico?" said Strange. "What was the play?"

"Thirty-one on two," said Rico, picking some turf off his helmet.

"And Thirty-one is?"

"Halfback run to the one-hole," said Joe Wilder.

"Joe, I know *you* know," said Strange. "I was askin' Rico."

"Like Joe said," said Rico.

"But you weren't headed for the one-hole, were you, son?"

"I got messed up in my head."

"Think," said Strange, tapping his own temple.

"You had your hands wrong, too," said Quinn. "When you're taking a handoff and you're going to the left, where's your right hand supposed to be?"

"On top. Left hand down at your belly."

"Right. The opposite if you're going right." Quinn looked to the linemen who had made the tackle. "Nice hit there. Way to wrap him up. Let's try that again."

In the huddle, Dante called a Thirty-five. The first number, three, was always a halfback run. The second number was the hole to be hit. Odd numbers were the left holes, one, three, and five. Evens were the two-, four-, and six-holes. A number larger than six was a pitch.

They executed the play. This time Rico took the ball smoothly and found the hole, running low off a clean Joe Wilder block, and he was gone.

"All right, good." Quinn tapped Joe's helmet as he ran back to the huddle. "Good block, Joe, way to *be*."

Joe Wilder nodded, a swagger in his step, his wide smile visible behind the cage of his helmet.

❐

Close to dark, Strange blew a long whistle, signaling the boys into the center of the field.

"All right," said Blue, "take a knee."

The boys got down on one knee, close together, looking up at their coaches.

"I got a call today," said Dennis Arrington, "at work. One of you was asking me how to make his mouth guard from the kit we gave you. Course, he just should have asked me before he did it, or better yet, listened when I explained it the first time. 'Cause he went and boiled it for three minutes and it came out like a hunk of plastic."

"Tenderized it," said Blue, and some of the boys laughed.

"You put it in that boiling water for twenty seconds," said Arrington. "And before you put it in your mouths to form it, you dip it in some cold water. You don't do that, you're gonna burn yourselves fierce."

"You only make that mistake one time," said Strange.

"Any questions?" said Blue.

There were none.

"Want to talk about somethin' tonight," said Strange. "Heard you all discussing it between yourselves some and thought I ought to bring it up. One of your teammates got himself in big trouble at school today, something to do with a knife. Now I know you already got the details, what you heard, anyway, so I won't go into it, and besides, it's not right to be talkin' about this boy's business when he's not here. But I do want to tell you that he is off the team. And the reason he is off is, he broke the deal he made with his coaches, and with you, his teammates, to act in a certain way. The way you got to conduct yourselves if you are going to be a Panther. And I don't mean just here on the field. I'm talking about how you act at home, and in school. Because we are out here devoting our time to you for no kind of pay, and you and your teammates are working hard, sweating, to make this the best team we can be. And we will not tolerate that kind of disrespect, to us or to you. Do you understand?"

There was a low mumble of yesses. The Pee Wee center, a

quiet African kid named Prince, raised his hand, and Strange acknowledged him.

"Do you need to thee our report cards?" said Prince. The boy beside him grinned but did not laugh at Prince's lisp.

"Yes, we will need to see your first report card when you get it. We're especially gonna be looking at behavior. Now, we got a game this Saturday, y'all know that, right?" The boys' faces brightened. "Anybody hasn't paid the registration fee yet, you need to get up with your parents or the people you stay with, 'cause if you do not pay, you will not play. I'm gonna need all your health checkups, too."

"We gettin' new uniforms?" said a kid from back in the group.

"Not this season," said Strange. "I must answer this question every practice. Some of you just do not listen." There were a couple of "Dags," but mostly silence.

"Practice is six o'clock, Wednesday," said Blue.

"What time?" said Dennis Arrington.

The boys shouted in unison, *"Six o'clock, on the dot, be there, don't miss it!"*

"Put it in," said Quinn.

The boys formed a tight circle and tried to touch one another's hands in the center. *"Petworth Panthers!"*

"All right," said Strange. "We're done. You that got your bikes or live close, get on home now before the dark falls all the way. Anyone else needs a ride, meet the coaches up in the lot."

❐

THERE were about ten parents and other types of relatives and guardians, dedicated, enthusiastic, loving, mostly women and a couple of men, who came to every practice and every game. Always the same faces. The parents who did not show were too busy trying to make ends meet, or hanging with their boyfriends or girlfriends, or they just didn't care. Many of these kids lived with their grandparents or their aunts. Many had absent fathers, and some had never known their fathers at all.

So the parents who were involved helped whenever they could. They and the coaches watched out for those kids who needed rides home from practice and to and from the games. Running a team like this, keeping the kids away from the bad, it was a community effort. The responsibility fell on a committed few.

Strange drove south on Georgia Avenue. Lamar and Joe Wilder were in the backseat, Wilder showing Lamar his wrestling figures. Joe usually brought them with him to practice. Lamar was asking him questions, patiently listening as Joe explained the relationships among all these people, whom Strange thought of as freaks.

"You gonna watch Monday Nitro tonight?" asked Joe.

"Yeah, I'll watch it," said Lamar.

"Can you come over and watch it?"

"Can't, Joe. Got my sister to look after; my moms is goin' out." Lamar punched Joe lightly on the shoulder. "Maybe we can watch it together next week."

Strange brought Lamar along to practice to keep him out of trouble, but he was also a help to him and the other coaches. Both Lamar and Lionel were good with the kids.

Next to Strange sat Prince, the Pee Wees' center. Prince was one of three Africans on the team. Like the others, Prince was well behaved, even tempered, and polite. His father drove a cab. Prince was tall for ten, and his voice had already begun to deepen. Some of the less sensitive boys on the team tended to imitate his slight lisp. But he was generally well liked and respected for his toughness.

"There's my office," said Strange, pointing to his sign on 9th. Whenever he could, Strange reminded his kids that he had grown up in the neighborhood, just like them, and that he owned his own business.

"Why you got a picture up there of a magnifying glath?" said

Prince. He was holding his helmet in his hands, rubbing his fingers along the panther decal affixed to the side.

"It means I find things. Like I look at 'em closer so other people can see better. That make sense?"

"I guess." Prince cocked his head. "My father gave me a magnifying glath."

"Yeah?"

"Uh-huh. One day it was thunny, and me and my little brother put the glath over some roach bugs that was outside on the alley porch, by the trash? The thun made those bugs smoke. We burned up those bugs till they died."

Strange knew that here he should say that burning bugs to death wasn't cool. But he said, "I used to do the same thing."

Prince lived on Princeton Place, in a row house in Park View that was better kept than those around it. The porch light had been left on in anticipation of his arrival. Strange said good night to Prince and watched him go up the concrete steps to his house.

Some boys hanging on the corner, a couple years older than Prince, made some comments about his uniform, and then one of them said, "Pwinth, why you steppin' so fast, Pwinth?"

They were laughing at him, but he kept walking without turning around, and he kept his shoulders erect until he made it to the front door and went through.

That's right, thought Strange. *Head up, and keep your posture straight.*

The light on the porch went off.

Strange returned to Georgia Avenue, drove south, and passed a small marijuana enterprise run by a half dozen kids. Part of the income made here funneled up to one of the two prominent gangs that controlled the action in the neighborhood. South of the Fourth District, below Harvard Street, was a smaller, independent operation that did not encroach on the turf of the gang business up the road.

At Park Road, Strange cut east and then turned into the Section Eight government-assisted housing complex called Park Morton. Kids sat on a brick wall at the entrance to the complex, their eyes hard on Strange as he drove by.

The complex was dark, lit only by dim bulbs set in cinder-block stairwells. In one of them a group of young men, and a few who were not so young, were engaged in a game of craps. Some held dollars in their fists, others held brown paper bags covering bottles of juice halved with gin, or forties of malt liquor and beer.

"That your unit, Joe?" said Strange, who always had to ask. There was a dull sameness to these dwellings back here, broken by the odd heroic gesture: a picture of Jesus taped to a window, or a string of Christmas lights, or a dying potted plant.

"Next one up," said Lamar.

Strange rolled forward, put the car in park, and let it idle.

"Walk him up, Lamar."

"Coach," said Joe, "you gonna call Forty-four Belly for me in the game?"

"We'll see. We'll practice it on Wednesday, okay?"

"Six o'clock, on the dot," said Joe.

Strange brushed some bits of lint off of Joe's nappy hair. His scalp was warm and still damp with sweat. "Go on, son. Mind your mother, now, hear?"

"I will."

Strange watched Lamar and Joe disappear into the stairwell leading to Joe's apartment. Ahead, rusted playground equipment stood silhouetted in a dirt courtyard dotted with Styrofoam containers, fast-food wrappers, and other bits of trash. The courtyard was lit residually by the lamps inside the apartments. A faint veil of smoke roiled in the light.

It was a while before Lamar returned. He rested his forearms on the lip of the open passenger window of Strange's car.

"What took you so long?"

"Wasn't no one home. Had to get a key from Joe's neighbor."

"Where his mom at?"

"I expect she went to the market for some cigarettes, sumshit like that."

"Watch your mouth, boy."

"Yeah, all right." Lamar looked over his shoulder and then back at Strange. "He'll be okay. He's got my phone number he needs somethin'."

"Get in, I'll ride you the rest of the way."

"That's me, just across the court," said Lamar. "I'll walk it. See you tomorrow, boss."

Strange said, "Right."

He watched Lamar move slowly through the courtyard, not too fast like he was scared, chin level, squared up. Strange thinking, You learned early, Lamar, and well. To know how to walk in a place like this was key, a basic tool for survival. Your body language showed fear, you weren't nothin' but prey.

Driving home, Strange rolled up the windows of the Brougham and turned the AC on low. He popped a War tape, *Why Can't We Be Friends,* into the deck, and he found that beautiful ballad of theirs, "So." He got down low in the bench, his wrist resting on the stop of the wheel, and he began to sing along. For a while, anyway, sealed in his car, listening to his music, he found some kind of peace.

7

SUE Tracy sat in a window deuce, watching the foot traffic on Bonifant Street in downtown Silver Spring, as Terry Quinn arrived at the table carrying two coffees. They were in the Ethiopian place close to the Quarry House, the local basement bar where Quinn sometimes drank.

"That good?" said Quinn, watching her take her first sip. She had asked for one sugar to take the edge off.

"Yeah, it's great. I guess I didn't need the sugar."

"They don't let the coffee sit out too long in this place. These people here, they take pride in their business."

"That bookstore you work in, it's on this street, isn't it?"

"Down the block," said Quinn.

"Near the gun shop."

"Yeah, and the apartments, the Thai and African restaurants, the tattoo parlor. Except for the gun place, it's a nice strip. There aren't any chain stores on this block, it's still small businesses.

Most of which have been wrecking-balled or moved, tucked under the rug to make way for the New Downtown Silver Spring. But this street here, they haven't managed to mess with it too much yet."

"You got something against progress?"

"Progress? You mean the privilege of paying five bucks for a tomato at our new designer supermarket, just like all those suckers on the other side of town? Is that the kind of progress you're talking about?"

"You can always stick to Safeway."

"Look, I grew up here. I know a lot of these shop owners; they've made a life here and they won't be able to afford it when the landlords up the square-foot price. And where are all these working people who live in the apartments going to go when their rents skyrocket?"

"I guess it's great if you own real estate."

"I don't own a house, so I couldn't really give a rat's ass if the property values go up. I walk through this city and every week something changes, you know? So maybe you can understand how I don't feel all warm and fuzzy about it, man. I mean, they're killing my past, one day at a time."

"You sound like my father."

"What about him?"

"He thinks that way, too, is all." Tracy looked Quinn over, held it just a second too long, so that he could see her doing it, and then reached down to get something from the leather case at her feet.

He was still looking at her when she came back up, holding some papers in her hands. She wore a scoop-neck white pullover with no accoutrements, tucked into a pair of gray blue slacks that looked like work pants but were probably expensive, meant to look utilitarian. Her breasts rode high in her shirt, its whiteness set off by her tanned arms. Black Skechers, oxfords with white stitching, were on her feet. Her blond hair was pulled back, held in place by a blue gray Scunci, with a stray rope of blond falling forward over one cheek. He wondered if she had planned it to fall out that way.

Quinn wore a plain white T-shirt tucked into Levi's jeans.

"What?" said Tracy.

"Nothing."

"You were staring at me."

"Sorry."

"I don't know why I mentioned my father."

"I don't either. Let's get to work, okay?"

Tracy handed Quinn a stack of flyers exactly like the one Strange had given him the night before. "You might need more of these. We've got 'em posted around town, but they get ripped down pretty quick."

Quinn picked up the Paper Mate sitting atop the notepad he had brought along with him. "What else can you tell me about her?"

Tracy pushed another sheet of paper across the table at Quinn. "Jennifer ran away from her home in Germantown several months ago."

Quinn scanned the page. "This doesn't say why."

"She hit her teens and the hormones kicked in. Add to that, the kids she was hanging with were using drugs. It's the usual story, not so different from most that we hear. From interviews we did with her friends out in the county, it sounds like she started hooking before she split."

"In the outer suburbs?"

"What, you think that part of the world is immune to it? It starts out, girl will take a ride with an older guy and fellate him so she can buy a night of getting high for her and her friends. Or maybe she lets herself get penetrated, vaginally or even anally, for a little more cash. She doesn't get beat up or ripped up those first couple of times — she doesn't *learn* something, I mean — it accelerates pretty quickly after that. It gets easy."

"She's only fourteen."

"I'm hip."

"Okay, so she leaves Germantown. What makes you think she's in the District?"

"Her friends again. She told them where she was going. But they haven't heard from her since."

"You said she was using drugs. What kind?"

"Ecstasy was her favorite, what we heard. But she'd use anything that was put in front of her, if you know what I mean."

"Anything else?"

"We haven't done a thing except interview her parents and a few of her friends. Like we told Derek, we're up to our ears in county business right now. That's why we were looking to hook up with you guys for the D.C. side of things. My partner wanted to meet you, but she's out rounding up a girl she found as we speak."

"Rounding up?"

"Basically, we yank 'em right off the street when we find them. We've got this van, no windows —"

"This legal, what you do?"

"As long as they're minors, yeah. They have no domain over themselves, and if the parents sign a permission form for us to go after them it's all straight. If there are any repercussions, we deal with it later. We work with some lawyers, pro bono. Basically, we're out to save these kids."

"That's nice. But this work here, Derek didn't say anything about it being pro bono. And on top of our hourly rate, I'm gonna need expense money."

"Keep detailed records and you got it."

"It could get rich."

"We're covered by the APIP people."

"They must have some deep pockets."

"Grant money."

"Because I got a feeling I'm going to have to pay some people to talk."

"Okay. But I'm still going to need those details."

Tracy's hand kept going into a large leather bag set on the table. She had been fondling something inside of it, then removing her hand, then putting it back in again.

"What've you got in there?"

"My cigarettes."

"Well, you might as well stop romancing that pack. You can't light up in here."

"You can't light up anywhere," she said, adding by way of explanation, "It's the coffee."

"Gives you that urge, huh?" Quinn reached into a pocket and dropped a pack of sugarless gum between them. "Try this."

"No, thanks."

"We'll be done in a minute, you can step outside." Quinn tapped his pen on the notepad. "The one thing I'm wondering is, a girl runs away from home, there's got to be good reason. It can't just be galloping hormones and drugged-out friends."

"Sometimes there's an abusive parent involved in the equation, if that's what you're getting at. Emotional or physical or sexual abuse, or a combination of the three. Part of what me and Karen do is, we spend considerable time in the home, trying to figure out if that's the best place for the kid to go back to. And sometimes the home's not the best environment. But you're wrong about one thing: It often is just hormones and peers, and accelerating events, that make a kid run away. With Jennifer, we're convinced that's the case."

"Where do you suggest I start?"

"Start with stakeouts, like we do. The Wheaton mall, it's near D.C. and it's been good for us before. The overground rave clubs, trance, jungle, whatever they're calling it this week. The ones play a mix of live and prerecorded stuff. What's that place, in Southeast, on Half Street?"

"Nation."

"That one. Platinum is good, too, over on Ninth and F."

"I don't like stakeouts. I'd rather get out there and start talking to people."

"No one likes stakeouts. But suit yourself, whatever works for you."

"Anything else?"

"Just in general terms. White-girl runaways tend to start out in far Northwest, where they're around a familiar environment."

"Other white kids."

"Right. Places like Georgetown. They get hooked into drugs in a bigger way, they get taken in by a pimp —"

"They move east."

Tracy nodded. "It's gradual, and inevitable. Last stop is those New York Avenue flophouses in Northeast. You don't even want to know what goes on in those places."

"I already know. I was a patrol cop in the District, remember?"

Tracy turned her coffee cup slowly on the table. "Not just any cop."

"That's right. I was famous."

"It's not news to me. We ran your name through a search engine, and there were plenty of hits."

"Some people can't get past it, I guess."

"Maybe so. But as far as you and me are concerned, this is day one."

"Thanks."

"Anyway, first impression, you seem like an okay guy to me."

"You seem like an okay guy to me, too."

"I bought a tomato at Fresh Fields once."

"You probably spent too much for that shirt you're wearing, too."

"It's a blouse. I paid about forty bucks for it, I think."

Quinn touched his own T-shirt. "This Hanes I got on? Three for twelve dollars at Target, out on Twenty-nine."

"I better get out there before they run out."

Quinn tapped the stack of flyers on the table. "I'll phone you, keep you caught up."

"You ready for this?"

"Been a while," said Quinn. "But yeah, I'm stoked."

She watched him step out of the coffee shop, studying the way he filled out the seat of his Levi's and that cocky thing he did with his walk. Talking about her father, giving up something of herself to this guy who was, after all, a stranger, it was not what she would normally do. Add to that, Christ, she should have known better, he was a cop. But there was a connection between them already, sexual and probably emotional; it happened right away like that with her if it happened at all. She had known it two minutes after they had sat down together, and, she had seen it in his damaged green eyes; he had known it, too.

❐

STRANGE looked over the file on Calhoun Tucker that Janine had dropped on his desk.

"Nice work."

"Thanks," said Janine. She was sitting in the client chair in Strange's office. "I ran his license plate through Westlaw; everything came up easy after that. People Finder gave me the previous addresses."

Strange studied the data. Tucker's license plate number had given them his Social Security number, his date of birth, his assets, any criminal record, and any lawsuits. Janine had printed out his credit history, with past and present employment, as well. Credit drove the database of information; it was the foundation of computerized modern detective services. It was useless for getting histories on indigents and criminals who had never had a credit card or made time-payment purchases. But for someone like Tucker, who was part of the system, it worked just fine.

Janine had fed Tucker's SS number into People Finder, a subprogram of Westlaw. From this she had gotten a list of his current neighbors and the neighbors of his previous addresses.

"He looks pretty straight, first glance."

"No criminal record," said Janine. "Apart from a default on a car loan, he's barely stumbled."

Strange read the top sheet. "Graduate of Virginia Tech. Spends a few years in Portsmouth after college, working as an on-site representative for a company called Strong Services, whatever that's about."

"I'll find out."

"Looks like he owned a house in Portsmouth. Check on that, too, will you? Whose name was on it, any cosigners, like that."

"I will."

"Then he moved over to Virginia Beach."

"Most likely that's where he got into entertainment," said Janine. "Got involved in promotions in clubs, hookups with fraternities, like that. Looks like that's what he's doing up here now, with the Howard kids along U Street and the upscale club circuit over around Ninth and on Twelfth."

"That Audi he's driving —"

"Leased. Maybe he's beyond his means, but hey, he's in a business where image is half of what you are."

"I heard that." Strange dropped the file onto his desk. "Well, let me get on out of here, see what I can dig up. Can't tell much until you face-time."

"Tucker looks pretty clean to me."

"I hope you're right," said Strange. "There's nothin' I'd like better than to give George Hastings a good report."

Strange got up from his chair and walked around the desk. His office door was closed. He touched Janine on the cheek, then cupped his hand behind her neck, bent down, and kissed her on the mouth.

"You taste good."

"Strawberry," said Janine.

Strange clipped his beeper onto his belt and picked up the file.

"Terry phoned in," said Janine. "He was in Georgetown when he called. Asked Ron to run some girl's name, see if she has an arrest record in the District."

"He's workin' a job those county women farmed out to us. Did you bill them for that one I did the other night?"

"It went out yesterday."

"All right, then." Strange headed for the door. "See you later, baby."

"Tonight?" said Janine to his back.

Strange kept walking. "I'll let you know."

8

QUINN parked his Chevelle on R Street along Montrose Park, between Dunbarton Oaks and Oak Hill Cemetery in north Georgetown. He walked over to Wisconsin Avenue with a stack of flyers, a small staple gun, and a roll of industrial adhesive tape that he carried in a JanSport knapsack he wore on his back.

Foot traffic was moderate in the business district, with area workers breaking for lunch, along with college kids and the last of summer's visitors window-shopping the knockoff clothiers and chain stores. There wasn't anything here that couldn't be had elsewhere and at a better price. To Quinn, and to most of D.C.'s longtime residents, Georgetown during the day was a charmless tourist trap and a parking nightmare to be avoided at any cost.

Quinn went along Wisconsin and west to the residential side streets, stapling the flyers to telephone poles and taping them to city trash cans. He knew the flyers would largely be gone, ripped down by residents and foot cops, by nightfall, maybe sooner. It was a long shot, but it was a start.

South of the P Street intersection he stopped to talk to a skinny man, all arms and legs, built like a spider, who was leaning in the doorway of Mean Feets, D.C.'s longtime trendsetting shoe boutique, dragging on a Newport. Inside the shop, Quinn saw a handsome older man smoothly fitting a shoe onto the foot of a young woman as a D'Angelo tune came from the open front door.

As a former cop, Quinn knew that urban shoe salesmen spent a good portion of their day standing outside their shops, talking to women walking down the sidewalk, trying to get them inside, into their web. As it was an occupational necessity, they tended to remember not just shoe sizes but faces and names as well. They also serviced many of the city's hookers and their pimps.

Quinn greeted the skinny man, then opened a leather holder, flashing his badge and license. To the public, it looked like a cop's badge. Beside a picture of the D.C. flag, it actually read, "Metropolitan Police Department," over the words "Private Investigator." It was Quinn's habit, suggested to him by Strange, to show the license and badge long enough for the flag and MPD moniker to register, then put it away just as fast.

"Investigator, D.C.," said Quinn. Strange had taught him this, too. It wasn't against the law. It wasn't even a lie.

"What can I do for you, officer?"

"Name's Terry Quinn. You?"

"Antoine."

Quinn unfolded a flyer he had kept in his back pocket and handed it to Antoine. Antoine squinted through the smoke curling up from the cigarette dangling from his mouth.

"Any chance you've seen this girl?"

"Don't look familiar."

"You sell shoes to prostitutes from time to time, don't you?"

"Sure, I got my regular ladies, come in for their evening shoes. But I don't recognize this one. Been doin' this a long time in the District, too. She hookin'?"

"Could be."

"I don't recall ever seeing one this young in my shop. Not that I knew of, anyway."

"Do me a favor. Put this up in the back room, by the toilet, whatever." Quinn handed Antoine his card. "You or your coworkers, they see her, even if she's walking down the street, you give me a call."

Antoine dropped the cigarette, ground it out. He reached for his wallet, slipped Quinn's card inside, and retrieved a card of his own, handing it to Quinn.

"Now you do *me* a favor, officer. You need a pair of boots or somethin', get you out of those New Balances you got on, some-thin' a little more stylin', you give *me* a call, hear? Antoine. You walk in here, don't be *askin'* for anyone else."

"I got a wide foot."

"Oh, I'll fit you, now. Antoine can *stretch* some shoes."

"All right," said Quinn. "I'll see you around."

"The name is Antoine."

Quinn walked north to a strip club up the hill on Wisconsin, stopping at an ATM along the way. He entered without paying a cover and was seated by a bouncer at a table in the middle of a series of tables set tightly in a row throughout the depth of the nar-row club, facing one of several stages. Three men wearing ties, their shirtsleeves rolled back off their wrists, occupied the table. The men did not acknowledge Quinn. A nice-looking young woman in a sleeveless dress quickly arrived and took his order. She cupped her ear to hear him over the Limp Bizkit, their cover of "Faith," booming through the speakers.

Quinn checked out the dancers, working the poles on their stages, into the music, smiling politely at the audience but with their eyes someplace else. Thin, young, toned, and generally pleasant to look at. One of them was straight-up attractive, with a cheerleader's bright face and ruby red nipples. Connoisseurs claimed this place had the finest, cleanest-looking dancers in town. It was all perception and taste; Quinn knew men who swore by that joint near Connecticut and Florida Avenues. Quinn had been there once and judged it to be a skank-house.

The woman returned with a bottle of Bud, for which he paid dearly. He showed her the flyer. She barely looked at it and shook her head. Quinn paid her, tipped her, and asked for a receipt.

There were several bouncers working the room, all wearing radio headsets. The customers could go to the stages and tip the dancers, but they couldn't linger in the aisle, and if they did, one of the bouncers told them to get back to their seats. Patrons judged to be nursing their beers were encouraged to drink up and reorder or leave. This was the New World Order of strip clubs. To Quinn, it was all too bloodless and it didn't seem to be much fun.

Quinn recognized one of the bouncers, a black Asian-featured guy now standing by the front door, as a moonlighting cop. He didn't know the cop personally and didn't know his name. Quinn waited for his receipt, left his beer untouched, and walked over to the bouncer. He introduced himself, shook the guy's hand, and showed him the flyer.

"I don't know her," said the cop. He looked closely at Quinn. "Where'd you say you were at?"

"In the end, I rode Three-D."

The cop got that look of recognition then, the clouding over of the eyes, that Quinn had seen many times.

"Keep the flyer," said Quinn, handing the cop his business card as well. "You see her, do me a favor and give me a call."

Quinn walked out, Kid Rock screaming at his back. He knew the bouncer would throw the flyer and his card in the trash. He was one of those guys, once he figured out who Quinn was, he

didn't want to have anything to do with him. He'd never get past
the fact that Quinn had killed a fellow cop.

Quinn returned to his car and drove east, over the P Street
Bridge and onto the edge of Dupont Circle. He found a spot on
23rd Street, walked past a gay nightclub that had been there since
disco's first wave, and stopped at a coffeehouse at the next intersection. It was near P Street Beach, a stretch of Rock Creek Park
that in years past had been known for sunbathing, cruising, and
open-air sexual activity. Quinn remembered from his patrol days
that this was also an area where ecstasy could be easily scored, as
the 18th Street clubs were in the vicinity. It was a perimeter that
young hustlers worked as well.

He bought a cup of regular and took it out to where tables
were set on the sidewalk. He found a seat and checked out the
crowd. Teenagers were interspersed in the mostly adult customer
base of coffee drinkers and smokers. Some of the teenagers sat
with friends; others, both boys and girls, sat with older men.
Quinn guessed that some of these kids were cutting school, just
slumming, and some were runaways who crashed wherever they
could around town. That left the few who had gone professional
and were working the crowd.

Quinn had the feeling, from the eye contact he was getting,
that a couple of the kids had marked him as a cop. Strange claimed
you never lost the look. Quinn was way too old to be one of them,
too young to be a john, and, he told himself, too attractive to look
like the type who would pay for it. He was mulling over all of this,
sitting there trying to decide how to approach one of these kids.

Fuck it, he thought, getting up and crossing the sidewalk
patio to a table where two teenage girls sat, empty cups in front of
them, ashing the pavement with their cigarettes.

"Hey," said Quinn, "how you ladies doing?"

Both of the girls looked up, but only one of them kept her
eyes on him.

"We're fine, thanks." The girl, who had the look of hard money, someone who had been taught never to thank the waitress, said, "Something we can help you with?"

Quinn had obviously made a mistake. "I was wondering, can I snag a cigarette from you?"

She rolled her eyes and gave him one from her handbag without looking at him further. He thanked her and returned to his table, noticing a boy and his female friend laughing at him, feeling a flush of anger and trying to stifle it as he adjusted himself in his seat. Holding a cigarette and without even a match to complete the ruse.

He retrieved his cell from his pack and phoned the office. Janine switched him over to Ron Lattimer.

"Any luck?" said Ron.

"Nothing yet. Our girl got a sheet?"

"Jennifer Marshall. Got it right here."

"Solicitation?"

"Man wins the Kewpie doll."

"What about an address?"

"Listed as five seventeen J Street, Northwest. You might have a little trouble finding it, unless someone went and built a J Street in the last week or so —"

"There is no J Street in D.C."

"No *shit*."

"She's got a sense of humor, anyway."

"Or the one who told her to write it like that does."

"Thanks, Ron. I'll look over the rest of it when I come in. Derek around?"

"Uh-uh, he's out doing a background check."

"Tell him I was looking for him, hear?"

"Call him on his cell."

"He doesn't keep it on most of the time."

"You can leave a message on it, man."

"True."

"I see him, I'll tell him."

Quinn was replacing his cell in his bag when he noticed a girl standing before him. She wore boot-cut jeans and a spaghetti-string pink shirt with a cartoon illustration of a Japanese girl holding a guitar slung low, à la Keith. Her shoulder bag was white, oval, and plastic. Her dirty-blond hair fell to her shoulders. Her hips were narrow, her breasts small, mostly nipple and visible through the shirt. She was pale, with bland brown eyes and a tan birthmark, shaped like a strawberry, on her neck. She wore wire-rim prescription eyeglasses, granny style. She was barely cute, and not even close to pretty. Quinn put her in her midteens, maybe knocking on the door of seventeen, if that.

"You gonna smoke that?"

Quinn looked at the cigarette in his hand as if he were noticing it for the first time. "I don't think so."

"Can I get it from you, then?"

"Sure."

She sat down without invitation. He handed her the cigarette. "You got a light?"

"Sorry."

"You need a new rap," she said, rooting through her shoulder bag for a match. Finding a book, she struck a flame and put fire to the cigarette. "The one you got is lame."

"You think so?"

"You be hittin' those girls up for a smoke, you don't ask 'em for a light, you don't even have a match your *own* self?"

Quinn took in the girl's words, the rhythms, the dropping of the g's, the slang. Like that of most white girls selling it on the street, her speech was an affectation, a strange in-and-out blend of Southern cracker and city black girl.

"Pretty stupid, huh?"

"And if you was lookin' to score some ass, you went and picked the only two girls out here ain't even had their boots knocked yet. Couple of Sidwell Friends girls, trying out the street for a day before they go back to their daddy's Mercedes, got it parked around the block." She grinned. "You prob'ly don't even smoke."

"I tried it once and it made me sick."

"But you want something," she said, no inflection at all in her voice, just dead. It made Quinn sad.

"I'm looking for a girl."

"You a cop?"

"No."

"You have to tell me if you are. It's entrapment otherwise."

"I'm not a cop. I'm just looking for a girl."

"I can *get* you some pussy, now." She lowered his eyes, magnified behind the lenses, suggestively. "Shit, you can have this pussy right here, that's all you want."

Quinn found a flyer in his knapsack and slid it across the table. "I'm looking for her."

He watched her examine the face and data on the flyer. If she recognized Jennifer Marshall, her eyes did not give it up.

"I don't know her," said the girl. "But maybe I can hook you up with someone who does."

"You work the middle," said Quinn.

"When I can. It's rough out here, you know; I'm talkin' about the competition. My looks are, like, an acquired taste. Guys don't make passes at girls who wear glasses, and all that. My mother, when she was dolin' out one of her famous pearls of wisdom, used to remind me all the time. But contacts hurt my eyes. So here I am, lookin' like a magnet-school geek tryin' to peddle her ass. And my tits are too little, too. White johns like that black pussy, and with this kiddie pelvis I got, the brothers just tear my shit up. So maybe I'm not cut out for the life. You think I am?"

Quinn gave the girl a chin nod. "What's your name?"

"Stella. Yours?"

"Terry Quinn. You were gonna hook me up, Stella."

"It's gonna cost you fifty."

"For a name?"

"It's a good name."

"How do I know?"

"'Cause I ga-ran-tee it, dude. Now how about that fifty?"

Quinn paid her discreetly. She finished her cigarette and dropped it to the concrete.

"There's a girl dances over at Rick's, on New York Avenue, on the way out of town, past North Capitol?"

"I know the place."

"Black girl, goes by Eve. They call her All-Ass Eve; you see her, you'll know why. She knows this girl."

"How do you know that she knows her?"

For the first time, Stella's confidence was visibly shaken. She recovered quickly, though, smiling crookedly like a child caught in a lie. And Quinn saw the little girl then, just for a moment, that someone had rocked to sleep, bought presents for, loved. Maybe not always — maybe the mother or the father had fucked up somewhere along the way. But he had to believe that this girl had been loved at one time.

"Okay, I don't know for sure that Eve knows this girl right here, but listen to me: This is the *kind* of girl Eve gets to know. She cruises through this intersection, and in bus stations and malls, lookin' for new talent so she can steer it to her pimp. Everyone workin' this area knows who she is. The ones been around know to stay away from her and stick to this side of the creek. But the girl in this picture right here? She is fresh meat. I mean, she looks like she don't know jack. It's the dumb ones, the desperate ones that go with Eve. I'm just connecting things, is all. Anyway, Eve don't work out for you, you come back, we'll start again."

"For more money."

Stella shrugged. "I'm strugglin', dude."

"How do I reach you?"

Stella gave Quinn her cell number. He used his to phone her right there at the table. Her cell rang in her shoulder bag. She fished it out and answered.

"Hellooo? Officer Quinn?"

"Okay." He killed the call on his cell and gave her one of his cards. "You want to talk, you call me, hear?"

"Talkin' don't pay my bills." She looked him over. "I'll suck your dick for another fifty, though."

"This pans out, there's another fifty in it for you just for giving me the lead."

"I'll take it. But don't use my name when you're talking to Eve."

"You don't need to tell me that. Eight years on the force, I never once lost a snitch."

"Knew you were a cop."

"In another life," said Quinn, getting up and stepping back from the table. "Let's stay in touch, all right?"

chapter

9

CALHOUN Tucker was tall and lean and visibly muscled beneath a crisp beige shirt tucked into tailored black slacks. He had a thin Billy D mustache and some kind of pomade worked into his close black hair that gave it shine. He wore expensive-looking shades and a small, new-tech cell clipped to his waistband. All of this Strange could see through his 10×50 binoculars as he sat in his Chevy, surveilling Tucker across the street from his residence, a rental town house near a medical park between Wheaton and Silver Spring.

Tucker went down the sidewalk toward his car, a cherry red S4, Audi's hopped-up model in the 4-series line, their version of the BMW M3. Tucker's complexion was a deep brown, not so dark as to hide his features, not so light as to suggest white blood. He walked with confidence, chin up, like the handsome young man he undoubtedly knew he was. He had the package women liked; the confidence thing, they liked that, too. Strange could see right away why Alisha Hastings had been attracted, surface-wise, to Tucker.

Tucker fired up the Audi and pulled out of his space. Strange followed him south, making sure there were plenty of cars between them all the way. Just over the District line, Tucker shot right on Alaska, then another right up 13th, into the cluster of "flower-and-tree" streets, where he cut a left onto Iris. He was heading for George Hastings's house. Strange went around the block, counter to the route Tucker had taken, and parked in the alley behind Juniper. He got out of his car and left the alley on foot, his binos in his hand.

By the time Strange made it to the intersection of Iris and 13th, Alisha Hastings had come out of her father's house and was leaning into the driver's-side window of Tucker's ride, idling out front behind George's Volvo. Alisha had on some kind of casual, wear-around-the-house hookup that looked spontaneous but had probably been planned. Tucker had probably called her from his cell and told her he would be stopping by on his way into town. Strange didn't blame Tucker for wanting to get a look at her before he started his day; Alisha was radiant and poised, with deep dimples framing her lovely smile. Tucker had his hand on her forearm and he was lightly stroking it, talking to her, making her laugh, making her so happy she had to look away. Seeing the two of them there, it reminded Strange of a girl he had loved hard back in the early seventies. He watched them kiss. A twinge of guilt snapped in his chest, and he went back to get his car.

He followed Tucker down into Shaw. Tucker parked on U Street, and Strange put his Chevy in a spot along a construction fence on 10th. He jogged up to the corner and saw Tucker walking west, carrying a briefcase of some kind. He followed Tucker until he went up the steps and into a nightclub that was a quiet bar and lunch joint during the day. Tucker came out ten minutes later and walked farther west to a similar club. He entered, and Strange stood back and leaned against a parking-meter pole stripped of its head. Back from where he'd come, he could see the lunch crowd going in and out of Ben's. His felt his mouth water and a rumble in his stomach, and he looked the other way.

It took Tucker a while to come out of the club. Strange knew the place. He used to drink there occasionally when it was a neighborhood bar, just a few short years ago. In the summer the management had strung speakers outside, and on some nights, driving slowly down U Street, Strange could hear James Brown doing "Payback," or a Slave tune, or Otis and Carla singing "Tramp," and that was enough to cause him to pull over and stop in for a beer. All types were in the bar then, even a few whites; you could wear what you wanted to, it was cool. But then they changed things over, instituting a dress code, and a race code, it seemed, as one night Strange had seen some fancy brothers punk out this one young white dude who was sitting at the bar quietly drinking a beer. The white dude, he wasn't bothering anyone, but he wasn't the right color and he wasn't wearing the right clothes, and they hard-eyed him enough to make him feel like he wasn't wanted, and soon he was gone. Strange hadn't gone back since. The truth was, he was too old for the crowd himself, and he preferred a working-class atmosphere when he sat down to have his drinks. Mostly, he didn't dig that kind of intolerance, no matter who was on the giving or the receiving end. He'd seen too much in his life to excuse that kind of behavior from anyone, even his own people. If this was the New U, then it wasn't for him.

Strange retrieved his car and kept it running on the street, waiting for Tucker to come out of the bar. Soon Tucker walked down the steps of the club, slipping his shades on, and went to his car. He pulled out onto U, and Strange followed.

Tucker went east, over to Barry Place, parking his Audi between Sherman and 9th, not far from Howard University. Strange kept going and circled the block.

He parked on the Sherman / Barry corner and got his AE-1,

outfitted with a 500mm lens, out of his trunk, keeping his eye on Tucker, who was now walking down the street, talking on his cell. Strange returned to the driver's seat of his Chevy, where he had a clear view of Tucker, and snapped several photographs of him walking up the steps of a row house and waiting at its door. He got a last shot of Tucker going though the open door, and of the woman who let him in. He used the long lens to read the address off one of the brick pillars fronting the porch of the house. He used his cell to phone in the address to Janine. Janine had a reverse-directory program on her computer that would give them a phone number and name for the residence.

Strange sat there for an hour or so, sipping water from a bottle, listening to Joe Madison's talk show on WOL, while he thought of what was going on in the house. Maybe that was a business appointment in there, or it was a friend and the two of them were having lunch. More likely, right about now Tucker was knocking the back end out of that woman Strange had seen in the open door. Strange was disappointed but not surprised. Thinking about that young man and woman in there, it stirred something in him, too. He'd done enough today. He was hungry and he had to pee.

Strange ignitioned the Chevy and drove over to Chinatown, where he parked in an alley behind I Street. A man whom Strange recognized, a heroin addict who worked the alley, appeared like a phantom, and Strange handed him a five to look after his car. Then he went in a back door next to a Dumpster, down a hall where he passed a kitchen and several closed doors, and through a beaded entranceway into a small dining area where dulcimer music played softly. He took a deuce and ordered some hot-and-sour soup and Singapore-style noodles from an older woman who called him by his name. He washed the lunch down with a Tsingtao.

"Everything okay?" said the hostess.

"Yes, mama, it was good. Bring me my check."

"You want?" she said, her eyes moving to the beaded curtain leading to the hall. "Your friend here."

Strange nodded.

He paid cash and went down the hall to a door opposite the kitchen. He went through the door and closed it behind him. He was in a white-walled room lit by scented votive candles. The music from the dining area played in the room. A padded table was in the center of the room, with a small cart set beside it holding lotions, towels, and a washbasin.

Strange went through another door, turned on a light, and undressed in a room containing a toilet, sink, and tiled shower stall. He hung his clothing on a coat tree and took a hot shower, wrapping a towel around himself when he was done. Then he returned to the candlelit room and lay facedown on the padded table. Soon he heard a door open and saw light spear into the room. The light slipped away as the door was closed.

"Hello, Stwange."

"Hello, baby."

Strange heard the squirt of an applicator and next felt the woman's warm, slick hands. She kneaded the lotion, some sweet-smelling stuff, into his shoulder muscles and his lats. He felt her rough nipples graze his back as she bent in to whisper in his ear.

"You have good day today?"

"Uh-huh."

She hummed to the music as she massaged his back. The sound of her voice and the sensation of her touch made him hard. He turned over, the towel falling open. She massaged his chest, his calves, his upper thighs, working her way up to his balls. The lotion was warm there; Strange swallowed.

"You like?"

"Yeah, that's good right there."

She applied more lotion to her hands and fisted his cock. Her movement was slow. As her hand went up his shaft, she feathered the head with her fingers. Strange opened his eyes.

The woman was in her twenties, with carelessly applied lipstick and eyes like black olive pits. She wore red lace panties and nothing else. She was short and had the hips of a larger woman. Her breasts were small and firm. He brushed his fingers across one nipple until it was pebble hard, and when the fire rose up in his loins he pinched her there until she moaned. He didn't care if it was all fake.

"Go now," he said, and she pumped him faster.

His orgasm was eye-popping, his own jism splattering his stomach and chest.

"You need," said the woman, chuckling under her breath.

As she wet-toweled him, Strange said, "Yes."

Dressed again, he left forty-five dollars in a bowl by the door.

Out in the alley, his beeper sounded. It was the office number. He debated whether or not to return the call. He got into his car and used his cell to dial the number. Quinn's voice came through from the other end.

"I stopped by the office to pick up Jennifer Marshall's sheet from Ron," said Quinn. "Where you at?"

"Chinatown," said Strange.

"Uh-huh."

"Had some lunch."

"Okay."

Strange had spilled his guts to Quinn one night when both of them had put away too many beers. Giving up too much of himself to Quinn had come back to him in a bad way. It was always a mistake.

"I'm headed down to Rick's, on New York Avenue," said Quinn, then explained the reason. "You wanna join me?"

"Yeah, okay."

"C'mon over to the office. We can drive down together."

"I'll meet you at Rick's," said Strange. "Say, half hour?"

"Fine," said Quinn. "Bring some dollar bills."

Strange cut the line. He didn't want to go back to the office and have to small-talk Janine. He was relieved it hadn't been her on the phone when he'd called in.

On his way east, he drove by the row house on Barry Place, the site of Calhoun Tucker's afternoon tryst. Tucker's Audi was gone.

chapter

10

RICK'S was a stand-alone A-frame establishment located a few miles east of North Capitol on New York Avenue, a bombed-out-looking stretch of road that was the jewel-in-the-crown introduction to Washington, D.C., for many first-time visitors who traveled into the city by car.

The building now holding Rick's had originally been built as a Roy Rogers burger house. It had mutated into its current incarnation, a combination sports bar and strip joint for working stiffs, when the Roy's chain went the way of corded telephones.

The conversion had been simple. The new owners had gutted the fast-food interior, keeping only a portion of the kitchen and the bathroom plumbing, and hung some Redskins, Wizards, and Orioles memorabilia on the walls. The omission of Washington Capitals pennants was intentional, as hockey was generally not a sport that interested blacks. The final touch was to brick up the windows that had once wrapped around three sides of the structure.

Bricked windows generally meant one of three things: arson victim, gay bar, or strip joint. Once the word got around on which kind of place Rick's was, the owners didn't even bother to hang a sign out front.

Rick's had its own parking lot, an inheritance from the Roy's lease. A couple of locals had been shot in this parking lot in the past year, but pre-sundown and in the early evening hours, before the liquor turned peaceful men brave, then violent, the place was generally safe.

Strange pulled his Caprice alongside Quinn's blue Chevelle, parked in an empty corner of the lot. Quinn got out of his car as Strange stepped out of his. They met and shook hands. Quinn made a show of sniffing the air.

"Damn, Derek. You smell kinda, I don't know, *sweet*. Is that perfume?"

"I don't know what you're talkin' about, man."

It was the lotion that girl had rubbed on him back in Chinatown. Strange knew that Quinn was remarking on it, in his own stupid way.

They walked toward Rick's.

Strange nodded at the JanSport hanging off Quinn's shoulder. "What, we goin' mountain climbing now? Thought we were just gonna have a beer or two."

"My briefcase."

"You been waitin' on me long?"

"Not too long," said Quinn.

"You coulda gone inside," said Strange, giving Quinn a long look. "I bet I would have spotted you right quick."

"I'd be the one on the bottom of the pile."

"With the red opening in his neck, stretchin' from one ear to the other."

"Not too many white guys in this place, huh?"

"Seeing a white guy at Rick's be like spottin' a brother at a Springsteen concert."

"I figured I'd just wait for you to escort me in."

"No need to tempt fate. It's what I been telling you the past two years. You're learning, man."

"I'm trying," said Quinn.

They went into Rick's. Smoke hovered in the dim lights. The place was half filled, just easing into happy hour. A bar ran along one wall where the order counter for Roy's had been, and beyond it was a series of doors. Guys sat at the stick, watching the nostalgia sports channel, Packers uniforms dancing in a flurry of snow, "Spill the Wine" playing on the stereo throughout the house. In two corners, women danced in thongs, nothing else, for groups of men seated at tables. Waitresses wearing short shorts and lacy tops were servicing the tables. Big men with big shoulders and no headsets were stationed around the room.

Floor patrons fish-eyed Strange and Quinn as they stepped up to the bar. Those seated at the bar barely noticed their presence, as their eyes were glued to the television set mounted on the wall.

Strange nodded up at the set. "You want to get a man's attention, put on any Green Bay game where it got played in the snow. Guy'll sit there like a glassy-eyed old dog, watchin' it."

"It's like when they run *The Good, the Bad and the Ugly* on TNT."

"You mean, like, every week?"

"Tell me the truth; if you're scanning the channels with the remote and you see Eastwood, or Eli Wallach as Tuco —"

"'Otherwise known as the Rat.'"

"Right," said Quinn. "So, when you recognize that movie, have you ever been able to scan past it? I mean, you always sit there and watch the rest of the film, don't you?"

"*The Wild Bunch* is like that, too," said Strange. "How many times you figure you've seen that one?"

Quinn pumped out two short strokes with his fist. "With my pants on, or with them around my ankles?"

Strange chuckled as the bartender, a young guy with a hard face, arrived before them. "What can I get y'all?"

"I'll take a Double R Bar burger and a saddle fulla fries," said Quinn, but the bartender didn't smile.

"Heineken for me," said Strange.

"Bud," said Quinn.

"In bottles," said Strange. "And we're gonna need a receipt."

The tender returned with their beers. Quinn paid him and dropped a heavy tip on the bar, placing his hand over the cash. "Which one of the girls is Eve?"

"That's her right there," said the bartender, chinning in the direction of a big-boned dancer working one of the corners of the room.

"When does she stop?"

"They work half hours."

"Any idea how long she's been at it?"

" 'Bout ten years, from the looks of her."

"I meant tonight."

"Ain't like I been clockin' her."

"Right," said Quinn. He took his hand off the money, and the bartender snatched it without a word. He had never once looked Quinn in the eye.

Strange saw two men get up from their table near Eve's corner. He folded the bar receipt, put it in his breast pocket, and said to Quinn, "There we go, that's us right there."

They crossed the floor, one of the stack-shouldered bouncers staring hard at Quinn as they passed. "Sweet Sticky Thing" came forward from the house system. Quinn and Strange had a seat at the deuce. Strange leaned forward and tapped his beer bottle against Quinn's.

"Relax," said Strange.

"I get tired of it, is all."

"You expect all the brothers to show you love, huh?"

"Just respect," said Quinn.

They drank off some of their beers and watched the work of the woman the bartender had identified as Eve. She was squatting, her back to a group of men, her palms resting atop her thighs, working the muscles in her lower back. Her huge ass jiggled rapidly, seemingly disconnected from the rest of her. It moved wildly before the men.

"Someone ought to give that a name," said Strange.

"She does have a nickname: All-Ass Eve."

"Bet it didn't take long to come up with it."

"You like it like that?"

"Is seven up?"

"She doesn't hold a candle to Janine."

"That's what I know. You don't have to tell me, man." Strange smiled and pointed to one of the speakers suspended from the ceiling by wires. "Listen to this right here. The third verse is comin' up."

"So?"

"The horn charts behind this verse are beautiful, man. The Ohio Players never did get much credit for the complexity in their shit."

"That's nice," said Quinn. "You know, Janine was askin' where you were when I was back in the office."

"You tell her I was in Chinatown?"

"I don't like lying to her." Quinn's eyes cut off Strange's stare. "No, I didn't say where you were."

Strange had a sip of beer. "You met with Sue Tracy, right?"

"Yeah."

"What'd you think?"

"She's a pro. She's nice."

"Bet you didn't find her all that hard to look at, either."

"Knock it off."

"Just wanted to make sure you still had some red blood runnin' through your veins. While you're sittin' over there judgin' me with your eyes."

Quinn didn't respond. Strange said, "Ron give you the sheet on the Marshall girl?"

"I got it."

"What did it tell you?"

"She got popped for solicitation. It's a no-paper, so we won't be finding her in court."

"She put an address on the form?" said Strange.

"A phony. But the spot where she wrote down her contact was interesting. A guy named Worldwide Wilson."

"Worldwide."

"Yeah, looks like she gave up the name of her pimp."

"She give out his phone number, too?"

"She did write one down. But it's got one of those number symbols after it."

"Must be his pager."

"Genius."

"Just tryin' to help you out, rookie."

"Anyway, I'll find out tonight."

They watched the rest of Eve's performance. The music programmer stuck with the Ohio Players and moved into "Far East Mississippi" and "Skin Tight." Strange and Quinn ordered two more beers. Eve finished her shift and walked off through one of the doors behind the bar, accompanied by the stack-necked bouncer who had hard-eyed Quinn. A woman arrived, built similarly to Eve, and she began to dance in the same way Eve had danced, this time to a tune by the Gap Band. The woman's behind rippled as if it were in a wind tunnel.

"This here must be strictly an ass joint," said Quinn.

"And they asked me when I took you on, Will he make a good detective."

"It's like their signature dish."

"Ledo's Pizza got pizza. The Prime Rib's got prime rib. Rick's got ass."

"You black guys do love the onion."

"Was wonderin' when you were gonna get to that."

Soon Eve came out of the back room wearing a sheer top with no bra and matching shorts showing the lines of her thong. She was going around to the tables, shaking hands with the men, some of whom were slipping her money in appreciation of her performance. The stack-necked bouncer was never far from Eve. He had braided hair and a gold tooth. Quinn thought he looked like Warren Sapp, that football player. He was big as one.

"She'll be here in a second, Terry. I'll ask the questions, you don't mind."

"My case. Let me handle it, all right?"

Eve was a large woman, in proportion with her backside. Her nose was thick and wide, and her lips, painted a bright red, were prominent; her hands and feet had the size of a man's. She had sprayed herself with some kind of sweet perfume, and it was strong on Strange and Quinn as she arrived at their table.

"Did you gentlemen like my performance?" she said, giving them a shy smile, her hand out.

"I did," said Strange.

Quinn extended his hand, a twenty-dollar bill folded in it so that she could see the denomination. He pulled it back as she reached out for it.

"C'mon back when you have a minute," said Quinn. "My friend and I want to talk to you."

Eve kept her smile, but it twitched at one corner. Strange noticed her bad teeth, a common trait among hos.

"Management says I can't sit down with the customers," said Eve, " 'less they buy me a cocktail."

"Bet you like those fruity ones," said Strange, "loaded up with all kinds of rums."

"Mmmm," said Eve, licking her lips clumsily.

"We'll see you in a few," said Quinn.

The bouncer gave him one long, meaningful look before he and Eve went off to the next table full of suckers.

"That drink's gonna cost you, like, another seven," said Strange.

"I know it."

"Won't even have no liquor in it."

"Thanks, Dad."

"Make sure you get a receipt. We'll charge it to your girl Sue."

Eve returned after a while and pulled a chair over from another table, sliding it in between Strange and Quinn. She carried a collins glass filled with pinkish liquid and held it up by way of salute to her new friends before taking a sip. The bouncer had a seat on a stool positioned a table away and stared at Quinn. Kool and the Gang's "Soul Vibration" played loud on the sound system. Strange watched the dancers bring it down a notch to catch the groove of the song.

"Thanks for the drink," said Eve. She wiped her mouth and placed the drink on the table. Her lipstick had made a kiss mark on the glass. "You two wouldn't be police officers, would you?"

"We're not with the police," said Quinn, pushing the yellow flyer he had taken from his pack across the table. He dropped the twenty on top of the flyer, careful not to cover the photograph of Jennifer Marshall. "You recognize this girl?"

Eve's eyes held their neutral vacancy. "No."

"You sure?"

"I said no. Was I talkin' too soft for you?"

"I can hear you fine. I don't believe you is what it is."

Eve's smile, like a death rictus, remained upon her face. "You're cuttin' me deep, white boy."

Strange looked over at the bouncer, then around the room. He recognized one guy, an older cat with a cool-fish handshake he'd seen at church now and again. Anything went down, this cat would be no help at all.

Quinn leaned forward. "You never seen her, like at a bus station, nothin' like that? How about over by P Street Beach?"

Eve's smile faded, and with it any facade of love.

"Ever hear of a guy named Worldwide Wilson?" said Quinn.

Eve's eyes were dead now, still on Quinn. She shook her head slowly.

"You steer girls over to Wilson, Eve. Isn't that right?"

Eve reached for the twenty on the table. Quinn put a hand over her wrist and pushed his thumb in at her pressure point. He pressed just enough for her to feel it. But if she felt it, it didn't show. In fact, the smile returned to her face.

"All right, Terry," said Strange. "Let her go."

The bouncer was still staring at Quinn but hadn't moved an inch. Eve slowly pulled her hand free. Quinn let her do it.

"You know why you still conscious?" said Eve, her voice so soft it was barely audible above the sounds in the club. "'Cause you don't mean a *mother*fuckin' thing to nobody up in here."

"I'm lookin' for this girl," said Quinn just as softly, tapping his finger on the flyer.

"Then look to the one who gave you my name."

"Say it again?"

"Do I look like I hang on P Street to you?" Eve took the twenty off the table and slipped it into the waistband of her shorts. "White boy, you got played."

Eve stood out of her chair, letting her eyes drift over Strange, then walked away.

"You done?" said Strange. "Or you want another beer?"

"I'm done," said Quinn, looking past Strange into the room.

"We could buy the house a round. Sing some drinking songs with all your new friends, like they do in those Irish bars —"

"Let's go."

As they moved toward the bar, Quinn's and the bouncer's eyes met.

"Check you later, slim," said the bouncer, and Quinn slowed his step. It was something you said to a girl.

Strange tugged on Quinn's T-shirt. At the stick, Strange settled the tab while Quinn kept his back at the bar, watching the patrons in the house, many of them now staring at him. Some were grinning. He felt the warmth of blood that had gone to his face. He wanted to fight someone. Maybe he wanted them all.

"We're gone," said Strange, handing the receipt to Quinn.

Vapor lights cast a bleached yellow on the lot outside the club. They walked the asphalt to their cars.

"That was good," said Strange. "Subtle, like."

Quinn kept looking back to the door of the club.

"Wanna go back in, huh?"

"Drop it."

"Terry, one thing you got to learn to do is, don't take all this bullshit too personal."

"Guess I ought to be more detached, like you."

"You need to manage some of that anger you got inside you, man."

"Tomorrow's Wednesday. We got practice in the evening, right Derek?"

"Six o'clock on the dot," said Strange.

"I'll see you then."

Quinn drove his Chevelle out of the lot while Strange killed some time, fumbling with his car radio and such. When Quinn was out of sight, Strange locked up his car and walked back into Rick's.

c h a p t e r

11

"Girl," said Strange, "you gonna bleed me dry."

"House rules," said Eve with a shrug. "You want me to sit down with you, you gotta buy me one of these drinks."

"Tell the truth, though. There's no liquor in that glass, right?"

"You *know* it ain't nothin' but sugar and juice."

"Figured it was some kinda hustle," said Strange.

They were seated at the far end of the bar, away from the sports junkies, near the service station. Eve's bouncer was nearby, talking to one of the dancers, keeping one eye on the house, one on Eve.

"That your man?" said Strange.

"Yeah. You got to have one, and he's as good as any I've had. Never has raised a hand to me once."

Eve slid a cigarette from a pack the bartender had placed before her as she took her seat. Strange struck a match and gave her a light.

"Thank you, sugar."

"Ain't no thing."

"Say your name again?"

"Derek Strange."

She dragged on the smoke, then hit it again. Strange took a
ten from his wallet and placed it on the bar between him and Eve.
Eve's head was moving to the Tower of Power coming from the
house system as she slipped the ten into her shorts.

"'Clever Girl,'" said Strange.

"I ain't all that. Would I be here if I was?"

"I'm sayin', that's the name of this song. Lenny Williams up
front. Ain't no question, he was the best vocalist this group had,
and they had a few."

"Little before my time."

"I know, darling." Strange leaned in close to Eve. "Let me
just go ahead and ask you straight up, you don't mind. Do you
know the girl in the flyer?"

Eve shook her head. "No."

"I didn't think you did."

"I *told* your boy."

"But you do know this cat Worldwide."

"He was my pimp at one time."

"Was?"

"I stopped trickin' last year. I can make a better living doing
this right here. Plus, I got this thing at Lord and Taylor's, up in
Chevy Chase? Givin' out perfume samples, like that."

"Always wondered where they found those pretty girls in
places like that."

"Thank you," said Eve, lowering her eyes for a moment and
then fixing them again on Strange.

"Sounds like you're doin' all right."

"I'm makin' it."

"You just walked away from trickin', huh?"

"Worldwide specializes in those young girls. It wasn't like I went off to another pimp. That's something he wouldn't let happen, understand what I'm sayin'? What it was, he couldn't use me no more. I got old, Strange. So I clean-breaked and came on over here."

"You're like, what, thirty? That ain't old."

Eve tapped ash off her smoke. "I'm twenty-nine. That's old for World."

"What about the one who gave Quinn your name? You know her?"

"Oh, yeah. Had to be this little white bitch, name of Stella."

"She told him you steered girls over to Wilson."

"I ain't never done that. It's what *she* does. Can't sell her own ass; ain't nobody even wants that pussy for free. Trick-ass bitch hustled your boy out of his money, bringin' him my way. I knew straight off, he mentioned P Street, it was her. 'Cause that's her corner, right? She gets next to those young white-girl runaways and puts them up with World. She was doin' that shit when *I* was with him, and she still is, I guess. Thought she could make some quick change, givin' up my name. That's her, all the way."

"Where's Worldwide base his self?"

"Uh-uh." Eve took a final drag off her cigarette and crushed it dead in the ashtray. "Look, I talked too much already. And I got to get myself back to work."

"I need you, I can get up with you here, right?"

"Door's open, long as you just wanna watch me dance. Far as this goes, though, we are done. You do come back, don't be bringin' your Caucasian friend with you, hear?"

"Boy's got some anger management problems is what it is."

"Needs to learn some manners, too." Eve stood and straightened her outfit. "Listen, you do run into World —"

"I don't know you no way. I never met you, and I don't even know your name."

Eve's eyes softened. She looked younger then, and when she moved in and rested her hand on Strange's shoulder, it felt good.

"Somethin' else, too," she said. "Don't you even have a dream of fuckin' with that man. This is *not* somethin' you want to do."

"I hear you, baby."

Eve kissed him lightly on the cheek. "You smell kinda sweet for a man, y'know it?"

Strange said, "Take care of yourself, all right?"

She moved away and went through one of the doors behind the bar. Strange settled his tab and got his receipt. On his way out he stopped by the bouncer with the braided hair. He stood before him, looked him up and down, and smiled.

"Damn, boy," said Strange, "you got some size on you, don't you?"

"I go about two forty," said the bouncer.

"Looks like most of it's muscle, too. Can you move?"

"I'm quick for my size."

"You a D.C. boy, right?"

"Uh-huh."

"Played for who?"

"Came out of Ballou in ninety-two."

"The Knights. No college?"

The bouncer spread his hands. "I ain't had the grades."

"Well, all that natural talent you got, you ought to be doin' somethin' 'stead of standing in this bar, breathing in all this smoke."

"I heard that. But this here is what I got."

"Listen," said Strange, "thank you for handling that situation the way you did."

"I don't reach out for trouble. But I only give out one get-out-of-jail card per customer, see what I'm sayin'? You need to tell your boy, he comes back in here again, I *will* kick his motherfucking ass."

Strange put a business card into the bouncer's left hand, shook his right. "You ever need anything, the name's Strange."

Strange walked out, thinking on one of those golden rules his mother used to repeat, that one about the honey always gettin' the flies. His mother, she was full of those corny old sayings. Him and his brother, when he was alive, used to joke about it with her all the time. She'd been gone awhile now, and more than anything, he missed hearing her voice. The longer he lived the more he realized, damn near everything she'd taught him, seemed like it was right.

❐

QUINN showered at his apartment on Sligo Avenue, then walked up to town, passing the bookstore on Bonifant, stopping to check the lock on the front door before he went on his way. He drank two bottles of Bud at the Quarry House, seated next to a dwarfish regular who read paperback novels, spoke rarely, but was friendly when addressed. Quinn had gotten a taste at Rick's and knew his evening would not be done without a couple more. These days, he almost always walked into bars by himself. He hadn't had a girl-friend since things between him and Juana, a law student and waitress up at Rosita's on Georgia Avenue, had fallen apart over a year ago. But he still frequented the local watering holes. He liked the atmosphere of bars, and he didn't like to drink alone.

After his beers, Quinn walked up to Selim Avenue, trying but failing to not look in the window of Rosita's, then crossed the pedestrian bridge spanning Georgia that led to the B&O train station alongside the Metro tracks. At this time of night the gate leading to the tunnel that ran beneath the tracks was locked, so he stayed on the east side. As he often did, he stood there on the platform, admiring the colored lights of the businesses and the pale yellow haloing the street lamps of downtown Silver Spring. A freight train approached, raising dust as it passed, and he closed his eyes to feel the stir of the wind. When the sound of the train faded he opened his eyes and went back in the direction of his place.

He came up here to the tracks nearly every night. The platform reminded him of a western set, and he liked the solitude, and the view. A construction crew had been working on the station, probably converting it into a museum or something, a thing to be looked at but not used, another change in the name of redevelopment and gentrification. Of course, he didn't know for sure what they were doing to the station, but recent history convinced him that it was something he would not like. In the last year Quinn's breakfast house, the Tastee Diner, had been moved to a location off Georgia, and he rarely ate there anymore as it was out of his foot range. Also, with its new faux-deco sign out front, it now looked liked the Disney version of a diner. He wondered when the small pleasure of his nightly walk would be taken from him, too.

❐

BACK at his apartment, Quinn checked his messages and returned a call from Strange, who had phoned from Janine's place. Strange told him what he had learned from Eve.

"Sounds like you ought to go back to that girl Stella," said Strange.

"I will," said Quinn. "Thanks."

Quinn was a little jealous that Strange had been able to get what he could not, but he was cognizant of his own limitations, and grateful that Strange had made the extra effort on his behalf.

After hanging up with Strange, he sat on his couch, rubbing his hands together, looking around at the spartan decor of his apartment, which was no decor at all. He was high from the beers and a little reckless from the high, and he felt as if his night was not done. He dragged his knapsack over to the couch, found Stella's phone number, and then saw Worldwide Wilson's number on Jennifer Marshall's sheet. He reached for his phone and dialed the number Jennifer had scribbled down.

It was a pager number, as he knew it would be. Quinn left his home phone number, waited for the tone that told him the number had been received, and cut the line.

He stared at the phone in his hand, looked around the room, stared at the phone some more, then dialed Stella's cell. She answered on the third ring.

"Hellooo. Officer Quinn?"

"You psychic or something?"

"Caller ID, duh."

"I ought to get one of those 'number unknown' things."

"Bet you're too cheap to pay for the service, Quinn."

"It always comes back to money for you."

"Well, yeah."

"Why'd you do it, Stella?"

"You musta talked to Eve."

"I had the pleasure."

"She bugged on you, huh?"

"I guess I ought to ask you another way. Why'd you send me to her? You could've put me onto somebody who didn't know anything at all."

"That's true. But I wanted you to come back to me. I wanted to see how bad you wanted Jennifer, baby doll. And I can see that you do. I mean, you didn't come looking to kick my ass or nothin' like that. You're callin' me like a gentleman and you don't sound angry. Are you angry at me, Quinn?"

"No," he said, but it was a lie. "Can you deliver Jennifer?"

"I'd deliver my mother for a price. Shit, I'd give you my mother for free, everything she done to me."

"What's the price?"

"Five hundred will get you your girl."

"How you gonna do that, Stella?"

"I got somethin' of hers. Somethin' I know she wants."

"You stole from her?"

"Oh, *my* bad."

"You're a piece of work."

"Always good to have a little somethin' someone wants, information or merchandise, you know what I'm sayin'? Like I told you, it's rough out here."

"What about Worldwide?"

Quinn heard the snap of a match and the burn of a cigarette.

"What about him?" said Stella.

"You're working for him. I don't think he'd take too kindly to you setting up one of his girls to get taken off the street."

"Course not. Worldwide is a bad motherfucker, for real. But he ain't never gonna know, green eyes, 'less you thinkin' on tellin' him. You don't have to worry about me, 'cause I have done this before. Made some large money on it, too. Parents pay more than ex-cops, but I take whatever's there."

"Always playing the middle."

"When I can."

"I won't worry about you, Stella. But I do want this girl. So I'll get you the money, with one condition. That you'll be right there with me when I make the snatch. Because I don't trust you, understand? I won't get burned by you again."

"Fair enough."

"When can we set it up?"

"Soon as you want, lover."

"I need to get my hands on the money and a van. How's tomorrow night sound?"

"Sounds good."

"I'll call you tomorrow, hear?"

Quinn hit "end." He phoned Sue Tracy and got her on her cell.

"Sue, it's Terry." He cleared his throat. "Quinn."

"Hey, Terry." There was a rasp to her voice, and he heard a long exhale before she said, "What's up?"

"Listen, I got a strong line on Jennifer Marshall. But I'm gonna need a half a yard to buy the last piece of the puzzle."

"I can get it."

"Good. I think I might be able to make a grab tomorrow night."

"We can do that."

"We?"

"Well, one person generally can't do this right, Terry. I'll bring the van."

"Okay, then. Okay."

"Hold on a second."

Quinn heard a rustling sound and waited for Tracy to get back on the line.

"Tell me where and when," she said.

"You all right?"

"I'm in bed, Terry."

"Oh."

"I had to find paper and pen. Go ahead."

"I don't know yet. What I mean is, I'll let you know."

"You been out tonight?"

"Well, yeah."

"You sound like you been drinking a little."

"Just a little."

"I bet you drink alone."

"I don't like to," said Quinn.

"Tell you what. We get this girl tomorrow, I'm gonna buy you a beer. You don't mind sitting next to a woman when you drink, do you?"

Quinn swallowed. "No."

"Good work, Quinn."

Quinn sat there for a while thinking of the velvet sandpaper in Sue Tracy's voice, the sound of her long exhale, the way his stomach had kind of flipped when she'd said "I'm in bed." How "Good work, Quinn" had sounded like "Fuck me, Terry" to him. Well, he was just a man, as stupid as any other. He looked down, saw his hand resting on the crotch of his jeans, and had to grin. He was too tired to jerk off, so he went to bed.

◻

STRANGE sat on the edge of the bed, Janine's strong thighs over his. She moved slowly up and down on his manhood, gyrating on the upstroke, that thing she did that made him feel twenty-one all over again. One of his hands grasped her ass and the other was flat on the sheets, and he pushed off, burying himself all the way inside her.

"You going for my backbone, sugar?"

"A man can try."

She gave him her hips. "Shit, yeah."

"C'mon, baby."

"I am on the way."

She kissed him deep, her eyes wide and alive. She kept them open when they kissed. He liked that.

Strange licked and sucked at one of her dark nipples, and Janine laughed low. Quiet Storm was coming from the clock radio by the bed, playing Dorothy Moore. Strange had turned it up before undressing her, so that Lionel, in the next room over, could not hear them making love.

He shot off and kept himself in motion. She was almost soundless when she came, just a short gasp. Strange liked that, too.

Later, he stood in his briefs by the bedroom window, looking through the blinds down to the street. Greco had nosed his way through the door and was sleeping on a throw rug, his muzzle resting between his paws.

"Come to bed, Derek."

He turned around and admired Janine, her form all woman beneath the blanket on the bed.

"I'm just wondering what's goin' on out there. All those kids, still walking around."

"You're done working for today. Come to bed."

He slid under the sheets and rested his thigh against hers.

"You better go to sleep," said Janine. "You know how you get cranky when you don't get enough."

"Oh, I *got* enough."

"Stop it."

"Look, it's just, at the end of the day, all these things go racing through my mind."

"Like?"

"Thinkin' on you, you want the truth. How I don't tell you enough what a good job you do. And what you mean to me."

Janine ran her fingers through the short wiry hairs on Strange's chest. "Thank you, Derek."

"I mean it."

"Go ahead."

"What?"

"Usually, when you start going that way with me, it means you need to unload something off your mind. So what is it?"

"Ain't nothin' like that," said Strange.

"Is it Terry?"

"Well, he's still a little rough around the edges. But he's all right."

"Is it the job you're doing for George Hastings?"

"Uh-uh. I'm nearly done with that."

"I'm almost done on my end with it, too," said Janine. "Got one more thing to check up on. You didn't find anything, did you?"

"No," said Strange, and reached over to the nightstand and turned off the lamp.

He wasn't sure why he had lied to her. So Calhoun Tucker was a player, so what? But something about snitching on a guy about that to a woman didn't sit right with most men. It was a kind of betrayal, in an odd way. One betrayal too many in the day for Strange.

❏

QUINN was disoriented from sleep when the phone rang by his bed. He reached over and picked up the receiver.

"Hello?"

"You called?" The voice was smooth and baritone. There was music playing in the background against the sound of a car's engine.

"Who is this?"

"Who's *this*? You called *me*. But you, uh, declined to leave your name."

Quinn got up on one elbow. "I'm looking for a girl."

"You done called the right number then, slick. How'd you get it, by the way?"

"I'm looking for one girl in particular," said Quinn. "Girl named Jennifer, I think."

"You think?"

"It's Jennifer."

"Asked you how you got my number."

"Why is that important?"

"Let's just say I like to know if my marketing dollars are well spent. You know, like, do I re-up with the Yellow Pages or do I go back heavy on those full-page ads in the *Washington Post*?"

The man on the other end of the line laughed then. It was a cut-you-in-the-alley kind of laugh, and the sound of it made Quinn's blood tick. His hand tightened on the receiver. He looked down at some CDs stacked carelessly on the floor. An old Steve Earle was atop the stack.

"A friend of mine, guy named Steve, recommended I call you. Said you could hook me up."

"Oh, I can hook you up, all right. Your name is?"

"Earle."

"Okay, Earle. But I'm a little curious; it's in my nature, if you don't mind. White boy like you, usually when I get a request from one, it's for some black pussy, understand what I'm sayin'? And Jennifer, it's the same girl we both thinkin' of, she's white all the way."

"That's what I want. She's young, too, isn't she?"

"Oh, Jennifer's young, all right. They call her Schoolgirl, matter of fact. She'll be good to you, too. But I guess your boy Steve told you that."

"He did."

"Sure he did. Satisfied customer's the very best form of advertising. Steve, he mention specifics?"

"Just that he had a good time. That she'll do things."

"Any goddamn thing you want. You can bring your friends and roll some videos, too. Have your own private record of the occasion. Fuck her mouth or her pussy. Ass-fuck her, you got a mind to. Course, you gonna pay for all that."

"Look, I'm talkin' about a private party. You deliver her and you name the price. I got money."

"You're gonna need it, Earle. 'Cause this is some fresh turnout here. And I can't be givin' pussy this new away."

Quinn kicked off his top sheet, swung his legs over the bed, and sat up. He reached for the pencil and pad he kept on the nightstand. Maybe he could make this happen without Stella. He didn't need her now that he had gotten through to Wilson.

"How do I hook it up?" said Quinn.

"Well, let's see. Where'd your boy Steve have his party?"

"He didn't say."

"Oh, come on, Earle, you can tell me. See, I need to know, to satisfy that curiosity I was tellin' you about. Steve must have bragged on it. Man don't tell another man ass stories without goin' into the details."

"It was out on New York Avenue," said Quinn, feeling the sweat break upon his forehead. "I think it was one of those motels they got out there on the way out of town."

"You think?"

"It *was*."

The man on the other end of the line laughed heartily. It ended with a chuckle, long and low.

"What's so funny?" said Quinn.

"Just that, you know, you done gone and fucked up right there. You talked too much, see? 'Cause I don't use those trick pads over on New York Avenue. Never have."

"What difference does it make? I said I thought it was there —"

"You said it *was*. And I did like the way you said it, Earle. It *was*. So sure of yourself. So tough. So *much* like the rough and tough man you must be. Bet you got your little chest all puffed up, right about now. Got your fists balled up, too? So easy to be tough when you're speaking on the phone. Isn't it? *Earle.*"

His voice was singsong and mocking. Quinn unclenched his jaw and spoke through barely parted lips.

"My name's Terry Quinn."

"Oh, I got your phone number now, so it would have been easy to get your name right quick. But thanks for providin' it for me; I'll remember it for sure. What're you, Vice, sumshit like that? You must be new, 'cause I got the patrol boys on my strip taken care of."

"I'm not a cop."

"Don't matter to me what you are, anyway. You don't mean nothin' more to me than some dog shit on my shoe. Look here, I better be goin'. I'd put your girl on the line, but she's suckin' a dick right now, makin' me some money."

"Wilson —"

"So long, white boy. Maybe we'll meet someday."

"We will," said Quinn. But the line was already dead as the words came from his mouth.

So now Wilson had his name and number. It would be easy for him to get Quinn's address. In his mind, Quinn shrugged. When he was a cop, the threat that he'd be tracked down to his place of residence had been made many times. He'd lost count of those threats long ago.

Quinn turned off the nightstand lamp. He stood and went to the bedroom window. His hands were shaking at his sides. It wasn't fear.

Tomorrow night the girl would be his.

chapter

12

ON Wednesday morning, Garfield Potter had Carlton Little and Charles White drop him at the Union Station parking garage, where he spotted a car he liked, a police-package, white-over-blue '89 Plymouth Grand Fury with a 318 engine and a four-barrel carb. Potter used a bar to break into the vehicle and a long-handled flat-head to pop out the ignition. He hot-wired the Plymouth and rolled down to the exit. Potter wore a skully and shades so that the booth camera could record very little of his face. As he didn't have a ticket, he paid the full-penalty parking fee and drove out of the garage.

Potter followed Little and White out to Prince George's County, pulling up behind them on a gravel shoulder running alongside a football field in Largo. He waited for his boys to wipe the prints out of the interior and off the exterior handles of the beige Caprice, as he had instructed them to do, and when they joined him inside the Fury he turned the car back toward D.C.

Potter and Little both had priors: possession, intent to distribute, and aggravated-assault beefs. Also, there had been one sodomy-rape charge on Potter, dropped when the victim would not testify. Eventually, they knew, some judge would have to give them time. Like many of his peers, Potter often bragged on the fact that violent death or a jail cell awaited him. But he didn't want to go down on something as mundane as grand theft. A charge like that was a bitch charge, and it bought you no respect inside the walls. So he was always careful to cover his tracks when he got rid of one of his stolen cars.

Old police cars, or those outfitted for police specifications, were the vehicle of choice for many young men in and around D.C. Potter heard you could buy them cheap off lots in Virginia, in places like Manassas and Nokesville, wherever that was. But he didn't like to cross over into Virginia for any reason, and anyway, lately he hadn't been buying shit. You could steal a car easily in the District, and if you rotated it out, say, once a week, you'd never get caught. Well, he hadn't been caught at it yet.

Potter looked at it like this: What you had to do was, you had to target a car owned by a young brother who lived in the city or near the PG County line. Some young brothers got their shit stole, they didn't even report it to the police, on account of they knew damn near nothing would come of it anyway, and there was also this unwritten thing about not talking with the MPD. Many of them didn't carry insurance either, so there wasn't no money reason to report it. Sure, the ones got their cars took kept their ears open and their eyes out for the thief, looking to get some street justice if they could. But so far, Potter, Little, and White had escaped that as well.

Potter floored the gas as he got on the entrance ramp to the Beltway.

"Shit moves," said Potter.

"Better than that hooptie we done had, D," said Little.

"Gonna buy us a Lex soon, though. I'm fixin' to own me a nice whip."

"When?" said Little.

"Soon."

Charles White sat in the backseat, letting the wind from the open window hit his face. He was listening to that song "Bounce with Me," done by that singer they called Lil' Bow Wow, who dressed like a gangster but wasn't nothin' much more than a kid. White was still up there from the hydro him and Carlton had smoked on the way out to Largo, and the song sounded good. He was into music; it was, like, his hobby. Sometimes he made tapes of himself over beats. Maybe someday he'd take some of the money they were making and go into a studio, lay somethin' down for real. But he figured that was for other people to do, like Bow Wow, had someone showin' him how to make it and all that. Someone to guide him, like.

In his true mind Charles White knew that he was stuck with what he had right here. The only family he had now, except for his grandmother, was the boys he'd come up with. Garfield and Carlton, before both of them turned cold and all the way hard, like they were now.

White's hand instinctively dropped to his side, but there was nothing there. He still thought of Trooper all the time. He missed him. He wished Trooper were sitting warm beside him on the backseat.

Potter looked in the rearview at White, breathing through his mouth, looking out the window with the wind beatin' on him, slumped in the backseat. Dumb-ass motherfucker, probably still stressin' over that stupid dog. Potter thought of White as a dog, too, in a way, a thing that just kind of followed him and Carlton around.

He was stuck with White. White still acted and thought like a kid sometimes. He hadn't changed much since the three of them had been tiny, growing up in the Waterfront Gardens, the Section Eight housing units down off M Street by the Southeast / Southwest line. Wasn't no "waterfront" about it, though sometimes the seagulls did drop in from Buzzards Point and pick at the trash. Some government type actually did have the nerve to name that shit hole a Garden, too. One of those jokes you couldn't even laugh at. Not that Potter was crying about it or nothin' like that. If it wasn't for what he didn't have, and he never did have one good thing, he wouldn't have the ambition and drive he had today.

He could have used a father, he supposed, someone to throw a football to or sumshit like that. His mother didn't even have the strength to lift a ball, eighty-eight pounds of no-ass crackhead like she was, at the end.

He wasn't gonna cry about that either. Family and all that bullshit, it meant nothing to him, and it didn't get you anything when you counted the chips up at the end of the day. It was like them books his teachers was always tellin' him to read before they gave up on his ass, back about the fifth grade. He couldn't hardly read, and still he had a shoebox full of cash money in the closet at his place, clothes, cars, bitches, *everything*. So what was the point of books, or some piece of paper, said you went to school?

He had a good business going now. Him and Carlton, he guessed he had to call Charles a partner, too, they had some runners down on Georgia, below Harvard Street, and they sold the *shit* out of some dime bags of marijuana on that corner there. Marijuana, the good shit that was goin' around, the stuff grown hydroponic, was the way to go. In D.C., didn't matter whether you were in possession of a dime bag or ten pounds, it wasn't nothin' but a misdemeanor. You did go to court, most of the time it was no-papered, everyone in the life knew that. Black juries didn't want to send a young black man into the deadly prison system for some innocent charge like holding a little marijuana. Innocent, *shit*, Potter had to laugh at that. Young brothers killed one another over chronic just as dead as they did over crack and heroin. The people in charge would change the laws, make them tougher again when they figured all this out, but until then, hydro was the game.

So Potter had this business and he liked to keep it small. He didn't call him and his boys a "crew" or a "mob" or nothin' like that. You got into turf beefs and eyeball beefs that way; shit just got too complex. Potter was basically into having fun: stealing cars, taking off dumb motherfuckers who could get took, robbing crap games, shit like that. But he never fucked with those he knew to be hooked into crews, or their kin. Never that he knew, anyway. Only fuck with the weak, those who had no strength in numbers, that was his plan. He figured he hadn't made any big mistakes yet. He was still alive.

"Where we goin'?" said Little.

"Dime the rest of that key out and get it out to our troops," said Potter. "Maybe tonight we'll slide by Roosevelt, see if our boy Wilder is hangin' with his nephew on that football field."

"You still on that?"

"Told you I wouldn't forget."

They went back to their place, a row house they rented month-to-month on Warder Street in Park View, and dimed out the shit. They smoked a couple of Phillies while they worked. White went out for a bag of McDonald's, and when he returned there were a couple of young local girls up in the crib who'd dropped by. The new Too Short was up loud, and everyone was on the get-high and drinking gin and grapefruit. This pretty young thing, Brianna, was with Little, and they were laughing and then just gone, up in Carlton's room. Potter took the other one, couldn't have been more than thirteen, away with him next, kind of pulling on the sleeve of her Tweety Bird shirt. To White she didn't look like she wanted to go. A little while later White heard the bedsprings from back in Potter's room against the crying of that girl. White turned up the stereo so he didn't have to hear it, but he could still hear it deep in his head. So he went outside and sat on the stoop, where he rubbed at his temples and tried to remember if there had ever been a time in his life when he felt right.

❐

POTTER and the rest drove down to Harvard Street and found his main boy, kid named Juwan, sitting on a trash can. Juwan was one of those, like Gary Coleman, had a man's head on a boy's body. They took Juwan back to where the fence ran along the McMillan Reservoir. Juwan, sitting next to White in the backseat, passed a large Ziplock bag full of money, which he had taken from his knapsack, up to Little. Little took the money out, separated some for Juwan, and filled the Ziplock with dimed-out bags of marijuana. Juwan slipped the package back into his knapsack.

"Everything all right, little man?" said Potter.

"It's good, D. One thing, though. You know William, that boy got one leg shorter than the other? The po-lice took him in last night. William be like, *thick* and shit. I done told him, Don't be carryin' when you steerin', you know what I'm sayin'? But he don't listen. I know he'll be out today, but —"

"Say what's on your mind."

"Was gonna ask you, I got this cousin, just moved up from Southeast? He was lookin' to get put on, yo."

"Put him on then, Jew. What I been tellin' you, man? Someone don't work out, go ahead and find someone else. Always gonna be kids out there wanna get in."

They dropped Juwan back on Harvard and Georgia. Then Potter stopped at a market and bought a few forties of malt. They drove around some more, drinking the malt and getting smoked up. Little found a cassette tape, a Northeast Groovers PA mix that had been left in the glove box by the Plymouth's owner, and he slipped it in the deck.

"Shits ain't got no bass," said White from the backseat.

Potter ignored White and turned up the volume. At a stoplight he stared down some young boy in a rice burner who he thought had been staring at him. The young boy looked away.

"Where we goin'?" said Little.

"Swing on up to Roosevelt," said Potter.

"I don't want to be drivin' around all night lookin' for some ghost."

"You got somethin' better to do?"

"Brianna," said Little. "I might just meet her again tonight, she can get out her mother's house. I tossed the *shit* out of that bitch today, boy."

"She ain't look too satisfied to me."

"Bull*shit*."

"That's too much girl for you, man."

"Shit, she was singin', 'Say my name, say my name' this afternoon. You saw her smilin' when she walked out the crib. Not like that girl you was fuckin', had tears on her face when she left."

"I gave her the anaconda, she couldn't help but cry. Anyway, your girl Brianna wasn't smilin', she was *laughin'*."

"At what?"

"At that itty-bitty thing you got between your legs."

"Shit, I'm thick as a can of tuna fish down there, man."

Potter side-glanced Little. "*Long* as one, too."

They drove up to Roosevelt High and parked on Iowa. Potter walked down the driveway entrance to the lot, where several cars were parked, and went to the fence bordering the stadium. Kids in football uniforms were doing calisthenics on the field. Their call-and-response chant echoed up to the parking lot.

"*How y'all feel?*"

"*Fired up!*"

Potter didn't see Lorenze Wilder in the group of parents and relatives sitting in the stands. A bunch of men, looked like coaches, stood around on the field. One of them he recognized as the older dude with the gray in his natural, had been bold enough to study him and Little that time before. Potter spit on the ground and walked back to the car. He got behind the wheel of the Plymouth, his face gone hard.

They went back to their place. They got their heads up and

drank some more and watched UPN and something on the WB. Little tried to sweet-talk Brianna out again, but her mother got on the telephone line and told him she was in for the night. Potter suggested they go out again, and Little agreed. White didn't want to, but he got up off the couch. Potter slipped his .357 into his waistband and put a Hilfiger shirt on, tails out, over his sleeveless T. He fitted his skully back on his head. White slipped on a bright orange Nautica pullover, his favorite, and followed Potter and Little out to the street.

They drove around, up and down Georgia. They checked on the troops. Potter drank another forty, and his face got more humorless and he drove from a lower position in the seat. It had been a long day of getting high and doing nothing, and it felt late to White. Anyway, it was full dark. Potter rolled the Plymouth into the Park Morton complex, driving real slow. Some kids were out, sitting like they always did on the entrance wall.

"Lorenze Wilder's sister live here," said Potter.

Little said nothing. Like White, he was tired, and right about now would rather have been in front of the television, or in bed. He didn't like being out with Garfield when he'd been drinkin', had all that liquid courage inside him. Truth was, Little was kinda drunk, too.

Potter slowed the car. A lanky young man was walking across the narrow street, onto a plot of dirt that passed for a playground. He wore khaki pants, a pressed white T-shirt, and wheat-colored Timberland boots.

"Ask him he knows her," said Potter.

"Yo," said Little out the window. They were alongside the young man now. He was still walking, and the Plymouth was keeping pace.

"What?" said the young man, who looked at them briefly, for just the right amount of respect time, but kept his step.

"You know a woman name of Wilder lives here?" said Little. "Got a little boy, kid plays football, sumshit like that. I got this friend owes her money, he asked me to swing by and tell her he'd be payin' it back to 'er next week."

The young man looked at them again, scanned the front and backseat, his sight staying on the odd-looking young man in the bright orange pullover for what he feared might be a moment too long, then cut his eyes. "I ain't know no one around here, no lie. I just moved up *in* here, like, last week."

"Aiight then."

"Aiight," said the young man, moving off into the playground, walking with his shoulders squared, his head up, turning a corner and disappearing into the night.

"Maybe I ought to talk to that boy my own self," said Potter, the lids of his eyes heavy, half shut.

"He said he didn't know, D," said Little. "Let's just let this shit rest for tonight."

Potter kept the Plymouth cruising slow. He went around a kind of long bend that took him to the other side of the housing complex. They could see a group of people back in a stairwell lit pale yellow. Potter braked, steered the Plymouth up on the dirt, and cut the engine.

Potter said, "C'mon."

They got out of the car and followed him across the dirt to the stairwell entrance. There were three men crouched down there and a pink-eyed woman leaning against a cinder-block wall. In one hand the woman held both a cigarette and a bottle wrapped in a paper bag. Smoke hung in the yellow light.

Older cats, all of 'em, thought Potter. Didn't know nobody, didn't have nobody gave a fuck about 'em.

The dice-playing men looked up briefly as Potter approached, Little and White behind him. The oldest of the players, vandyked, wearing a black shirt with thin white stripes and a black Kangol cap, eyed Potter up and down, then rolled dice against the wall. The dice came up sixes. There was some talk about the boxcar roll, and money changed hands. Money was spread out on the concrete.

"Y'all want in," said the roller, staring down the lane to the wall, shaking the dice in his hand, "you're gonna have to wait."

Potter didn't like that the man didn't look him in the eye when he spoke.

"That your woman?" said Potter, staring at the lady leaning on the wall. She took his stare, even as Potter smiled and licked his lips.

The dice man didn't answer. He made his roll.

"Asked you if that was your woman."

"And I told you to wait," said the man.

The other men laughed. One of them reached into his breast pocket and extracted a cigarette. None of them looked at Potter.

"Get up," said Potter. "Stand your tired ass up and face me."

The dice man sighed some, then stood up. He grunted and rubbed at one knee as he did. He was old. But he was bigger than Potter expected, both in the shoulders and in height. He had a half foot on Potter if he had an inch. Now his eyes were twinkling.

"You got somethin' you want to say to me?"

Potter reached under his shirttail and drew the Colt. He held it at his hip, the muzzle on the midsection of the man. The man's eyes were calm; they didn't even flare.

"Give it up," said Potter. "All the cash."

"Shit," said the man, drawing it out slow, and he smiled.

"I'm gonna take your money," said Potter. "You want, I'll dead you to your woman, too."

"Son?" said the man. "I done had guns pointed at me, by real men, while I was layin' in rice paddies and mud, for two solid years. And here I am standin' before you. Do I look like I'm worried about that snub-nose you got in your hand?"

"This here?" Potter looked at the gun as if it had just showed up in his hand. "Old-time, I wasn't gonna *shoot* you with it."

Potter swung the barrel so quickly that it lost its shape in the light. He slashed it across the brow of the man, the blow knocking the cap off his head. The man's hand went to his face, blood seeping through his fingers immediately, and he stumbled back against the wall. Potter flipped the gun in the air and caught it on the half turn, so that he held it now by the barrel. He moved forward, ignoring the other men who had stood suddenly and backed away, and smashed the butt into the man's cheekbone. He hit him in the nose the same way, blood dotting the cinder blocks as the man's head whipped to the side. Potter laughed against the woman's screams. He reared back to beat the man again and felt someone grab his arm. Looking over his shoulder with wild eyes, he saw that it was Charles White who held him there.

"Man, *get* your got-damn hands off me, man!" yelled Potter.

"Let's just take the money," said Little, moving into the light. "You about to kill a motherfucker, boy."

"Get the money, then," said Potter. He smiled and spit on the man lying bloodied before him. "You ain't standin' now, *are* you, Old-time?" Potter barked a laugh and raised his voice in elation. "Can't nobody in this city fuck with Garfield Potter?"

Little and White gathered the cash up off the concrete. They backed up into the grassy area, turned, and walked quickly to the car. No one followed them or shouted for help.

Little counted the cash as they drove out of the complex. White looked in the rearview. A grin had broken, and was frozen, on Garfield Potter's face.

❏

Lamar Williams said good night to his mother, a thirty-two-year-old woman with the face and body of a forty-year-old, who was leaning against the stove in their galley-sized kitchen, smoking a cigarette.

"Where you been at, Mar?"

"Practice with Mr. Derek. I was watchin' wrestlin' with that kid Joe Wilder after that, over at his mother's."

"I'm gonna need you in tomorrow night. I got plans."

"Aiight."

Lamar went down a hall and pushed open the door to his baby sister's room. She was lying atop her bed, stretched out in those pj's of hers, the ones had little roses printed on them. On her feet were those furry gold slippers she wouldn't take off, with Winnie the Pooh's head on the front. What was she now, almost four? Lamar covered her with a sheet.

He went back to his room, turned on his radio, sat on the edge of his bed, and listened to DJ Flexx talkin' to some young girl who'd called in with some shout-outs for her friends. Then Flexx played that new Wyclef Jean joint that Lamar liked, the one with Mary J., where they was talkin' about "Someone please call 911." That one was tight. It made him feel better, to hear that pretty song.

Lamar lay back on the bed. He could still feel his heart beating hard beneath his white T-shirt. He'd done right, not giving up anything to those boys who'd tried to sweat him from the open windows of that car, because whatever they wanted with Joe Wilder's mother, it was no good. But it was hard to keep doing right. Hard to have to walk a certain way, talk a certain way, keep up that shell all the time out here, when sometimes all you wanted to do was be young and have fun. Relax.

Lamar was tired. He rested the palm of his hand over his eyes and tried to make himself breathe slow.

chapter

13

STRANGE spent Wednesday morning clearing off his desk, his noontime testifying for a Fifth Streeter down in District Court, and his afternoon finishing his background check on Calhoun Tucker. He hit a couple of bars on U Street and then drove over to a club on 12th, near the FBI building, where George Hastings had said that Tucker had done some promotions.

All he spoke to that day told him that Tucker was an upstanding young businessman, tough when he had to be but fair and with a good reputation. At the 12th Street club, the bartender, a pretty, dark-skinned woman setting up her station, said that Tucker was "a good guy," adding that he did have "a problem with the ladies, though."

"What kind of problem?" said Strange.

"Being a man, you probably won't think of it as one."

"Try me out."

"Calhoun, he can't just be satisfied with one woman. He's a

player, serial style. It's cool for a young man to be that way, but he's the type, he's gonna be a player his whole life, you understand what I'm sayin'? After a while you gotta check yourself with that, 'cause you are bound to hurt people in the end."

"Did he hurt you?"

The bartender stopped slicing limes, pointing her short knife at Strange. "It's my business if he did."

Strange placed his card on the bar. "You think of anything else you want to tell me about him, you let me know."

Strange went back to his place, hit the heavy bag in his basement, showered, fed Greco, and got on the Internet, reading the comments on a stock chat room while he listened to the *Duck, You Sucker* sound track he had recently purchased as an import.

"See you later, good boy," said Strange, patting Greco on the head before he headed out the door. "Gotta get over to Roosevelt."

❐

THEY ran the team hard that night, as their game was coming up and the night-before practice would be light. The kids looked good. They weren't making many mistakes, and they had their wind. The Midgets were in numbers on one side of the field with Lydell Blue, Dennis Arrington, and Lamar Williams, and the Pee Wees occupied the other. Near dark, after the drills, Strange called the Pee Wees in and told them it was time to run some plays. Strange took the offense aside as Quinn gathered the defensive unit.

The offensive huddle broke and went to the line. Dante Morris took the snap from Prince on the second "go" and handed off to Rico, who hit the five-hole off a Joe Wilder block, broke free from a one-handed tackle attempt, and was finally taken down twenty yards down the field.

Quinn took the kid who had missed the tackle aside. "None of this one-handed-tackle stuff. You can't just put your arm out and say, Please, God, let him fall down. It doesn't work that way, you hear me?"

"Yes."

"Hit him in the stomach. Wrap him up and lock your hands."

The kid nodded. Quinn tapped him on the helmet with his palm, and the kid trotted back to the defensive huddle.

Joe Wilder slowed down as he passed Strange on the way to the offensive huddle. "Forty-four Belly, Coach Derek?"

"Run it," said Strange. "And nice block there, Joe."

Wilder ran the play into Dante Morris, who called it on one. It was a goal-line play, a simple flanker run direct through the four-hole. Wilder executed it perfectly and took the ball into the end zone. He did the dirty bird for his teammates and jogged back to Strange, a spring in his step.

"I be doin' that on FedEx Field someday, Coach Derek."

"It's *I will* be doing that," said Strange, who then smiled, thinking, I believe you will.

After practice, Strange talked with Blue awhile, then caught Quinn getting into his Chevelle.

"Where you off to so fast, Terry?"

"Got plans tonight."

"A woman?"

"Yeah."

"Thought you were gonna try and close that Jennifer Marshall thing tonight."

"I am," said Quinn. "I'll let you know how it pans out."

Prince, Lamar, and Joe Wilder were standing by Strange's Brougham. He put his football file into the trunk, let them in the car, and drove off the school grounds.

Strange turned up Prince's street, not far from the football field.

"There go my houth right there," said Prince.

"I know it," said Strange, stopping the car. "Get in their straight away, boy, don't make no detours. Those boys on that corner over there, they try to crack on you, you ignore 'em, hear?"

Prince nodded and got out of the car. He went quickly up the steps to his place, where the light on the porch had been left on.

As they drove south on Georgia, Joe Wilder held two action figures in his hand. He was making collision sounds as he pushed their rubber heads together like warring rams.

"I thought those two was friends," said Lamar, sitting beside Wilder.

"Uh-uh, man, Triple H be the Rock's *enemy*. H is married to the commissioner's daughter." Joe Wilder looked up at Lamar. "Will you come inside and watch it with me tonight?"

"Okay," said Lamar. "I'll watch it with you some."

After Strange dropped them off, he popped a tape into the dash, a Stevie Wonder mix Janine had made him. Kids sat on the wall and dead-eyed him as he passed through the exit to the housing complex, Stevie singing "Heaven Is 10 Zillion Light Years Away" from the deck. Strange couldn't help thinking how beautiful the song was. Thinking, too, how for those who'd been born in the wrong place through no fault of their own, how sad that it was true.

❏

SUE Tracy picked up Terry Quinn at his apartment somewhere past ten o'clock that night. She stood in the doorway of his place while he shook himself into a waist-length black leather jacket over a white T-shirt. As he did this he blocked her way, his body language telling her to come no further. She watched him fumble his badge case into one jacket pocket and his cell into the other. Clearly he was anxious to slip out before she had a chance to get a good look at his crib. But Tracy had taken in enough to know that there was nothing much to see.

They walked out of the squat, three-story brick building, toward an old gray Econoline van parked on Sligo Avenue.

"Hey, Mark," said Terry to a mixed-race teenage boy standing with a group of boys his age outside a beer-and-cigarette market on the corner.

"Wha'sup," said the boy, not really looking at Quinn, muttering the greeting in a grudging, dutiful way.

Tracy stopped to light a cigarette. She dropped the spent match to the ground and exhaled smoke out the side of her mouth. "Kid really likes you, Terry."

"He does like me. It's just, you know, the code. He can't act like we're friends when he's hanging with his boys, you know what I'm sayin'? I have this gym set up in the basement of the building; I let some of these neighborhood guys work out with me, long as they show me and the equipment respect."

They stood by the van, Tracy finishing her cigarette before getting in, Quinn letting her without comment.

"And you coach a football team, too."

"I kinda help out, is all."

"You're not so tough, Terry."

"It's a way to kill time."

"Sure." Tracy ground out her cigarette. "Where to first?"

"We'll pick up Stella. I got it all set up."

The van dated back to the 1970s. It had front and rear bench seats and little else. The three-speed manual shift was a branch coming off the trunk of the steering wheel. A tape deck had been mounted where the AM radio had been, its faceplate loose, its wires exposed and swinging below the dash.

"I bet you only fly first class, too," said Quinn.

"It was a donation," said Tracy.

She wore a black nylon jacket over a black button-down blouse tucked into slate gray utilitarian slacks. She found a gray Scunci in her jacket pocket, put it in her mouth while she gathered her hair behind her, and formed a ponytail. The Scunci picked up the gray of the slacks. She pulled a pair of eyeglasses with black rectangular frames from the sun visor and slipped them on her face.

"Cool."

"This van? Bet there's a bong around here somewhere, too, if you're interested."

"I was talking about your glasses."

"They'll keep us from getting killed. My night vision is for shit."

They drove down into Northwest, cutting into Rock Creek Park at 16th and Sherrill and heading south. Tracy slipped a Mazzy Star compilation tape into the deck. Chicks and their chick music, thought Quinn, but this was guitar driven and pretty nice.

They didn't talk much on the ride into town. It wasn't uncomfortable. Quinn didn't feel like he did around most women, like he had to explain who he was, why he'd chosen the path he'd taken, the one that had put him on the way to becoming a cop. The singer's voice, breathy but unforced, was relaxing him, and arousing him, too. He looked over at Tracy, at the tendons in her neck, the elegant cut of her jaw as it neared her ear.

"What?" said Tracy.

"Nothing."

"You're staring at me again, Terry."

"Sorry," said Quinn. "I was just thinking."

After a while they came up out of the park. Stella emerged from the shadows of a church at 23rd and P as they pulled the van along the curb.

"That her?"

"Yeah."

"She looks fifteen."

"Cobras live to be fifteen, too," said Quinn.

"They do?"

"I'm making a point."

"The back doors are open," said Tracy. "Tell her to get in there."

Quinn rolled down his window as Stella reached the van. She wore black leather pants and a white poplin shirt, with a black bag shaped like a football slung over her shoulder. Her eyeglasses sat crooked on her face.

"You like?" said Stella, looking down at her pants. Her eyes were magnified comically behind the lenses of her glasses. "I wore 'em for you, Officer Quinn. They're pleather, but that's okay. I get paid tonight, I'm gonna buy me a pair of leather ones on the for-real side."

"You look nice," said Quinn.

"What color should I get? The black or the brown?"

"The back door's open. Let's go."

They drove east. Quinn introduced Stella to Sue Tracy. Stella was cool to her questions. She only became animated when responding to Quinn. Clearly she was eager for his attention. It was plain to Tracy that Stella had a crush on Quinn, or it was a daddy thing, but he was ignoring it. More likely, as with many men, the obvious had eluded him.

On 16th they saw some girls working the stroll, a stretch of sidewalk off the hotel strip south of Scott Circle.

"Around here?" said Tracy.

"Those aren't World's," said Stella.

"Where, then?" said Quinn.

"Keep goin'," said Stella. "He ain't into that visiting-businessmen trade. They talk too much, take too much time. Worldwide's girls walk between the circles. The Logan-and-Thomas action, y'know what I'm sayin'?"

Quinn knew. "That's old-school turf. I remember that from when *I* was a teenager."

Tracy shot him a look from across the seat.

"Strictly locals," said Stella. "Husbands whose wives won't blow 'em, birthday boys lookin' to get their cherry broke, barracks boys, like that. World's got some rooms nearby."

"We're gonna try and take her in Wilson's trick-house?" said Quinn. "Why?"

"Because she don't trust me," said Stella. "She won't meet me anywhere else."

Tracy steered the van around Thomas Circle.

"North now," said Stella, "and make a right off Fourteenth at the next block."

The landscape changed from ghost town–downtown to living urban night as soon as they drove onto the north side of the circle. Small storefronts, occupying the first floors of structures built originally as residential row houses, low-rised the strip. The commercial picture was changing, new theater venues, cafés, and bars cropping up with regularity. In fact, it had been "changing" for many years. White gentrifiers tried to close down the family-run markets, utilizing obscure laws like the one forbidding beer and wine sales within a certain proximity to churches. The crusading gentrifiers cited the loiterers on the sidewalks, the kinds of unsavory clientele those types of businesses attracted. What they really wanted was for their underclass dark-skinned neighbors to go away. But they wouldn't go away. The former Section Eights were up the street, and so were families who had lived here for generations. It was their neighborhood. It was a small detail that the gentrifiers never tried to understand.

There weren't any hookers walking the 14th strip. But as they turned right and drove a block east, Quinn could see cars double-parked ahead wearing Maryland and Virginia plates, their flashers on, girls leaning into their driver's-side windows.

"Pull over," said Stella.

Tracy curbed the van and cut the engine. Quinn studied the street.

A half block up, a couple of working girls, one black and one white, were lighting smokes, standing on the sidewalk outside a row house. One of them, the young white girl with big hair, wearing white mid-thigh fishnets and garters below a tight white skirt, walked up the steps of the row house and through the front door. A portly black man in an ill-fitting suit got out of his car, a late-model Buick, and went into the same house shortly thereafter.

"These all Wilson's?" said Quinn.

"Not all," said Stella. "You got a few independents out here, out-of-pocket hos. Long as they don't look him in the eye, disrespect him like that, then they gonna be all right. But those are World's trick-pads over there. All his. He rents out the top two floors, got, like, six rooms."

"What about the car action?"

"That's okay for a quick suck. World gets money for the room, too, so he tells his ladies, Make sure you take 'em upstairs. Anyway, you don't want to be fuckin' a man in a car down here. Even the pocket cops, they see that, they got to take you in. This ain't the Bronx."

"That where you come from, Stella?" said Tracy.

"I'm from nowhere, lady."

"We waitin' on Jennifer?" said Quinn.

"You already saw her," said Stella. "She was that white girl with the white stockings, went inside."

"It didn't look like her," said Quinn.

"What, you think she'd still be wearing her yearbook clothes?" Stella laughed joylessly, an older woman's laugh that chilled Quinn. "She ain't no teenager now. She ain't nothin' but a ho."

"We could have grabbed her off the street."

"We got to do this my way. I told you I'd come along, but I don't want nobody spottin' me, hear?"

"Keep talking."

"I called Jennifer up. Soon after I met her, I boosted her Walkman and a few CDs she had. She never went anywhere without her sounds. I told her when I called her, I found her shit in some other girl's bag and I was lookin' to get it back to her."

"Where?"

"Told her I'd meet her at eleven-thirty, up in three-C. That's the third-floor room nearest the back of the house. There's a fire escape there, goes down to the alley. The window leads out to the fire escape, one of those big windows, goes up and down —"

"A sash," said Quinn.

"Whatever. World always tells the girls, leave that window open, hear, case you need to get out quick."

Quinn checked his watch: close to eleven by his time.

"Think I'll drop in on her a little early," said Quinn.

"I'm coming with you," said Tracy.

"Who's gonna drive the van?" said Quinn, head-motioning over his shoulder. "Her?"

Tracy looked out her window for a moment, then at Quinn. She reached back and pulled her leather briefcase from under the back bench. Her hand went into the briefcase and came out with a pair of Motorola FRS radios. She handed one to Quinn.

"Walkie-talkies?"

"That's right."

"These come with a decoder ring, too?"

"Quit fuckin' around, Terry. You keep the power on, hear? There's a call alert; you'll hear it if I'm tryin' to get through to you."

"All right." Quinn turned the power on so that Tracy could see he had done it. He slipped the radio into his jacket.

"How long you gonna need in there?" said Tracy.

"Jennifer's where Stella says she is, I'd say ten minutes tops."

"I'm gonna take the van back in the alley, but I'm gonna give you five minutes before I roll. I don't like alleys. I've seen too much shit go wrong in alleys, Terry —"

"So have I."

"I don't want to get jammed up in there."

"All right. I'll bring the girl down the fire escape. See you in ten, right?"

"Ten minutes."

Quinn got out of the van and crossed the street. Go-go music came loudly from the open windows of one of the double-parked cars. The girl outside the row house, black girl with red lipstick and a rouged face, her ass cheeks showing beneath her skirt, looked him over and smiled as he approached.

"You datin' tonight, sugar?"

"I'm taken, baby. My girl's waitin' on me inside."

Her eyes went dead immediately, and Quinn walked on. He took the row house steps and opened the front door, stepping into a narrow foyer. The door closed softly behind him. He looked up a flight of stairs to the second floor. The foyer smelled of cigarettes, marijuana, and disinfectant. He could hear voices above. Footsteps, too.

Quinn's blood was up. It was a high for him, to be back in the middle of it again. And to be in this place. It reminded him of his own first time with a prostitute, fifteen years earlier, in a house very much like this one, just a few blocks away from where he now stood.

He took the two-way radio out of his pocket and turned the power button off. He didn't need any gadgets. He didn't need any "call alerts" or anything else to distract him while he was looking for the girl.

Quinn started up the stairs.

c h a p t e r

14

WORLDWIDE Wilson cruised down 14th in his '92 400SE, midnight blue over palomino leather, the music down low. He had that Isley Brothers slo-jam compilation, *Beautiful Ballads,* on the stereo, Ronald singing all sweet, talkin' about, "Make me say it again, girl," coaxin' that man in the boat to show himself and drown.

Wilson had the seat back all the way. Still, even with that, his knees were high, straddling the wheel. He switched lanes, cutting the wheel quick to avoid hitting the dumb-ass in front of him who was making a sudden left without using the turn signal God gave him. As he swerved, the little tree deodorizer he had hung on the rearview swung back and forth.

He had recently had the steering wheel covered in fur, but the Arab he'd given the job to up at the detail shop, he'd fucked it all up. Put some cheap shit on there, so that the hairs were always coming off in his hands and flyin' around the car. Someone didn't know better, they'd think he owned a cat, some bullshit like that. Teach him to give his business to an Iraqi. And he should've known not to trust a man had a girl's name: Leslie.

Wilson's given name was Fred. Frederick, Freddie, he didn't like it any way you put it, what with the kids always callin' him Fred Flintstone and shit when he was a kid. Till he got the reputation, he would fuck them up good they said it again. Worldwide, that was more like it. He'd given himself that name after he returned from Germany, where he'd served in the army back in the late seventies. He'd put together his first little stable over there. Light-skinned girl with Asian eyes, and couple of blond bitches, too. German girls could lay a stamp on a black man, didn't even think twice about his color. Another thing he liked about being overseas.

Wilson punched numbers into the grid of the inverted phone he'd installed in the Mercedes. He liked the way the numbers lit the cabin up green at night. This was one pretty car, real classy, not a ride with too much flash, like those wanna-be pimps, just comin' up, were driving around. The fur steering wheel, that was the only thing he'd added. Oh, yeah, there was a working television and VCR in the backseat, and those stainless steel DNA exhaust pipes he'd recently put on. And the phone. And the Y2K custom wheels he had on this motherfucker. Those rims set the whole joint off right.

Wilson got through on the line and lifted the phone out of its cradle.

"What's goin' on, baby?"

"Slow."

"I'm comin' in."

Wilson turned off 14th. He went slowly down the block, checking out the action. Wasn't much. He passed a shitty old van and a couple other hoopties parked on the street, and went around a double-parked Chevy Lumina, where one of his women stood leaning in the driver's window. That particular girl, she talked too much, and when she did talk she had nothin' to say. One of those special-ed bitches, wore his shit out. Time he got that mouth of hers straightened around.

He pulled up in front of his row house, where Carola, another of his girls, his best producer but getting to be on the old side, stood. Wilson hit a button and let the window drop. Carola came over and leaned on the door.

"Where Jennifer at?"

"Schoolgirl's inside. Trickin' some old Al Roker–lookin' sucker."

"What else?"

"I don't know. Some white boy just went in. I axed him for a date, but he said he already had a girl. Thing is, I didn't see him follow no one in."

"He high?"

"Didn't look to be."

"Vice?"

"He wasn't wearin' no sign if he is."

"Okay. Why you standin' around, though?"

"Told you there wasn't nothin' goin' on."

"Well, get out there and *make* somethin' go on. Get on back to the tracks and get a date."

"I'm tired."

"I'm tired, too. Tired of you talkin' about *bein'* tired and not earnin' shit. Now go on out there and market that pussy, girl."

"My feet hurt, World."

"C'mere." Carola leaned forward to let Wilson stroke her cheek. "You my bottom baby. You *know* this, right?"

"I know it, World."

Wilson's eyes dimmed. "Then don't *make* me get out this car and take a hand to your motherfuckin' ass."

Carola stood straight and backed up a step. "I'm goin'."

"Good, baby." Wilson smiled, showing a row of gold caps. "I'll give you a foot massage later on, hear?"

But Carola was already off, walking down the block, Wilson thinking, Glad I got me that degree in pimpology. All you had to do was use a little psychiatry on these bitches, worked every time.

He cut the engine on the Mercedes and untangled his frame from the car. Big man like he was, it was a struggle to get out of these foreign rides. But his time in Berlin had given him a permanent love for German automobiles, and, though they were more roomy, he never had liked the way Cadillacs and Lincolns drove.

He stood beside his car, smoothed out the leather on his coat, and adjusted his hat. Before he closed the door of the Mercedes, he put one foot up on the rocker panel, then the other, and buffed the vamps of his alligator shoes with the palm of his hand. What was the point of spending five hundred dollars on a pair of gators if they didn't have a nice shine? He closed the door and stood straight.

Now he'd have to see what Carola was talkin' about. See what some white boy was doin' wandering around in his house without a woman he'd paid to fuck.

❒

"Oh, shit," said Stella, leaning forward, blinking hard behind her glasses. "There go World."

"Where?"

"That's his ride right there, the blue Mercedes. He's talkin' to Carola, up in the window there."

Sue Tracy watched the girl step away from the tricked-out car and walk off down the block. Then she watched Worldwide Wilson get out of his car. He wore a full-length leather coat with tooled-out skin, and a hat with a matching tooled band. Wilson stood tall, a good six three, his shoulders filling out the soft cut of the coat. He had the walk of a big cat.

Tracy keyed the mic on the radio in her hand. There was no response.

Wilson walked up the row house steps. He pulled on the front door and moved fluidly through the space. The door closed behind him, and he disappeared into the house.

She tried the radio again and tossed it on the seat beside her. "*Shit*, Terry."

"What?" said Stella.

Tracy didn't answer. She ignitioned the van and slammed the tree up into first. She drove to the corner and cut a hard left.

⌐

QUINN'S hand came off the shaky wooden banister as he stepped up onto the second-floor landing. The banister continued down a straight, narrow hall. The doors to the rooms, all closed and topped with frosted-glass transoms, were situated opposite the banister. Television cable ran from one room to the other in the hall, going transom to transom. Quinn heard no activity on the second floor. He took the hall to the next set of stairs.

Sounds from above grew louder as he ascended the stairs. It was the sound of furniture moving on a hard floor. Talk from a radio and the human bass of a man's voice and the unformed voice of a young girl.

Up on the landing, Quinn checked the sash window at the back of the house. It was open a crack, and he lifted it further and looked down through the mesh of the fire escape to the alley below. The alley was unlit, unblocked, and looked to be passable by car.

Quinn went to the first door, marked 3C in tacked-on letters broken off in spots. From behind the door came the talk radio and the man-girl sounds and the sound of bedsprings. The knob in his hand turned freely, and Quinn pushed on the door and walked inside.

A fat middle-aged black guy was on top of Jennifer Marshall on the bed. His fat ass and his fat sides jiggled as he pumped at her, and Quinn was on him just as he turned his head. He pulled him back by the shoulders and then pushed him roughly against the wall that abutted the bed. The man's head, bald on top and patched with black sides, made a hollow sound as it hit the wall.

Quinn speed-scanned the room: high ceilings and chipped plaster walls. A bed and a nightstand that held a lamp and a radio, with a bathroom coming off the room. Clothing lay in a pile beside the bed.

Jennifer had removed her skirt and panties only. She sat up against the headboard, her legs still spread. Her sex was pink and sparsely tufted with reddish brown hair. Quinn looked away.

"Get your clothes on," said Quinn to the man, "and get your ass out of here, *now*."

The man, naked except for a pair of brown socks, didn't move. His face was still, and his swollen penis, sheathed in a condom, was frozen in place.

"I told you to get going."

"What the fuck's goin' on?" said Jennifer.

Quinn picked up Jennifer's skirt and panties and tossed them before her on the bed. "Put 'em on." And to the man he said, "Move."

The man began to dress. Jennifer slipped on her panties and got off the bed, her skirt in her hands. She was thin of wrist, with skinny legs. Up close the heavy makeup could not conceal her age. She looked like a child who had gotten into her mother's things.

"Hurry up," said Quinn.

"Who *are* you?" said Jennifer.

"I'm an investigator," said Quinn. "D.C."

The door opened. Worldwide Wilson stepped into the room.

"An investigator, huh?" Wilson's gold-capped smile spread wide. "You won't mind then, motherfucker, if I have a look at your badge."

❐

SUE Tracy pulled the van alongside the back of the building. Eyes glowed beneath a Dumpster, frozen in the fan of the headlights. As Tracy cut the engine and the headlights the alley went black. She let herself adjust to the sudden change of light. Lines of architecture began to take shape. A rat, then another, scampered across the alley in front of the van.

Residual light bled out from the curtained windows of a sleeper porch on the second floor and a window topping the fire escape on the third.

"That's it, right?"

Stella managed to get her head close to Tracy's window and look up. "I guess it is."

Tracy took a wad of cash from her briefcase and stuffed it into the pocket of her slacks. "Wait here."

"You're not gonna leave me, are you?"

"I'll be right back," said Tracy.

"Don't leave me here in the dark," said Stella.

"You jet, you don't get your money. Just remember that."

Tracy stepped out of the van and carefully pushed on the driver's-side door. It closed with a soft click.

❐

WILSON reached behind him, not turning his head, and closed the bedroom door. It barely made it to the frame. The man on the bed averted his eyes. He struggled from the sitting position to put on his pants. Some change slipped from the trouser pockets and dropped to the sheets. Quinn kept his posture straight and his eyes on Wilson's.

"I didn't do nothin', World," said Jennifer.

Wilson took a few steps into the room, one hand in his leather, stopping several feet shy of Quinn. He looked down on Quinn and he looked him over and smiled.

"So what you *doin'* in here, man?"

Quinn didn't answer.

"You ain't datin'," said Wilson, his voice smooth and baritone.

Quinn said nothing.

"What'sa matter, white boy? Ain't you got no tongue?"

"I came for the girl," said Quinn.

"You must be . . ." Wilson snapped the fingers of his free hand. "Terry Quinn. Am I right?"

Quinn nodded slowly.

The room was suddenly small. There was no window, and Quinn knew he'd never make it to the door. Wilson was a big man, but his fluid movement suggested he would be unencumbered by his size. The only way to bring him down, Quinn reasoned, was to hit him low and wrap him up. It was what he always told the kids. Quinn edged one foot forward and put some weight on that leg's knee.

"Now you gettin' ready to rush me, little man? That's what you fixin' to do?"

Wilson produced a switchblade knife from his coat pocket. Four inches of stainless blade flicked open, the pearl handle resting loosely in Wilson's hand.

"Picked this up over in Italy," said Wilson. "They make the prettiest sticks."

The man on the bed clumsily drew on his shirt. Jennifer began to step into her skirt.

Wilson's eyes flared. "You scared, *Terry?*"

Again, Quinn did not reply.

"Terry. That's a girl's name, ain't it?" Wilson laughed and stepped forward. "Don't matter much to me, Terry. I need to, I cut a bitch up just as good as a man."

The door was kicked open. Sue Tracy kicked it again on the backswing as she walked into the room. One arm was extended and holding a snub-nosed .38 Special. The other hand held her license case, flapped open.

"Fuck is that toy shit?" said Wilson.

"I'm an investigator," said Tracy.

"Aw," said Wilson, "now y'all are gonna play like you police, huh?"

"Shut up," said Tracy, the muzzle of the revolver pointed at Wilson's face. "Drop that knife."

Even as the words were coming from her mouth, Wilson was tossing the knife to the floor. He was still smiling, though, his eyes lit with amusement, going from Tracy back to Quinn.

"Get outta here," said Tracy to the fat man. She had a surge of adrenaline then, and she shouted, "Get the fuck back to your wife and kids!"

The man picked what was left of his clothing up off the floor and quickly left the room.

Wilson chuckled. "Damn, baby. You are like . . . you are like a *man*, you know it?" He head-motioned in the direction of Quinn. "You got a lot more man to you than this itty-bitty mother-fucker right here, I can tell you that."

Tracy saw Quinn's face flush. "Terry, get her out of here. I'm right behind you, hear?"

Quinn stood frozen for a moment, his eyes dry and hot.

"Take her!" said Tracy, still holding the gun on Wilson.

"Cavalry gonna hold the Indians back while the women and children leave the fort," said Wilson.

Jennifer Marshall finished fastening her skirt. Quinn reached over and took her firmly by the elbow. She was shaking beneath his touch.

"I didn't do nothin', World."

Wilson didn't even look at the girl. He was smiling at Quinn, who was moving Jennifer out of the room, going around Tracy, careful not to impede the sight line of her gun.

"Next time, *Theresa*," said Wilson.

Tracy heard their footsteps out in the hall. She heard them going out the open window. The sound of their bodies knocking the window frame faded. She kept her gun arm straight.

"You got a name, too?" said Wilson.

Tracy waited. She could hear them on the fire escape and soon that sound faded, too. Then there was the man talking from the radio and Wilson's stare and smile.

Wilson studied her shape. "Look here, I didn't mean nothin', callin' you a man like I did. Blind man can see you're all woman. I mean, you got some fine titties on you, baby. Can tell by the up-curve, even through that shirt. I bet they stand up real nice when you unfasten that brassiere. Do me a favor, turn around and let me get a look at that pretty ass."

Tracy felt a drop of sweat slide down her forehead. It snaked off her brow and stung at her eyes.

"You got a nice pussy, too?"

Tracy snicked back the hammer on the .38.

"Go on, now," Wilson said softly. "I ain't gonna follow you or nothin' like that. I don't care to hurt a woman 'less she makes me. You ain't gonna make me, are you, darlin'?"

She backed out of the room. She backed down the hall and backed through the open window. She quickly looked down at the idling van in the alley as she got onto the fire escape, but she kept her eyes on the third floor and her gun pointed at the window all the way as she backed herself down the iron stairs.

15

QUINN drove out of the city, keeping to the speed limit and stopping for yellow lights. He had thanked Tracy when she got in the van, but they had barely spoken since. She knew that he was grateful for what she'd done. She also knew what kind of man Quinn was, and that he had been shamed.

Jennifer and Stella argued loudly, sitting beside each other on the back bench, for most of the way out of D.C. But as they crossed the line their voices grew quieter, and their conversation softened further still as Quinn took the ramp onto the Beltway. By the time Quinn was on 270 North, he looked in the rearview mirror and watched them embrace. For the first time since the row house snatch, Quinn loosened his grip on the wheel.

Tracy lit a cigarette and dropped the match out the window. "You all right?"

"I'm fine."

"Can I have my radio back?"

Quinn took it from his jacket and handed it over. "This thing works for shit, y'know it?"

"Next time turn it on." Tracy moved her hand to the tray and tapped ash off her cigarette. "You don't have a problem with what happened back there, do you?"

"No problem," lied Quinn. "I'd be a class-A jerk if I did. I mean, you saved my ass."

Tracy grinned. "And the rest of you, too."

"That was pretty smooth, you bustin' in like that. And you didn't even tell me you were carrying a gun."

"My father gave it to me a long time ago. He bought it hot downtown. It's an old MPD sidearm, before they went to the Glocks."

"It's, uh, illegal to have one of those in the District. You know it?"

"Really."

"Yeah, you could get in a world of trouble, you get caught with it on your person. You could lose your license."

"It's better than the alternative."

"Just letting you know, is all."

"I wouldn't walk into a situation like that without it."

"Okay."

"You tellin' me you don't own one?"

"I do own one. I'm just surprised that *you* do, that's all."

"I wanted to kill him, Terry. I mean, I was close. It scared me a little, back there. Even more than he did, you know? You ever get a feeling like that?"

"All the time," said Quinn.

In fact, Quinn was visualizing the room in the row house and Worldwide Wilson now.

"Anyway," said Tracy, "nice work. You found her quick. Even the hero stuff you pulled back there. Good, solid work."

"Hero? Christ, what about you?"

Tracy smiled crookedly. "What?"

Quinn looked her over. "Bad-ass."

Tracy pointed to the detention center across the highway that had become visible on their left. Quinn put the van into the right lane and took the next exit.

He parked in the lot of Seven Locks station. In the backseat, the two girls talked quietly. Stella was reaching into her football-sized handbag, pulling out a Walkman and then several CDs.

"I'm gonna be a while," said Tracy. "I don't have to, but I think I ought to wait for her mother and father to get here while the cops process the paperwork. I like to talk to the parents when I can."

"No problem. You still want to grab a beer?"

"Sure."

"Bars'll be closed by the time we're done here. Thought I'd go snag a six while you're inside."

"Make it a twelve-pack."

"I'll be out here waiting," said Quinn.

Jennifer climbed out of the back of the van. Tracy tossed her pack of cigarettes back to Stella. Jennifer did not speak to Quinn as she passed by his window and went with Tracy up the sidewalk to the station. Tracy kept her hand on Jennifer's elbow all the way.

"Think we can find a beer store out here in Potomac?"

"*I* want one," said Stella.

"Forget it," said Quinn.

It took a while to locate a deli. When they returned to the lot Quinn cracked open a can of beer and took a long swig. Stella sat beside him and smoked one of Tracy's cigarettes. She had Quinn half turn the ignition key so that she could get some power to the van, and she pushed the Mazzy Star tape back into the deck.

"This is old," she said, "but it still sounds pretty cool."

"Yeah, it's nice."

"Bet it's your partner's tape."

"That's right." Quinn closed his eyes as he drank off some of his beer. It was cold and good.

"You're more like the Springsteen type."

"Uh-huh." He looked at the brick building lit by spots, remembering back to that time in high school when he'd spent a night out here in one of the cells. A D&D charge at a house party that had gone on way too long. He'd beaten up the host's father. Quinn wondered if the kid ever got over seeing his father on the ground, getting punched out by a seventeen-year-old boy. And all because the old man had looked at Quinn the wrong way and smiled.

"Hey, you listenin'?"

"Yeah, sure."

"My father likes Springsteen. The old Springsteen, he says, which means, like, the stuff that's one hundred years old. Not that I'm comparing you to my father. You're younger than him, for one." Stella dragged on her cigarette. "My father was 'weak and ineffectual.' That's what the shrink my parents took me to said. This shrink, he wasn't supposed to say stuff like that to me, I know. But I was suckin' his little dick right there in his office, so he said all kinds of stuff."

"I don't want to hear about it," said Quinn.

"He said that I 'gravitated toward strong men' 'cause my father was weak. What do you think of that?"

"No clue."

"It's why I hooked up with World, I guess. Couldn't find a much stronger man than him. He turned me out quick, too." Stella double-dragged on her smoke and pitched it out the window. "But I couldn't produce for him. Nobody wanted to pay for this stuff, not that I blame them. I'm not much of a woman, *am* I, Terry? Do you think I am?"

"You're fine," said Quinn.

"Yeah, I'm a beauty, all right. Anyway, that's how I got into the recruitment biz for World."

"Stella —"

"I do like strong men, Terry. The shrink was right about that."

She slid over on the seat so that she was close to him. Quinn could feel her warm breath on his face.

"That's not a good idea," he said.

"Don't worry, green eyes, I'm not gonna hurt you. I was just lookin' for a little love. A hug, is all." She moved back against the passenger-side door, her face colored by the vapor lights of the lot. Quinn could see that her eyes had teared up behind the lenses of her glasses.

"I'm sorry, Stella."

"Ain't no big thing," she said, a catch in her voice. She turned her face away from him and stared out the window.

They sat awhile longer, watching the uniformed cops moving in and out of the station. A minivan pulled into the lot. A man and a woman got out of it and hurried inside. Stella laughed joylessly, watching them.

"I love happy endings," said Stella. The hard shell had returned to her face.

"You don't have to go back to working for Wilson. You know that, don't you?"

"Yeah, I know. Damn right, I am somebody, and all that."

"I'm serious. And we both know it's not safe. One of these days he's gonna find out you been playin' him for the middle."

"You didn't give me up to him back there, did you? You didn't say my name or nothin' like that."

"No."

"Course not. There wasn't nothin' in it for you."

"That's not the only reason people do or don't do what they do," said Quinn.

"Yeah, okay, whatever." Stella lit another cigarette. "Just so I get paid."

A half hour later Tracy emerged from the station. Stella climbed into the back and Tracy took the shotgun seat.

"Everything go okay?" said Quinn.

"The parents have her," said Tracy. "They're taking her home. I can't tell you if it's going to stick."

She drank a beer and Quinn drank another as they drove back into D.C. Quinn parked the van on 23rd, alongside the church.

Tracy gave Stella five hundred-dollar bills, along with her card.

"It was a pleasure doin' business with y'all," said Stella. "You want your smokes back?"

"Keep 'em," said Tracy. "I got another pack. And, Stella, you need to talk, anything like that —"

"I know, I know, I got your number right here."

"Stay low for a few days," said Quinn.

Stella leaned forward from the backseat and kissed Quinn behind the ear. Then she was out of the van's back door and walking across the church grounds. They watched her move through the inky shadows.

"Where do you suppose she's going?" said Quinn.

"Don't think about it."

"I shouldn't even care, right? I mean, she's steering girls over to Wilson so he can turn them out."

"Stella's a victim, too. Try to think of it like that. And remember, we got Jennifer off the street."

"So how come I feel like we didn't accomplish shit?"

"You can't save them all in one night," said Tracy. "C'mon, let's go."

Quinn looked back to the church grounds. Stella was gone, swallowed up by the night. Quinn put the van in gear, rolled to the corner, hooked a left, and headed uptown.

❐

SUE Tracy invited herself into Quinn's apartment. He was relieved that she took the initiative but not surprised. He snapped on a lamp in the living room, gathering up newspapers and socks as he moved about the place, and told her to have a seat.

Quinn went into the kitchen to put the beer in the refrigerator, opened two, and brought them back out to the living room along with an ashtray. Tracy was on her cell, talking to her partner, telling her what had gone down. Karen, it went fine, and Karen this and Karen that. He heard Tracy say where she was, then listen to something her partner said. Tracy laughed, saying something Quinn couldn't make out, before she ended the call.

Tracy lit a smoke and tossed a match in the ashtray. "Thanks. You don't mind if I smoke in here, do you?"

"Nah, it's fine."

Quinn was by his modest CD collection, trying to figure out what to put on the carousel. It struck him, looking to find something that would be appropriate, that most of the music he owned was on the aggressive side. He hadn't really noticed it before. He settled on a Shane MacGowan solo record, the one with "Haunted" on it, his duet with Sinéad. Good drinking music, and sexy, too, like a scar on the lip of a nice-looking girl.

Quinn had a seat on the couch next to Tracy. She had taken off her Skechers and tucked her feet under her thighs.

"To good work," she said, and tapped her green can against his. They drank off some of their beer.

"What were you laughing about on the phone there. Me?"

"Well, yeah. Karen bet me I was gonna spend the night here. I took the bet."

"And?"

"I told her I'd pay up the next time I saw her."

Tracy stamped out her smoke and pulled the Scunci off her

ponytail. She shook her head and let her hair fall naturally past her
shoulders. Some strays fell across her face.

"Do I have anything to say about it?" said Quinn.

"Both times we've been together, you've been staring at me
like you were from hunger. And Terry, I'm not as obvious as you
are, but I've been looking at you the same way."

"Christ, you got some balls on you."

"It's not like I make a habit of this." She unfolded her legs and
swung them down to the hardwood floor. "But, you know, when it's
so obvious like it is right here, I mean, why dance around it?"

"You talked me into it."

Tracy leaned into Quinn. He brushed hair away from her
face and she kissed him on the mouth. Their tongues touched and
he bit softly on her lower lip as she pulled away.

"Let's have another beer," said Tracy. "Relax a little, talk.
Listen to some music. Okay?"

"You're in charge."

"Stop it."

"No, it's cool." Quinn breathed out slow. "Relax. That
sounds nice."

They drank their beers and Quinn went off for two more.
Tracy was lighting a cigarette when he returned. He sat close to
her on the couch. Quinn had downed three beers and was working on his fourth. His buzz was on, but he was still amped from
the grab.

"Thought you were gonna relax."

"I am."

"You got your fist balled up there."

"So I do."

"Forget about what happened tonight with Wilson, Terry.
He pushed my buttons, too. But he's history and we got the job
done. That's the only thing that matters now, right?"

Quinn nodded. He *was* thinking about Wilson. Sitting here
drinking a cold beer with a fine-looking woman he liked, ready to

go to bed with her, and not able to stop thinking of the man who had punked him out.

"What makes you think I had Wilson on my mind?"

"I asked around about you, talked to a couple of guys Karen knew in the MPD."

"Yeah? What'd they say?"

"Well, everyone's got a different opinion on what happened the night you shot that cop."

"That black cop, you mean. Why didn't you just ask Derek? He did his own independent investigation into the whole deal."

"That how you two hooked up?"

"Yeah."

"The department said you were right on the shooting."

"It's more complicated than that. You know what I'm sayin'; you were a cop yourself. But a whole lot of cops I come across, they're not too willing to forget about it. Some guys still think that shooting was a race thing. By extension, that I'm some kind of racist."

"Well?"

"Sue, I'm not gonna sit here and tell you that I have no prejudice. For a white guy to say he sees a black man and doesn't make some kind of assumptions, it's bullshit, and it's a lie. And the same thing goes in reverse. Let's just say I'm no more a racist than any other man, okay? And let's leave it at that."

"You know, even the ones who had that opinion of you, they also admitted that you were well-liked, and a good cop. You did have a reputation for violence, though. Not bully violence, exactly. More like, if anyone pushed you, you weren't willing to let it lie."

Quinn drank deeply of his beer and stared at the can. "You always background check the guys you're interested in?"

"I haven't been interested in anyone in a long time." Tracy took a drag off her smoke and ashed the tray. "Now you. Ask me anything you want."

"Okay. First day I met you, I had the impression you had some daddy issues."

"You're wrong," said Tracy, shaking her head. "Not like you mean. I loved my father and he loved me. I never felt I had to prove anything to him. He was always proud of me. I know 'cause he told me. He even told me the last time I saw him, in his bed at the hospice."

"Was he a cop?"

"No. He did come from a family of them, but it wasn't something he wanted for himself. He was a career barman at the Mayflower Hotel, downtown."

"They're all, like, Asian guys behind the bar down there."

"That's now. Frank Tracy was all Irish. Irish Catholic. Just like you, Quinn."

"And you."

"Not quite. The Tracy part of me is. My mother was Scandinavian, where I got the name Susan and my blond hair."

"You're a natural blonde?"

"Don't be rude."

"I was just wondering."

Tracy smiled. "You'll find out soon enough."

"You are something," said Quinn.

They undressed each other back in his room, standing face to face before the bed. She helped him off with his T-shirt and then slipped out of her slacks, leaving on her black lace panties. They were cut high, and her thigh muscles were ripped up to the fabric. He unbuttoned her shirt and peeled it back off her strong shoulders. She wore a black brassiere that fastened in the front. He unfastened it and let it drop to the floor. He pinched one of her pink nipples and flicked his tongue around it.

"These are nice," said Quinn.

"I've been told."

He swallowed. "I mean it, baby."

"They hold my bra up," said Tracy.

Quinn chuckled and kissed her lips. He got down to his knees and drew her panties down and kissed her sex. He blew on her pubis and kissed her there and split her with his tongue. Her fingers dug into his shoulder until it hurt. He sucked her flesh into his mouth and tasted her silk and she came standing there.

They moved to the bed and fucked on the edge of it, Quinn on top. His orgasm was like a punch in the heart. They talked for a while and took a shower and fucked again. Quinn lay beside Tracy and they looked at each other for a long time without speaking. He watched her eyelids slowly drop. In sleep she had a small smile.

Quinn got out of bed and walked to the window. It was late, nearly four. The street was still. A cop car from the station up the street blew down Sligo Avenue and was gone. He wondered if the guy was on a call, or if he was just driving fast, looking for the next piece of action. He wondered if he was that kind of cop, the kind Quinn had been.

It had happened fast with Tracy. He knew it would when he'd met her the first time, in the coffee shop. It had been simple, as simple as her uttering those few words. *Irish Catholic. Just like you, Quinn.* Nothing much needed to be said between them after that, as all was understood. There was her father, as much a part of her as the blood in her veins, and now him, equally familiar. He wondered, as he often did, if it wasn't more natural for people to stick with their own kind. Well, anyway, it was easier. Of this he was sure.

Tracy had been a cop, too, just like him. With her, he didn't have to pretend that he didn't care about the action, that he didn't crave it all the time. There wouldn't be any of that bullshit fronting, the mask he'd felt he had to wear when he was with other women. In that way, they were good for each other. She took him for who he was.

Quinn stood there looking out the window to the darkened street, picturing Wilson in that trick-house, seeing that gold-capped smile and hearing his smooth baritone and trying to forget. Trying to figure out where he was headed with this problem of his. Trying to figure out, himself, who he was. Who he was and where it would take him in the end.

16

O<small>N</small> Saturday morning the team gathered at Roosevelt High School for a roster check. Strange and Blue wanted to be sure the kids were outfitted with the proper pads and mouthpieces, so that there would be no surprises before game time or injuries on the field of play. When they were done checking on those details, the kids got into the cars of the coaches and the usual group of parents and guardians and drove across town and over the river to the state of Virginia, where the Petworth Panthers' first game was to be played.

Their destination was a huge park and sports complex in Springfield that held tennis and basketball courts, picnic areas, and several soccer and football fields. A creek ran through the woods bordering the property. Complexes like this one were typical and numerous in the suburbs, especially farther out, where there was land and money. The kids from the Panthers had rarely seen playing fields as carefully tended as these, or sports parks situated in such lush surroundings.

"Dag, boy," said Joe Wilder, his eyes wide, "this joint is tight; check out those lights they got!"

"Look at thoth uniforms," said Prince, pointing to a team warming up on a perfect green field, with big blue star decals on their helmets. "They look just like the Cowboys!"

The kids were on a path between the road and the field, alongside a split-rail fence. Strange, Blue, Lionel Baker, Lamar Williams, Dennis Arrington, and Quinn were walking among them. Rico, the cocky running back, was telling the quarterback, Dante Morris, what he was going to do to the opposing team's line, and Morris was nodding, not really listening to Rico but keeping quietly to himself. Later, just before the first whistle, Morris would say a silent prayer.

There were several teams on and around the two main fields. Many had their own cheerleading squads and booster clubs. A game was ending on one of the fields. As the Panthers went through an open chain-link gate, they passed a group of boys in clean red-and-white uniforms, decked out in high-tech equipment, their gleaming helmets held at their sides.

"Y'all the Cardinals?" said Joe Wilder.

"Yeah," said one of the boys, mousse in his studiously disheveled hair, looking down on Wilder and looking him over.

"We're playin' y'all," said Wilder.

"In those uniforms?" said the kid, and the Cardinal next to him, pug nosed and with an expensive haircut like his friend, laughed.

"What, did you find those in the trash or somethin'?" said pug nose.

Wilder looked over at Dante Morris, who shook his head, Wilder taking it to mean, correctly, that Morris was telling him to keep his mouth shut. Rico took a step toward the two Cardinals, but Morris pulled on his sleeve and held him back.

Strange, who had heard the exchange and seen this kind of thing before, said, "C'mon, boys, you follow me."

The Cardinals were a team of white kids and the Panthers were all black. But it wasn't a white-black thing. It was a money–no money thing, a way for those who had it to show superiority over those who did not. Plain old insecurity, as old as time itself.

Blue checked in the team rosters to a guy in a Redskins cap whom he knew to be the point man for the league, then met Arrington, Lionel, and the Midgets for their pregame warm-ups. Strange and Quinn led the Pee Wees under the shade of a stand of oaks beside the main stadium and had them form a circle. Strange told Joe Wilder and Dante Morris, the designated captains, to lead the team in calisthenics. Lamar Williams stood by and made sure that they kept the circle tight.

"How y'all feel?"

"Fired up!"

"How y'all feel?"

"Fired up!"

"Breakdown."

"Whoo."

"Breakdown."

"Whoo!"

Strange watched the Cardinals warming up down on the edge of the field. He watched their coach, a fat white man in Bike shorts, yelling out the calisthenics count to his team. Strange remembered this guy from a scrimmage late in the summer, a heart attack waiting to happen, and how he coached his kids to be intimidating and mean.

"You hear what went down back there?" said Quinn.

"I heard it," said Strange.

"I hope we beat the shit out of these guys, Derek, I swear to God."

There was only so much money in the program. The kids had to come up with fifty dollars to play for the squad, and some of them hadn't even been able to raise that. Dennis Arrington, who was flush from his job in the computer industry, had donated a couple of thousand dollars to the team. Strange, Blue, and Quinn had come up with a grand between them. It bought good pads and replacement helmets and mouthguards, but it didn't buy new jerseys and pants. The Panthers' green uniforms were faded, mismatched, and frayed. The number decals on their scarred helmets rarely matched the numbers on their jerseys.

"It's not the attitude we're trying to convey to the boys," said Quinn, "but I can't help feeling that way, even though I know it's wrong."

"It ain't wrong," said Strange. "But we got what we got. Game time comes, it's not the uniforms gonna decide the contest. It's the heart in these kids gonna tell the tale."

Strange called them in. They gathered around him and Quinn. Quinn talked about defense and making the big plays. Strange gave them instructions on the general offensive game plan and a few words of inspiration.

"Protect your brother," said Strange when he was done, trying to meet eyes with most of the boys kneeling before him. "Protect your brother."

The boys formed a tight group and put their hands in the center.

"Petworth Panthers!" they shouted, and ran down to the field.

Both teams were rusty at the start of the opening quarter. Morris fumbled an errant Prince snap in the first set of downs but fell on the ball and recovered. They went three-and-out and punted. On first down the Cardinal halfback was taken down behind the line of scrimmage, and on second down he was stripped of the ball. A Panther named Noah picked up the ball off its bounce and ran ten yards before he was dropped. It was the gasoline on the fire the Panthers needed, a wake-up call that would carry them the rest of the game.

The offensive line began to make their blocks and open the holes. Rico hit those holes, and the chains began to move as the team marched down the field. The Cardinals' coach called a time-out and yelled at his defensive line. Strange could see the veins on the man's neck standing out from across the field.

"No heart," said Strange.

"Their hearts are pumpin' Kool-Aid," said Blue.

The line tightened its play and stopped a thirty-five-run call on the next play. Strange had Joe Wilder run in the next play to Morris, a triple-right. Morris lobbed a pass in the direction of the three receivers — halfback, end, and flanker — who had lined up on the right and gone out to the flats. Rico caught it and took it in, freed by a Joe Wilder block on the Cardinals' corner.

Strange stuck with the running game but took it to the out-side. The Cardinals' left side was weak and seemed to be grow-ing weaker the more the coach screamed at his players. At flanker, Wilder was taking out the defensive man assigned to him, push-ing him inside, allowing Rico to turn the corner and just blow and go.

By halftime, the Cardinals were totally demoralized and the Panthers were firing on all cylinders. Barring an act of God, the game was theirs, Strange knew.

The second half went the same way. Strange played the bench and rested his first-stringers. The Cardinals managed a score against the Panthers' scrubs, causing an anemic eruption from the cheerleaders on the other side of the field. But the drive was just a spark, and even their coach, who threw his hat down in disgust when his team turned the ball over on their next posses-sion, knew they were done. The Panthers moved the ball into Car-dinal territory easily and were threatening again with a minute left to play.

Strange brought Joe Wilder out of the game and rested his hand on his shoulder. "Next play, I want you to tell Dante to down the ball. Just let the clock run out, hear?"

"Let me take it in, Coach," said Wilder. He was smiling at Strange, his eyes eager and bright. "Forty-four Belly, that's my play."

"We won, Joe. We don't need to be rubbin' it in their faces."

"C'mon, Coach Derek. I ain't touched the ball all day. I know I can run it in!"

Strange squeezed Wilder's shoulder. "I know you can, too, son. You got real fire in you, Joe. But we don't do like that out here. Those boys been beat good today. I don't like to put the boot to someone's face when they're down, and I don't want you doin' it either. That's not the kind of man I want you to be."

"Okay, then," said Wilder, the disappointment plain on his face.

"Go on, boy. Run the play in to Dante like I told you."

The game ended the way Strange had instructed. At the whistle, the players gathered on the sideline. Wilder got a hug from Quinn and a slap on the helmet from Strange.

"Line up," said Strange. "Now, when you go to shake their hands, I don't want to hear a thing except 'Good game.' No trash-talking, you understand? You said all you needed to on the field. After what you did out there, don't shame yourselves now, hear?"

The Panthers met the Cardinals in the center of the field, touched hands as they went down the line. The Panthers said 'Good game' to each player they passed, and the Cardinals mumbled the same words in reply. Dante Morris stared into the eyes of the pug-nosed boy who had cracked on their uniforms, but Morris didn't say a word, and the boy quickly looked away. At the end of the line the Cardinals' coach shook Strange's hand and congratulated him through teeth nearly clenched.

"All right," said Quinn, as the team returned and took a knee before him. "I liked the way you guys played today. A lot of heart. Just remember, it's not always going to be this easy. We're going to be playing teams who have better athletes and are better coached. And you need to be ready. Ready in your minds, which means you keep your heads in the books during the day. And ready physically as well. That means we're going to continue to practice as hard as we ever have. We want the championship this year, right?

"Right!"

"I didn't hear you."

"Right!"

"What time is practice Monday night?" said Strange.

"Six o'clock on the dot, be there, don't miss it!"

"I'm proud of you boys," said Strange.

c h a p t e r

17

LATER that afternoon, Quinn sat behind the counter of Silver Spring Books reading *The Pistoleer*, a novel by James Carlos Blake. His coworker, Lewis, was back in the military history room, straightening the shelves. A homeless intellectual whom everyone in the area called Moonman was sitting on the floor in the sci-fi room, reading a paperback edition of K. W. Jeter's *The Glass Hammer*. A customer browsed the mystery stacks nearby.

Quinn had put *Johnny Winter And* on the turntable, and the molten blues-metal classic was playing at a low volume throughout the store. Syreeta, the owner of the business, who was rarely on site, had instructed the employees to play the used vinyl in stock to advertise the merchandise. This disc, with its faded black-and-white cover portraits, had recently been inventoried as part of a large purchase, a carton of seventies albums.

Quinn cherished these quiet afternoons in the shop.

The mystery customer, a thin man in his early forties, brought a paperback to the register and placed it on the glass counter. It was Elmore Leonard's *Unknown Man No. 89*, one of the mass-market publications Avon had done with the cool cover art depicting a montage of the book's elements; this one displayed a snub-nosed .38, spilled-out shells, and an overturned shot glass.

"You ever read his westerns?" said Quinn. "They're the best, in my opinion."

"I go for the crime stuff set in Detroit. There's a lot of different Leonard camps and they've all got opinions." The customer nodded to one of the speakers mounted up on the wall. "Haven't heard this for a while."

"It just came in. The vinyl's in good shape, if you want it."

"I own it, but I haven't pulled it out of the shelf for a long time. That's Rick Derringer on second lead."

"Who?"

"Yeah, you're too young. Him and Johnny, the two of them were just on fire on this session. One of those lightning-in-a-bottle things. Listen to 'Prodigal Son,' the cut leads off side two."

"I will." Quinn gave the man his change and a receipt. "Thanks a lot. And take it easy, hear?"

"You, too."

Quinn figured this guy had a wife, kids, a good job. You'd pass him on the street and think he was your average square. But one thing you learned working here was that just about everyone had something worthwhile to say if you took the time to listen. Everyone was more interesting when you got to know them a little than they initially appeared to be. That was the other thing he liked about working in a place like this. The conversations you got into and the people you met. Of course, he had met plenty of people on a daily basis in his former profession. But it almost always started from an adversarial place when you met them as a cop.

Quinn read some more of his novel. A little while later, Quinn watched Sue Tracy cross Bonifant Street on foot. She was wearing her post-punk utilitarian gear and had a day pack slung over her shoulder. Quinn's heart actually skipped, watching her walk. He was imagining her naked atop his sheets.

The small bell over the door rang as she walked in. Quinn let his feet drop off the counter, but he didn't get up out of his seat.

"Hey."

"Hey."

"New in town?"

"I missed you."

"I've been missing you, too."

"Got on the Metro and walked up from the station. Can you get away?"

"I can probably sneak out, sure."

"It's a beautiful day."

"I've got my car here. We can, I don't know, go for a ride."

Tracy looked down at the book in Quinn's hand. "What's that, a western?"

"Yeah, sort of."

"What's with you and your partner? Strange went on about some scene from *The Magnificent Seven*."

"That would be the one with Coburn shooting the rider instead of the horse."

"Uh-huh."

"He does go back to that one a lot."

Lewis came forward from the back of the shop. His black hair was long, greasy, and tangled, and his thick glasses had surgical tape holding one stem to the frame. Yellow perspiration marks stained the armpits of his white shirt.

"Lewis, meet my friend, Sue Tracy."

"My pleasure," said Lewis. Tracy and Lewis shook hands.

"I'm gonna punch out for the day, Lewis. That okay by you?"

Lewis blinked hard behind the lenses of his glasses. "Fine."

Quinn gathered his things, marking the Leonard paperback off in the store's inventory notebook before he came around the counter.

"This Johnny Winter?" said Tracy.

"How'd you know that?"

"Older brothers. I had one played this till the grooves wore out on the vinyl."

"That's Rick Derringer on second lead right here."

"Who?"

"You're too young."

They left the shop and walked up Bonifant.

"Lewis gonna be all right back there, all by himself?" said Tracy.

"He's the best employee Syreeta's got. A little lonely, though. Any suggestions?"

Tracy laced her fingers through Quinn's. "I'm spoken for."

"Maybe your partner, then."

"He's not Karen's type."

"What type is that?"

"The type who runs a comb through his hair every so often. The type who showers."

"Picky," said Quinn.

They stopped at his car, parked in the bank lot.

"Sweet," said Tracy. Quinn had recently waxed the body, scrubbed the Cragar mags with Wheel-Brite and wet-blacked the rubber. The Chevelle's clean lines gleamed in the sun.

"You like, huh?"

Tracy nodded. "You got the Flowmasters on there, huh?"

"I bought it like that off the lot."

"What's under the hood, a three ninety-six?"

"Now you're making me nervous."

"My older brothers."

"C'mon, get in."

She got into the passenger side. Quinn saw her admiring the shifter, a four-speed Hurst.

"You want to drive?"

"Could I?"

"I knew there was something else I liked about you. Aside from you being a natural blonde, I mean."

"What can I say? I like fast cars."

"Bad-ass," said Quinn.

Tracy drove down into Rock Creek Park. They parked near a bridle trail on the west side of the creek and took the path up a rise and all the way to the old mill. On the walk back they sat on some boulders in the middle of the creek. Quinn took his shirt off, and Tracy removed her socks and shoes. She let her feet dangle in the cool water. They talked about their pasts and kissed in the sun.

Late in the afternoon they went back to Quinn's apartment and made love. They showered and re-dressed and had dinner at Vicino's, a small Italian restaurant Quinn liked up on Sligo Avenue. Quinn had the calimari over linguini, and Tracy had the seafood platter, and they washed it down with a carafe of the house red. They stopped for another bottle of red on the way back to Quinn's place and drank it while listening to music and making out on his couch. They fucked like teenagers in his room, and afterward they lay in bed, Tracy smoking and talking, Quinn listening with a natural smile on his face.

The day had been a good one. The kids had won their game, and in his mind Quinn could still see the look of pride on their faces as they had run off the field. Then Sue Tracy had surprised him and stopped by the shop.

Quinn looked at his hands and saw that they were totally relaxed on the sheets. He hadn't been thinking of the streets or if anyone had looked at him the wrong way or anything else but Sue, his girlfriend, lying beside him. He hadn't felt this comfortable with a woman for some time.

❐

STRANGE dropped off Prince, Lamar, and Joe Wilder, then dropped Lionel at Janine's house uptown.

"You comin' for dinner tonight?" said Lionel, before getting out of the car.

"I haven't spoken to your mother about it," said Strange.

"My mom wants you to come over, I know. Saw her marinating some kind of roast this morning before you picked me up."

"Maybe I'll see you, then."

"Whateva," said Lionel, turning and going up the sidewalk toward his house.

Strange watched the boy and his loping walk.

Boy's still got that way of stepping. Had that walk since I been knowing him, back when he wasn't nothing much more than a kid. Thinks he's a man, but he's still a boy inside.

He grinned without thinking, watching him, and waited until Lionel got inside the house before driving away.

Strange picked up the Calhoun Tucker photos from the Safeway over on Piney Branch. Safeway was cheap and they did a good-enough job on the processing. It took a little longer when you used them, but he wasn't in any hurry on this particular job.

Back in his office, he inspected the photographs. The woman in the doorway, Tucker's somethin' on the side, was plain as day in the shot, letting him into her crib. Janine had gotten her name from the crisscross program, based on her street address. It was in the file he was building on Tucker, the one he was preparing for his friend George Hastings. Strange found the file and slipped the photographs inside it. He was just about done with the background check. He'd need to report on all this to George. Soon, thought Strange, I will do this soon. He wondered what was stopping him from getting George on the phone right now. Strange turned this over in his mind as he locked the file cabinet, then his office door.

Walking through the outer office, he noticed his reflection in the mirror nailed to the post, and stopped to study himself. Damn if his natural wasn't nearly all gray. The years just . . . they just *went*. Strange was bone tired and hungry. He thought about having a nice meal, maybe some Chinese. And a hot shower, too; that would do him right.

❒

AT dinner that night, Strange sat at the head of Janine's table, as he always did, in the one chair that had arms on it. It had been her father's chair. Lionel sat to his left and Janine to his right. Greco played with a rubber ball, his eyes moving to the dinner table occasionally but keeping control of himself, staying there on his belly, lying on the floor at Strange's feet.

Janine had *Talking Book* on the stereo, playing softly. She did love her Stevie, in particular the breakout stuff that he'd done for Motown in the early seventies.

"Where you off to tonight?" said Strange, eyeballing Lionel, clean in his Nautica pullover and pressed khakis.

"Takin' a girl to a movie."

"What, you gonna walk her there?"

"Gonna pull her in a ricksha."

"Don't be playin'," said Strange. "I'm just asking you a question."

"He's taking my car, Derek."

"Yeah, okay. But listen, don't be firin' up any of that funk in your mother's car, hear?"

"You mean, like, *herb?*"

"You know what I mean. You get yourself a police record, how you gonna get to be that big-time lawyer you always talking about becoming?"

Lionel put his fork down on his plate. "Look, how you gonna just *suppose* that I'm gonna be out there smokin' some hydro tonight? I mean, it's not like you're my father, Mr. Derek. It's not like you're here all the time, like you know me all that well."

"I know I'm not your father. Didn't say I was. It's just —"

"I wasn't even thinkin' about smokin' that stuff tonight, you want the truth. This girl I'm seein', she's special to me, understand, and I wouldn't do nothin', *anything*, that I thought would get her in any kind of trouble with the law. So, all due respect, you can't be comin' up in here, part-time, lookin' to guide me, when you don't even know me all that well, for real."

Strange said nothing.

Lionel looked at his mother. "Can I be excused, *Mom*? I need to pick up my girl."

"Go ahead, Lye. My car keys are on my dresser."

Lionel left the room and went up the hall stairs.

"I guess I messed that up pretty bad."

"It is hard to know what to say," said Janine. "Most of the time, I'm just winging it myself."

"I do feel like a father to that boy."

"But you're not," said Janine, her eyes falling away from his. "So maybe you ought to go a little easier on him, all right?"

Janine got up out of her seat and picked up Lionel's plate off the table. She head-motioned to Greco, whose eyes were on her now and pleading. "C'mon, boy. Let's see if you can't finish some of this roast."

Greco's feet sought purchase on the hardwood floor as he scrabbled toward the kitchen, his nub of a tail twitching furiously. Strange got up and went to the foyer, meeting Lionel, who was bounding down the stairs.

"Hey, buddy," said Strange.

"Hey."

"You got money in your pocket?"

"I'm flush," said Lionel.

"Look here —"

"You don't have to say nothin', Mr. Derek."

"Yeah, I do. Don't want to give you the impression that I'm just assuming you're always out there looking to get into trouble, doing somethin' wrong. Because I do think that you're a fine young man. I appreciate you helping out with the team like you do, and the way you help your mother around here, too."

"I know you do."

"I guess what I'm trying to tell you is, I'm proud of you. I give you advice you don't need, I guess, because I care about you, see? I'm looking to play some kind of role in your life, but I'm not quite sure what that is yet, understand?"

"Uh-huh."

They stood there in the foyer looking at each other. Lionel put his hands in his pockets and took them out again and shuffled his feet.

"Anything else?" said Lionel. " 'Cause I gotta bounce."

"That's it, I guess."

Strange shook Lionel's hand and then hugged him clumsily. Lionel left the house, looking over his shoulder at Strange one time before continuing on down the sidewalk. Strange watched him through the window and made sure he got safely into Janine's car.

"How'd that go?" said Janine, standing behind him with a cold bottle of beer in one hand and two glasses in the other.

"Uh, all right, I guess."

"C'mon back out to the living room, then, and put your feet up."

Strange followed her out of the foyer, through a hall. He watched her strong walk and the back of her head of hair. He could see she'd been to the beauty salon that day, and he hadn't even complimented her on it. He thought of how much he did love her, and the boy. And he thought of the stranger who had jacked his dick off on a massage table just a few hours earlier in the day.

"Goddamn you, Derek," he said under his breath.

Janine looked over her shoulder. "You all right?"

"I'm fine, baby," said Strange.

He wished that it were so.

18

GARFIELD Potter, Carlton Little, and Charles White spent most of Monday driving around Petworth, Park View, and the northern tip of Shaw, checking on their troops, looking for girls to talk to, drinking some, and staying high. Early in the evening they were back in their row house, hanging out in the living room, where the smoke of a blunt Little had recently fired up hung heavy in the air.

Potter had been trying to get up with a girl all afternoon, but he hadn't been able to connect. He paced the room as Little and White sat on the couch playing Madden 2000 while an Outkast cut on PGC came loud from the box. White saw the shadow that had settled on Potter's face, the look he got when the girl thing hadn't gone his way. Truth was, most girls were afraid to be with Garfield Potter, something that had never crossed his mind.

Potter was working on his third forty of malt. He'd been drinking them down since early in the day.

"Y'all gonna play that kid shit all night?" said Potter.

"It's the new one they got," said Little.

"I ain't give a good fuck about no cartoon football game," said Potter. "Let's go up to that field and see some real football."

"That again?"

"I feel like smokin' someone," said Potter. He rubbed his hands together as he walked back and forth in the room. "Lorenze Wilder is gonna be got."

"Ah, shit, D," said Little. "Let me and Coon just finish this one game."

Potter went over to the PlayStation base unit and hit the power button. The game stopped and the screen went over to the cable broadcast. Potter stood in front of the couch and stared at his childhood friends. Little started to say something but thought better of it, looking into Potter's flat eyes.

"You want to go," said Little, "we'll go."

Potter nodded. "Bring your strap."

Charles White didn't protest. He hoped they would not find this Lorenze Wilder up at the football field. He told himself that they would not. After all, they had gone back to the practice field a couple of times, and except for the first go-round when Wilder had been there, there hadn't been nothin' over there but a few parents, coaches, and some kids.

They met a few minutes later at the front door of the house, Potter wearing his skully. Both he and Little had dressed in dark, loose clothing. White had slipped on his favorite shirt, the bright orange Nautica pullover in that soft fleece, the one felt good against his skin.

"Take that shit off," said Potter, looking at White's shirt. "Like you wearin' a sign says, Look at me."

"Why you buggin'?" said White.

"'Cause I don't want no one to remember us later on," said Potter, talking carefully as he would to a child. "Could you be more stupid than you is?"

❐

LORENZE Wilder stood by the stadium seats, leaning on the chain-link fence, watching the kids practicing while his hand dipped into a bag of french fries doused in ketchup. He shoved a handful of fries into his mouth and licked ketchup off his fingers. He hadn't thought to get some napkins from the Chinese chicken house he'd stopped into up on the strip. Cheap-ass slope who owned the shop, he was probably hiding the napkins in the back anyhow.

Wilder nodded to one of the parents of the kids who was seated nearby. Man barely gave him the time of day, just a kind of chill-over with his eyes. One of those bourgeois brothers, Wilder guessed, thought he was somethin' with his low-grade government job. Maybe he didn't like Wilder's T-shirt, had a big picture of a marijuana leaf on the front. Didn't like him wearing it in front of all these kids. Well, fuck him, too.

The coaches were working these boys tonight. That white-boy coach they had, he had set up three of those orange cones road crews used in the center of the field. The kids were running to the cones, and the white boy had the pigskin, and he was shouting "Right" or "Left," and the kid would cut that way without looking over his shoulder and get the pass from that coach. The pass would always be there, on the money. Wilder had to admit, the white boy had an arm on him, but he should've thrown it much harder, taught those boys what it was like to feel the sting of a bullet-ball. That's what Wilder would do if he was the coach. He wouldn't mind getting out there himself, show them all how it was done.

The one named Strange was out there, talking to another coach, a brother with a gray mustache who looked even older than him. Wilder didn't care much for this Strange, who he could tell didn't want him hangin' around his little nephew, Joe. First time they'd met, Strange had given him one of those chill-looks, too.

Now the kids were being told to come in and take a knee. It had gotten near to dark, and Lorenze Wilder guessed the practice was coming to an end. Wilder had brought his car with him tonight. He wasn't gonna let Strange talk him out of spending time with his nephew. Joe was his own kin, after all. And Lorenze Wilder needed to speak to him about something important. He'd been looking to get up with the little man on it for a long time.

◻

CHARLES White sat in the backseat of the Plymouth and watched Garfield Potter return from the fence bordering Roosevelt's stadium. In the passenger seat, Carlton Little ate a Quarter Pounder, his eyes closed as he chewed. He had made them stop at the McDonald's near Howard before doubling back up here to the high school. Little always got hungry behind the herb.

Potter crossed the lot slow, putting a down-dip to his walk, a kind of stretched-back grin spreading on his face. The things that made Potter smile were not the things that made other people smile, and White felt a tightening in his chest.

Potter leaned into Charles White's open window.

"You drivin', Coon. Get out and take the wheel. Roll over to Iowa and park on the street. We'll wait there for him to pull out."

"Wilder's here?" said Little, looking up from his meal.

"Yeah," said Potter. "And we gonna dead this motherfucker tonight."

◻

STRANGE gave his usual closing talk to the Midgets and Pee Wees, and answered their questions patiently. Then he asked them for the starting time of the next practice, on Wednesday night.

"Six o'clock on the dot, be there, don't miss it!"

"See you then," said Strange. "Those of you on your bikes, get home now. If you're waitin' on a ride from one of the coaches or parents, you wait over there by the stands, or at the parking lot if you know the car."

Strange looked over to the stands, saw the parents and

guardians grouped together, waiting for their kids and for those who were not theirs but who depended on them for a lift home. He noticed Joe Wilder's no-account uncle standing apart from the rest, leaning on the fence, a brown bag of trash at his feet. He probably just dropped it there, thought Strange. Wouldn't think to move a few feet and throw it in a can.

Prince and Joe Wilder were walking together toward the stands.

"Prince! Joe! Y'all wait for me, hear?"

Joe Wilder turned his head, made a small wave back to Strange, and kept walking. Strange could see the boy's eyes blink under his helmet as he took out his mouthguard and fitted it in the helmet's cage. He was holding one of those wrestling figures of his tight in his hand.

If Lionel or Lamar were there, he'd tell them to go ahead and get up with the boys, make sure they waited up by his car. But Lamar was baby-sitting his little sister, and Lionel had stayed home to catch up on his schoolwork.

"Derek," said Lydell Blue, coming up beside him and startling him with his voice. "Can I talk to you a minute? Need some advice on what to do with my offensive line. I mean, they did nothin' on Saturday. You and Terry been handlin' yours pretty well."

"I can't talk long," said Strange.

"This won't take but a minute," said Blue.

Some of the boys had stayed on the field and were throwing long passes, tackling one another, clowning around. Strange glanced over at Arrington and Quinn, who were gathering up the equipment on the far sideline.

"All right," said Strange, "but let's make it quick. I gotta get these boys back in their homes."

❑

JOE Wilder saw his uncle Lorenze standing by the fence as he neared the stands. Joe's mom was mad at his uncle or something, and Joe hadn't seen him around the apartment for quite some time.

"Little man," said Lorenze.

"Hey, Uncle Lo," said Joe with a smile.

"How you been doin'? You lookin' strong out there, Hoss."

"I been doin' all right."

"I got my car. C'mon, boy, I'll drive you home tonight."

"Thanks, but I was gonna ride with Coach Derek."

"You like ice cream, don't ya?"

"Yeah?"

"Well, c'mon, then. We'll grab a cone or a cup or somethin', and then I'll run you home."

"*I* like ithe cream," said Prince.

"Sorry, youngun," said Lorenze. "Only got enough to spring for me and my man here. Next time, okay?"

Joe Wilder looked back at Coach Strange, who was still on the field, talking with Coach Blue. His uncle seemed pretty nice. He wouldn't let anything happen to him or nothin' like that. And an ice cream sounded good.

"Tell Coach Derek I got a ride home with my uncle," said Joe to Prince. "All right?"

"I'll tell him," said Prince.

Prince had a seat on the lowest aluminum bench in the stands and waited for Strange to finish what he was doing. Joe and his uncle climbed the concrete steps to the parking lot. The shadows of dusk faded as full dark fell upon the school grounds.

❐

"THERE we go," said Potter, looking through the windshield of the Plymouth from the passenger side. "There goes Wilder right there."

Lorenze Wilder was letting a uniformed boy into the passenger side of his car. As he went around to the driver's side, he looked around the parking lot, studying the cars.

Potter chuckled under his breath, then took a deep swig from a forty-ounce bottle of malt liquor. He slid the bottle back down between his legs.

"He got some kid with him," said White. "That's his nephew, right?"

"Whateva," said Potter.

"Yo, turn that shit up, D," said Little from the backseat. He was busy rolling a fat number, his hands deep in a Baggie of herb.

Potter turned up the volume on the radio.

"That's my boy DJ Flexx right there," said Little. "They moved him into Tigger's spot."

"Put this shits in gear, Coon," said Potter. "They're pullin' out."

"We gonna do this thing with that kid in the car?" said White.

"Just stay on Wilder. He probably gonna be droppin' that boy off at his mother's, sumshit like that."

"We don't need to be messin' with no kids, Gar."

"Go on, man," said Potter, chinning in the direction of the royal blue Oldsmobile leaving the parking lot. "Try not to lose him, neither."

❏

LORENZE Wilder's car was a 1984 Olds Regency, a V8 with blue velour interior, white vinyl roof, and wire wheel covers. The windows were tinted dark all the way around. It reminded Wilder of one of those Miami cars, the kind those big-time drug dealers had down there, or a limousine. You could see out, but no one could see inside, and for him it was the one feature of the car that had closed the deal. He had bought it off a lot in Northwest for eighteen hundred dollars and financed it at an interest rate of 24 percent. He had missed the last three payments and had recently changed his phone number again to duck the creditors who had begun to call.

Lorenze saw Joe running his hand along the fabric of the seat as they drove south on Georgia Avenue.

"You can get your own car like this someday, you work hard like your uncle." In fact, Lorenze Wilder hadn't had a job in years.

"It's nice," said Joe.

"That's like, *velvet* right there. Bet your father got a nice car, too."

Joe Wilder shrugged and looked over at his uncle. "I ain't never met my father, so I don't know what he drives."

"For real?"

"Mama says that my father's just . . . She say he's *gone*."

Of course, Lorenze knew all about the family history. It was this very thing Lorenze and his sister had argued about, that had set her shit off. She didn't want the boy to know about his father, that was her business. But here it was now, affecting him, Lorenze. Standing in *his* way. All he wanted was a little somethin', a way in. Lorenze tried not to think on it too hard, 'cause it only made him angry.

He glanced over at his nephew. Joe Wilder's helmet was next to him on the bench seat. He held an action figure in his hand, some guy in tights. Sunglasses had been painted on the man's rubber face.

Lorenze let his breath out slow. He hadn't been around kids too much himself. But as kids went, his nephew seemed all right. Lorenze made himself smile and tried to put a tone of interest in his voice.

"Who's that, Joe?"

"The Rock."

"That's that Puerto Rican boy, right?"

"I don't know what he is, but he's bad. I got a whole rack of wrestlers like this at home."

"Bet you ain't got no good ice cream at your mama's place."

"Sometimes we do."

"What kind of ice cream you like?"

"Chocolate and vanilla. Like, when they mix 'em up."

"I think I know where this one place is." They were south of Howard University now, and Lorenze turned the wheel and went east on Rhode Island Avenue. "Let's see if it's open, okay?"

Had Wilder bothered to look in his rearview, he would have seen a white Plymouth following him from four or five car lengths back.

❐

"He ain't droppin' that kid off," said White.

"Just keep on doin' what you're doin'," said Potter.

Carlton Little passed the fat bone over the front seat to Potter. Potter took it and hit it deep. He kept the smoke in his lungs for as long as he could stand it. He exhaled and killed the forty of malt and dropped the bottle at his feet. The music from the radio was loud in the car.

In the Edgewood Terrace area of Northeast, still on Rhode Island, Potter saw the blue Olds slow down up ahead. It turned into a parking lot where a white building stood, fronted with glass and screens.

"Keep drivin' by it," said Potter.

As they passed the building, Potter saw that it was a take-out ice-cream joint, had a sign out front looked like a kid had drawn it. Next to it was a 7-Eleven with plywood over its windows and red condemnation notices stuck on the boards.

"Drive around the block, Coon."

White made a left at the next intersection, and the next one after that. Potter reached into his waistband and drew the .357 Colt that he had there. He broke the cylinder and checked the load. He jerked his wrist to snap the cylinder shut, as he had seen it done in the movies, but it did not connect, and he used his free hand to finish the job. He tightened his fingers on the revolver's rubber grip.

"Get your shit ready, Dirty," said Potter.

"I'm tryin' to," said Little, with a nervous giggle. He had his 9mm automatic out from under the front seat. He had released the magazine and was now trying to slide it back in. Little had gotten this Glock 17, the current sidearm of the MPD, from a boy he knew who owed him money, a drug debt erased. But Little hadn't practiced with it much.

"Boy," he said, "I am *fucked up*." The magazine found its home with a soft click.

White brought the car back out to Rhode Island, about fifty yards south of the ice-cream place.

"Park it here and let it run," said Potter.

As they pulled along the curb, Potter watched Lorenze Wilder and his nephew up at the screen window of the joint, the place where you ordered and paid. Wasn't but one other car in the lot, a shitty Nissan. Well, it *was* September. The nights had cooled some.

"What're we gonna do?" said White.

"Wait," said Potter.

The person worked in the ice-cream place, had a paper hat on his head, Potter could see it from back on the street, was taking his time. Potter looked around the block. He didn't see anyone outside the few residences that were situated around the commercial strip, but there could have been some people looking out at them from behind curtains and shit, you never knew. Later on, they might remember their car.

"Take it around the block again, Coon," said Potter. "I don't like us just sittin' here like this."

Potter pulled the trans down into drive and rolled out into the street. As they neared the ice-cream shop, Potter saw Wilder and his nephew walk toward the Olds. Then he saw the kid hand Wilder his cone and head back toward the shop. The kid was going around the side, where they had hung some swinging signs over a couple of doors.

"Keep goin'!" shouted Potter, and then he barked a laugh. "Oh, shit, that boy's goin' to the bathroom! Hit this motherfucker, man, go around the block quick. Just drive straight into that ice-cream lot when you get back onto Rhode Island, hear?"

White's foot depressed the gas. He fishtailed the car as he made the left turn, and the tires squealed as he made the next one.

"You ready, Dirty?" said Potter.

"I guess I am," said Little, his voice cracking some on the reply. He bunched up the McDonald's trash by his side and flung it to the other side of the car. He thumbed off the Glock's safety and racked the slide.

"Motherfucker thinks he gonna rise up and take me for bad," said Potter. "He's gonna find out somethin' now."

White made the next turn, and Rhode Island Avenue came up ahead. His hands were shaking. He gripped the wheel tightly to make the shaking stop.

❐

JOE Wilder went around to the side of the building. He had to pee, and his uncle had told him they had a bathroom there. His uncle said to go now so he could enjoy his ice cream without squirming around in the car. But when Joe got to where the men's room was, he saw that someone had put one of those heavy chains and a big padlock through the handle of the door.

He could hold it for a while. And the thought of that ice cream, the soft chocolate-and-vanilla mix, made him forget he had to go. He went back to the car and got inside.

"That was quick," said Lorenze, handing Joe his cone.

"It's all locked up," said Joe. "But it's all right." He licked at the ice cream and caught some that had melted down on the cone.

"Good, huh?"

"Yeah, it's tight." Joe smiled. His tongue showed a mixture of white and brown.

"Listen, Joe . . . you need to get up with your moms about your father and all that."

"What about him?"

"Well, he ain't exactly gone, like *gone* gone, know what I'm sayin'?"

"Not really."

"You really ought to meet your father, son. I mean, every boy should be in contact with his pops."

Joe Wilder bit off the crest of the mound of ice cream sitting atop the cone.

"When you do meet him," said Lorenze, "what I want you to do for me is, I want you to tell him how nice I been to you. Like what we did right here tonight."

"But my moms says he's gone."

"Listen to me, boy," said Lorenze. "When you do talk to him, *wheneva* you do, I want you to tell him that Uncle Lo wants to be put on. Hear?"

Joe Wilder shrugged and smiled. "Okay."

Lorenze looked up at a tire sound and saw a white police-looking car pull very quickly into the lot. The car stopped in front of his Olds. Well, it wasn't no police. The car was too old, a fucked-up Plymouth, and anyway, it looked like a bunch of young boys just driving around. Dumb ones, too, if they thought he was gonna let them block his way when there were plenty of other spaces in the lot.

Both passenger-side doors opened on the car, and two of the young men jumped out, one coming around the hood and the other around the tail of the Plymouth. Lorenze's eyes widened as he recognized Garfield Potter at the same time that Potter and a boy with cornrows showed their guns and raised them, stepping with purpose toward the Olds.

"Hey," said Joe Wilder, "Uncle Lo."

Lorenze Wilder heard popping sounds and saw fire spit from the muzzles of the guns. He dropped his ice cream and threw his body across the bench to try to cover his nephew just as the windshield spidered and then imploded. He felt the awful stings and was twisted and thrown back violently and thought of God and his sister and Please don't take the boy, God in that last long moment before his brain matter, blood, and life blew out across the interior of the car.

19

F RIENDS, relatives, police, and print and broadcast media heavily attended Joe Wilder's showing at a funeral parlor near the old Posin's Deli on Georgia Avenue. At one point, traffic had been rerouted on the strip to accommodate the influx of cars. Except for a few acquaintances and a couple of black plainclothes homicide men assigned to the case, few came to pay their respects to Lorenze Wilder on the other side of town.

The boy and his uncle were buried the next day in Glenwood Cemetery in Northeast, not far from where they had been murdered.

Because of the numbing consistency of the murder rate, and because lower-class black life held little value in the media's eyes, the violent deaths of young black men and women in the District of Columbia had not been deemed particularly newsworthy for the past fifteen years. Murders of young blacks rarely made the lead-off in the TV news and were routinely buried inside the Metro section of the *Washington Post*, the details consisting of a paragraph or two at best, the victims often unidentified, the follow-up nil.

Suburban liberals plastered Free Tibet stickers on the bumpers of their cars, seemingly unconcerned that just a few short miles from the White House, American children were enslaved in nightmare neighborhoods, living amid gunfire and drugs and attending dilapidated public schools. The nation was outraged at high school shootings in white neighborhoods, but young black men and women were murdered without fanfare in the nation's capital every single day.

The shooting death of Joe Wilder, though, was different. Like a few high-profile cases over the years, it involved the death of an innocent child. For a few days after the homicide, the Wilder murder was the lead story on the local television news and made top-of-the-fold Metro as well. Even national politicians jumped into the fray, denouncing the culture of violence in the inner cities. As the witness at the ice-cream shop had mentioned the loud rap music coming from the open windows of the shooters' car, these same politicians had gone on to condemn those twin chestnuts, hip-hop and Hollywood. At no time did these bought-and-sold politicians mention the conditions that created that culture, or the handguns, as easily available as a carton of milk, that had killed the boy.

Strange was thinking of these things as he pulled his Brougham into Glenwood Cemetery, coming to a stop behind a long row of cars that stretched far back from Joe Wilder's grave site. Lydell Blue was beside him on the bench. Lamar Williams and Lionel Baker sat quietly in the back of the Cadillac.

Strange looked in his rearview. Dennis Arrington was pulling up behind him in his Infiniti. He had brought along Quinn and three of the boys from the team: Prince, Rico, and Dante Morris. Some of Joe's other teammates had attended the church service, a ceremony complete with tears-to-the-eyes gospel singing, in the Baptist church where Joe and his mother had attended services.

Strange looked out at the automobiles, and the people getting out of them and crossing the lawn. Joe Wilder's mother, Sandra Wilder, was stooped in the middle of a group of mourners who were helping her along to the grave site. She had just gotten out of an expensive German car. Lorenze's casket and Joe's, half the size of his uncle's, were up on platforms under a three-sided green tent beside two open graves.

Most of the cars parked along the curb and up on the grass had been waxed and detailed out of respect. There was a van in the mix that Strange knew to be a police van, its occupants taking photographs of the funeral's attendees. This was fairly routine in killings believed to be of the serial variety, as serial killers often showed up at the wakes and funerals of their victims.

Strange knew, and the police knew, that the killers would not show up here today. He was fairly certain what this had been about. This wasn't a serial killing. It was a gang killing, or turf beef, or eyeball beef, or a death collect on a drug debt. The target was Lorenze Wilder; his nephew Joe just happened to have been in the car. A simple, everyday thing.

Again, Strange studied the cars. Many of them were not just clean. Many of them were drug cars. High-priced imports tricked out in expensive customized options. The men getting out of them were very young and flashily dressed. Strange didn't even have to turn it over in his mind. It wasn't black-on-black racism. He had lived in the city his whole life. It was real.

"You thinking what I'm thinking?" said Blue.

"All kinds of young drug boys here," said Strange. "Question is, why?"

"No idea."

"Joe wasn't even close to being in the life. I know his mother, and she's straight."

"You see that car she got out of?"

Strange had seen it. It was a three-series BMW, late model, the middle of the line.

"I saw it."

"She's got, what, a thirty-five-thousand-dollar car and she's living in government-assisted housing?"

"Could be a friend's car," said Strange.

"Could be."

"Something to think about. But this ain't the time or the place."

They got out of the car. Lamar and Lionel joined Quinn, Arrington, and the boys from the team. They walked as a group to the gravesite. Strange and Blue walked behind.

"You okay?" said Blue.

"Yeah," said Strange. But to Blue's eyes his friend looked blown apart, both depleted and seething inside.

"I'm on midnights tonight," said Blue. "Was gonna take a car out. Was wonderin' if you wanted to do a ride-along."

"I do," said Strange.

"Just thought I'd see what's out there."

"I'll be there."

"Meet me at the station at around eleven-thirty. You're gonna need to sign some papers."

"Right," said Strange.

Dennis Arrington had asked the group to form a circle. He took the hand of Quinn, who was standing beside him, and the rest of the boys joined hands until the unbroken circle went back to Arrington. They all bowed their heads, and the young deacon led Quinn and the boys in a quiet prayer. Nearby, Strange and Blue also lowered their heads and prayed.

When Strange was done he looked over to the grave site and saw Joe's mother, Sandra, talking to a young man with closely cropped hair, immaculately dressed in a three-button suit. The young man looked over at Strange as Sandra Wilder talked. He kept his eyes on Strange and said something to the well-dressed young man beside him. His friend nodded. These two young men, Strange decided, were also in the life.

"Let's go, Derek," said Blue. "Looks like they're about ready to say the final words."

Blue and Strange walked to the site. Fifteen minutes later, Joe Wilder, eight years old, was lowered into his grave.

❐

STRANGE woke from a nap at about ten o'clock that night, showered and changed, fed Greco, and locked the house. He had called Janine before he left, telling her that he would be out most of the night and would probably not be back in the office until the following afternoon. He had not spent the night at Janine's place that week.

Strange drove north toward the Fourth District station house at Georgia, between Quackenbos and Peabody. Lydell Blue had already filled him in on the developments of the Wilder case. In the three days that had elapsed since the murders, much had been learned.

The ice-cream shop, called Ulmer's, carried two employees in the fall and winter seasons, a young Salvadoran named Diego Juarez and the owner, Ed Ulmer, African American and fifty-nine years old. On the night of the shooting, Juarez was on the clock. His car, a black Nissan Sentra, was the only one in the lot when Lorenze Wilder pulled in and parked his Olds. After serving Wilder and his nephew, Juarez noticed that the boy tried to use the bathroom around the side of the building but quickly returned to the Oldsmobile. Ulmer had padlocked the bathroom doors after several incidents of vandalism.

Shortly after the boy got into the Olds, joining the older man, a white Plymouth, stripped down like an old police vehicle, came into the parking lot at a high rate of speed. Driven by a young black man with "a long nose, like a beak," the Plymouth stopped in front of the Olds, blocking its forward path. Juarez stated that the "rap music" coming from the open windows of the car was quite loud. Very quickly, two young black men got out of the car, one from the passenger seat and one from the backseat, drew handguns, and began firing into the windshield of the Olds.

Diego Juarez mentally recorded the sequence of letters and numbers on the D.C. license plate of the Plymouth before retreating into the back of the shop. At this point, he phoned the police and then locked himself in the employee bathroom until he heard the squad cars arrive, five minutes later. He had nothing to write with in the bathroom, and in his nervous excitement he had forgotten one of the license plate's two letters and most of its numerals. When he came out of the bathroom, he could recall none of the numerals. By then, of course, the shooters were gone.

One of the shooters, apparently, had vomited a mixture of alcohol and hamburger meat on the asphalt of the parking lot before he'd gotten back into the Plymouth.

Both victims had been shot several times. Lorenze Wilder had been shot in the back as well as the face and neck, indicating that he had initially tried to protect the boy. This was before the force of the bullets had spun him around. Joe Wilder had taken five bullets, one in the groin area, two in the stomach and chest, and two in the face and head. Both victims, lying in melted ice cream and blood, were dead when the police arrived. A rubber action figure, also covered in blood, was found near the boy's hand. A football helmet with a mouthguard wedged in its cage was found at his feet.

Ten 9mm casings were found in the lot consistent with those that would be ejected from an automatic weapon. Their ejection pattern suggested that they came from the gun of the shooter on the right, described by Juarez as the one with "the braids in his hair." There were no casings found from the gun of the second shooter. Either he had picked them up, highly unlikely, or they had remained in the chambers of his gun. If the latter was the case, the weapon he used was a revolver. Indeed, the slugs that had done the most damage to the bodies would later be identified as hollow-points fired from a .357.

Juarez described the second shooter as "a tall and skinny black" with light skin and a skully. Juarez said that the shooter was smiling as he fired his weapon, and it was this smile that had persuaded him, Juarez, to retreat into the back of the shop. He had since worked extensively with police artists to come up with drawings that would closely resemble his brief recollection of the faces on the young men he had seen.

There were no other witnesses to the shooting, and none of the occupants of the nearby residences claimed to have seen a thing.

The white Plymouth was found the next morning on a rural stretch of road bordering a forest in Prince George's County. The car had been doused in gasoline and burned. The smoke rising above the trees had been seen by a resident of a community situated on the other side of the woods, which had prompted him to call the police. The first letter of the license plate matched the letter recalled by Juarez. This was the shooters' car. The arson job had been thorough, obliterating any evidence save for some clothing fibers; the automobile had been wiped clean of prints.

The Plymouth was registered to a Maurice Willis of the 4800 block of Kane Place in the Deanwood section of Northeast. Squad cars and homicide detectives were dispatched to his address, where Willis was taken in without resistance for questioning. The Plymouth belonged to Willis. It had been stolen from the Union Station parking lot while he was attending a movie at the AMC. He had not reported the theft, he explained candidly, because he had been driving the car without insurance. Based on his recollection of the movie he had seen and his certainty of its time, the detectives were able to pinpoint a two-hour window for the theft.

By the end of this next day, the surveillance tapes from the pay booth at the parking garage had produced a photographic record of the one who had stolen the Plymouth. The image was of a light-skinned young black man wearing a sheer black skullcap and shades. On top of these visual obstacles, the suspect had deliberately kept his face partially turned away from the camera while he paid the parking fee. The camera evidence wouldn't find them the shooter, but it would be useful in court.

Detectives continued to canvass the neighborhood where the shooting had occurred. They posted sketches of the suspects and kept the sketches on hand when interviewing potential wits. They interviewed friends and relatives of Lorenze and Joe Wilder extensively, focusing on the acquaintances of the uncle. Most important, the police department had issued a ten-thousand-dollar reward for any information leading to the arrest and conviction of the shooters. This was the most important element and effort of the investigation. In the end, Strange knew, it would be a snitch who would give them the identity of the killers.

They're doing a good job. A damn good job so far. They're doing everything they can.

Strange pulled into the parking lot behind the Fourth District station, found a spot, and cut the engine on his car.

❐

STRANGE went around to the front of the station house, named in honor of Charles T. Gibson, the uniformed officer slain outside the Ibex Club a few years earlier. He went directly to the front desk in the unadorned, flourescent-lit lobby. The police officer on desk duty, a woman he did not recognize, phoned Lieutenant Blue in his second-floor office while Strange signed two release forms for insurance purposes. These were required of all citizens requesting ride-alongs.

Blue appeared in uniform. He and Strange went back through the locker room and down a flight of stairs to the rear entrance. Blue told a sergeant, out in the lot catching a cigarette, that he was taking the Crown Victoria parked leftmost in a row of squad cars facing the building. He mentioned the car's number, displayed on its side and rear, to the sergeant as well.

Blue got behind the wheel of the Crown Vic, and Strange sat beside him. They drove out onto Georgia at just past midnight and headed south.

The Fourth District, known as 4-D, ran north-south from the District line down to Harvard Street, and was bordered by Rock Creek on the west and North Capitol Street on the east. It included neighborhoods of the wealthy and those of the extreme lower class. With a high rate of sexual assault, auto theft, and homicide, 4-D had become one of the most troubled districts in the city. Chief Ramsey had been considering an eighth police district to break up the Fourth, probably in the form of a substation near 11th and Harvard. It had gotten that bad.

The crime rate in the city, despite the propaganda issued to the media about "New Day D.C.," was rising once again. In the first six months of the new century, homicides were up 33 percent; rapes had increased by over 200 percent. In '97, detectives had been transferred and reassigned citywide after an independent investigation had reported substandard performance. Anyone who knew anything about police work knew that results came from a network of informants and neighborhood contacts, and confidences, built up over time. The reassignment had destroyed that system. The result was that the current homicide closure rate was at an all-time low. Two out of three murders in the District of Columbia went unsolved — a closure rate of 31 percent.

The streets were fairly quiet. The temperature had dropped to sweater weather, and it was a work night, and kids had school the next day. But still, kids were out. They were out on the commercial strip and back on the corners of the residential streets, sitting on top of trash cans and mailboxes. A curfew law came and went in D.C., but even when it was in effect it was rarely enforced. No one was interested in locking up a minor who had stayed out too late. Police felt, rightly so, that it wasn't their job to raise other people's kids.

"Anything new since the funeral?" said Strange.

"Nothing on the forensic side," said Blue. "The detectives are doing some serious recanvassing of the neighborhood over there around Rhode Island. And they're heavily interrogating Lorenze Wilder's associates and friends."

"He have any?"

"He had a few. The plainclothes guys at Lorenze's wake got some information until they got made. And they do have the sign-in book from the funeral home, has the names and addresses of those who bothered to use it."

"Anything yet from those interrogations?"

"Lorenze was one of those fringe guys. Didn't work for the most part, least not in payroll jobs. Even his friends admit he was no-account. But none of 'em say he was a target. He wasn't mixed up in no big-time crews or anything like that. That's what they're telling our people, anyway."

"I'd like to get a list of his friends," said Strange.

"You know I can't do that, Derek."

"All right."

Blue had said it. He had to say it, Strange knew. And Strange let it lie.

They drove back into the neighborhoods between Georgia and 16th. Blue stopped to check on a drunken Hispanic man who was standing in the middle of Kenyon Street, his face covered in alcohol sweat. He said he had "lost his house." Blue talked to him carefully and helped him find it. At 15th and Columbia he slowed the patrol car and rolled down his window. A man sat on the stoop of a row house, watching a young boy dribble a basketball on the sidewalk.

"He's out kinda late, isn't he?" said Blue.

The man smiled. "Aw, he's just hyped. You know kids."

"I hear you," said Blue, smiling back. "But you need to get him inside."

"Aiight then," said the man.

Blue drove away. Strange noted how relaxed he was behind the wheel. Blue had always liked working midnights. He said that the danger in these hours was greater, but the respect between the citizens and cops actually increased between midnight and dawn. The squares had all gone home and were sleeping, leaving an uneasy alliance for those who remained.

Blue took a call on a domestic disturbance at 13th and Randolph. He asked the woman if she wanted the husband, whom she had accused of striking her, to spend the night in jail. She said she didn't want that, and this call, like most domestics the police answered, ended in peace.

"How's Terry doing?" said Blue, as he cruised east toward the Old Soldiers' Home.

"He's been quiet," said Strange. "Got a new girlfriend, I think, and he's been spending time with her. It's been good for him to be with a woman this week."

"And you and Janine?"

"Fine."

"Good woman. That son of hers is a fine young man, too."

"I know it," said Strange.

"Lionel gonna be at the game on Saturday?"

"I guess he is." Strange hadn't thought much on the game.

"You know we got to play it."

"Right."

"Think we ought to have a short practice tomorrow night. Talk to the kids."

"That's what we ought to do."

"They need to pick themselves up, right about now," said Blue. "They're gonna see a lot of death in their young lives. I want them to remember Joe, but I don't want this to paralyze them. You agree?"

"Yes," said Strange.

Blue looked over at his friend. They had hugged and patted each other's backs when they'd first seen each other after Joe

Wilder's murder. The both of them felt extreme guilt, Blue for
tying Strange up after practice, and Strange for letting Joe out of
his sight. But they had been tight since childhood, and this was
not something that needed to be apologized for or discussed. Blue
was dealing with it in his own way, but he wasn't sure about how
deeply it had burrowed into Strange.

"Listen, Derek —"

"I'm okay, Lydell. Just don't want to talk about it much right
now, all right?"

Blue turned up Warder Street in Park View. They passed a
group of row houses, all dark. Inside one of them, Garfield Potter,
Carlton Little, and Charles White slept.

❐

BLUE drove around the Fourth. They bought coffee at the all-
night Wings n Things at Kennedy Street and Georgia, and drove
around some more. They stopped to tell some kids to get off the
streets, and answered a domestic. Blue answered another domestic
on 2nd but was called suddenly to a disturbance a block away.

A fight had broken out in a bar on Kennedy at closing time,
and it had spilled onto the street. Several squad cars were already
on the scene. Officers were holding back the brawlers and trying
to quiet some of the neighbors and passersby who had been
incited by the police presence. The patrolmen carried batons. A
guy shouted "cracker motherfucker" and "white motherfucker"
repeatedly at the white policeman who had cuffed him. The
policeman's partner, a black officer, was called a "house nigger" by
the same man. Blue got out of the car and crossed the street.
Strange stepped out and leaned against the Crown Vic.

Down the street was the Three-Star Diner, Billy Georgelakos's place. Strange's father had worked there as a grill man for
most of his career. A riot gate covered the front of the diner.
Nearby, concertina wire topped the fence surrounding the parking
lot of a church.

Blue returned to the Crown Vic with sweat beading his forehead. Most of the bystanders on Kennedy had disappeared. Whatever this had been, it was over without major incident. It would go unreported to the majority of the city's citizens, safely asleep at home in their beds.

Strange asked Blue to make a pass through Park Morton, where Joe Wilder had lived, and Blue agreed. In the complex, few people were out. A boy sat on a swing in the playground of the dark courtyard, smoking a cigarette. Dice players and dope smokers moved about the stairwells of the apartments.

"We put flyers with the artist's renderings of the suspects in the mailboxes here," said Blue. "Gonna post them around the neighborhood as well."

"That's good."

"Most of the time we don't get much cooperation up in here. Drug dealers get chased by the police, they find a lot of open doors, places to hide, in this complex."

"What I hear."

"They even got community guns buried around here somewhere. We know all about it, but it's tough to fight."

"You sayin' you think no one will come forward?"

"I'm hoping this case here is gonna be different. We're mistrusted here, maybe even hated. I got to believe, though, anyone with a heart is gonna want to help us find the people who would kill an innocent kid."

On the drive out, Blue went by the brick pillars and wall that were the unofficial gateway to the housing complex. Two children, girls wearing cartoon-character jackets, sat atop the wall. The girls, no older than eleven or twelve, cold-eyed the occupants of the squad car as they passed.

"Where are the parents?" whispered Strange.

20

On Saturday morning, the Petworth Panthers defeated a Lamond-Riggs team on the field of LaSalle Elementary by a score of twenty to seven. Joe Wilder had not been mentioned by name in the pregame talk, but Dennis Arrington had led a prayer for their "fallen brother." The boys went to one knee and bowed their heads without the usual chatter and horseplay. From the first whistle, their play on the field was relentless. The parents and guardians in attendance stood unusually quiet on the sidelines during the game.

Afterward, as they were gathering up the equipment, Quinn put his hand on Strange's shoulder.

"Hey."

"Hey, Terry."

"You feel like gettin' a beer later this afternoon?"

"I gotta drop these kids off."

"And I've got to work a few hours up at the store. Why don't you meet me up at Renzo's, say, four o'clock? You know where that is, right?"

"Used to be Tradesman's Tavern, up on Sligo Avenue, right?"

"I'll see you there."

Lamar Williams, Prince, and Lionel Baker were waiting by Strange's Cadillac, parked on Nicholson. Lydell Blue's Park Avenue was curbed behind it. Strange told the boys to get in his Brougham as he saw Blue, holding a manila folder, approaching him from behind.

"Derek," said Blue, holding out the folder. "Thought you might want this Migdets roster back for your master file."

Strange took it and opened his trunk. He started to slip the folder into his file box as Blue began to walk away. Strange saw some notation written in pencil on the Pee Wees folder. He pulled it and studied his own writing, the description of a car and a series of letters and numbers, on the outside of the folder. He thought back to the evening he had written the information down.

"Lydell!" he said.

Blue walked back to Strange, still standing by his open trunk. Strange took the papers out of the Pee Wee folder and handed the folder to Blue, pointing at the notation.

"Probably nothin'," said Strange, "but you ought to run this plate here through the system."

Blue eyed the folder. "Why?"

"Not too far back, a week or so, I noticed some hard-looking boys up in the Roosevelt lot one night when we had practice. Thinking back on it, it was a night that Lorenze Wilder was down on the field, waitin' on Joe. I wrote down the plate number and car description out of habit. The car was a Caprice. I guessed on the year, but I do know it was close to the model year of the one I own. I put down it was beige, too."

Strange flashed on the image of the boys. One of them wore his hair in close cornrows, like those on one of the shooters the ice-cream employee had described. But that meant nothing in itself, like noting he wore Timberlands or loose-fitting jeans; a whole lot of young boys around town kept their hair the same way.

"A beige Caprice. Why you got 'beige-brown' on here, then?"

"Had one of those vinyl roofs, a shade darker than the body color."

"Okay. I'll get it into the system right away."

"Like I say, probably nothin'. But let me know it if turns up aces."

"I will."

Strange watched Blue go back to his car. He took the papers from the Pee Wee folder and decided to put them together with the Midget papers in the folder Blue had just given him. He opened the folder. Inside was a mimeographed list of Lorenze Wilder's friends and acquaintances, along with notations describing interview details, taken from the official investigation.

Strange turned his head. Blue had ignitioned his Buick and was pulling off the curb. Strange nodded in his direction, but Blue would not look his way. Strange put the papers together, slipped the folder into his file box, and closed the lid of his trunk.

❑

STRANGE drove Lionel to his mother's house on Quintana. As Lionel was getting out of the car, he asked Strange if he was coming over for dinner that night. Strange replied that he didn't think so, but to tell his mother he'd "get up with her later on." Lionel looked back once at Strange as he went up the walk to his house. Strange drove away.

Prince was the next to be dropped. He had been quiet during the game and had not spoken at all on the ride. The boys who were always cracking on him were on their usual corner, across from his house. Prince asked Strange if he would mind walking along with him to his door. At the door, Strange patted Prince's shoulder.

"You played a good game today, son."

"Thanks, Coach Derek."

"See you at practice, hear? Now go on inside."

Lamar Williams rode shotgun for the trip down to Park Morton. He stared out the window, listening to that old-school music Mr. Derek liked to play, not really paying attention to the words or the melody. It was always that blue-sky stuff about love and picking yourself up, how the future was gonna be brighter, brother this and brother that. Lamar wondered if everyone had been more together back then, in the seventies or whenever it was. If those brothers weren't killin' each other every day, like they were now. If they were killin' on kids "back in the day." Anyway, that kind of music, it sure didn't speak to the world Lamar was living in right now.

"You thinkin' of Joe?" said Strange.

"Yeah."

"It's okay. I was, too."

Lamar shifted in his seat. "That boy was just good. I never thought he'd die. You'd think he'd be the last one living in my complex who'd go out like that. "

"Just because he was a good boy? You know better than that. I've told you before, you always got to be aware of what's going on around you, living where you do."

"I know. But I don't mean that, see? Word was, Joe was protected. Even the ones liked to step to everybody, they kept their hands off that boy. I mean, he was a tough little kid and all. But the word was out; everybody knew not to fuck with Joe."

Strange started to correct Lamar from using the curse word, but he let it pass. "Why you think that was?"

"No idea. Was like, people got the idea in their heads he was connected to someone you didn't want to cross. It was just one of those things got around, and you knew."

"I saw some fellas at his funeral," said Strange, "had to be drug boys."

"I saw 'em, too," said Lamar.

"Any idea why they were paying their respects?"

"Uh-uh."

"Was his mother involved with those people?"

"Not so I knew."

"What about that car she came in?"

"Everybody drivin' a nice car these days, seems like. Don't make you in the game."

"True. But you never saw her hangin' with people you thought were in the life?"

"No. There *was* these young boys, was lookin' for her one night. They rolled up on me when I was walkin' through the complex. Said they owed her money. I didn't tell 'em where she lived, though. They didn't look right."

Strange looked over at Lamar. "How *did* they look?"

"I don't recall, you want the truth. Don't mind tellin' you, Mr. Derek, I was scared."

"Did one of them have cornrows?"

"I don't remember. Look, I didn't even want to meet their eyes, much less study on 'em. I only remember this one boy in the backseat, 'cause he was, like, goofy lookin'. Had a nose on him like one of those anteaters and shït."

"What about their car?"

"It was white," said Lamar. "Square, old. That's all that registered in my mind. That's all I know."

"You did right not to meet their eyes, Lamar. You did good."

"Yeah." Lamar snorted cynically. "It's all good. Good to be livin' in a place where you can't even be lookin' at anyone long for fear you're gonna get downed."

Strange pulled into Park Morton and went slowly down its narrow road.

"You got be positive, Lamar. You got to focus on doing the things that will get you to a better place."

Lamar looked Strange over. His lip twitched before he spoke. "How I'm gonna do that, huh? I can't read all that good, and I'm barely gonna graduate high school. I got no kinda grades to get me into any kind of college. Only job I ever had was dustin' your office and taking out your trash."

"There's plenty of things you can do. There's night school and there's trade school . . . whole lotta things you can do, hear?"

"Yessir," said Lamar, his voice devoid of enthusiasm. He pointed to the road going alongside the playground in the courtyard. "You can drop me right here."

Strange stopped the car. "Listen, you been good to me, Lamar. Conscientious and efficient, and I'm not gonna forget it. I'll help you in any way I can. I'm not going to give up on you, young man, you hear me?"

Lamar nodded. "I'm just all messed up over Joe right now, I guess. I miss that boy."

"I miss him, too," said Strange.

He watched Lamar cross the courtyard, pushing on a rusted swing as he walked past the set. Strange thought about the description that Lamar had just given him: the white car, and the kid with the long nose. Juarez, the ice-cream-parlor employee, had described the Plymouth's driver as having a nose "like a beak."

Strange had the strong suspicion that this was not a coincidence. He knew he should phone Lydell Blue right now and give him the information he had just received. But he had already decided to keep Lamar's story to himself.

Strange was not proud of his decision, but he had to be honest with himself now. He was hoping to find the murderers of Joe Wilder before they were picked up by the police. He knew that if these little pieces were coming to him, a private cop, it would not be long before the police, fully mobilized, would have suspects in custody. He was wondering how much time he had before they took the killers in. Wondering, too, what he would do to them if he found them first.

◻

STRANGE hit the heavy bag in his basement, showered and dressed, fed Greco, and locked down his row house. He drove uptown toward the District line. In his rearview he thought he saw a red car, vaguely familiar, staying with him but keeping back a full block at all times. The next time he checked on the car, up around Morris Miller's liquor store, it was gone, and Strange relaxed in his seat.

The events of the past week had elevated his sense of street paranoia. People living in certain sections of the city, Strange knew, felt the fear of walking under this kind of emotional sword every day. But he didn't like to succumb to it himself.

Strange parked on Sligo Avenue. As he was crossing the street, the beeper on his hip sounded, and he checked the numbered readout: Janine. He clipped the beeper back onto his belt.

Strange walked into Renzo's, an unbeautiful neighborhood beer garden in downtown Silver Spring. Renzo's housed a straight-line bar, stools along a mirrored wall, a pool table, and keno monitors. Bars like this one were common in Baltimore, Philly, and Pittsburgh, but rare around D.C. Quinn sat on a bar stool, reading a paperback and nursing a bottle of Bud in the low light. A heavy-set guy in a flannel shirt, a guy in camouflage pants, and several keno players, huffing cigarettes, sat with him along the stick. The bartender was a woman, nearly featureless in the low light, wearing a Nighthawks T-shirt and jeans. Smoke hung heavy in the air.

Strange got up on a stool next to Quinn. He ordered a Heineken from the tender.

"From a bottle," said Strange. "And I don't need a glass."

"This is you," said Quinn, producing a record album he had propped up at his feet.

Strange took it and studied the cover. He smiled at the photograph of Al Green decked out in a white suit, white turtleneck, and white stacks, sitting in a white cane chair against a white background. A green hanging plant and a green potted plant, along with the singer's rich chocolate skin, gave the cover its color. It looked like Al was wearing dark green socks, too, though some argued that the socks were black.

"I'm Still in Love With You."

"You don't have to say it," said Quinn. "It's understood."

"Al freaks called this 'The White Album,'" said Strange, ignoring Quinn. "Has 'Simply Beautiful' on it, too."

"You don't have it, do you? I thought it might be one of those you lost in that house flood you had."

"I did lose the vinyl, you're right. I own the CD, but the CD's got no bottom."

"Funny thing is, it came in with this carton of seventies rock, a lot of hard blues-metal and also weird stuff some pot smoker had to be listening to. I found Al Green filed alphabetically, after Gentle Giant and Gong."

"Herb smokers used to listen to Al, too. People used to listen to all sorts of music then, wasn't no barriers set up like it is now. Young man like you, you missed it. Was a real good time."

"I think you might have mentioned that to me before. Anyway, I'm glad you like it."

"Thank you, buddy."

"It's all right."

Strange and Quinn tapped bottles. Strange then filled Quinn in on the ongoing investigation. He told him about the Caprice in the parking lot and the white car and its occupants that had rolled up on Lamar Williams. He told him about Lydell Blue's list.

"You get up with Joe's mother," said Quinn, "she might be able to narrow down the number of names for us."

"I called Sandra a couple of times and left messages," said Strange. "She hasn't got back to me yet."

They discussed the case further. Strange drank two beers to Quinn's one. Quinn watched Strange close his eyes as he took a deep pull from the bottle.

"Janine's been trying to get up with you," said Quinn.

"Yeah?"

"She called me at the bookstore, said she's been beeping you. Something about finding the last piece of the puzzle on Calhoun Tucker."

Strange drank off some of his beer. "I'll have to see what that's about."

"What's goin' on between you two?"

"Why, she say somethin' was?"

"Only that you've been avoiding her this week. Outside of work stuff, she hasn't been able to get through to you at all."

"I'm not sure I'm right for her right now, you want the truth. Her *or* Lionel. When I get like this . . . Ah, forget it." Strange signaled the bartender.

"You're not done with that one yet," said Quinn, nodding to the bottle in front of Strange.

"I will be soon. But thanks for pointing it out." Strange's elbow slipped off the bar. "At least you're doin' all right with Sue. Seems like a good woman. Looks good, too."

"Yeah, she's cool. I'm lucky I found her. But Derek, I'm talkin' about you."

"Look, man, everything's been boiling up inside me, with Joe's death and all. I know I haven't been dealing with it right."

"Nobody knows how to deal with it. When a kid dies like that, you look around you and the things you thought were in order, your beliefs, God, whatever . . . nothing makes sense. I've been fucked up about it myself. We all have."

Strange didn't say anything for a while. And then he said, "I should've let him run that play."

"What?"

"Forty-four Belly. He wanted to run it in at the end of the game. Boy never did get to run that touchdown play, the whole time he played for us. He would've scored that day, too, 'cause he had the fire. Can you imagine how happy that would've made him, Terry?"

Strange's eyes had filled. A tear threatened to break loose. Quinn handed him a bar napkin. Strange used it to wipe his face.

Quinn noticed that the guy in the flannel shirt was staring at Strange.

"You want somethin'?" said Quinn.

"No," said the guy, who quickly looked away.

"I didn't *think* you did," said Quinn.

"Settle down, Terry. I'd be starin', too. Grown man, actin' like a baby." Strange balled up the napkin and dropped it in an ashtray. "Anyway. It's all water passed now, isn't it?"

"You did right," said Quinn, "telling Joe not to run up that score. You were teaching him the right thing."

"I don't know about that. I don't know. I thought he had a whole lifetime of touchdown runs ahead of him. Out here, though, every day could be, like, a last chance. Not just for the kids. For you and me, too."

"You can't think like that."

"But I do. And it's selfish of me, man, I know. Plain selfish."

"What is?"

Strange stared at his fingers peeling the label of the bottle of beer. "These feelings I been having. About my own mortality, man. Selfish of me to be thinkin' on it, when a boy died before he even got started and I been fortunate enough to live as long as I have."

"Men are always thinking about their mortality," said Quinn. He sipped his beer and placed the bottle softly on the bar.

"Shit, man, death and sex, we think about it all the time. It's why we do all the stupid things we do."

"You're right. Every time I start thinkin' on my age, or that I'm bound to die, I start thinking about getting some strange. Makes me want to run away from Janine and Lionel and any kind of responsibility. It's always been like that with me. Like having a different woman's gonna put off death, if only for a little while."

"You need to be runnin' *to* those people, Derek. The ones who love you, man. Not to those girls down at those massage parlors —"

"Aw, here we go."

"Just because they don't walk the street doesn't make 'em any different than streetwalkers. Those girls ain't nothin' but hookers, man."

"For real?"

"I'm serious. Look, I've been with whores. So I'm not looking down on you for this. Just about every man I know has been with 'em, even if it was just a rite-of-passage thing. But what I've been seeing lately —"

"Your girl Sue got you converted, huh? Now you got religion and seen the light."

"No, not me. But it's wrong."

"Terry, these ladies I see, they got to make a living same as anyone else."

"You think that's what they want to be doing with their lives? Putting their hands on a man's dick they got no feelings for? Letting a stranger touch their privates? Shit, Derek, these Asian girls in those places, they've been brought over here and forced into that life to pay off some kind of a debt. It's like slavery."

"Nah, man, don't even go there. White man starts talkin' about, *It's like slavery,* I do not want to hear it."

"Ignore it if you want to," said Quinn. "But that's exactly what it's like."

"I got to relieve myself, man," said Strange. "Where's the bathroom at in this place?"

218 • G E O R G E   P.   P E L E C A N O S

Quinn drank the rest of his beer while Strange went to the men's room. When Strange returned, Quinn noticed that he had washed his face. Strange did not get back on his stool. He placed one hand on the bar for support.

"Well, I better get on out of here."

"Yeah, I need to also. I'm seeing Sue tonight."

Strange withdrew his wallet from his back pocket. Quinn put his hand on Strange's forearm.

"I got it."

"Thanks, buddy." Strange picked up his album and put it under his arm. "And thanks again for this."

"My pleasure."

"Monday morning, I plan on getting started on that list Lydell slipped our way. You with me?"

"You know it. Derek —"

"What?"

"Call Janine."

Strange nodded. He shook Quinn's hand and pushed away from the bar, unsteady on his feet. Quinn watched him go.

21

STRANGE stopped by Morris Miller's and bought a six. He opened one as he hit Alaska Avenue and drank it while driving south on 16th. Dusk had come. He didn't know where he was headed. He kept driving and found himself on Mount Pleasant Street. He parked and went into the Raven, a quiet old bar he liked, not too different from Renzo's, to get himself off the road. There, seated in a booth against the wall, he drank another beer.

When he came out he was half drunk, and the sky was dark. He said "hola" to a Latino he passed on the sidewalk and the man just laughed. Strange's beeper sounded. He scanned the readout and looked for a pay phone. He had brought his cell with him, but he didn't know where it was. Maybe in the car. He didn't care to use it anyhow. He knew of a pay phone up near Sportsman's Liquors, run by the Vondas brothers. He liked those guys, liked to talk with them about sports. But their store would be closed this time of night.

Strange walked in that direction, found the phone, and dropped a quarter and a dime in the slot. He waited for an answer as men stood on the sidewalk around him talking and laughing and drinking from cans inside paper bags.

"Janine. Derek here."

"Where are you?"

"Calling from the street. Somewhere down here . . . Mount Pleasant."

"I been trying to get up with you."

"All right, then, here I am. What've you got?"

"You sound drunk, Derek."

"I had one or two. What've you got?"

"Calhoun Tucker. You know how I been trying to finish out checking on his employment record? I finally got the word on that job he had with Strong Services, down in Portsmouth? They were no longer operating, so I was having trouble pinpointing the nature of the business —"

"C'mon, Janine, get to it."

There was a silence on the other end of the line. Strange knew he had been short with her. He knew she was losing patience with him, rightfully so. Still, he kept on.

"Janine, just tell me what you found."

"Strong Services was an investigative agency. They specialized in rooting out employee theft. He worked undercover in clubs, trying to find employees who were stealing from the registers, like that. Which is how he moved on into the promotion business, I would guess. But my point is, at one time, Tucker was a private cop. He might have done other forms of investigation as well."

"I get it. So now that completes his background check. Anything else?"

There was another block of silence. "No, that's it."

"Good work."

"Am I going to see you tonight, Derek?"

"I don't think so, baby. It'd be better for both of us if I was alone tonight, I think. Tell Lionel . . . Janine?"

Somewhere in there Strange thought he'd heard a click. Now there was a dial tone. The line was dead.

Strange stood on the sidewalk, the sounds of cars braking and honking and Spanish voices around him. He hung the receiver back in its cradle. He walked back down toward the Raven and tried to remember where he had parked his car.

❐

STRANGE parked in the alley behind the Chinese place on I Street and got out of his Caddy. The heroin addict who hustled the alley, a longtime junkie named Sam, stepped out of the shadows and approached Strange.

"All right, then," said Sam.

"All right. Keep an eye on it. I'll get you on the way out."

Sam nodded. Strange went in the back door, through the hall and the beaded curtains, and had a seat at a deuce. He ordered Singapore-style noodles and a Tsingtao from the mama-san who ran the place, and when she served his beer she pointed to a young woman who was standing back behind the register and said, "You like?"

Strange said, "Yes."

❐

HE walked out into the alley. He had showered and he had come, but he was not refreshed or invigorated. He was drunk and confused, angry at himself and sad.

A cherry red Audi S4 was parked behind his Cadillac. A man stood beside the Audi, his arms folded, his eyes hard on Strange. Strange recognized him as Calhoun Tucker. He was taller, more handsome, and younger looking up close than he had appeared to be through Strange's binoculars and the lens of his AE-1.

"Where's Sam at?" said Strange.

"You mean the old man? He took a stroll. I doubled what you were payin' him to look after your car."

"Money always cures loyalty."

"Especially to someone got a jones. One thing I learned in the investigation business early on."

Tucker unfolded his arms and walked slowly toward Strange. He stopped a few feet away.

Strange kept his posture and held his ground. "How'd you get onto me?"

"You talked to a girl down in a club on Twelfth."

"The bartender."

"Right. You left her your card. She was mad at me the day she spoke to you. She ain't mad at me no more."

The alley was quiet. A street lamp hummed nearby.

"You've been easy to tail, Strange. Especially easy to follow today. All that drinkin' you been doing."

"What do you want?"

"You got a nice business. Nice woman, too. And that boy she's got, he seems clean-cut, doesn't look like no knucklehead. Living up there on Quintana. You spend the night there once in a while, don't you?"

"You've been tailing me awhile."

"Yeah. Let me ask you somethin': Does your woman know you get your pleasure down here with these hos like you do?"

Strange narrowed his eyes. "I asked you what you wanted."

"All right, then, I'll get to it. Won't take up much of your time. Just wanted to tell you one thing."

"Go ahead."

Tucker looked around the alley. When he looked back at Strange, his eyes had softened.

"I love Alisha Hastings. I love her deep."

"I don't blame you. She's a fine young lady. From a real good family, too. You got yourself a piece of gold right there. Somethin' you should've thought of when you were runnin' around on her."

"I *think* of her all the time. And I plan to be good to her. To take care of her on the financial tip and be there for her emotionally, too. This is the woman who is gonna be the mother of my children, Strange."

"You got a funny way of preparin' for it."

"*Look* at yourself, man. Is it you who should be judging me?"

Strange said nothing.

"I'm a young man," said Tucker. "I am young and I have not taken that vow yet and until I do I am gonna *freak*. Because I am only gonna be this young and this free one time. But, you got to understand, that ceremony is gonna mean somethin' to me. I saw a bond between my mother and my father that couldn't be broken, and it set an example for me. For my brothers and sisters, too. I know what it means. But for now, I'm just out here having fun."

"George Hastings is a friend of mine."

"Then *be* a friend to him. I'm lookin' you in the eye and telling you, there is nobody out here who is going to love and respect his daughter, for life, like I know I am going to do."

"I can only report your history and what I've seen."

"You're not listening to me, Strange. Hear me and think about what I'm telling you. I *love* that girl. I love her fierce enough to make me do something I don't care to do. You want to take me down, fine. But you're gonna go right down with me."

"You threatenin' me?"

"Just telling you how it's gonna be."

Strange looked down at his feet. He rubbed his face and again met Tucker's eyes. "Whatever I'm gonna do with regards to you, young man, I am going to do. You standing there talking bold, it's not gonna influence me either way."

"Course not." Tucker looked Strange over. "You got principles."

"You don't know me that well to be talking to me that way."

"But I do know your kind."

"Now wait a minute —"

"Let me put it another way, then. This is all about what kind of husband I'm gonna be to Alisha, right? Well, I can promise you this: I ain't gonna end up like you, Strange. Sneakin' around down here in your middle age, paying to have some girl you don't even know jack your dick. Out here tellin' on others when you got a fucked-up life your own self. So do whatever you think is right. I've said what I came to say. You want to listen, it's up to you."

Tucker walked back to his car, got behind the wheel, and lit the ignition. Strange watched the Audi back out of the alley. Then it was just Strange, standing on the stones under the humming street lamp, alone with his shame.

❐

JANINE Baker came down the stairs and unlocked the front door of her house at a little past one in the morning. She had been lying awake in bed and had recognized the engine on Strange's Cadillac as he had cruised slowly down her block.

He was out there on the stoop, one step down from the doorway. She looked down on him, rumpled and glassy-eyed, as she stood in the frame.

"Come on in. It's cool out there."

"I don't think I should," said Strange. "I just came by to apologize for being so short with you on the phone."

Janine pulled the lapels of her robe together against the chill. Behind her, Strange could see Lionel coming down the staircase. He stopped a few steps up.

"Tell him to go back to bed," said Strange softly. "I don't want him seeing me like this."

Janine looked over her shoulder and directed her son to return to his room. Strange waited for Lionel to go back up the stairs.

"Well?"

"I'm all turned around," said Strange.

"And you're trying to say what?"

"I just don't feel . . . I don't feel like I'm right for you now. I know I'm not right for the boy."

"You're looking to give up on us, is that it?"

"I don't know."

"I haven't given up on *you*."

"I know it."

"Even while I knew how you been cheatin' on me these past couple years."

Strange looked up at her. "It's not what you think."

"*Tell* me what it is, then. Don't you think I been knowin' about your, your *problem* for a while now? I might be forgiving, but I am human, and I still have my senses. Smelling sweet like lilacs or somethin' every time you come back from seeing her. Smelling like perfume, and you, a man who doesn't even wear aftershave."

"Listen, baby —"

"Don't *baby* me. Derek, I can smell it on you *now*."

Her voice was almost gentle. It cut him, Janine being so steady with him, so strong. He wanted her to raise her voice, let it out. But he could see she wasn't going to do that. It made him admire her even more.

Strange shifted his feet. "I never loved another woman the whole time I been lovin' you."

"That supposed to mean something to me? Should I feel better because you only been, what, cattin' around with hos?"

"No."

"What about respectin' me? What about respecting yourself?"

Strange cut his eyes. "When my mother was dying, that whole time . . . that was when I started. I couldn't face it, Janine. Not just her passing, but lookin' at my own death, too. Seeing that my turn was coming up, not too far behind."

"And now Joe Wilder's been killed," said Janine, completing his thought. "Derek, don't go dishonoring that little boy's memory by connecting the one thing to the other. All these bad things out here ought to lead you to the ones who love you. In the face of all that, family and your faith in the Lord, it's what keeps you strong."

"I guess I'm weak, then."

"Yes, Derek, you are weak. Like so many men who are really just boys on the inside. Selfish, and so afraid to die."

Strange spread his hands. "I love you, Janine. Know this."

Janine leaned forward and kissed him on the mouth. It was a soft kiss, not held long. As she pulled back, Strange knew that the feel of her lips on his would haunt him forever.

"I won't share you anymore," said Janine. "I am not going to share you with anyone else. So you need to think about your future. How you want to spend it, and who you want to spend it with."

Strange nodded slowly. He turned and walked down the sidewalk to his car. Janine closed the door and locked it, and went into the hallway and leaned her back against the plaster wall. Here she was out of sight of Lionel and Strange. For a very short while, and quietly, she allowed herself to cry.

❐

TERRY Quinn sat naked in a cushioned armchair set by the window. His bedroom was dark, and outside the window the streets were dark and still. He stared out the window at nothing, his fist resting on his chin. He heard a rustling sound as Sue Tracy moved under the sheets and blanket. Her nude form was a lush outline as she brought herself to a sitting position in his bed.

"What's wrong, Terry? Can't you sleep?"

"I'm thinking about Derek," said Quinn. "I'm worried about my friend."

c h a p t e r

22

THE next morning, Strange willed himself out of bed and down to the kitchen, where he brewed a cup of coffee and slipped the sports page out of the Sunday *Post*. He drank the coffee black while reading Michael Wilbon's latest column on Iverson and a story on the upcoming 'Skins / Ravens contest, set for that afternoon. Strange then drove with Greco up to Military and Oregon, where he hung a left into Rock Creek Park. He and many others ran their dogs in a field there by a large parking lot.

Greco ran the high grass field with a young Doberman named Miata, a black-and-tan beauty whose primary markings were a brown muzzle, chest, and forelegs. Generally, Greco preferred the company of humans and chose his few canine playmates carefully. But he took to this one quickly, finding Miata to be an energetic and able-bodied friend. The dog's owner, Deen Kogan, was an attractive woman with whom Strange found it very easy to talk. In another life, he might have asked her out for a scotch, maybe a bite to eat. But she wasn't Janine.

Back on Buchanan, Strange showered and dressed in one of the two suits he owned. He emptied a full can of Alpo into Greco's dish and headed up to the New Bethel Church of Christ, on Georgia and Piney Branch. Driving north, he realized that he was being followed by a black Mercedes C-Class, a fine factory automobile cheapened in this case by the custom addition of a spoiler and over-elaborate rims. Up around Fort Stevens he circled the block, came back out on Georgia, and looked in his rearview: The Mercedes was still behind him. After his encounter with Calhoun Tucker, he could no longer blame his feeling of dread on paranoia. This was real.

Strange took a seat in a pew far back in the church, coming in at the tail end of the service. He could see Janine and Lionel in their usual place, a few rows up ahead. Strange prayed hard for them and for himself, and closed his eyes tightly when he prayed for Joe Wilder. He believed, he had to believe, that the spirit of that beautiful boy had gone on to a better place. He told himself that the corpse lying in the ground in that small box wasn't Joe, but was just a shell. He felt his emotions well up, more from anger than from sadness, as he prayed.

Outside the church Strange shook hands with the parishioners he knew, and with a few he was meeting for the first time. He felt a hand drop onto his shoulder and he turned. It was George Hastings, his daughter by his side.

"George," said Strange. "Alisha. Sweetheart, you look lovely today."

"Thank you, Mr. Derek."

"Honey," said Hastings, "give me a moment alone with Derek here, will you?"

Alisha gave Strange a beautiful smile and found a friend to talk to nearby.

"Haven't heard from you in a while," said Hastings.

"Been meaning to get up with you, George," said Strange.

"You could stop by for the game. You got plans for the day?"

"No, I . . . All right. Maybe I'll drop by later on."

Hastings shook Strange's hand and held the grip. "My sympathies on that boy from your team."

Strange nodded. He had no idea what he would say to his friend when they next met.

Strange caught up with Janine and Lionel as they walked to her car and asked them if they'd like to have breakfast with him at the diner. It was their Sunday morning ritual. But Janine said she had a busy afternoon planned and that she ought to get a jump on it. Lionel did not protest. Strange told him he'd pick him up for practice Monday night. Lionel only nodded, double-taking Strange with what Strange took to be a look of confusion before dropping into the passenger side of Janine's car. Strange hated himself then for what he knew he was: another man who was about to drift out of this boy's life. He wondered what Janine had told Lionel, and what he would tell Lionel himself if he had the chance.

On the way over to the Three-Star Diner, going east on Kennedy, Strange noticed the Mercedes, once again, in his rearview. The tricked-out car was only two lengths back. They're not even worried about being burned, thought Strange, and for one young moment he considered taking a sudden turn and punching the gas. He could lose them easily; he'd come up around here, and no one knew these streets and alleys like he did. But he let them follow him, all the way down to First, where he parked his Caddy in a space along the curb. The Mercedes pulled up behind him.

Strange locked his Brougham and walked toward the Mercedes, memorizing the car's license plate and confirming the model as he approached. Strange reached the car as the driver's-side window slid down. Behind the wheel was a handsome, typically unfriendly looking young man with close-cropped hair. His suit and the knot of his tie were immaculate. Strange recognized him as one of the men who had attended Joe Wilder's funeral. He had been talking to Joe's mother, Sandra Wilder, by the grave.

In the passenger bucket was a man of the same age, same unsmiling expression, more flashily dressed. He sat low, with one arm leaning on the sill of his window, talking on his cell.

"What can I do for you fellas?" said Strange.

"A man needs to speak with you," said the driver.

"Who?"

"Granville Oliver."

Strange knew the name. The city knew Granville Oliver's name. But with Strange it was more; he had a history with Oliver's bloodline.

"And you are?"

"Phillip Wood."

Wood's partner lowered the cell and looked across the buckets at Strange. "Granville wants to see you *now*."

Strange did not acknowledge this one or give him any kind of eye contact at all. He glanced over his shoulder through the plate glass fronting the diner. He could see Billy Georgelakos coming around the counter, his girth pushing against his stained apron, holding the pine baton that Strange knew had been hollowed out and filled with lead. Strange shook his head slightly at Billy, who stopped his forward path at once. Strange returned his gaze to the driver, Phillip Wood.

"Tell you what," said Strange. "I'm gonna go on in there and eat my breakfast. When I come out, y'all are still out here? We can talk."

Strange gave them his back, left the idling Mercedes curbside, and walked into the Three-Star. The sound of gospel music, coming from the house radio, hit him like cool water as he entered the diner.

"Everything all right, Derek?" said Georgelakos, now behind the counter again.

"I think so."

"The usual?"

"Thanks, friend," said Strange.

❐

STRANGE ate a feta-cheese-and-onion omelette sprinkled with Texas Pete hot sauce, and a half-smoke side, and washed it down with a couple of cups of coffee. Some after-church types were at the counter and some sat in the old red-cushioned booths. The diner was white tiles and white walls, kept clean by Billy and his longtime employee, Etta.

Billy Georgelakos, his bald head sided by patches of gray, ambled down the rubber mat that ran behind the counter and leaned his forearms on the Formica top.

"Where's Janine and the boy?"

"Busy," said Strange, sopping up the juice left on the plate with a triangle of white toast.

"Uh," grunted Georgelakos. His great eagle nose twitched. His glance moved through the window to the street, then back to Strange. "What about it? They're waiting for you, right?"

"I *told* them to wait," said Strange. He closed his eyes as he swallowed the last of his breakfast. "Billy, you can't get a better egg and half-smoke combination in all of D.C. than you can right here."

"The omelette was my father's recipe, you know that. But your father taught us all how to grill a half-smoke."

"However it happened, it's beautiful music, that's for damn sure."

"You sure you gonna be all right?"

"Pretty sure. Lemme see your pen."

Georgelakos drew his Bic from where it rested atop his ear. Strange wrote something down on a clean napkin he pulled from a dispenser.

"In case I'm wrong," said Strange, "here's the license plate number of their car. It's a C two thirty, a two thousand model, in case it comes up."

Georgelakos took the napkin, folded it, and slipped it under his apron. Strange left money on the counter and shook Georgelakos's hand.

On the way out, Strange stopped by the photograph of his father, Darius Strange, wearing his chef's hat and standing next to Billy's father, Mike Georgelakos, in the early 1960s. The photograph was framed and mounted by the front door. He stared at it for a few moments, as he always did, before reaching for the handle of the door.

"*Adio,* Derek," said Georgelakos.

"*Yasou, Vasili,*" said Strange.

◻

OUT on the street, Strange stood before the open window of the Mercedes.

"Get in," said Phillip Wood.

"Where we goin'?"

"You'll find out, chief," said Wood's partner.

Strange looked at Wood only. "Where?"

"Out Central Avenue. Largo area."

"I'll follow you out," said Strange, and when Wood didn't answer, Strange said, "Young man, it's the only way I'll go."

Wood's partner laughed, and Wood stared at Strange some more in that hard way that was not working on Strange at all.

"Follow us, then," said Wood.

Strange went to his car.

◻

STRANGE followed the Mercedes east to North Capitol, then south, then east again on H to Benning Road. Farther along they found Central Avenue and took it out of the city and into Maryland.

As he drove, Strange mentally recounted what he knew of Granville Oliver.

Oliver, now in his early thirties, had come up fatherless in the Stanton Terrace Dwellings of Anacostia, in Southeast D.C. His mother was welfare dependent and a shooter of heroin and cocaine. When he was eight years old, Granville had learned how to tie his mother off and inject her with coke, a needed jolt when her heroin nods took her down to dangerously low levels. He was taught this by one of her interchangeable male friends, hustlers and junkheads themselves, always hanging around the house. One of these men taught him how to go with his hands. Another taught him how to load and fire a gun. At the time, Granville was nine years old.

Granville had an older brother, two cousins, and one uncle who were in the game. Cocaine at first, and then crack when it hit town around the summer of '86. The brother was executed in a turf dispute involving drugs. The cousins were doing time in Ohio and Illinois prisons, dispersed there after the phase-out of Lorton. Granville's mother died when he was in his early teens, an overdose long overdue. It was the uncle, Bennett Oliver, who eventually took Granville under his wing.

Granville dropped out of Ballou High School in the tenth grade. By then he was living in a row house with friends in Congress Heights, south of Saint Elizabeth's. He had been a member of the notorious Kieron Black Gang in the Heights, but it was small change, a you-kill-one-of-us-and-we-kill-one-of-you thing, and he wanted out. So Granville went to his uncle, who took him on.

From the start it was apparent that Granville had a good head for numbers. After he had proven himself on the front lines — he was allegedly the triggerman in four murders by the time he was seventeen years old — he quickly moved into operations and helped grow the business. Through ruthless extermination of the competition, and Granville's brains, the Oliver Mob soon became the largest crack and heroin distribution machine in the southeast quadrant of the city.

The center of the operation was a small rec center anchoring a rocky baseball field and rimless basketball court on the grounds of an elementary school in the Heights. There Bennett and Granville got to know the kids from the surrounding neighborhoods of Wilburn Mews, Washington Highlands, Walter E. Washington Estates, Valley Green, Barnaby Terrace, and Congress Park.

For many of the area's youths, the Olivers, especially the young and handsome Granville, were now the most respected men in Southeast. The police were the enemy, that was a given, and working men and women were squares. The Olivers had the clothes, the cars, and the women, and the stature of men who had returned from war. They gave money to the community, participated in fund-raisers at local churches, sponsored basketball squads that played police teams, and passed out Christmas presents in December to children in the Frederick Douglass and Stanton Terrace Dwellings. They were the heroes, and the folk heroes, of the area. Many kids growing up there didn't dream of becoming doctors or lawyers or even professional athletes. Their simple ambition was to join the Mob, to be "put on." Working out of the rec center, the elder Oliver had the opportunity to observe the talent and nurture it as well.

Granville and Bennett's hands no longer touched drugs. In the tradition of these businesses, the youngest shouldered the most risk and thereby earned the chance of graduating to the next level. The Olivers rarely killed using their own hands. When they did, they didn't hold the weapon until the moment of execution. The gun was carried by an underling; the squire, in effect, handed it to the knight at the knight's command.

So the Olivers were smart, and it seemed to the newspaper-reading public and to some of the police that they would never be stopped. There were possibilities: tax evasion was one, as were wires and bugs planted to record their conversations. The more likely scenario was that they would be ratted out by snitches: guys who needed to plead out or guys who had previously been raped in jail and would do anything to avoid being punked out again. The Olivers knew, like all drug kingpins knew, that they would go down eventually. And snitches would be the means by which they would fall.

In August of 1999, one week before he was scheduled to go on trial for racketeering after a wire recorded him discussing a major buy, Bennett Oliver was found murdered behind the wheel of his car, a new-style Jag with titanium wheels, idling a block from the rec center. Two bullets had entered his brain, one had blown out an eye, and a fourth had bored a tunnel clean through his neck. The Jag was still idling when the police rolled up on the scene. There were no bullet holes in the palms of the hands, no defensive marks at all, indicating that Bennett knew and maybe even trusted his attacker and had been surprised by his own murder. The word on the street was that Bennett's nephew Granville, expecting his uncle to roll over and implicate him on the stand, had pulled the trigger or had ordered it pulled.

Granville Oliver had kept a relatively low profile since the murder of Bennett. Though he was still very much in the business, his name, and the name of his operation, had not appeared recently in the news. He had moved to a new home outside the city, in Largo, where he was said to be recording an album in a studio he had built in the basement of the house.

Strange steered his Cadillac off the main highway. He supposed that he was headed toward Granville Oliver's house now.

He parked behind the Mercedes in a circular drive in front of a large brick colonial. Another brand-new Mercedes, less adorned than the one Phillip Wood drove, was parked there, facing out.

The house was on a street with two similar houses, one of which appeared to be unoccupied. It wasn't a neighborhood, exactly, certainly not one of those gated communities favored by the new African American wealth of Prince George's County.

Maybe Granville wanted the privacy. More likely, those kinds of people had moved behind the gates to get away from the Granville Olivers of the world. There were unofficial covenants protecting them; real estate agents working certain neighborhoods knew to discourage sales to his kind.

Wood's partner remained in the car. Strange followed Wood to the front door. He noticed an open garage, totally empty, attached to the side of the house. Beside the garage, a boy no older than twelve raked leaves.

They walked into a large foyer in which a split staircase led to the upper floor. Two hallways on either side of the staircases reached a state-of-the-art kitchen opening to a large area holding cushiony couches, a wide-screen television, and stereo equipment. They went through this area, past a dining room introduced by French doors, and into another sort of foyer that led to an open door. Wood was talking on his cell all the way. He made a gesture to Strange and stepped aside so that Strange could go, alone, through the doorway.

The room was a kind of library, with framed photographs on the walls and books shelved around a huge cherry-wood desk, and it smelled of expensive cologne. Granville Oliver sat behind the desk. He was a large man with light brown eyes, nearly golden, and handsome in an open-neck shirt under a dark suit. Strange recognized him by sight.

"Go ahead and close that door," said Oliver.

Strange closed it and walked across the room.

Oliver stood, sized Strange up, leaned forward, and shook his hand. Strange had a seat in a comfortable chair that had been placed before the desk.

"This about Joe Wilder?" said Strange.

"That's right," said Oliver. "I want you to find the ones who killed my son."

chapter

23

"Y OU'RE Joe's father?"

"Yeah."

"He never mentioned it."

Granville Oliver spread his hands. "He didn't know."

The Motorola StarTAC on Oliver's desk chirped. Oliver picked up the cell, flipped it open, and put it to his ear. Strange listened to "uh-huh" and "yeah" over and over again. He was too wired to sit in the chair and digest what had been revealed. He got up out of the chair and walked around the room.

The wall cases were filled with books. Judging by the tears on the corners of the frayed jackets and the cracks in the spines of the paperbacks, the books had been read. Except for a few classic works of fiction by writers like Ellison, Himes, and Wright, most of Oliver's collection consisted of nonfiction. The subjects dealt with black nationalism, black separatism, and black empowerment. All were penned by black authors.

The photographs on the walls were of Oliver with local sports celebrities and politicians. One showed him with his arm slung over the shoulder of D.C.'s former mayor. There was a rumor, unsubstantiated, that Oliver had periodically supplied the mayor with both women and drugs. Another photo had Oliver standing on an outdoor court, presenting a trophy to a basketball team wearing black shirts with red print across the chests. The shirts read, "Dare to Stay Off Drugs."

The cell phone made a sound again as Oliver ended his call.

"You sponsor a team?" said Strange.

"Gotta give back to the community," said Oliver, with no apparent irony.

Strange could only stare at him. Oliver nodded in the direction of his cell phone, which he had placed on a green blotter. "I had to take that, but it's turned off now. We can talk."

Strange sat back down in his chair.

"So what do you think?" said Oliver, waving his hand around the room, the gesture meant to include the entire house, his land, all his possessions. "Not bad for a Southeast boy, right?"

"It is something."

"Check this out." Oliver shook a black-and-white photograph out of a manila envelope and slid it across the desk to Strange. It was a head shot of a scowling Oliver wearing a skully and chains, his arms crossed across his chest, a Glock in one hand and a .45 in the other.

Strange dropped the photograph back on the desk.

"That's my new promo shot," said Oliver, "for this record I just made. I brought this boy down from New York, used to run the mixin' board up there for some of the top acts. This boy put some beats behind me, made my flow tight. I got a studio right here in my basement, man. All new equipment, all of it the best. I mean, I got everything."

"It does make an impression," said Strange. "But I hope you'll understand if I don't seem too impressed."

"So now you gonna tell me, It's not what you have, it's how you got it, right?"

"Somethin' like that. All these pretty things you own around here? There's blood on 'em, Granville."

Oliver's eyes flared, but his voice remained steady. "That's right. I *took* it, Mr. Strange. Wasn't no one gonna give me nothin', so I just went out and grabbed it. White man gonna try to keep a black man down from birth. But Bobo, he couldn't do it to this black man."

"Okay, then. In your mind, you've done all right."

Oliver blinked his eyes hard. "I have. Despite the fact that I got born into that camp of genocide they used to call the ghetto. Poverty is violence, Mr. Strange, you've heard that, right?"

"I have."

"And it begets violence. Poor black kids see the same television commercials white boys and white girls see out in the suburbs. They're showed, all their young lives, all the things they should be striving to acquire. But how they gonna get these things, huh?"

Strange didn't reply.

Oliver leaned forward. "Look, I got a good head for numbers, and I know how to manage people. I've always had that talent. Young boys wanted to follow me around the neighborhood when I wasn't no more than a kid. But do you think anyone in my school ever said to me, Take this book home and read it? Keep reading and get yourself into a college, you can run your own company someday? Maybe they knew, black man ain't never gonna run nothin' in this country 'less he takes it and runs with it his own self. Which is what I been doin' my whole adult life.

"So poor kids with nothin' are gonna want things. They start by gettin' into their own kind of enterprise, 'cause they figure out early there ain't no other way to get it. And these enterprises are competitive, like any business. Once you start gettin' these things, see, you're gonna make sure you keep what you got, 'cause you can't never go back and live the way you were livin' before. And now Bobo gonna act surprised when the neighborhoods he done herded us into start runnin' with blood."

"You don't have to lecture me about being black in this country, Granville. I been around long enough to remember injustices you haven't even dreamed of."

"So you agree."

"For the most part, yes. But it doesn't explain the fact that a lot of kids who grew up in the same kinds of places you did, the same way you did, with no kind of guidance, got out. Got through school, went on and got good jobs, careers, are raising kids of their own now who are gonna have a better chance than they ever did. And they're doin' it straight. By hanging with it, by being there for their children. Despite all the roadblocks you talked about."

"Didn't work out that way for me," said Oliver with a shrug. "But it sure did work out. So I hope you'll understand *me* if I'm not too ashamed."

"That what you tell that young boy you got working for you, the one I saw outside?"

"Don't worry about that boy. That boy is gonna do just fine."

Strange leaned back in his chair. "Say why you called me out here."

"I told you."

"Okay. You claim Joe was yours."

Oliver nodded. "He was one of my beef babies, from back when the shit was wild. When I was out there getting into a lot of, just, *battles* and mad shit like that. Used to crib up with different girls I knew from around the way, just to go underground, keep myself safe until the drama cooled down. In those two or three years, I must have fathered three babies like that."

And you think that makes you a man.

"But you were never there for Joe," said Strange.

"His mother, Sandra, wanted it like that. She didn't want him to know about me. Didn't want him lookin' up to someone like me, Mr. Strange. It speaks to what you were just *lecturin'* me on just now. She wanted the boy to grow up with some kind of chance."

God bless her, thought Strange.

"You gave her money?"

"She wouldn't take much. Didn't want me anywhere near the boy; no presents at birthday time, nothin' like that. She did take a whip I gave her, though. Told her I didn't want no son of mine ridin' around in that broken-down hooptie she was drivin'. A nice BMW. She couldn't turn that down."

"I saw it," said Strange. "Why did you pick me?"

"Sandra says you all right. You been havin' that business down in Petworth for years, and you got a good reputation behind it. And she says you always were good to the little man." Oliver smiled. "Boy could play some football, couldn't he?"

"He had a heart," said Strange, speaking softly. "You missed out on the most beautiful thing that ever could've happened to your life, Granville. You missed."

"Maybe. But now I want you to help me make it right."

"Why? Okay, so you fathered Joe. But you never were any kind of father to him for real."

"True. But some people know he was mine. Man in my position, he can't just let this kind of thing go. Everyone needs to know that the ones who took my kin will be got. You lose respect in this business I'm in, there ain't nothin' left."

"The police are close," said Strange. "I'd say they're gonna find the shooters in a few days. They've got likenesses and they're putting them around the neighborhoods. This isn't your normal street beef where everybody keeps their mouths shut. The police aren't the enemy in a case like this. A child was murdered. Someone's gonna come forward soon and talk."

"I want you to find them first."

"And do what?"

"Gimme some names."

"I've been working on it," said Strange. "I'm planning on talking to Lorenze Wilder's friends."

"You got a list?"

"Somethin' like that."

"Sandra will help you narrow it down."

"I've tried to talk to her. She didn't seem to want to."

"She'll talk to you now. I just got off the phone with her before you showed. She's waitin' on you to come by when we get done here."

There was a knock on the door. Oliver raised his voice and said, "Come in."

Phillip Wood appeared as the door swung open but stood back behind the frame. "You got an appointment in fifteen."

"We'll be done by then," said Oliver.

Wood nodded and pulled the door shut.

"There's an example of what I was talkin' about right there," said Oliver to Strange. "That boy, Phil Wood? Boy can't even read. But he's *drivin'* a Mercedes. He's *wearin'* twelve-hundred-dollar suits with designer tags. Young man is gainfully employed, Mr. Strange, 'stead of lyin' around in his own pee, which is where he was headed if I hadn't put him on."

"Where you think he's headed now?"

"True. We all know what waits for us. But we can't be thinkin' on tomorrow all that much, can we? The thing you got to do is enjoy the ride."

"It's all good, right?"

"No, not all. Take Phil, for example. I'm gettin' near to the point, I got to be making a decision on his future. Phil Wood's taken a fall two times. The Feds know this, and they're lookin' to see him stumble, 'cause the third fall is gonna be long time. And Phil can't do no long time. He's weak that way. I know it, and he knows it, too."

"You're afraid he's gonna roll over on you."

"He will. Fond as I am of that young man, he will. Gonna be one of those 'You too, Brutus' motherfuckers in the end. My very own Judas, gonna sell out Granville Oliver for his thirty pieces."

"You comparing yourself to the Lord?"

"Matter of fact, the first example was out of *Julius Caesar*. I read a lot, case you haven't noticed. But, nah, it's just . . . You know what I'm sayin'. I got a decision to make. Just tellin' you, you know, this ain't all fun and games."

Strange looked at his watch.

"Yeah, okay," said Oliver. "So, we got ourselves a deal, right?"

"No," said Strange.

"What's that?"

"I don't think I'll be working for you."

"You got a problem with my kind."

"That's right."

"Forget about me, then. Think about the boy."

"I am."

"Don't you want to see justice done?"

"I told you, the police will have this wrapped up quick."

"We ain't talkin' about the same thing."

"The cycle never ends, does it?"

"Oh, it'll *end,* you do what I ask you to do. That's my point. There ain't no death penalty in the District of Columbia, Mr. Strange. You want to see those shooters go to prison, get warm meals, get to sleep real comfortable, maybe walk out in twenty, twenty-five? You think my son's ever gonna get to walk out his grave? Gimme some names, like I said. I'll make sure justice gets served."

"You can't trade a bad life for a good."

"What's that?"

"Something someone told me a long time ago."

"I'm givin' you straight talk," said Oliver, "and you're over there talkin' proverbs and shit. Talkin' about *cycles*."

244 • GEORGE P. PELECANOS

Strange looked into Oliver's eyes. "I knew your father."

"Say it again."

"They always say that D.C.'s a small town. Well, it's true. I knew your father, over thirty years ago."

"You got one up on me, then, chief. 'Cause I never did get to meet the man. He died in sixty-eight, during the riots. Right around the time I was born."

"He had light eyes, just like you."

Oliver cocked his head. "Y'all were tight?"

"He knew my brother," said Strange. "My brother passed about the same time as your father."

"So?"

"Cycles," said Strange, leaving it at that.

Strange got up out of his chair. Granville Oliver handed him a business card. It was for his record company, GO Entertainment. Under the logo, Oliver's cell number was printed.

"You call me," said Oliver, "you find anything out. And somethin' else: Sandra says you got a white boy, helps you coach that football team. Says he works with you, too. Well, I don't want him workin' on none of this, hear?"

Strange slipped the business card into his suit pocket.

"My sympathies on the death of your uncle," said Strange.

"Yeah," said Oliver. "That was a real tragedy right there."

Strange walked out of the house. He nodded to the boy raking leaves and received only a scowl. Phillip Wood and partner were leaning against their Mercedes in the circular drive. Strange passed them without a word, got into his Cadillac, and drove back into D.C.

24

THE Park Morton complex looked different during the day. There were children using the playground equipment, and mothers, aunts, and grandmothers watching over them. A group of girls was doing double Dutch by the entrance, and the ones sitting on the brick wall nearby were actually smiling. Strange knew that Sundays were quiet time, even in the worst neighborhoods, and the fact that the sun was full in a clear blue sky, its rays highlighting the turning leaves, added to the illusion of peace. Also, most all the men around town, even the bad ones, were indoors watching the Redskins game.

Strange had been listening to it on the radio, the pregame and then the play-by-play, Sonny, Sam, and Frank on WJFK. The Ravens were in the house at FedEx, and the contest had just gotten under way.

Strange got the list Lydell Blue had given him out of his trunk and locked down the Brougham. He walked across the brown grass of the courtyard to the stairwell leading to Sandra Wilder's apartment. He noticed flyers with the likenesses of the shooters taped on the stairwell wall.

Strange knocked on the door of the Wilder residence. He waited patiently for a while and did not knock again. Then the door opened and Sandra Wilder stood in its frame. She gave Strange warm eyes.

"Sandra."

"Derek." She reached out and touched his arm. "Come on in."

They settled in a kind of living room the size of a den, at the end of a hall broken by an open entrance to a galley-style kitchen. The couch Strange sat on was marked with food stains and its piping was torn away from the fabric. A television sat on a stand past the rectangular table set before the couch; it was on and showing the game at a very low volume. On the wall behind the set were photographs torn from magazines and newspapers, taped crookedly, of Keyshawn Johnson and Randy Moss, along with a close-up of Deion wearing a do-rag. Tellingly, a poster of Darrell Green at the ready was the largest and most prominently displayed. It would be like Joe to honor the tireless workhorse above the flash. Strange could see him sitting on this couch, eating a snack or a microwaved dinner prepared by his mom, watching the game on a Sunday afternoon. He guessed that that was how the stains had gotten on the couch.

Strange drank a glass of instant iced tea, quietly watching the 'Skins move the ball upfield. Sandra sat beside him, leaning forward and making marks on the list Strange had given her, which she had placed on the table. Her lips moved as she read the names.

Though Sandra Wilder was in her mid-twenties, she appeared at first glance to be ten years older. She was heavy in the hips and waist, and her movements were labored. She had big brown eyes, freckles, a full mouth, and straight teeth. She was pretty when she smiled. Strange guessed she had given birth to Joe when she was about sixteen.

Today Sandra wore a pair of jeans with an untucked T-shirt showing a computer-generated photograph of a grinning Joe. The words "We will not forget you" were printed beneath his image. Entrepreneurs offered T-shirts like this at the wakes and funerals of young people citywide, usually in the form of bulk sales to the grieving families. It had become a cottage industry in D.C.

"Here you go," said Sandra, handing Strange the sheet of paper. "Why are those Social Security numbers next to the names?"

"My friend hooked me up. I'll be using those numbers in my computer to get addresses, job histories, like that."

"I circled the ones still come to mind."

Strange studied the list. Sandra had highlighted three names: Walter Lee, Edward Diggs, and Sequan Hawkins.

"These your brother's closest friends?"

"The ones I recall. The ones who used to be around our house most when we were coming up."

"Were they still tight with Lorenze?"

"I have no idea. I didn't have much contact with my brother these past few years. But you say these names came off the funeral home list, that book you sign when you pay your respects? So I figure, at least they're still around. Far as where they live or how to get in touch with 'em, I don't have a clue."

"I can find them," said Strange. "You don't have to worry about that."

"My mother would know. She had this address book, she used to keep all our friends' names in it, 'cause me and Lorenze, when we were young? We were, like, always slipping out, and she had to have a way of finding us. 'Specially Lorenze; that boy was buck wild, you couldn't keep him in the house at all."

"Can I speak to your mother?"

"She's dead."

Strange turned on the couch so that he was facing her. "Where'd y'all come up, Sandra?"

"Manor Park, over there around North Dakota Avenue. South of Coolidge?"

"I know it," said Strange, something catching his eye over Sandra's shoulder. On an end table abutting the couch sat a framed photograph of Joe in his uniform, his face shiny with sweat, a football cradled against his chest.

"Anything else?" said Sandra.

"You say you were out of contact with your brother. Why was that, you don't mind my askin'?"

"Lorenze was no-account. I loved him, but that's what he was. He wanted some of that bling-bling, but he couldn't even do that right, for real. He was always calling me, trying to get me to hook him up with Granville. Tellin' me he wanted Granville to put him on. But when Joe got born, I didn't want to have anything to do with Granville anymore. I didn't want Joe to know about him at all. Lorenze wouldn't leave it alone, so I broke things off with my own blood. You know I took a car from Granville, and I am not proud of that, but I swear to you, that's all I had to do with that man."

"You don't need to apologize for anything."

"But I do want you to know. I've been straight all the way. I been having the same job for years now and I'm never late on my bills. . . . It's been hard, Derek, but I have been *straight*."

"I know you have," said Strange. "Did Lorenze have enemies you knew of?"

"It's like I told the police. He didn't go lookin' for trouble. But it found him sure enough. It was his way. He just didn't take anything serious. Couldn't hold a job, and still, he always felt free to put out his hand. Never did take care of his debts. *Never* did. Laughed it off most of the time. He thought it was all a joke, but the ones he was laughin' at, they didn't see it that way. To them, Lorenze was tryin' to take them for bad."

"You think that's why he was killed?"

"I expect."

Strange folded the list and slipped it into the inside pocket of his suit coat. He took one of Sandra Wilder's hands. It felt clammy and limp in his.

"Listen," said Strange. "You did right by keeping your son away from Oliver, and away from your brother, too. And don't you ever think that you could have prevented what happened. Because you did right, and you did good. That boy was as special as they come, Sandra. And it's because of you."

A smile broke upon her face. The smile was perfect, and her hair was beauty-shop done and in place, and her makeup was perfectly applied. Cosmetically, Sandra Wilder was completely intact. But Strange could see that her eyes were jittery and too bright, and her mouth twitched at the corners as he tried to hold the smile.

Strange put his arms around her and drew her toward him. She fell into his embrace without resistance, Strange catching the foulness of her breath. It was quiet in the room except for the faint voice of the announcer calling the game. After a while he felt Sandra's shoulders shaking beneath him and her hot tears where she had buried her face in his neck. He held her like that until she was cried out, and he left her there when he knew that there was nothing left.

❐

THE 'Skins / Ravens game was tied up three to three, a pair of field goals the only score, as Strange drove north. A pass interference call against Washington put the Ravens on the Redskins' one yard line with ten seconds to go in the half. From the radio, Sonny Jurgensen and Sam Huff discussed the most likely call for the next play. It would certainly be a run, Jamal Lewis up the middle. If he was stopped, there would still be time on the clock for a field goal to put the Ravens ahead before the end of the first half.

Strange pulled his Cadillac to the curb and let the motor run. He clockwised the volume dial.

"Come on," said Strange. "Hold 'em."

Ravens quarterback Tony Banks did not hand the ball off to Lewis. He attempted a pass into the flat of the end zone to Shannon Sharpe, who was in the company of two burgundy jerseys. It was a bad play to call — if Banks were to throw it at all he should have thrown it away. Redskin linebacker Kevin Mitchell picked off the pass.

Strange's holler was one of disbelief. The roar of FedEx and the laughter of Sonny and Sam were in the car as Strange pulled down on the tree and continued uptown.

❐

"DEREK, come on in," said George Hastings. "You see that last play?"

"I been listenin' to it on the radio," said Strange.

They walked through the hall of Hastings's brick tudor in Shepherd Park. Hastings wore a Redskins cap, but he was otherwise cleanly dressed in an expensive sweater and slacks. His house was just as clean.

"You believe that call Billick made?" said Hastings, looking over his shoulder as he led Strange into his den. "You got Jamal Lewis, a tough young back, on the one yard line, and all you got to do is give it to him and let him run it up the gut, and you call a *pass?*"

"Tony Banks ain't exactly one of your top-tier NFL quarterbacks either."

"Not yet, anyway."

"Should have pitched it out of the end zone when he saw the coverage. That was his inexperience showing right there."

Hastings pointed to one of two big loungers in the den. A large-screen Sony was set in a wall unit in the room; the second half was under way. "Sit down, Derek. Can I get you something? I might have a cold beer myself."

"Nothin' with alcohol in it for me, not today. A Co-Cola if you got it, George."

Hastings returned with the drinks and had a seat. Both teams went scoreless in the third.

"Our defensive linemen got fire in their eyes today," said Strange.

"Yeah, this is one of those classic defensive battles we got goin' right here," said Hastings.

"They've stopped Stephen Davis, and we got hardly any receivers left except Albert Connell. Fryar's out."

"Your boy Westbrook is gone for the season, too. *Again*."

"And I thought it was gonna be his year, too," said Strange sadly. "Next year, maybe."

At the start of the fourth quarter, Stephen Davis left the field with a pinched nerve in his shoulder. Skip Hicks replaced him for three downs at tailback and then Davis came back in. On second and seven, the teams lined up on the Baltimore thirty-three, with the Ravens showing blitz. Davis took the handoff from Brad Johnson and hit a hole provided by tackle Chris Samuels and fullback Larry Centers. Davis was off with only safety Rod Woodson between him and the goal line. Davis stiff-armed Woodson, dropped him to the turf, and sailed into the end zone.

Strange and Hastings were on their feet with instant high fives.

"Just like Riggo," said Strange.

"Thought you said they were stoppin' Davis."

"You can't stop that boy for long."

George looked at his friend. "Good to see you smiling, man."

"Was I?" said Strange. "Damn. Guess it's been a while since I have."

They watched the rest of the game, knowing the contest was over with the Davis touchdown. The 'Skins had broken Baltimore's back with that one play. When the whistle sounded, Hastings hit the mute button on the remote and sat back in his lounger.

"All right, man," said Hastings. "Gimme the bad news."

"Well, I don't think you can call it bad," said Strange. "Your future son-in-law is clean."

"For real?"

"Don't look so disappointed."

"What about all that Calhoun Enterprises jive?"

Strange spread his hands. "Can't fault a man just 'cause he picks a bad name for his business. Far as his work ethic goes, and his reputation, the man is golden. He comes from a solid family who gave him a good example, by all accounts. I got no reason to think he won't be anything but a good provider for your daughter."

"What else?"

"Huh?"

"I been knowin' you too long, Derek, and you know I can read your face. There's somethin' else, so why don't you say it?"

"Well, Calhoun Tucker likes the ladies."

"Course he does. What, you think some *faggot*'s gonna be fallin' in love with my girl?"

"I don't mean that. I mean, he's got an eye for 'em."

"Say what you're gettin' at, man."

Strange looked down at his hands. He had been rubbing them together and he made himself stop.

"I don't know what I'm getting at exactly, George. I guess . . . I was wondering, not to get into your business, understand, but I was wondering how it was between you and Linda. The whole time you were married, I mean. Did you ever, you know, stumble? Did you ever find yourself steppin' out on her or anything like that?"

"Never," said Hastings. "You know me better than that, Derek."

"But I remember how you were, back when the two of us were out there. When we were single and coming up, I mean. You had a lot of girlfriends, George. Wasn't like you ever just stuck to one."

"Until I met Linda."

"Right. But you and her were together for like, *two years* before you put the ring on her finger. How was it for you and other women in that time?"

"Well, naturally, you know, I continued to see other girls while I was dating Linda. I never did consider that to be any kind of sin. But once I made a pledge to her and the Lord in the church, though, that was it. I looked hard at plenty of women, but as far as lyin' down with someone other than my wife, after I was married? It was never an option for me again."

"So you don't see nothin' wrong with cattin' around up to the wedding day."

"Young man's only gonna be young once. You tellin' me Calhoun Tucker's a player?"

If he were to bring it up, now would be the time. But he had been leaning one way already, and this conversation with George had made up his mind. Strange shook his head.

"I guess I strayed off the topic some. To tell you the truth, I was askin' about it because . . . because I been having some problems with Janine. I been stumblin' like that with regards to her, George. Not just once or twice, understand, but as a matter of habit. It came to a head between us last night."

"Sounds like you need to make some decisions. But you know, Derek, everybody's got to make those kinds of choices their own selves."

"I hear you."

"Anything else about Tucker?"

"Just this: I talked to some people who know him, here in
D.C. They told me, to a one, how much he goes on about Alisha
all the time, how deep he loves her. Sounds like he's sincere
to me."

"Who wouldn't love that girl?"

"True. But I thought you might like to know. Far as what
kind of husband he's gonna be, only thing I can say is, neither one
of us is gonna know that until time tells us. Right?"

"Yeah, you're right. I guess I been wantin' to find something
wrong with that young man. It's like you told me back in your
office: Maybe the only thing wrong with him is that he's getting
ready to take away my little girl."

"Maybe. Wouldn't anybody blame you for feeling that way,
though. The thing is, you just got to support her decision now and
see what happens. Don't you agree?"

Hastings reached over and shook Strange's hand.

"Thank you, Derek."

"I'll have a written report for you next week."

"Send a bill along with it."

"You know I will."

Hastings removed his Redskins cap and rubbed the top of
his head. "Any progress on finding that boy's killers?"

"It won't be long," said Strange. "One way or another, they'll
be got."

❐

STRANGE walked out the front door of the Hastings residence.
Calhoun Tucker's Audi was parked behind Strange's Cadillac.
Tucker, all Abercrombie & Fitch, leaned against the car. Alisha
Hastings was with him, her eyes alight as she followed his every
word, both of them beside the waxed Audi parked beneath the
fiery colors of an oak. The tableau was like some advertisement for
beauty and youth.

"Come here, Mr. Derek," said Alisha. "I want you to meet someone."

Strange crossed the lawn and went to the couple. He kept his eyes on Tucker's as Alisha introduced them to each other. They shook hands.

"I bet you and my daddy were in there watching the game," said Alisha. "I can't understand how you two could stay inside and watch television on a beautiful day like this."

"It's always a beautiful day when the Redskins win," said Strange.

"Y'all catching up on old times in there?" said Tucker.

"Just being a friend to my old buddy George."

"Oh?"

"Been meaning to get by and congratulate him on the engagement of his lovely daughter here. Congratulations to the both of you as well."

Tucker's eyes softened. "Thank you, Mr. Strange."

"Make it Derek."

They shook again. Strange tightened his grip on Tucker's hand.

"Good to meet you, young man."

"You don't have to worry," said Tucker, moving in close to Strange's face.

"See that I don't," said Strange, his voice very low. He released Tucker's hand.

Strange kissed Alisha, hugged her and held her tightly. He kissed her again and walked toward his car.

"What was that about?" said Alisha. "I couldn't hear what you two were saying, but it looked intense. You two don't know each other, do you?"

"No. It was nothing. Just, you know, pissin'-contest stuff between men."

"Stop it."

"I'm kiddin' you. He seems like a good guy. He coming to the wedding?"

"Yes. Why?"

"Looking forward to seeing him again is all."

Tucker flexed his right hand to alleviate the pain. He watched Strange drive away, orange and red leaves rising from the street in the Caddy's wake.

❐

STRANGE stopped by the house to pick up Greco and a couple of CDs, then drove down to his place of business. In his office, he slipped *The Sons of Katie Elder* sound track into his CPU as he settled into his chair. The message light blinked beside his phone.

Lydell Blue had called to tell him that the beige Caprice had been found in an impound lot in Prince George's County. The Chevy was determined to have been a stolen vehicle, wiped down of prints. Clothing fibers, orange threads of a fleece material, found in the Chevy matched those found in the Plymouth driven by the shooters.

Strange was certain now that the boys he had seen in the Caprice idling in Roosevelt's parking lot were the killers of Lorenze and Joe Wilder. He had caught a look at the driver and especially the boy with the braids, and their faces loosely matched those of the artist's renderings posted around town.

He knew this. But he didn't phone Lydell Blue back to tell him what he knew.

Strange got into Westlaw and fed the names Walter Lee, Edward Diggs, and Sequan Hawkins, along with their Social Security numbers, into the program. It took a couple of hours to find what it would have taken Janine a half hour to find. Despite his rudimentary knowledge of the programs, Strange was still old world, and much better at his job when out on the street. He also tended to seek out distractions when he should have been working nonstop behind his desk. In those two hours he played with

Greco, thought of Janine, and ate a PayDay bar she had left for him on his mouse pad. But finally he got the information he needed.

Using PeopleFinder and the reverse directory, he had secured the current addresses and phone numbers of the men. Also the names and addresses of their current neighbors. The Social Security numbers had given him their past and present employment data.

Strange phoned Quinn and got him on the third ring.

"Terry, it's Derek. You see the game?"

"I saw some of it."

"Some of it. Your girlfriend over there, man?"

"Yes, Sue's here."

"Been there all day, huh? Y'all even get a look at the sunshine today, man?"

"Derek, what's on your mind?"

"Wanted to make sure you were gonna be ready to go in the morning."

"Told you I would be."

"Meet me down at Buchanan at nine, then. We'll roll out together in my car."

"Right."

"And Terry?"

"What?"

"Bring your gun."

chapter

25

CARLTON Little swallowed the last of his Big Mac and used his sleeve to wipe secret sauce off his face, where it had gathered like glue on the side of his mouth. He had another Mac in the bag on the table in front of him and he wanted to kill it right now. The grease stain on the bottom of the bag, just lookin' at it made him hungry.

He was hungry all the time. Not hungry for real like he had been when he was a kid, but hungry just the same. Loved to eat anything you could take out of somebody's hand from a drive-through window. Taco Bell, Popeyes, and the king of it all, *Mac-*Donald's. Little knew guys who had trouble with their movements, but not him. All the food he ate, the kind came in damp cartons and grease-stained bags? Damn if he didn't take three or four shits a day.

He supposed his love for food had somethin' to do with the fact that he didn't have any when he was a boy. His aunt, who he stayed with, she sold their food stamps most of the time to pay for her crack habit. She had food in there from time to time, but the men she was hangin' with, who were pipeheads, too, and always leaving a slug's trail around the house, ate it or stole it themselves. There was cereal sometimes, but the milk went fast, and he couldn't fuck with eatin' no dry cereal. Before he grew some, when he weighed, like, sixty pounds, Carlton used to hide the milk outside his bedroom window, on this ledge that was there, so it wouldn't get used up. In wintertime the milk froze and in summer it went sour, so you couldn't do it all the time. But it was a good trick that worked half the year. This teacher taught him how to do that after he collapsed one time at school 'cause he was so weak. Weak from not eating. Not that he was cryin' about it or nothin' like that. He had money now, and he wasn't weak anymore.

Man on the TV said that one third of the kids in D.C. lived below the poverty level, the same way he had. Well, fuck those kids. Nobody ever gave him nothin', and he made out all right. They'd have to figure a road out their own selves. If they *were* to ask him, he'd say that there was one thing he knew for sure about this life out here. You acted the punk, you were through. You wanted to make it, you had to be hard.

Little laid himself down on the couch.

Potter sat low in one of those reclining rocking chairs he loved. Potter had bought two of them at Marlo's, along with the couch Little lay on now, filled out the no-payment-till-whenever paperwork and had them delivered the next day. That was a year ago, and Potter had still not made a payment and never would. No Payments Till Forever, that's the way the sign read to him. Potter had given the African or whatever he was a different billing address than the delivery address, and the dude hadn't even noticed. Stupid-ass foreigners they hired out there, workin' those sucker jobs.

"You gonna eat that?" said Potter, one hand pointed lazily at the paper bag holding the last Mac.

"I was thinkin' on eatin' it right now," said Little.

"I wouldn't even be feedin' that shits to a dog."

"It's good."

"You gonna throw it up out in the street, like you did the other day?"

"I ain't ashamed. Made me sick to see what happened to that kid."

"Well, he shouldn't't've been in that car."

"Yeah, but those bullets you used done fucked him up for real."

"Oh, it was just *mines* now."

"It was those hollow points out of that three-five-seven you was holdin', did all that damage."

"Couldn't handle lookin at it, huh?"

"Shit was just nasty is all."

"Yeah, well, you keep eatin' that *Mac*Donald's, gonna make you worse than sick. Gonna kill you young."

"I be dyin' young anyway."

"True."

They had been in the living room all day. Charles White had gotten into his Toyota at lunchtime and brought them back a big carton of Popeyes and biscuits for the Redskins game, and they had gotten high and eaten the chicken, and then they had watched the four o'clock game and told White they were hungry and to go out again. White had returned with a bag of McDonald's for Little and some Taco Supremes from the Bell for Potter, because Potter didn't eat McDonald's food.

Now the eight o'clock game was coming on ESPN, and the sound was off on the television because neither Potter nor Little could stand to hear Joe Theismann, the color man for the Sunday night games, speak. They put on music during the games, but the Wu-Tang Clan CD they had been listening to had ended. For the first time that day, it was quiet in the room.

Potter and Little had been keeping a very low profile since the murders. They sent White out for all their food and beer. He was scared, they could tell it from his face and the way his voice kinda shook these past few days. But they knew him to be weak, knew that he would do as they asked.

Juwan, their main boy down in the open-air market, had been delivering the daily take to their place on Warder. Their dealer in Columbia Heights had agreed to drop off the product, as needed, at the house. They had burned the Plymouth and abandoned it, and dropped the guns off the rail of the 11th Street bridge into the Anacostia River. Far as evidence went, Potter reasoned, their asses were covered good.

Since the shooting, Potter had gone out twice. Once to buy a couple of straps from this boy he knew who arranged straw purchases out of that gun store, where you could pay junkies and their kind to buy weapons real easy, over in Forestville. The other time he went out was to buy a car, a piece of garbage sitting up on that lot on Blair Road in Takoma, across from a gas station and next to a caterer. Place where all the cars had $461 scrawled in soap on the windshields, all the same price, looked like a kid had written it. Potter bought something, he didn't even bother to look at it close, and paid cash. The salesman tellin' him how to get plates, get insurance, get it inspected, all that, Potter not even listening because he knew he wouldn't have the car long enough to worry about it anyway. Insurance, what the fuck was that? Shit.

So they were keeping low. Their pictures, drawings made to look like them, anyhow, were posted all around the neighborhood. Potter figured, who that could connect the pictures to their names was gonna rat them out? Wasn't anyone that stupid, even if the reward money was printed right there on the drawings, because that person had to know that if they did this, if they snitched on them, they would die. It was a good idea to stay indoors for a while, but Potter wasn't worried in a serious way, and if Little was worried he didn't act it. It was Charles White who was the loose end.

"Where Charles at?" said Potter.

"Up in his room," said Little. "Why?"

"You and me need to talk."

"Well, talk."

"Go put some music on the box. I don't want him to hear us."

"He can't hear us. You know that boy's up in his bed with his headphones on, listening to his beats."

"I expect."

Potter fired a Bic up in front of the Phillie in his hand and gave the cigar some draw. He held the draw in and passed the blunt over to Little.

Little hit the hydro and exhaled slowly. He blew a ring of gray smoke into the room. "So talk."

Carlton Little knew what was about to come from Potter's mouth. He expected it, and didn't like it, but he would go along with it, because he knew Potter was right. Though Little fully expected to die on the street or in prison, it didn't mean he was in any hurry. He wasn't exactly afraid to die. He had convinced himself that he was not. But he did want to live as long as he could. His friend Charles White was fixin' to cut his life short, one way or another. Charles had to go.

"We got a problem with Charles," said Potter. "Boy gets picked up for somethin', he is gonna roll on us. Or maybe his conscience is gonna send him to the po-lice before that. You *know* this, right?"

"I do." Little sat up on the couch and rubbed at his face. "Shame, too. I mean, me and Coon, all of us, D, we go back."

"I'll take care of it, Dirty."

"Wish you would."

"You know, Charles is like that dog of his," said Potter. "Good to hang around with, wags his tail when you be walkin' into a room and shit. But like that dog, he's a cur. And a cur needs to be put down."

"When?" said Little.

"I was thinkin', later tonight, after we watch this game, get our heads up some? We take Charles out for a ride."

❐

CHARLES White had been lying in bed, listening to a Roc-a-Fella compilation through the headphones of his Aiwa, when the cups on the phones started to hurt him some. His ears got sore when he kept the phones on too long, and he had been having them on his head most of the day. He took the headphones off and moved onto his side, staring out the window at the night out behind the house. Wasn't nothin' but dark and an alley back there. He looked at it a little while, then got off the bed and walked out to the bathroom in the hall.

White could hear them playing the first Wu-Tang, the one that mattered, down in the living room. It was that last track the Clan had, "Tearz," before that spoken thing they did to close the set. This was the bomb, the kind of classic shit he wanted to record his own self when he got the chance. But of course, he knew deep down he would never get the chance.

White figured he better go downstairs and see what Dirty and Garfield was up to. See if they wanted him to run out for some burgers or malt or sumshit like that. But first he needed to get those dirt tracks off his face. He had been crying a little while ago, back in his room. Some of it had been over what they'd done to that kid, but most of it had been just cryin' for himself.

He bent over the bathroom sink, washed his face, toweled off the water, and checked himself in the mirror. He must have lost weight or something, what with the way he'd been stressin' since they'd killed that boy. His nose looked bigger than usual, his cheeks on either side of it nothin' but some flabby skin hanging on to bone. But you couldn't tell he'd been crying, now that he'd cleaned up. He looked all right.

White went along a hall, hearing their voices below and smelling the smoke of the cheeva they were hittin' drifting up the stairs. It was strange for things to be so quiet in this house. He heard Dirty say, "So talk," and then Garfield say, "We got a problem with Charles."

White's heart had kicked up and his fingers were shaking some as he went down the stairs halfway. There was a wall there that blocked a view from the living room, and carpet on the steps to muffle the sound of his descent.

He listened to their conversation. He heard his friend Carlton say "When?" and Garfield, quick and cold in his reply, answered, "Later tonight." He said something else about watching the game and getting high, and then he said, "We take Charles out for a ride."

You ain't takin' me a *mother*fuckin' place, thought White as he backed himself slowly up the stairs.

❐

CHARLES locked his bedroom door. They came up and asked why he'd locked himself in, he'd deal with it then.

He got into his Timbies and laced them tight. He found an old Adidas athletic bag, the size of a small duffel, in his closet. He stuffed it with underwear and a few pairs of jeans and some shirts, and one leather jacket, but he left most of the cold-weather stuff on the hangers because he had already decided that he was headed south. He had grabbed his toothbrush and shaving shit from the vanity over the sink on the way to his room, and he dropped it all in. There was still some room in the bag. He put his Aiwa in along with all the CDs, the newer joints, he could fit. He found some older stuff he still listened to, *Amerikkka's Most Wanted* and *Doggystyle,* and jammed those in there, too.

White went to his bedroom mirror, where he had taped a photograph of his mother to the glass. In the original shot, some Jheri-curled sucker, all teeth and sweat, lookin' like he walked off the *Street Songs* cover, had his arm around White's mom. White had scissored the man off the picture so that now you could only see the hustler's hand. His mother was smiling in the photo, had a low-cut dress on, red, you could see her titties half hangin' out, but that was all right. At least she looked happy. Not like she looked when they'd cuffed her right at the apartment for robbery, the last of her offenses in a long line of them, and taken her off to that women's prison in West Virginia. Last time White had seen her, ten years back, before he went to live with his grandmother. Gran-moms had been okay to him, but she wasn't his moms. He had no idea who his father was.

White carefully took the photograph down and slipped it into his wallet, along with eighteen hundred dollars in cash he found where he'd hidden it, under some T-shirts in the bottom of his dresser.

He opened the window by his bed and dropped the Adidas bag into the darkness. He heard it hit the alley and he closed the window tight.

White slipped himself into his bright orange Nautica pullover, swept the keys to his Toyota off his scarred dresser, and walked out of his room. He walked quickly, so he wouldn't have much time to think on what he was about to do. Wasn't like he could just drop himself out that bedroom window and ghost. He needed to talk to those two, act like everything was chilly. He needed to do this and be gone.

And now he was going down the stairs. And now he was down the stairs and into the living room, and he was twirling his car keys on his finger, wondering why he was doing that, tipping them off so soon that he was headed out the door.

"Where you off to, Coon?" said Little, lying on the couch. He said it casual, like he was still White's friend. White could see in Carlton's eyes that he was higher than a motherfucker, too.

"I'm hungry. *You* hungry, right?"

"I still got me a Mac."

"I was gonna roll on up to the Wings n Things, man." His

voice shook some and he closed his eyes, then forced them open quick.

"Bring me some malt back," said Potter.

"You got money?" said White.

He moved to the lounger where Potter sat.

Be hard, Charles. Give 'em somethin' bold to remember you by. Let 'em know you all there.

White opened his hand in front of Potter's face. Potter slapped the hand away. "Man, *get* that shit out my face! Bring me some Olde English back, hear? Two forties of that shits."

"And some wings," said Little.

Potter and Little laughed, and White laughed, too.

"Aiight, then," said White. He headed for the door.

"Coon," said Potter, and White turned.

"Yeah?"

"What I tell you about wearin' that orange shirt out, man? You *want* people to be noticin' you? Is that it?"

"Cold out, D. Shit keeps me warm."

"Damn, boy, you about the thickest motherfucker . . . Look, you ain't gonna be long, right?"

"Nah, I'll be back in like, an hour, sumshit like that."

"'Cause I thought we'd all roll out together for a while, later on."

White nodded, went out the door, and closed it behind him. He walked down to the corner and when he was out of window-sight he ran around to the alley. He found his Adidas bag there and ran with it back to the street, where he walked to his Toyota parked along the curb. His heart was fluttering like a speed bag as he put his key to the driver's-side door.

White tossed the Adidas bag in the backseat, got into the front, and turned the ignition. He put the stick into first and heard the tires squealing as he pushed on the gas and let off the clutch. First time this old shit box had ever caught rubber. White didn't look in the rearview. As he neared Georgia Avenue he began to laugh.

◻

WHITE stopped at a market on Georgia, one of those fake 7-Elevens, places those Ethiopians named Seven-One or Seven-Twelve, for a big cup of coffee to go. A 4-D cop was parked in the lot, but that meant nothing in this neighborhood, 'less you were out here committing some obvious mayhem. Shoot, someone was smoking cheeva in a nearby car, you could smell it in the lot, and the cop was just sitting there behind the wheel, smellin' it too, most likely, sipping from a large cup. Why would that cop care to stress his self, make an arrest, when the courts would just kick that smoker right back out on the street?

White went into the store. He bought his coffee and a couple of Slim Jims, some potato chips, and a U.S. road map, folded up wrong like someone had been using it without paying, which was in a slot next to the gun magazines they sold in that joint. White went back out to the lot, the map in one hand, the other stuff in a brown paper bag.

There was this boy standing near his Toyota, and when White came out the boy kind of backed away. He was wearing a white T-shirt and khakis, and White had the real feeling he knew this boy or he'd seen him before.

White wasn't a fighter and he wasn't brave, but when it looked like someone was fuckin' with your whip out here, ordinarily you had to say something. You couldn't let it pass, because then you were weak. Just a comment like, "You got some business lurkin' around my shit?" or somethin' like that. But White didn't need no drama tonight, what with the police right there, and he let it pass.

As he pulled out of the lot and back onto Georgia, he noticed that boy, standing on the corner, staring at him and his car. But White wasn't gonna worry about it now. He was gone.

❐

WHITE got over to 14th Street and headed south. He took the 14th Street Bridge over the Potomac River and into Virginia, where he followed 395 to 95 South. Soon he was out of anything that looked like the city and seeing signs for places like Lorton, which of course he had heard of, and Dale City, which he had not. Down around Fredericksburg, just an hour into his journey, he saw a Confederate flag sticker on the back window of a pickup truck and knew he was already very far away, maybe a whole world away, from D.C.

The coffee had done its job. He was wired and bright with thoughts of the future. He was sorry that the little boy had been killed, but he was convinced that he couldn't have stopped it, and he knew for certain that he couldn't change what had happened now.

This was his plan: He had a cousin in Louisiana, a nephew of his mother's who had come up and stayed with his grandmother a couple of summers back. That summer, White and this boy, Damien Rollins, had got kind of tight. Damien worked in a big diner down there on the interstate, outside New Orleans, and told White that he would hook Charles up if he ever came down south. He said that the man who owned the diner paid cash, under the table. Charles had the idea that this would allow him to work there without incident, under an assumed name, in case anyone was still lookin' for him up in D.C.

White had an address on his cousin, and he had held on to it. About halfway down, he'd give him a call and tell him he was on his way. He had money in his pocket, so he'd also tell cuz that he'd be stayin' with him and help out with half the rent. He'd get that job at the diner and he'd hold it. He wouldn't get into any kind of bad shit down there and he'd stay away from those who looked wrong.

Maybe he'd make manager someday at that job.

W ALTER Lee worked for a big-box electronics retailer up by Westfield Shopping Center, the fancy new name for the mall that everyone in the area still called Wheaton Plaza, a few miles north of the Silver Spring business district. Lee wrote up answering machines, mini–tape recorders, cordless phones, and portable stereos at a computer station after the customers had basically picked the units out themselves. The human resources department gave him the title of sales counselor, but there were few professional salesmen left in the business, and Walter Lee was a clerk.

Strange and Quinn entered the store late in the morning. There was a sea of maroon shirts in the place and few customers at this hour. Most of the employees looked like African Americans, African immigrants, and Indians of some variety, with some Hispanics thrown into the mix to cater to the Spanish-speaking clientele. Strange found himself wondering if the manager of the store was white.

No one approached them or asked if they needed help. In fact, several of the sales counselors had scattered when the two of them had walked through the doors. Strange went up to a tall young African and asked him if he could point out Walter Lee. Strange already knew that Lee was on the schedule; he'd phoned the store on the ride out to Wheaton.

Walter Lee stood by the rack of boom boxes, fiddling with a radio dial, as Strange and Quinn approached. Lee looked up and saw a strong middle-aged man in a black leather jacket, a beeper and a Buck knife and a cell on his belt line, with a younger white dude, also in a leather, had a cocky walk, coming toward him. Lee saw two cops.

"How you doin' today?" said Strange.

"Good. What can I get for you gentlemen?"

Quinn got too close to Lee, crowding him, like he used to do when he wore the uniform. Strange did the same to Lee on his opposite side and flipped open the leather case he drew from his jacket. He let Lee look at the badge and license and closed the case before he had looked at them too long.

"Investigators, D.C.," said Strange. "This here's my partner, Terry Quinn."

"What y'all want?"

" 'Bout a minute of your time," said Strange. "A few questions about Lorenze Wilder."

"I already talked to the police." Lee looked around the sales floor. He was in his early thirties and carried too much weight for his age. He wore a fade haircut that looked fine on Patrick Ewing but on Lee just looked tired. "This ain't too cool, you know."

"We won't be long," said Strange. "You were at the wake for Lorenze, right?"

"Sure."

"Y'all were tight?"

"I already told the police —"

"Tell us," said Strange.

"Tell us *again*," said Quinn, his tone softer than his partner's.

Lee looked over Strange's shoulder, then breathed out slow. "We hadn't been tight for, like, ten, fifteen. We ran together in high school, that was about it."

"Coolidge?"

"Yeah. I came out in eighty-six. Lorenze, I don't think he finished up."

"Lorenze have many enemies when you two were hangin' together back then?"

"Back then? I guess he did. He had this way about him, right? But if you're askin' me, Did he have enemies lately, or, Do I know who killed him? The answer is, I don't know."

"Y'all didn't swing in the same circles," said Strange.

"Like I said: not for a long time."

"You use drugs, Walter?"

Lee's eyes, directly on Strange, narrowed, and he lowered his voice. "This ain't right. You *know* this ain't right. Comin' up in here to a black man's workplace and tryin' to sweat him."

"*If* you do drugs," said Strange, plowing ahead, "and if you cop from the same people, then maybe you know who Lorenze owed. 'Cause it could've been a drug debt got him doomed."

"Look. I haven't been usin' any kind of drugs for a long time. Back in the eighties, yeah, I had a little problem with pow-der. Lotta people did. But I found my way out of it, see —"

"Let's get back to Lorenze."

"No, you're gonna let me finish. I found my way *out* of it. This isn't the only job I have. I got a night job, too. I been holdin' two jobs down now for the last ten years, and all the time doin' it straight. Takin' care of my little girl, raising her right."

"All right," said Strange. "You're so far away from all that, why'd you go to Lorenze's wake, then?"

"Because I'm a Christian. I went to say a prayer for my old friend. To pay my respects. Even you can understand that, right?"

"Did Lorenze still hang with some of the old crowd that you know?"

Lee relaxed his shoulders. It seemed he'd given up on reaching Strange's human side and now he just wanted this done. "Most of them grew up and moved on. A couple of them passed."

"Sequan Hawkins? Ed Diggs?"

"I haven't seen Sequan, so I don't know. Digger Dog? He's still around."

"That's Diggs's street name?"

Lee nodded. "I saw him at the funeral home. He's still livin' over there with his grandmother. He looks older, but the same, you know? He always was Lorenze's main boy."

"Thanks for your time," said Quinn.

"That it?" said Lee, his eyes still locked on Strange.

"That'll do it," said Strange. "We need you, I expect we can find you here."

Strange and Quinn walked toward the entrance to the store. They passed a white guy in a maroon shirt, small, with a belly and patches of hair framing a bald top, trying to calm an angry customer. The manager, thought Strange.

Out in the lot, Quinn glanced over at Strange on the way to the car. "You were kinda rough on him, weren't you?"

Strange stared straight ahead. "We got no time to be nice."

They drove out toward Potomac in Strange's white Caprice. Strange made a cell call to see if Sequan Hawkins was at his job. Then he phoned the office and got Janine. Quinn sipped coffee from a go-cup and listened to their short, businesslike conversation. Strange made another call, left a message on the machine at Lamar Williams's apartment, and left Lamar the number to his cell.

"What's going on?" said Quinn.

"Lamar's been trying to get up with me. Janine said he told her it was important."

"Well?"

"He's got his classes right now. I'll get him later."

"Any idea what he wants?"

"These boys rolled up on him a while back in Park Morton, lookin' for Joe's mother? Pretty sure it's the same hard cases I saw up at Roosevelt one night at practice. They were huntin' Lorenze, I'm certain of it now. Bet you they ain't nothin' but neighborhood boys, too. Maybe Lamar found out something more."

"If they're stupid enough to stay in the neighborhood, it won't be long until someone turns them in."

"You're right. If it doesn't happen today, it'll happen tomorrow, if you know what I mean. The police are gonna get those boys soon enough."

"What if we find them first?"

"I haven't figured that out yet, Terry. To tell you the truth, right now I'm just goin' on blind rage."

Strange kept the needle above eighty on the Beltway. Quinn didn't comment on the speed. He blew the steam off his coffee and took a long pull from the cup.

"You and Janine got some problems, huh?" said Quinn.

"Guess you heard that in my tone."

"You two gonna make it?"

"Haven't figured that one out yet, either," said Strange. "Anyway, it's not up to me."

Strange parked the Caprice in the lot of Montgomery Mall, near an upscale retailer that anchored the shopping center. In contrast to Westfield, the parking lot here was clean, and the multiethnic people walking from their luxury cars and SUVs to the mall might as well have had dollar signs stamped right on their foreheads.

Strange and Quinn went up to the second floor of the department store. The sound of piano met them as they reached the top of the stairs. A man in a tuxedo played the keys of a Steinway set near the escalators adjacent to a menswear section and a large layout of men's shoes. Middle-aged white men wearing pressed jeans and sweaters strolled the aisles. Strange wondered what they were doing here on a Monday, why they weren't at work. Living off the interest, he reckoned.

They walked along the display tables of shoes. Several well-dressed salesmen eyed them as they passed.

"You need any kicks?" said Strange.

"I got a wide foot," said Quinn, "and it's hard to fit. There's this salesman, though, at Mean Feets, down in Georgetown? Says he can fit me. Dude named Antoine."

"Skinny cat, right? Always standin' outside in the doorway there, hittin' a cigarette."

"That's him."

"I know him. They call him Spiderman."

"You know everyone in town?"

"Not yet," said Strange. "But it's a long life."

To the side of the shoe department was a shoe-shine stand, where a kneeling man in suspenders was buffing the cap-toes of a suited white man sitting in a chair above him, up on a kind of elevated platform.

Strange and Quinn waited in an alcove-type area beside the stand. They could hear the white man talking to the shoe-shine man about the Redskins/Ravens game, praising only the black players. They could hear the white man ending his sentences with "man" and they could hear him dropping his g's, talking in a way that he thought would endear him to the black man kneeling at his feet. Talking in a way he would never talk at work and in a way he would forbid his children from talking at the dinner table at home. Strange looked over at Quinn, and Quinn looked away.

Soon the white man left, and they went out to the stand, where the shoe shiner was straightening the tools of his trade.

"Sequan Hawkins?" said Strange, getting a short nod in return. "I'm Derek Strange, and this is Terry Quinn, my partner. We phoned you a little while ago."

Hawkins rubbed his hands clean with a rag that smelled of nail polish remover. He was a handsome, well-built man with a light sheen to his close-cropped hair and a careful hint of a mustache.

"Come on around here," said Hawkins, indicating with his chin the alcove where they had stood.

They went back to the alcove and Strange said, "This is about Lorenze Wilder, like I explained."

"Let me see some identification, you don't mind," said Hawkins.

Strange flipped open his leather case and produced his badge and license. Hawkins's mouth turned up on the right, a lopsided grin.

"You two are, like, cops."

"Investigators, D.C.," said Strange. "We knew the young man who was murdered alongside Lorenze."

"My sympathies," said Hawkins, the grin disappearing at the mention of the boy. "I got two of my own."

"You went to the funeral home for Lorenze's wake," said Quinn.

"That's right."

"You were friends with him?"

"A long time ago."

"What made y'all stop being friends?" said Strange.

"Geography," said Hawkins. "Ambition."

"Geography?"

"I haven't lived anywhere near the old neighborhood for the past ten years."

"Don't get back there much, huh?"

"Oh, I do. I drive over to the house I grew up in, like, once a month. Park outside of it at night sometimes and look through the windows. They got a new family in there now."

"Why would you do that?"

"To look at the ghosts."

Strange didn't feel the need to comment. He often went by his mother's house at night, parked on the street, and did the same thing. He didn't consider Hawkins's actions to be odd at all.

"You ever run into Lorenze Wilder on those trips?" said Quinn.

"Sure, I saw him now and again. He was still living in his mother's house; I guess it was paid for with life insurance after her death. He never did get a steady job I knew of. He was one of those . . . I don't like to speak ill of the dead. But it was plain Lorenze was never gonna make it."

"How about Ed Diggs?" said Strange.

"I saw him around the way, too. He was living with his grandmother last time I ran into him. Ed was the same way."

"Any other reason why you might have gone back?"

"What do you mean?"

"We're looking for someone who might have wanted to hunt down Lorenze," said Strange. "Maybe for a drug debt or somethin' like that."

"I wouldn't know about that."

"So, you'd go back to the neighborhood once a month for what, exactly?" said Quinn. "Couldn't be to just park outside your house."

"I went back to remember, Mr. . . ."

"Quinn."

"I'd see some of those guys still in the neighborhood, the ones who were already at that dead end, who weren't even lookin' to get through it anymore, and it just served to remind me."

"Of what?"

"Of why I'm down on my knees here every day. See, I don't just work here. I *own* this concession. I got four of these around the Beltway and a couple downtown."

"You must be doin' all right," said Strange.

"Got a house on a couple acres out in Damascus, a wife I love, and a couple of beautiful kids. There's a Harley in my garage and a Porsche Boxster, too. It's not the Carrera, but I'm workin' on that. So yeah, I've done all right."

"You read about the murders," said Strange, "and you knew Lorenze. Any ideas?"

"I think you're talkin' to the wrong man. You want to know if Lorenze died because of a street beef, you need to be talking to Ed. They were still as tight as any two men could be, way I understand it. But Ed's not the type to talk to the police, or even to someone got a toy badge, tryin' to *look* like they're police."

"Okay," said Strange.

"Couldn't resist," said Hawkins. "You need to be flashing that license quick, so no one can look at it too close."

"Normally I do. Get back to Diggs."

"All I'm saying is, if there's any information to be got, Ed's the one to talk to. But you're gonna have to be creative." Hawkins looked them both over. "Y'all got a couple of pairs of shoulders on you. Use 'em."

"You say he still stays with his grandmother?"

"Far as I know."

Strange shook Hawkins's hand. "Thanks for your time."

Crossing the lot to the Caprice, Quinn said, "Just goes to show you, you can't judge a man by his appearance."

"You tellin' *me* that?"

"Oh, so now you're gonna tell me you didn't look at that guy and think, Shoe-shine Boy."

"Didn't see the word 'boy' flashin' through my head at any time, if that's what you mean."

"You know what I'm sayin'. Man shines shoes for a living and he's got a Porsche in his garage."

"It's not a Carrera, though."

"He's workin' on that," said Quinn.

Strange removed his keys from his pocket and tossed them to Quinn. "You drive. I need to make some calls."

"Right."

Quinn hit the Beltway and headed back toward the city. Strange phoned Lamar, got no answer, and left another message. He found the number for Ed Diggs on his list and phoned the house. Quinn heard him talking to a woman on the other end of the line; he could tell it was an older woman from the patient tone of Strange's voice.

"Any luck?" said Quinn, as Strange hit "end."

"His grandmother says he's on his way out the door. I figure he's still home, still wearin' his pajamas, and now she's gonna tell him to get his shit together and get himself out the house." Strange looked at the needle on the speedometer. "You can get there quicker, we might still catch him in."

"I'm already doin' seventy-five. Wouldn't want us to get pulled over. You might go showing that toy badge of yours to a real police officer, get us into a world of hurt."

"Funny. C'mon, Terry, speed it up. Car's got a three-fifty square block under the hood, and you're drivin' it like a Geo and shit."

"You want me to drive it like a race car, I will."

"Pin it," said Strange.

◗

LUCILLE Carter lived on a number street off North Dakota Avenue in Manor Park, in a detached bungalow fronted by a series of small roller-coaster hills that stopped at a stone retaining wall before they reached the sidewalk. There were plenty of cars parked along the curb on this workday. This, along with the condition of the raked lawns and the updated paint on the modest houses, indicated to Strange that the residents were mainly retirees holding on to their properties and sheltering their extended families.

Strange and Quinn went up the concrete steps to the porch of Lucille Carter's house. Strange knocked on the front door, and it soon opened. Carter, short, bespectacled, narrow in the hips, and not yet completely gray, stood in the frame. She knew who they were. Her eyes were unsmiling and her body language told them that she wasn't about to let them in. As agreed, Quinn stepped back and let Strange take the lead.

"Derek Strange. This is my partner Terry Quinn." Strange opened his badge case and closed it just as quickly. "Like I explained to you on the phone, we're investigating the Lorenze Wilder homicide. We need to speak with your grandson Edward."

"He already talked to the police."

"I told you we needed to speak with him again."

"And I told *you*, Mr. Strange, that he was on his way out. As I am about to be, shortly."

"Any idea where we can catch up with him?"

"He went out to his job —"

"He doesn't have a job, Miss Carter."

"He went out to his job *search*. If you had let me finish —"

"All due respect, I don't have the time or the inclination to let you finish. You told Edward that we were on our way over here, and now he's gone. So let me make this easy for you and tell you how it's gonna be. Me and my partner here are gonna be back in an hour with a subpoena. Edward's not in, we'll come back the hour after that. Same thing the hour after that. We have to, we'll be here on the hour around the clock. Now, what do you suppose your good neighbors gonna think of that?"

"This is harassment."

"Yes, ma'am."

"Would you like me to call your supervisors?"

"I can't stop you." Strange looked at his watch. "We'll see you in about sixty minutes, then. Thank you for your time."

They heard the door close behind them as they were walking down the steps.

"That was nice," said Quinn. "The Gray Panthers are gonna give you their humanitarian award for that one."

"You want to find a man in this city, shake down his grandmother," said Strange. "Black man like Diggs always gonna respect the matriarch who treated him right. Plus, she's stronger than he is, and the last thing he's gonna want is to incur her wrath."

"That cop knowledge?"

Strange shook his head. "My mother always said it. 'Kick the bush and the quail comes flyin' out.'"

"So Diggs flies out of the bush. Then what? I mean, the cops have already talked to this guy."

"They didn't know how close he was to Lorenze. And they didn't *talk* to him the way I'm gonna talk to him."

"Okay, what now?"

"Let's get my car out of view so we can regroup."

Strange pulled the Caprice around the corner and parked it a block south of the Carter residence and out of its sight lines. He phoned Lamar's apartment and this time he got him on the line. Strange made a writing sign in the air and snapped his fingers. Quinn handed him a pen. Strange wrote down a series of numbers, asked Lamar some questions, nodded as he listened to the answers, and said, "Good work, son," before ending the call.

"What?" said Quinn.

"Lamar saw one of those boys last night, one of the three who rolled up on him at Park Morton." Strange was punching numbers into the grid of his cell as he talked. "Said this boy was wearing the same bright shirt he had on when he saw him the first time."

"Lotta bright shirts out here."

"His face was hard to forget, had a nose like an anteater."

"And?"

"Boy had a duffel bag in his backseat and a road map in his hand when Lamar saw him coming out the market, over there near the Black Hole. Looked to Lamar like he was runnin'."

"What else?"

"Lamar got the license number off this boy's Toyota, too." Strange gave him the hold-up sign with his hand as his call connected. "Janine. Derek here. I need you to run a plate for me quick. You get an address on the owner of the car, I'm gonna need a phone number from the reverse directory, too." Strange gave her the information and nodded as if Janine were in the room. "I'll be waiting. Right."

Strange hit "end." "Janine will get it quick. She sends a Christmas card every year to this guy she's been knowin', over at the DMV? One of those little things she does, small gestures of kindness. Gets results."

"She is good."

"The best." Strange pointed his chin up the block. "You want the alley or the front of the house?"

"The alley."

"Where's your gun at, case I need it?"

"Right here, under the seat."

"Is it loaded?"

"Yeah."

"You got your cell?"

"In my pocket."

"Keep it live." Strange kept the pen Quinn had given him and slipped a notepad into his jacket. "The old lady will be going out, I expect. Either he's in there or she's gonna find him and tell him to get back to the house and take his medicine. But I don't trust him to do what she says. If you get sight of him, you call me."

"What if you see him first?"

"I'll do the same."

❐

STRANGE positioned himself a half block east of the Carter home, his 10×50 binos around his neck.

Quinn walked down the alley, found the Carter bungalow, and quickly opened the link gate at the end of the weedy concrete path to the back porch of the house. Then he walked back and stood three houses away on the stones of the alley. A pit bull in a cage barked at him from a neighboring yard. No one came out to see what the barking was about, and no curtains moved from the back windows of the houses.

Quinn paced the alley for an hour. Then his phone chirped. He flipped it open.

"Yeah."

"The old lady just left. She's drivin' off in her Ford right now."

"Okay," said Quinn.

Another thirty minutes passed. Then a sad sack of a man in oversize jeans and a T-shirt came out from the back of the Carter house. He stepped down off the peeling wood porch and reached into his jeans for a pack of cigarettes. He shook one out from a hole cut in the bottom of the pack and lit it with a match he tore from a book.

Quinn stepped back behind a tall lilac bush that still had leaves. He phoned Strange and kept his voice low.

"Derek, he's out in the yard. How do you want to play it?"

"Hard," said Strange. "Strong-arm him into the house and keep that back door unlocked. How much time you figure before he goes back inside?"

"However long it takes to smoke a cigarette."

"Right," said Strange.

Strange ran to the Caprice. He dropped his binoculars to the floor. He found Quinn's automatic, a black Colt .45 with a checkered grip and a five-inch barrel, underneath the seat. He released the magazine and checked the load: a full seven shots. It had been a long time since Strange had had the weight of a gun in his hand. He felt that he needed one today.

❑

EDWARD Diggs took a last drag of his Kool, then a real last drag that burned his throat, and crushed the butt under his shoe. He picked up the butt and tossed it over the fence, into the yard of a neighbor who was also a smoker. Diggs's grandmother wouldn't let him smoke in the house, and she didn't like to see any evidence of it in her backyard. Mad as she had been this morning, he wasn't gonna do anything to get her back up more than it already was.

But fuck that shit if she thought he was gonna talk any more to the police. Let them deliver that subpoena. He had told them he didn't know shit about what had happened to Lorenze and that kid, and he didn't have to go on repeating it if he didn't want to. Far as telling them the truth, he had decided from the get-go to keep his mouth shut. Lorenze was his main boy, he loved him like a brother and all that, but all the talking in the world wasn't gonna bring Lorenze back. Diggs felt that the police wouldn't waste their time protecting a guy like him. All he wanted now was to live.

He turned and went back up the walkway, cracked and over-grown with clover and weeds. He thought he heard something behind him, but it couldn't be, it was just his own footsteps and that cur, wouldn't stop barking across the way.

His right hand was grabbed from behind and then bent at the wrist. A bolt of electric pain shot up to his neck, and the shock of it nearly dropped him to his knees. But the man behind him held him up.

"Let's go, Ed." A white man's voice, the one saying the words pushing him along the walkway to the back porch. "Inside."

"Fuck *is* this shit? You're hurtin' me!"

"Investigator, D.C. Move it."

"I'm 'onna get your badge number, man."

"Yeah, okay."

"This is assault right here!"

"Not yet," said Quinn. "Open that door, let's go."

Diggs did it and Quinn released him as they stepped inside. They were in a clean kitchen that held a small table and chairs. On the table was a coffee cup and the sports page of the *Washington Post*. A set of knives sat on the Formica counter, sheathed in a rub-ber stand. Diggs stood by the table, trying to give Quinn a hard glare. Quinn looked Diggs over carefully, thinking of the knives, deciding that Diggs would never make a play.

"Sit down," said Quinn, pointing to one of the chairs. Diggs pulled one away from the table and sat in it. He mumbled to himself as he stared at the linoleum floor.

Quinn moved to the rear window and looked through it. Strange was coming through the open gate and moving quickly up the walkway. His shirttails were out over his jeans. Then Strange was opening the door and he was in the kitchen and closing the door behind him. He walked toward Ed Diggs. Diggs stood from his chair.

"Meet Ed Diggs," said Quinn.

"Ed," said Strange, and as Strange reached him he threw a deep right into Diggs's mouth and knocked him back over the chair. Diggs slid on the linoleum and stopped sliding when the back of his head hit the kitchen cabinet beneath the sink. Strange yanked him up by his T-shirt, kept his left hand bunched on the T, and hit him with a short, sharp right to the same spot. Diggs's neck snapped back and his eyes fluttered. His eyes came back, and he stared up at Strange as blood flowed over his lower lip and dripped onto his shirt. Strange released him and Diggs dropped to the floor. Diggs staggered back up to his feet.

"We tell you to stand?" Quinn righted the chair. "*Sit* your ass down."

Strange pulled a chair over so it faced the one Diggs had been sitting on. He and Quinn listened to Diggs mumble and moan, and they waited for him to slouch across the room. Strange had split Diggs's lip wide, and blood came freely now from the cut.

Diggs sat down dead eyed, his shoulders slouched. Strange reached under his shirt and pulled the .45.

"Nah," said Diggs in the voice of a boy. "Uh-uh, man, nah, uh-*uh*."

"Who killed Lorenze?" said Strange.

"I don't know who did that." His diction was sloppy and wet.

"Somebody was huntin' him. Was it a drug debt?"

"I don't know."

Strange racked the receiver on the Colt.

"Why you want to do that, brother? I *told* you I don't know."

Strange got up out of his chair and with his free hand flat-palmed Diggs's chest. Diggs and the chair toppled back to the floor. Diggs grunted, and Strange crouched over him and forced the barrel of the .45 into his mouth.

"*You* know," said Strange. He withdrew the barrel, touched it gently to the corner of Diggs's right eye, and then pressed it there with force.

"They'll kill me," said Diggs.

"*Look* at me, Ed. *I'm* gonna kill you right now, I swear to God."

"Derek," said Quinn. It wasn't part of the act. Strange's eyes had long since veered from the script.

"*Look* at me, Ed."

Diggs did look. His lip quivered and he closed his eyes. When he opened them again a tear sprung loose and ran fast down his cheek.

"Lorenze," said Diggs, "he owed money to this boy for some hydro he copped. I was there when Lorenze bought it. He was gonna pay this boy in his own time. . . . Wasn't nothin' but a hunrid dollars. Boy stepped to me at a dogfight back by Ogelthorpe; I could tell he was serious. I mean, that boy had nothin' in his eyes."

"What'd this boy look like?"

"Tall and slim, light skinned, had this crazy smile."

"He had partners, right?"

"The ones he came with to the fight. Boy with cornrows and show muscles. 'Nother kid, one with the dog, boy had this funny-lookin' nose and shit."

"The main one, he say his name?"

"Garfield Potter."

"You know where he stays at?"

"He said he was up on Warder Street, near Roosevelt."

"What else you know?"

"Nothin' else." Diggs blinked hard. "You just doomed me, man. Don't you care nothin' about that?"

Strange slipped the Colt back under his shirt as he stood.

"Don't speak of this," said Strange. "Tell your grandmother you got jumped out on the street. Tell her you fell down and bounced a few times or anything you want. But don't tell her it was us came back. It's over for you, hear? You'll be fine."

They left him lying on the kitchen floor and walked out the back door of the house and to the alley.

Strange handed Quinn his gun. Quinn slipped it into his waistband and side-glanced Strange.

"You got some anger management issues you need to work on, Derek. You know it?"

"My anger's been working pretty good for me today so far."

"Thought you were gonna use the forty-five for a second back there."

"Couldn't have used it if I wanted to. I emptied the magazine before I came to the house."

"That gun felt too good in your hand, didn't it?"

"Scared me how good it felt," said Strange. "Your bullets are in the ashtray, back in the car."

❐

ON the way to the Caprice, Strange answered his cell. He continued his conversation with Janine as he got under the wheel of the car. Quinn slipped the .45 back under the seat. As Strange listened to his call, writing in his notebook, Quinn's cell chirped. He answered, got out of the Chevy, and leaned against the rear quarter panel as he took the call.

Strange waited for Quinn to get back inside. He noticed that some of the color had drained from Quinn's face.

"Janine got me a name and address on that boy Lamar saw," said Strange. "Charles White. And guess what? His credit record shows his last address is up on Warder Street. I bet you he was the only one of the three qualified to sign for the utilities. She got me the phone number there, too."

"Guess you got enough to call Lydell," said Quinn, his eyes showing he was somewhere else. "Time to send in the troops."

"I'm not ready to do that yet," said Strange, watching Quinn's stare go out the window. "Terry, you all right?"

"I just got a call from the MPD. They got a girl down in the ER at Washington Hospital Center, she's all fucked up. Beaten close to death. It's an informant of mine, helped me on that snatch I did. She gave my name as the first contact. Girl named Stella."

"You want to go there, then go. I can drop you at the hospital and pick this up my own self from here."

"All right," said Quinn. "Let's go."

Quinn phoned Sue Tracy as Strange turned off Georgia Avenue and headed east on Irving Street. Strange entered the complex of hospital buildings five minutes later and stopped the Caprice near the heliport adjacent to the ER entrance. Quinn opened his door and put one foot to the asphalt. He turned and shook Strange's hand.

"Don't do anything without me, Derek."

"I won't," said Strange.

Even as he said this, Strange was weighing a plan. It went against most everything he believed in. Still, he couldn't shake it from his mind.

27

QUINN went directly past the check-in desk, through the waiting area, and into the treatment facility. A security guard stopped him and walked him over to a plainclothes MPD cop who wore a black mustache. He held a go-cup of coffee in his thin, veined hand.

"You got a minute to talk?" said the cop.

"After I see the girl," said Quinn. "How is she?"

"According to the people here, she got beat up pretty bad. The man did it used his fists, but he didn't hold back. He punched right through her. Broke a few ribs, and she's bleeding inside. They're trying to stop that, and the doc thinks they will. Also, whoever this prince was, he carved up her face with a knife."

"She gonna live?"

The cop shrugged. He sipped from a hole torn in the lid of the cup and looked Quinn over. "You know, I recognized your name on the sheet, and then when you walked in, from the pictures they used to run in the papers. You're the same Terry Quinn used to be on the force, right?" The cop's eyes said curiosity rather than aggression.

"Yeah. Can I go?"

"Why'd she have you as contact number one?"

"I don't know why."

"No fixed address, no mention of parents. And she wants to talk to you?"

"That's right."

"Okay. She claims she got blindsided and never saw a thing. You got any idea who did this to her?"

"None."

"Here's my card."

Quinn took it and slipped it into his coat.

"Excuse me," said Quinn.

Stella was on a gurney behind a portable curtain, at the end of a row of makeshift stalls. Her forehead and cheeks were nearly covered in surgical tape, damp and brownish red in spots. Her thin right arm, lying outside the blanket, was bruised black with large defensive marks and also in several places where a nurse had tried to find a vein for the IV. Tubes ran from somewhere under the sheets and into her nostrils. The fluid in the tubes was dirty, and brown particles ran through it as Stella inhaled, her breath labored and ragged.

Quinn found a hard chair and placed it beside the gurney, where he took a seat and held her hand. A nurse came by and told him that they were preparing to move Stella to the ICU and he couldn't stay much longer. Ten minutes later, Stella opened her eyes, bloodied in the corners and ringed in black. Her head remained in place as her eyes moved to his, and she squeezed his hand.

"Hey, Stella."

"Green eyes."

Her voice was barely audible, and Quinn bent forward and moved his ear close to her mouth. "Say it again?"

"You came."

"Course I did," said Quinn. "We're friends."

Stella's lips began to move, but nothing came out. She tried again and said, "Ice."

A cup of ice chips sat beside Stella's eyeglasses on a stand next to the gurney. Quinn put the cup to her blistered lips and tilted it so that a few chips slid into her mouth. When he returned the cup to the table he saw a bag at the foot of the gurney containing Stella's clothing and shoes. A white plastic purse rested atop her possessions.

Quinn stroked her hand. "Wilson do this to you, Stella?"

She nodded, her eyes straining as she looked up at Quinn. Quinn took her glasses off the stand and carefully fitted them on her face.

"Better?"

Stella nodded.

"You tell anyone else that he did this?"

Stella shook her head.

"I don't want you to tell anyone else, not yet. Do you understand?"

Stella nodded.

"*Why* did he do this, Stella? Did Jennifer Marshall tell him you'd set up the snatch?"

"She called him," said Stella. "She's out again . . . mad at her parents . . . and she called World."

"All right," said Quinn. "That's enough." The tubes running into her nose were dense now with brown particles, and her hand felt hot beneath his.

"Terry . . ."

"Don't talk. Sue Tracy, remember her? She's on her way down. I want you to talk to *her* when she comes. You need to tell her how to get in touch with your people. Your parents, I mean."

"Home," said Stella.

"Sue's gonna take care of that."

The nurse returned and told Quinn he had to go. Quinn kissed Stella on her bandaged forehead, told her he'd be back to see her later, and walked out from behind the curtain. The cop was waiting for him by the swinging exit doors.

"She say anything?" said the cop.

"Not a word," said Quinn, hitting a wall button and going through a space in the opening doors. He yanked his cell off his belt clip and dialed Strange as he walked. He had Strange's location by the time he left the building and hit fresh air.

Quinn looked ahead. Sue Tracy was coming down the sidewalk toward him, a cigarette in her hand. She hit the smoke and pitched the butt onto the street as they met.

"What happened?" said Tracy.

"Wilson got to her. He worked on her with his hands and a knife."

"Why?"

"From what I can make out? Jennifer Marshall ran away from home again. She called Wilson and hipped him to Stella." Quinn looked around, distracted, nervous as a cat. "Listen, I gotta go."

"Wait a minute." Tracy grabbed his elbow. "I think you need to take a deep breath here."

"Go take a look at her yourself, Sue. See how peaceful it makes you feel."

"All right, it's rough. We've both seen plenty."

"Stay in neutral if that's what works for you."

"You got a history, Terry. Don't make this an excuse to settle some score just because some lowlife looked at you wrong and called you a girl."

"Right. Here's the part where you say, 'We live in two different worlds. Yours is too violent. I don't want to live in your world anymore.' Go ahead and say it, Sue, because I've heard it from women before."

"Bullshit. I'm not giving up, and I'm not looking to walk away. Don't put me down just because I'm worried about you."

Quinn pulled his arm free of her grasp. "Like I said, I gotta bounce."

"Where are you off to?"

"To hook up with Derek. We're working on something important and I can't leave him twisting out there."

"You sure that's where you're going?"

"Look: Stella wants to go home. You need to find her parents. She'll cooperate."

"I know what to do. You don't have to tell me, because I've been doing this for a long time. I hired you, remember?"

"There's a plainclothes in the ER; he'll be looking to talk to you. I didn't give him anything, understand?"

"You don't want me to talk to the police."

"Not yet. You'll know when the time's right."

"Why don't you want me to talk to them now?"

"Take care of Stella," said Quinn.

He put his arms around Tracy and kissed her on her lips. He took in the clean smell of her hair. They broke their embrace, and Tracy stepped back and pointed her finger at Quinn.

"Keep your cell on, Terry. I want to know where you are."

She watched him jog down the sidewalk toward a line of cabs idling near the main entrance of the hospital. She turned and walked into the ER.

Quinn got into the backseat of a purple Ford. The driver was talking on a cell phone and did not turn his head.

"Warder Street in Park View, off Georgia."

The African looked at Quinn in his rearview but kept talking on his cell. He did not touch the transmission arm coming off the steering column.

Quinn flipped open his badge case, reached over the front seat, and held the case in front of the cabby's face.

"Haul ass," said Quinn.

The cabby pulled down on the tree and fed the Ford gas.

⌐

"LYDELL, it's Derek."

"Derek, where you at?"

"Down near my office. Can you hear me?"

"Sure."

Strange sat behind the wheel of his Caprice, parked along the curb on Warder Street, facing east. He was a half block down from the row house where Charles White and, he expected, Garfield Potter and the boy with the cornrows lived. Strange's binoculars hung around his neck.

"Lydell, I wanted to get up with you. I don't think me and Terry are gonna make it to practice tonight."

"Why not?"

"We got a big surveillance thing we're working on. Can't break it; you know how that goes."

"That's a lot of boys for me and Dennis to handle."

"Call Lionel, and Lamar Williams; those two know the drills and the plays as good as we do. If you don't have their phone numbers, call Janine."

"Yeah, okay. But what's up with this surveillance thing? Thought you'd be out talking to Lorenze Wilder's associates today."

"We been doing that, too," said Strange, looking at the empty row house porch. "But nothin' yet."

"Well, *we* might have something."

"Yeah?"

"Woman called in, trying to get some of that reward money. Said she was out late one night, a few nights before the killings. Some male friends of hers was in a crap game got robbed by three young men, over there in Park Morton. One of the young men pulled a gun on one of her friends, man named Ray Boyer. Used it like a hammer and broke Boyer's nose. Woman says the one with the gun matched the description of the artist's drawing on the posters we put up in the neighborhood. And get this: She says the gun was a short-barreled revolver. You know that we've identified one of the murder weapons as a snub-nosed three fifty-seven."

"Could've been a thirty-eight that boy pulled on that crap game. Could've been anything."

"Could've been. But this is too much of a coincidence to leave alone."

"I don't suppose the gunslinger left his name."

"Matter of fact, this knucklehead did say his name. But she can't remember it. Admits she was too intoxicated and up on weed, and scared in the bargain. We're out looking for Ray Boyer right now. He didn't show up to his job today, so we're visiting the bars he likes to go to. Hoping that he'll remember this boy's name. Man's a Vietnam veteran, so I'm thinking he'll be able to identify the caliber of the gun as well."

"Sounds promising."

"Just a feeling, Derek, but it looks to me like we're gonna make an arrest on this today."

"Keep me posted on it, you don't mind. You got my cell number, right?"

"I got it."

"All right, then. Thanks, Lydell."

Strange slipped his cell into its holster on his side. In his rearview, he saw Quinn walking up Warder, two cups of coffee in his hands.

Strange reached over and opened the passenger door. Quinn dropped onto the seat and handed Strange one of the cups.

"Thank you, buddy," said Strange.

"I know you like to sip water on a surveillance."

"Coffee makes me pee."

"But you're gonna need the caffeine to make up for all the food we haven't eaten today."

"I forgot all about it. Not like me to forget being hungry."

Quinn chin-nodded up the street. "Which one is it?"

"Third one down from the corner there. Only one has a porch got nothin' on it. There, see?"

"They show themselves yet?"

"No. But I expect, they got any brains at all, they're staying inside."

"What about the one Lamar saw?"

"Charles White. His Toyota's not out here. Maybe Lamar's right about that boy leaving town." Strange sipped his coffee. "How's that girl, man?"

"Bad," said Quinn.

Quinn described what he had seen, and how he had kept what he knew from the police. Strange told Quinn that he had spoken to Lydell Blue, and that he had kept everything from his friend as well. He told Quinn that the police seemed very close to finding the killers. He told Quinn what he had in mind.

"So you're just giving up on those boys," said Quinn. "No possible hope, ever, is that what you're sayin'?"

"For them? That's right."

"You can call the MPD in now if you want to. End it right here."

"You think that would end it?"

"There's no death penalty in the District, if that's what you mean. But they'd do long time. They'd get twenty-five, thirty years. Maybe on a good day they'd get life."

"And what would that do? Give those boys a bed and three squares a day, when Joe Wilder's lying cold in the ground? Joe's gonna be dead forever, man —"

"Derek, I know."

"Then you're gonna read in the paper how the police solved the murder. The big lie. Can't no murder ever be *solved*. Not unless the victim gonna get out of his grave and walk, breathe in the air. Hug his mother and play ball and grow up to be a man and lie down with a woman . . . live a life, Terry, the way God intended him to. So how you gonna *solve* it so Joe can do that?" Strange shook his head. "I'm not lookin' to solve this one. I'm looking to *re*solve it."

"You telling me, Derek? Or are you trying to convince yourself?"

"A little bit of both, I guess."

"You do this," said Quinn, "you lose everything. You believe in God, Derek, I know you do. How you gonna reconcile this with your faith?"

"Haven't figured that one out yet. But I will."

Quinn nodded slowly. "Well, you're on your own."

"You don't want any part of it, huh?"

"It's your decision," said Quinn. "Anyway, I've got something I've got to do tonight myself."

Strange looked Quinn over carefully. "You're goin' after that pimp."

"I have to."

"It's not just what he did to the girl, is it? That pimp tried to punk you out."

"Like you said: It's a little bit of both."

"Sure it is." Strange smiled sadly. "Shit's older than time, man. Garfield Potter killed Joe Wilder 'cause he thought Joe's uncle disrespected him on a hundred-dollar debt. Now I'm gonna do what I think I have to, my idea of making it right. And all of it started 'cause this boy Potter thought he got took for bad."

Quinn finished his coffee and dropped the cup on the floor. "I gotta go."

"Go ahead, then. But don't forget your gun. It's under the seat there."

"I won't need it."

"Neither will I."

"I better leave it. Can't be carrying it around town now, can I?"

"Plus, you wouldn't feel right, would you, to have any kind of drop on that pimp?"

"That's not it."

"Okay. You need a ride?"

"I'll catch a Metrobus up Georgia. I can get off at Buchanan and pick up my car."

"You gonna hang out at the bus stop, in this neighborhood? At night?"

"I'll be all right."

Strange reached over and shook Quinn's hand. "I'm gonna pray that you will be."

"Keep your cell on," said Quinn, "and I'll do the same with mine. Let's talk later on, all right?"

Strange nodded. "See you on the other side."

Quinn got out of the car and shut the door. Strange eyed him in the rearview, walking down Warder in that cocky way of his, hands in his leather, shoulders squared, going by groups of young men moving about on the sidewalks and gathered on the corners.

Quinn went under a street lamp and passed through its light. Then he was indistinguishable from the others, just another shadow moving through the darkness that had fallen on the streets.

c h a p t e r

28

S TRANGE made a call on his cell. He spoke to the man on the other end of the line for a long while. When their conversation was done, Strange said, "See you then." He hit "end," punched Janine's number into the grid, pressed "talk," and waited to connect. He got Janine on the third ring.

"Baker residence."

"Derek here."

"Where are you?"

"Workin' this Joe Wilder thing. Sittin' in my car."

"*Where?*"

"Out here on the street."

"You're not drinking coffee, are you?"

"I did."

"You know how it runs through you."

Strange found himself smiling at the sound of her voice. "Just wanted to call and make sure Lionel got to practice."

"Lydell came by and got him. Told me to tell you, if we spoke, that they found this guy, Ray something, and picked him up."

"Ray Boyer. He say if Boyer gave him anything?"

"Not yet. Lydell said that Boyer wanted to lawyer up first. Something to do with making sure the paperwork's right so he gets the reward money."

Strange knew now that he didn't have much time.

"Why don't you knock off for the day?" said Janine. "Sounds like the police have this in hand."

"I think I'll stay out some, see what happens."

"Must be getting chilly in that car. And I know you're not lettin' the heat run. You, who's always telling Ron Lattimer that a running car kills a surveillance, what with the exhaust smoke coming out the pipes —"

"You know me too well."

"That I do."

"You asking me to come over and warm myself up?"

"Are you ready to do some serious talking?"

"Not yet," said Strange. "Soon. But I didn't just call about Lionel and practice."

"Well?"

"Wanted to ask you something. My mother used to tell me, You can't trade a bad life for a good. Do you think that's right, Janine?"

"Do I think it's right? I don't know. . . . Where *are* you, Derek? You don't sound right."

"Never mind where I'm at." Strange shifted his weight on the bench seat. "I love you, Janine."

"Us lovin' each other is not the issue, Derek."

"Good bye, baby."

Strange cut the call. He stared up the street at the row house. If he was going to do this, then he had to do it now. He found his notepad beside him, and on the top sheet, the phone number of the house. He punched the numbers into his cell. As he did, he went over in his head what he had planned. It was all risk, a long play. He couldn't waver or stumble now.

The phone rang on the other end. A silhouette moved behind the curtains of the row house window.

"Yeah."

"Garfield Potter?"

"That's right."

"Lorenze Wilder. Joe Wilder. Those names mean anything to you?"

"Who?"

"Lorenze Wilder. Joe Wilder."

"How'd you get my number?"

"Not too hard, once you find out where a person lives. I been followin' you, Garfield."

"Man, who the *fuck* is this?"

"Derek Strange."

"That supposed to mean somethin' to me?"

"If you saw me, you'd remember. I was coachin' the football team that little boy played on. The boy you killed."

"I ain't kill no boy."

"I'm the one you and your partners were crackin' on, callin' me Fred Sanford and shit while I was walking to my car. Y'all were smokin' herb in a beige Caprice. You and a boy with cornrows, and another boy, had a long nose. Remember me now? 'Cause I sure do remember you."

"So?"

Strange heard a crack in Potter's voice.

"I followed Lorenze and the boy the night you killed them. I was responsible for that boy, and I followed. Only, you weren't riding in a beige Caprice that night. It was a white Plymouth with a police package. Isn't that right, Garfield?"

"White Plymouth? That shit was on the news, any motherfucker own a television set gonna know that. You got somethin' serious you want to say, then say it, old-time."

"Maybe *you* want to say something, Garfield. You kill a boy —"

"Told you I ain't killed no kid."

"You kill a *boy*, Garfield, and you got to have somethin' to say." *Save yourself. If you want to live, young man, then now's the time.*

"What, some young nigger dies out here, I'm supposed to cry? I be dyin' young, too, most likely; ain't nobody gonna shed no tears for me."

Strange spoke softly as he closed his eyes. "I want to get paid."

"What? I just told you —"

"I'm tellin' *you*, I was a witness to the murders. I saw the event with my own eyes."

Strange listened to the hiss of dead air. Finally, Potter spoke. "You so sure of what you saw, why ain't you gone to the police? Get your reward money and slither on back into that hole you came out of?"

"Because I can get more from you."

"Why you think that?"

"Drug dealer like you, all that cash you got? Told you, I been followin' you, Potter."

"How much more?"

"Double the ten they're offering. Make it twenty." Strange squinted. "Since you been insulting my intelligence, might as well go ahead and make it twenty-five."

"Ain't even no murder gun no more. And I know you ain't gonna try and play me the fool and claim you got photographs or sumshit like that."

"Not photographs. A videotape. I own an eight-millimeter camera with a three-sixty lens. I was parked a whole block back from that ice-cream shop on Rhode Island, but with that zoom the tape came out clear as day."

"Tape can be doctored. Bullshit like that gets thrown out of court every day. Truth is, you can't prove a thing."

"I can try," said Strange.

More silence. "Aiight, then. Maybe we should hook up and talk."

"I don't want to talk about nothin'. Just bring the money. I'll give you the tape and we will be done."

"Where?"

"I got a house I keep as a rental property; it's unoccupied right now. Figure you're not stupid enough to try somethin' in a residential neighborhood. I got some business I got to take care of first, so it's gonna take me about an hour, hour and a half to get out there."

"Where is it?"

Strange gave Potter the directions. He repeated them slowly so that Potter could write them down.

"You still drivin' that black Cadillac that was parked outside Roosevelt?"

"You do remember me, then."

"You still drivin' it?"

"Yeah."

"I see any kind of police-lookin' vehicles outside that house, I am gone. I don't want to see nothin' but that Caddy, hear?"

"Bring the money, and come with your two partners. I want to keep my eye on all of you at once."

"Ain't but two of us now," said Potter.

"Hour and a half," said Strange. "I'll see you then."

Strange ended the call, ignitioned the Chevy, and put it in gear. He drove quickly up to Buchanan, where he washed his face, changed his shirt, and fed Greco.

Back on the street, Strange walked toward his Brougham. Quinn had parked his car behind the Cadillac earlier that morning. The Chevelle was gone.

❐

THE guns Garfield Potter had bought were a six-shot .38 Special and a .380 Walther, the PPK double action with the seven-shot capacity. The revolver, a blue Armscor with a rubber grip, was for Potter. He stayed away from automatics, fearing they would jam.

Potter checked the load on the .38. He jerked his wrist and snapped the cylinder shut. He had been practicing this action in the mirror just this afternoon.

"You ready, Dirty?"

"Uh-huh," said Little.

He was sitting on the couch, thinkin' on Brianna, how if she was here now how good it'd be to bust it out. He was flyin' like the eagle behind some hydro he'd just smoked, and his eyelids were heavy. He was happy. Hungry, too. He didn't really want to go out, but Garfield did. So there it was.

Little looked down at the automatic he held loosely in his hand. The grip was checkered plastic and had the Walther logo on it, the word written inside a kind of flag, like, looked like it was blowin' in a breeze. The safety was grooved, and there was this thing on the side, like a little sign, showed you when you had put one in the chamber, in case you forgot. Walther, they made a pretty gun.

"Dirty? You with me?"

"Yeah."

"Come on, then," said Potter, fitting his skully onto his head. He picked up two pairs of thin leather gloves off the table, one pair for him and one for Little. He knew Carlton would not think to bring a pair himself. "Let's get this done."

Little got up off the couch and looked in a mirror they had over a table by the stairs. His cornrows were lookin' raggedy and fucked. He wondered if maybe he ought to do those twisties in his hair, the short tips, like he'd seen the fellas around do. Little realized he had been staring at himself for a while and he chuckled. It sounded like a snort.

"Let's go, Dirty."

"Yeah, aiight."

Little got into his leather and holstered the Walther under

his shirt. Potter put his leather on and dropped the .38 in its side pocket. He looked at Little and smiled.

"Damn, boy, you just smoke too *much* of that shit, don't you?"

"It's good to me, D. Wish you had a player in that hooptie you bought, though. We could listen to some beats on the way out the county."

"We'll let Flexx roll on ninety-five point five. Anyway, I be havin' a Lex next time, with the Bose system in it, too."

"You been talkin' about that nice whip for, like, forever, man. When you gonna get it?"

"Soon."

Little and Potter laughed.

"Let's go," said Potter. "We need to take care of this tonight."

"Maybe we'll peep Charles while we're out."

"Coon's just hidin' somewhere, you know this." Potter pulled his car keys from the pocket of his jeans. "We do find him, we gonna down him, too."

Little head-motioned to the TV set, a UPN show playing with the volume up. "Should I turn it off?"

"Nah" said Potter. "We ain't gonna be gone all that long."

They walked from the row house, the laugh track from the sitcom fading as they shut the door behind them.

◘

QUINN did push-ups in his apartment while "Jackson Cage" played loud from his speakers. He did five sets of fifty and stopped when he had broken a sweat and felt the burn in his pecs. When he came out of the shower he dropped a Steve Earle into his player and listened to "The Unrepentant" as he dressed. His blood was up sufficiently now. He could feel his sweat again, cool beneath his flannel shirt.

Quinn slipped his cell into his jeans, put on his leather, and dropped a pair of cuffs into the side pocket. He locked the apartment down and walked out into the night air. A kid on the sidewalk nodded in his direction and Quinn said, "Hey," and kept walking without a pause in his step.

He got under the wheel of the Chevelle and fitted his key to the ignition. Quinn cooked it and headed downtown.

29

THE man at the used-car lot on Blair Road had told Garfield Potter that there might be some white smoke at first, coming out the exhaust pipes of the '88 Ford Tempo he was about to sell him, but not to worry.

"It just needs a good highway run," said the man, some kind of Arab, or a Paki, maybe; Potter couldn't tell one from the other. "Blow the cobwebs out, and it's going be just like new."

Potter knew the man was lying, but the price was right, and anyway, he was lookin' for something wouldn't attract much attention. An '88 Tempo? That was just about as no-attention-gettin' a motherfucker as you could get.

Looking in the rearview, going east on New York Avenue, he could see the white smoke trailing out behind the Ford. Carlton Little had made mention of it, as he always reminded Potter that what they were rolling in was a hoop, but he hadn't said much after that.

Little had turned the radio up loud. Flexx had a set going on PGC, the same list they played over and over every night, their most-requested jams. It had gone from Mystikal to R. Kelly to Erykah Badu since they'd left the house. Little had been kind of bobbing his head up and down, the same way no matter the beats, all the way. Potter didn't bother talkin' to him when he was chronicked out all the way, like he was now.

As he drove down the road, Potter saw a woman outside one of those welfare motels they had on New York. Woman had a boy by the hand and a cigarette hanging out her mouth, and she was leading the kid across the lot. Potter could see the boy's shirt, had one of those Pokémon characters on it, sumshit like that.

Potter had had a shirt with E.T. on the front of it when he was a kid. He was too young to have seen the movie in a theater, but his mother had bought the video for him from the Safeway on Alabama Avenue, and he had just about wore that tape out. He really loved that part where the boy kind of flew up in the sky on his bicycle against that big old moon. For a long time Potter had thought that if he had a special bike like that boy did, he could fly away, too. Until this man who was always hangin' around the apartment laughed at him one night when he talked about it, called him a dumb-ass little kid.

"You ain't flyin' *no* goddamn where," said the man, Potter still remembering his words. "You a project boy, and a project boy is all you will be."

His mother should've said something to that man. Told him to shut his mouth, that her boy could do anything he wanted to do. That he could fly against the moon, even, if he had a mind to. But she hadn't said a thing. Maybe she knew the man was right.

Potter got the Tempo on the Beltway and forced the car up to sixty-five. The new Destiny's Child was on the radio. Little was bobbing his head, kind of staring out through the windshield, his mouth open, his eyes set.

Potter's mother, she had this smell about her, sweet, like

strawberries, somethin' like that. It was these oils she used to wear. He remembered when she used to hold his hand like that woman was holdin' that kid's hand back in that lot. He could close his eyes and recall the way it felt. She had calluses on her palms from work, but her fingers were cushioned, like, sorta like that quilt blanket she'd cover him with at night. Her hand was always warm, like bein' under that blanket was warm, too. And sometimes when he couldn't sleep she'd sit by his bed, smoke a cigarette, and talk to him till he got drowsy. Once in a while, even now, he'd smell cigarette smoke somewhere, maybe it was the same brand she'd smoked, he didn't know, but it would remind him of her, sitting by his bed. When he was a kid and she was there for him, before she fell in love with that pipe. Forgetting she had a kid still needed her love, too.

But fuck it, you know. He wasn't no motherfuckin' kid no more.

"Dirty," said Potter.

"Huh?"

"Read them directions to me, man, tell me where we at."

Little squinted as he picked up the paper in his lap and tried to read Potter's handwriting, nearly illegible, in the dark of the car.

"Take the next exit," he said. "Take the one goes east."

They took the exit and the road off of it, brightly lit at first and then dark where the county had ended the lamps. They went along woods and athletic complexes and communities with gates.

"You ever think of your moms, Dirty?"

"My mother?" said Little. "*I* don't know. I think of my aunt some, 'cause she owes me money." He smiled as he heard the first few notes of a song coming from the radio. "This is that new Toni Braxton joint right here, 'Just be a Man'? I'd be a man to her, she let me."

Potter didn't know why he bothered talking to Carlton. But he figured he'd keep hangin' with him anyhow. He didn't have Dirty, he didn't have no one at all.

"Where we at?" said Potter.

Little looked at the notepaper. "Turn ought to be comin' up, past some church on the right-hand side." Little pointed through the windshield. "There go the church, right up there."

A half mile past the church, Potter made a turn into an ungated, unmarked community of large houses with plenty of space in between them. Many of the houses were dark, but that didn't mean anything. It was a Monday night, and it had gotten late.

"Right turn up there," said Little. "Then a left."

Potter made the first turn. Some light from a corner lamppost, made to look like one of those antique jobs, bled into the car and cast yellow on his face. Then his face was greenish from the light drifting off the dash.

"You know what to do," said Potter, "we get in there."

Potter made the second turn.

Little pushed out his hips, withdrew his Walther from where he had fitted it, and racked the slide.

"Kill Old-time," he said, refitting the gun under his shirt.

"Once we get the video," said Potter, "we'll down him quick. Put a couple in his head and get out."

Little put on his gloves. He held the wheel steady as Potter did the same. They were on a cul-de-sac now that had only three houses set on oversize lots. The first house was dark inside, with only a lamp on over the front door. They passed the second house, completely dark, with two black Mercedes sedans parked in its circular driveway.

"There's the Caddy," said Little, chinning toward the black Brougham parked in the circular drive in front of the last house on the street.

Potter parked the Ford along the curb and killed its engine.

They walked over grass and asphalt, then grass again, as they neared the steps of the brick colonial. The first-floor interior of the house was fully lit. An attached garage with a row of small rectangular windows across the top of its door was lit, too.

Potter and Little stood beneath a portico marking the center of the house. At Potter's gesture, Little rang the doorbell. Through leaded glass, Potter could see the refracted image of a man wearing black coming down a hall. The door opened. The football coach, the one who called himself Strange, stood in the frame.

"Come on in," said Strange.

They stepped into a large foyer. Strange closed the door and stood before them.

Potter licked his lips. "Somethin' you want to say to me?"

"Just wanted to have a look at you."

"You had it. Let's get on about our business."

"You got the money?"

"In my jacket, chief."

"Let me see it."

"When I see the tape."

Strange breathed out slow. "Okay, then. Let's go."

"Hold up. Want to make sure you're not strapped."

Strange spread his black leather jacket and held it open. Little stepped forward and frisked him like he'd seen it done on TV. He nodded to his partner, letting him know that Strange was unarmed.

"Follow me back," said Strange. "I've got a studio in the garage. The tape is back there."

They walked down one of the halls framing the center staircase, leading to a kitchen and then a living area housing an entertainment center and big cushiony furniture.

"Thought you said this house was unoccupied," said Potter.

"I rent it furnished," said Strange over his shoulder.

And it's all high money, too, thought Potter. And then he thought, Somethin' about this setup ain't right.

"What you do to get this?" said Potter, elbowing Little, who was clumsily bumping along by his side, away.

"I own a detective agency," said Strange. "Ninth and Upshur."

"Yeah," said Potter, "but what's your game? I mean, you can't be havin' all this with a square's job."

"I find people," said Strange.

They passed a door that was ajar and kept going, Strange stepping down into a kind of laundry room, then heading for another door and saying, "It's right in here."

"You can't be all *that* good at findin' people," said Potter, "to have all this."

"I found *you*," said Strange, and he opened the door.

Beyond the door was just darkness. Potter stared at the darkness, remembering the garage door and its little windows, remembering the light behind the windows as they'd walked toward the house.

"Dirty," said Potter, and as he reached into his leather for his .38 he heard steps behind him and then felt the press of a gun's muzzle against the soft spot under his ear.

Little was pushed up against a wall, his face smashed into it by a man holding a gun to the back of his head. The man found Little's gun and took it.

Potter didn't move. He felt a hand in his jacket pocket and then the loss of weight there as his revolver was slid out.

"Inside," said the voice behind him, and he was shoved forward.

Strange flicked on a light switch and moved aside as the four of them stepped down into the garage.

Potter saw a big man in a jogging suit with golden-colored eyes, standing with his hands folded in front of him. A young man in a dress suit stood beside him, an automatic in his hand. On the other side of the big man was a boy, no older than twelve, wearing an oversize shirt, tails out. Other than the people inside of it, the garage was empty. A plastic tarp had been spread on its concrete floor.

Potter recognized the big man as Granville Oliver. Everyone in town knew who he was.

Oliver looked over at Strange, still standing in the open doorway.

"All right, then," said Oliver.

Strange was staring at the young boy in the oversize shirt. He hesitated for a moment. Then he stepped back and closed the door.

A row of fluorescent lights, set in a drop ceiling, made a soft buzzing sound overhead.

"You Granville Oliver, right?" said Potter.

Oliver stepped forward with the others. The two who had braced Potter and Little had joined the group. Potter and Little retreated and stopped when their backs touched the cinder-block wall of the garage. One of the men reached out and tore Potter's skully off his head. He threw it to the side.

"What is this?" said Potter, hoping his voice did not sound weak. But he knew that it did. Little's hand touched his for a moment, and it felt electric.

Oliver said nothing.

"Look, you and me ain't got no kinda beef," said Potter. "I been careful to stay out the way of people like you."

The fluorescent lights buzzed steadily.

Potter spread his hands. "Have I been steppin' on your turf down there off Georgia? I mean, you tryin' to build somethin' up there I don't know about? 'Cause we will pack up our shit and move on, that's what you want us to do."

Oliver didn't reply.

Potter smiled. "We can work for you, you want us to." He felt his mouth twitching uncontrollably as he tried to keep the smile.

Oliver's eyes stayed on his. "You want to *work* for me?"

"Sure," said Potter. "Can you put us on?"

"Gimme my gun," said Oliver, and the young boy beside him reached under the tail of his shirt and withdrew an automatic. Oliver took the gun from the boy and jacked a round into the chamber. He raised the automatic and pointed it at Potter's face. Potter saw Oliver's finger slide inside the trigger guard of the gun.

Potter closed his eyes. He heard his friend beside him, sobbing, stuttering, begging. He heard Carlton drop to his knees. He wasn't gonna go out like Dirty. Like some bitch, pleadin' for his life.

Potter peed himself. It felt warm on his thighs. He heard the ones who was about to kill him laughing. He tried to open his eyes, but his eyes were frozen. He thought of his mother. He tried to think of what she looked like. He couldn't bring her up in his mind. He wondered, did it hurt to die.

❐

STRANGE walked through the kitchen toward the stairway hall. He slowed his step and leaned up against an island holding an indoor grill.

Even from here, even with that door to the garage closed, he could hear one of those young men crying. Sounded like he was begging, too. The one with the cornrows, if he had to guess. Strange didn't even know that young man's name.

It wasn't that one, though, or Potter, who had given him pause. It was the young boy standing next to Oliver. The one he'd seen raking leaves the previous day, the one he'd never seen smile. Like he was already dead inside at eleven, twelve years old. Quinn would say that you should never give up on these kids, that it was never too late to try. Well, Strange wasn't sure about Potter and his kind. But he knew it wasn't too late for that boy who'd lost his smile.

Strange walked back the way he'd come. He opened the door leading to the garage without a knock. He stepped down onto the plastic tarp and entered the cold room. All heads turned his way.

Granville Oliver was holding an automatic to the face of Garfield Potter. Saliva threads hung from Potter's open mouth, and his jeans were dark with urine. The smell of his release was strong in the garage. The one with the cornrows was on his knees, tears veining his face. His eyes were red rimmed and blown out wide.

"You ain't got no business back in here," said Oliver.

"Can't let you do this."

Oliver kept his gun on Potter. "You delivered our boys here. Now you're done."

"I thought I was, too," said Strange. "Can I get a minute?"

"You *got* to be playin'."

Strange shook his head. "Look at me, man. Do I look like I'm playin' to you? Gimme one minute. Hear me out."

Oliver stared hard at Strange, and Strange stared back.

"Please," said Strange.

Oliver's shoulders loosened and he lowered the gun. He turned to the man in the suit, Phillip Wood, standing beside him.

"Hold these two right here," said Oliver. To Strange he said, "In my office."

Strange said, "Right."

◗

A phone chirped as Strange sat in the chair before Granville Oliver's desk. Oliver reached into his jacket for his cell.

"That's me," said Strange, slipping his cell from its holster. "Yeah."

"Derek, it's Lydell. We got his statement."

"Whose?"

"Ray Boyer, the craps player. Said the boy who broke his nose did it with a three fifty-seven snub-nose."

"He remember the boy's name?"

"Garfield Potter. They're runnin' the name right now, should have a last-known on him any minute."

"Potter's the one."

"What?"

"I can give you his address," said Strange, looking over Oliver's shoulder through the office window to the street, where Potter had parked. Potter's car was gone. "But he ain't there just yet."

"What're you talkin' about, man?"

"Here it is," said Strange, and he gave Blue the Warder Street address. "It's a row house, got nothin' on the porch. They ought to be there in about a half hour. Both Potter and his partner, the one with the cornrows. Potter's driving a Ford Tempo, blue, late eighties. The third boy, I can't tell you where he is. I believe he's gone."

"How you know all this, Derek?"

"I'll explain it to you later."

"Trust me. You will."

"Get all your available units over there, Ly. Ain't that how they say it on those police shows?"

"Derek —"

"How'd practice go?"

"Say what?"

"Practice. The kids all right?"

"Uh, yeah. The boys all got home safe. Don't be trying to change the subject, man —"

"Good. That's good."

"I'm gonna call you later, Derek."

"I'll be waiting," said Strange.

Strange hit "end," made a one-finger one-moment gesture to Oliver, and punched in Quinn's number. Quinn had turned his cell off. Strange left a message and stared at the dead phone for a moment before sliding it back in place.

"You done?" said Oliver.

"Yeah."

"You know, what you did tonight ain't gonna change a thing in the end. Those two are gonna die. I'll make sure of that."

"But not tonight. Not by my setup. Not in front of that little boy you got workin' for you."

"Yeah, okay. We been all over that already."

"I just want that boy to have some kind of chance."

"So you said. But what would you have done if I had said no?"

"I was counting on reaching your human side. You proved to me that you have one. Thank you for hearin' me out."

Oliver nodded. "Boy's name is Robert Gray. You think I been ruinin' him, huh?"

"Let's just say that I don't see him hookin' up with your enterprise as an opportunity. You and me, we got a difference of opinion on that."

"Strange, you ought to see what kind of conditions he was livin' in when I pulled him out, down there in Stanton Terrace. Wasn't nobody doin' a *god*damn thing for him then."

Strange leaned back and scratched his temple. "This Robert, he play football?"

"What's that?"

"Can he *play*?"

"Boy can jook. He can hit, too." Oliver grinned, looking Strange over. "You're somethin', man. What, you tryin' to save the whole world all at once?"

"Not the *whole* world, no."

"You know, wasn't just my *human side* convinced me to let those boys walk out of here."

"What was it, then?"

"I'm gonna need you someday, Strange. I had one of those, what do you call that, premonitions. Usually, when I get those kinds of feelings, I'm right." Oliver pointed a finger at Strange. "You owe me for what I did for you tonight."

I owe you for more than that, thought Strange.

But he just said, "I do."

Strange drove back to the city in silence. Coming up Georgia Avenue, he tried to reach Quinn again on his cell but got a recording. He passed Buchanan Street and kept driving north, turning right on Quintana and parking the Cadillac in front of Janine's. She let him into her house and told him to have a seat on the living room couch. She joined him a few minutes later with a cold Heineken and a couple of glasses. The two of them talked into the night.

chapter

30

Q U I N N had been parked along the curb for half an hour when
Worldwide Wilson's 400SE came rolling down the street. Quinn
watched the Mercedes glide up in his rearview and he tucked his
chin in and turned his head a little as it passed. The Mercedes
double-parked, flashers on, as the driver's-side window came
down. A woman Quinn recognized, the black whore who'd asked
him for a date the night of the snatch, leaned into the frame. A
minute or so went by, and Wilson stepped out of the car.

He wore his full-length rust-colored leather over a suit. He
wore his matching brimmed hat and his alligator shoes. He
walked toward his row house, and the black whore got under the
wheel of his Mercedes and drove off to find a legal parking spot
for her man's car. Worldwide Wilson moved like a big cat onto the
sidewalk. He went up his steps and entered his house.

Quinn ignitioned the Chevelle and drove down the street,
hooking a left at the next corner, and then another quick left into

the alley. He parked the car in the alley along a brick wall. His headlights illuminated several sets of eyes beneath the Dumpsters. He cut the lights and in their dying moment saw rats moving low across the stones of the alley. He killed the engine and listened to the tick of it under the hood. He counted units and found the row house, lit by a single flood suspended from the roof. He saw a light go on in the sleeper porch on the second floor.

Quinn stepped out of the car and walked fast toward the fire escape. Dim bulbs lit the third-floor hall. He could see the third-floor window, but his long sight was gone, and he could not determine if the window was ajar.

He turned off his cell, got on the fire escape, and began his ascent. He could hear music from behind the wood walls of the sleeper porch as he climbed the iron mesh steps. The music grew louder, and he was grateful for that as he went low along the porch's curtained windows and kept going up. As he neared the third floor he could see the hall window clearly and he could see now that the window was open a crack.

He raised the sash and climbed into the hall. He could feel his sweat, and his blood pumping in his chest. The hall smelled of marijuana, tobacco, and Lysol. Behind one of the doors he heard thrusts and bedsprings, and the sounds of a man reaching his climax, and Quinn went on.

He moved down the hall, his hand sliding along the banister, and at the end of it he looked down the stairs to the second floor. The music, mostly bass, synthesizer, and scratchy guitar, was emanating from below. The music was loud and it echoed in the house. He started down the stairs. The music grew louder with each step he took.

❐

WORLDWIDE Wilson sat on a couch covered in purple velvet, swirling ice in a glass of straight vodka, listening to "Cebu," that bad instrumental jam ending side two of that old Commodores

LP, *Movin' On*. Wilson had owned the vinyl, on the Motown label, for over twenty-five years. He still had all his wax, racked up here in this finished porch, where he liked to kick it when he wasn't at home. At his crib he listened to CDs, but here he kept his records and turntable, and Bang & Olufsen speakers, and his old tube amplifier, made by Marantz. Box had a lotta clean watts to it, the perfect vehicle for his vinyl. You just couldn't beat the bottom sound of those records.

Wilson tapped some ash off his cigarette. He drank down some of the vodka, now that it had chilled some, and let it cool-burn the back of his throat.

Wilson loved his potato vodka. He bought that brand in the frosty white bottle, with the drawing of the bare tree on it, up there at the store on the District line. He was different from all those other brothers, felt they had to drink Courvoisier and Hennessy just because everyone else did, because the white man told you to. Shit was just poison. There was a word for it, even: carcino-somethin'. Gave you cancer, is what the word meant. And the Man pushed that bad shit into the ghetto, through billboards and bus ads and ads in *Ebony* and *Jet*, the same way they pushed death through cigarettes. Well, Wilson did like his tobacco, but the point was, he wasn't buyin' into all that, 'cause he was his own man all the way. His brother, who read a lot, had explained this all to him once after they'd smoked some Hawaiian at his mother's house on Christmas Day. So he wasn't into no con-yak. But he did love his expensive vodka. He'd gotten a taste for it overseas.

This room was nice. He'd insulated the room and put radiator heat in it for the wintertime. He had it carpeted with a remnant, hung some Africa-style prints he'd picked up at a flea market on the wall, and bought those thick curtains for the windows. The curtains gave him privacy and made him feel as if he was in his own private club. He'd brought in the furniture and even had a chandelier, had a couple of bulbs missing but it looked good, up in this motherfucker. You could bring a young country-type bitch up here, straight off the bus, and impress her in this room. Girl got a look at all this, you could turn her out quick.

Wilson put his feet up on the table and dragged on his cigarette. He looked at the windows and thought he saw some kind of shadow pass out there beyond the curtains. He had another sip of vodka, moved his head some to the sounds coming from the stereo, and finished his cigarette.

Wilson got off the couch, went to the windows, and spread the curtains. He looked out, down the fire escape, and then up to the third floor. Wasn't nothin' out there he could see. But he thought he'd go out to the hall for a minute, have a look out there. Never did hurt to double-check.

❏

QUINN had reached the bottom of the stairs and was standing on the landing when the door to the sleeper porch swung open at the end of the hall. Worldwide Wilson stood there, a drink in his hand, wearing a light green suit over a forest green shirt and tie. A look of perplexity creased his face. Then a smile of recognition broke upon it. His chuckle was long and low.

"Damn if it ain't Theresa Bickle," said Wilson. "You come to knock me for another woman? That why you came back? 'Cause I am fresh out of young white girls, *Theresa*."

Quinn moved quickly down the hall.

"Guess you ran into your friend Stella. Shame what that bitch made me do to her, huh?"

Quinn broke into a run.

"Now what?" said Wilson. "You gonna rush me now, little man?"

Quinn's stride reached a sprint, and he put his head down as Wilson dropped the glass and tried to reach into his jacket pocket. Quinn hit him low, wrapping his arms around Wilson and locking his fingers behind his back, and both of them went through the open door and into the room.

Quinn ran Wilson through the room and slammed him against the window. The window shattered behind the curtains, and shards of glass fell as Quinn whipped Wilson around, still holding on. Wilson was laughing. Quinn ran him into a stand holding a turntable, and as they toppled over the stand, Quinn's hands separating, there was the rip of needle over vinyl and the music that was pounding in their heads suddenly came to an end.

Quinn and Wilson stood up, six feet apart. Quinn saw blood on his hands. The glass from the window had opened up one of them or both of them. He didn't know which.

"You fucked up my box," said Wilson, incredulous.

"Let's go," said Quinn with a hand gesture, seeing the slice along his thumb now, seeing that it was bleeding freely and that the slice was deep.

Wilson stepped in. Quinn put his weight on his back foot, tucked his elbows into his gut, and covered his face with his fists. He took Wilson's first blows like that, and the punches moved him back and the pain of them surprised him. He took one in the side and grunted, losing his wind, and Wilson laughed and hit him in the same spot again. Quinn dropped his guard. Wilson hit him in the jaw, and the blow knocked Quinn off his feet. He rolled and came up standing. He moved his jaw, and the pain was a needle through his head. Wilson smiled, and his gold tooth caught the glow off the chandelier.

Quinn charged in. Wilson jabbed at his face as he advanced, but Quinn swatted it off and threw a right. The right glanced off Wilson's cheek, and as Wilson moved a hand up to fend off another blow, Quinn put one in his gut and buried it there. Wilson jacked forward, then squared himself straight. They traded body blows. Quinn threw a vicious uppercut in the space between Wilson's hands and connected square to Wilson's chin. Wilson's eyes rolled up, and Quinn hit him there again. Wilson staggered back. He shook the cobwebs out and kicked the table violently away from the couch. He wasn't smiling anymore.

There was a large space, cleared now, in the middle of the room. They circled the space and met in its center.

Wilson stepped on Quinn's foot and punched through his guard. Quinn's neck snapped back as he took the short right. He tasted the blood flowing over his upper lip, and Wilson threw the same jab. Quinn blocked it with his palm, quickly wrapped his arms around Wilson, and locked his hands behind him once again. Wilson ran him straight into a wall. Quinn felt a picture frame splinter behind his back. He reared back and butted his forehead into Wilson's nose. Wilson's blood mingled with his, and Quinn heard an animal sound that was his own and he butted Wilson again. Tears welled in Wilson's eyes, and Quinn released him. They both stepped back and tried to breathe.

Below his nose, blood covered Wilson's face. His blood was brown on his green suit. Quinn's shirt was slick with blood.

"Enough," said Wilson, reaching into his suit pocket. His hand emerged with a pearl-handled knife, and its blade flicked opened as Wilson walked toward Quinn. The scream of a woman now pierced the room.

Wilson's arm whipped forward. The blade winked in the light, and Quinn tried to move out of its arc, but as he felt the impact, like a punch, he knew that he had failed. Fresh blood warmed his face.

Wilson turned the handle in his hand so that the blade revolved and he tried to make a backswing, but Quinn caught his forearm and held it. Wilson's legs were spread wide, and Quinn kicked him in the balls, aiming for three feet behind them and following through. Wilson coughed. Quinn felt the tension go out of Wilson's forearm, twisted the arm behind him, and kicked Wilson's right leg out from under him at the shin. Wilson went down on one knee, and Quinn got his wrist and bent it forward until Wilson released the knife. The knife dropped to the carpet. Quinn put everything he had into it and kicked Wilson in the face. There was a wet cracking sound. Wilson's body jerked up, and blood arced up with it. Wilson fell on his side and then onto his back, where he remained. His face was featureless and ruined.

Quinn picked up the knife. He folded the blade into its handle and pocketed it. He dragged Wilson to the radiator and cuffed him to one of its tubes.

A woman was screaming obscenities at Quinn. She was standing in the doorway, ass-out in a short skirt and fishnets, but not attempting to enter the room.

Quinn reached into his jeans for his cell. He sat on the purple couch, squinting at the keyboard of the cell, and with a shaky hand punched in 911. He asked for squad cars and an ambulance and gave the dispatcher his general address. He ended the call and tried to think of Strange's number. He tried to think of Sue's. He couldn't bring either of their numbers to mind.

He breathed slowly. He knew that he was still bleeding because he could feel it going down his neck. He could feel the wetness of it on his upper chest and behind his collar. He wanted to bring his heart rate down to slow the flow of blood. The air was full on his wounds now, and the pain had ratcheted. He stared at the ripped curtains and the broken glass, and after a while he heard sirens and an odd sound coming from his lips.

Wilson said something from across the room. It was hard to hear him because the woman was still alternately sobbing and berating Quinn.

"What?" said Quinn.

"Somethin' funny?" said Wilson.

"Why?"

"You *laughin'*."

"Was I?" said Quinn.

It didn't surprise him. It didn't scare him or make him feel any way at all. Quinn let his head drop back to the couch. He closed his eyes.

31

O<small>N</small> the stoops of the row houses of Buchanan Street, the jack-o'-lanterns of Halloween had begun to wilt. Time and the weather had mutated the faces carved into the pumpkins, and hungry squirrels had mutilated their features. Gloves and scarves had come out of the closets, and lawn mowers had been drained of gas and put away in basements and sheds. Colors had exploded brilliantly upon leaves, then the leaves had dried and gone toward brown. One holiday was done and another was approaching. Thanksgiving was just a week away.

Strange drove his Cadillac up his block, waving to an old woman named Katherine who was out in a heavy sweater, slowly raking her small square of yard. Katherine had been an elementary school teacher in D.C. for her entire career, put two sons and a daughter through college, and had recently lost a grandson to the streets. Strange had been knowing that woman for almost thirty years.

Strange hooked a right on Georgia Avenue. He looked in his shoebox of tapes and slipped an old Stylistics mix into the deck. Bell and Creed's "People Make the World Go Round" began with a wintry prologue, Russell Thompkins Jr.'s incomparable vocal filling the car. As Strange drove south on Georgia he softly sang along. At a stoplight near Iowa, he noticed a flyer with the likenesses of Garfield Potter, Carlton Little, and Charles White still stapled to a telephone pole. By now, most of those flyers had been torn down.

Potter and Little had been arrested at their house on Warder Street without incident. They had been arraigned and were now incarcerated in the D.C. Jail, awaiting trial. The trial would not come for another six months. The whereabouts of the missing suspect, Charles White, would continue to be a source of speculation for the local media from time to time. A year and a half later, White's identity would surface in connection with another murder charge outside of New Orleans. White would eventually be shanked to death, a triangle of Plexiglas to the neck, in the showers of Angola prison. The story would only warrant a paragraph in the *Washington Post,* as would the violent fates of Potter and Little. As for Joe Wilder, the memorial T-shirts bearing his face had been discarded or used for rags by then. For most metropolitan-area residents, Wilder's name had been forgotten. "Another statistic." That's what hardened Washingtonians called kids like him. One name in thousands on a list.

Strange parked on 9th and locked the Brougham down. He walked by the barber shop, where the cutter named Rodel stood in the doorway, pulling on a Newport.

"How's it goin', big man?"

"It's all good."

"Looks like you could use a touch-up."

"I'll be by."

He went down the sidewalk and looked up at the logo on the sign hung over his place: Strange Investigations. There were a few dirt streaks on the light box, going across the magnifying glass. He'd have to get Lamar on that today.

Strange was buzzed into his storefront business. Janine was on her computer, her eyes locked on the screen. Ron Lattimer sat behind his desk, a porkpie hat angled cockily on his head. The color of the hat picked up the brown horizontals of his hand-painted tie. Strange stopped by his desk and listened to Lattimer's musical selection for the day, a familiar-sounding horn against a slamming rhythm section.

"Boss."

"Ron. This here is Miles, right?"

Lattimer looked up and nodded. *"Doo-Bop."*

"See, I'm not all that out of touch." Strange looked at the paperwork on Lattimer's desk. "You finishin' up on that Thirty-five Hundred Crew thing?"

"I'll be delivering the whole package to the attorneys next week. Major receivables on this one, boss."

"Nice work."

"By the way, Sears phoned in. They said your suit's been altered and you can pick it up any time."

"Funny."

"Serious business. The cleaner down the street called, said your suit and shirts are done."

"Thank you. I got a wedding to go to this weekend. You remember George Hastings, don't you? His little girl's."

"The dress I'm wearing is down there, too, Derek," said Janine, not taking her eyes off the screen. "Could you pick it up for me?"

"Sure."

"You don't mind my saying so," said Lattimer, "you goin' to a wedding, you *ought* to do something about your natural."

"Yeah," said Strange, patting his head. "I do need to get correct."

Strange passed Quinn's desk, littered with old papers and gum wrappers, and stopped at Janine's.

"Any messages?"

"No. You've got an appointment down at the jail, though."

"I'm on my way. Just stopped in to check up on y'all."

"We're doing fine."

"You comin' to the game this afternoon? It's a playoff game, y'know. Second round."

Janine's eyes broke from her screen, and she leaned back in her seat. "I'll be there if you want me to."

"I do."

"I was thinking I'd bring Lionel."

"Perfect."

Janine reached into her desk drawer and removed a PayDay bar. She handed it to Strange.

"In case you're too busy for lunch today."

Strange looked at the wrapper and the little red heart Janine had drawn above the logo. He glanced over at Ron, busy with his work, and back to Janine. He lowered his voice and said, "Thank you, baby."

Janine's eyes smiled. Strange went back to his office and closed the door.

Lamar Williams was behind Strange's desk, reaching for the wastebasket as Strange walked in. Strange came around and took a seat as Lamar stepped aside. Lamar stood behind the chair, looking over Strange's shoulder as he logged on to his computer.

"You getting into that People Finder thing?" said Lamar.

"Was just gonna check my e-mails before I go off to an appointment. Why, you want to know how to use the program?"

"I already know a little. Janine and Ron been showin' me some."

"You want to know more, I'll sit with you sometime. You and me'll get deep into it, you want."

"I wouldn't mind."

Strange swiveled his chair so that he faced Lamar. "You know, Lamar, Ron's not gonna be here forever. I know this. I mean, good people don't stay on in a small business like this one, and a fair boss wouldn't expect them to. I'm gonna need some young man to replace him someday."

"Ron's a pro."

"Yeah, but when he first came here, he was green."

"He had a college degree, though," said Lamar. "I'm strugglin' to get my high school paper."

"You'll get it," said Strange. "And we get you goin' in night school, you'll get the other, too. But I'm not gonna lie to you; it's gonna take a lot of hard work. Years of it, you understand what I'm tellin' you?"

"Yes."

"Anyway, I'm here for you, you want to talk about it some more."

"Thank you."

"Ain't no thing. You coming to the game?"

"I'll be there."

Lamar walked toward the door, the wastebasket in his hand.

"Lamar."

"Yeah," he said, turning.

"The sign out front."

"I know. I was fixin' to get the ladder soon as I emptied this here."

"All right, then."

"Aiight."

Strange watched him go. He picked up the PayDay bar he had placed on his desk. He stared at it for a while, and then he shut down his computer and walked out of his office. He stopped in front of Janine's desk.

"I was wondering," said Strange, "if Lionel couldn't just take your car home after the game. I thought, if you wanted to, you and me could go for a little ride."

"That would be good," said Janine.

"I'll see you up at the field," said Strange.

❏

STRANGE drove down to the D.C. Jail at 1901 D Street in Southeast. He parked on the street and read over the notes he had taken from the news stories he had researched on the Net.

Granville Oliver had recently been arrested and charged in one of the most highly publicized local criminal cases in recent history. He had fallen when Phillip Wood, his top lieutenant, was arrested for murder on an anonymous tip. The murder gun had been found, and Wood was charged accordingly. He had pleaded out and agreed to testify against Oliver on related charges. It was exactly what Oliver had predicted Wood would do when he and Strange had first met.

Oliver had been hit with several federal charges, including the running of a large-scale drug operation and racketeering-related murder. At a recent press conference, broadcast on all the local stations, the attorney general and the U.S. attorney had jointly announced that they would aggressively seek the death penalty in the case. Though the citizens of D.C. had gone to the voting booths and overwhelmingly opposed capital punishment, the Feds were looking to make an example of Granville Oliver and send him to the federal death chamber in Indiana.

Strange closed his notebook and walked to the facility.

He checked in and spent a long half hour in the waiting room. He was then led to the interview room, subdivided by Plexiglas partitions into several semiprivate spaces. There were two other meetings being conducted in the room between lawyers and their clients. Strange had a seat at a legal table across from Granville Oliver.

Oliver wore the standard-issue orange jumpsuit of the jail. His hands were cuffed and his feet were manacled. Behind a window, a guard sat in a darkened booth, watching the room.

Oliver nodded at Strange. "Thanks for comin' in."

"No problem. Can we talk here?"

"'Bout the only place we can talk."

"They treating you all right?"

"All right?" Oliver snorted. "They let me out of my cell one hour for every forty-eight. I'm down in Special Management, what they call the Hole. Place they put the high-profile offenders. You're gonna like this, Strange: Guess who else they got down there with me."

"Who?"

"Garfield Potter and Carlton Little. Oh, I don't see 'em or nothin' like that. They're in deep lockup, just like me. But we're down there together, just the same."

"You've got more to worry about right now than them."

"True." Oliver leaned forward. "Reason I'm telling you is, I got contacts all over. Last couple of years I made friends with some El Ryukens. You know about them, right? They claim to be descended from the Moors. Now, I don't know about all that. What I do know is, these are about the baddest motherfuckers walkin' the face of this earth. They fear nothing and take shit from no man. They got people everywhere, and like I say, me and them are friends. Wherever Potter and Little go, whatever prison they get sent to? They will be got."

"You don't need to tell me about it, Granville."

"Just thought you'd like to know."

Strange shifted his position in his chair. "Say why you called me here."

"I want to hire you, Strange."

"To do what?"

"To work with my lawyers. I got two of the best black attorneys in this city."

"Ives and Colby. I read the papers."

"They're going to need a private detective to help build my case against the government's. It's routine, but this case is anything but."

"I know how it works. I do this sort of thing regularly."

"I'm sure you do. But this here ain't the usual kind of drama. It's life and death. And I'll only have a black man working on my case. You do good work, so there it is. What those lawyers are gonna need is some conflicting testimony to the testimony the government is gonna get out of Phillip Wood."

"In a general sense, what's he saying?"

"I'll tell you specifically. He's gonna get up on the stand and say that I ordered the hit on my uncle. That I gave Phil the order directly, and he carried it out."

"Did you?"

Oliver shrugged. "What difference does it make?"

"None, I guess."

Oliver turned his head and stared at one of the room's blank white walls as if it were a window to the outside world. "They got Phil next door, you know that? In the Correctional Treatment Facility. He's in one of those low-number cells, like CB-four, CB-five, sumshit like that. The special cells they got reserved for the snitches. Phil got punked out the first stretch he did. Got ass-raped like a motherfucker, and he can't do no more prison. That's what all this is about. Course, he could be got the way Potter and Little gonna be got. But that would take some time, and time is something I do not have."

"Told you I don't need to know about that."

"Fine. But will you help me?"

Strange didn't answer.

"You wouldn't want to sit back and watch someone kill me, would you, Strange?"

"No."

"Course not. But they got me on these RICO charges, and that's what they aim to do. You remember that photo I showed you, that promo shot I did for my new record, with me holding the guns? The prosecution's gonna use that in court against me. You know why? Do you know why they picked *me* to execute, the only death penalty case in the District in years, instead of all the other killers they got in D.C.? Well, that picture says it all. They got a picture of a strong, proud, I-don't-give-a-good-fuck-about-nothin' black man holding a gun. America's worst nightmare, Strange. They can *sell* my execution to the public, and ain't nobody gonna lose a wink of sleep over it. 'Cause it's just a nigger who's been out here killin' other niggers. To America, it is no loss."

Strange said nothing. He held Oliver's stare.

"And now," said Oliver, "the attorney general wants to help me right into that chamber where they're gonna give me that lethal injection. She and the government gonna *help* me now. Wasn't no government lookin' to help me when I was a project kid. Wasn't no government lookin' to help *me* when I walked through my fucked-up neighborhood on the way to my fucked-up schools. Where were they then? Now they're gonna come into my life and *help me*. Little bit late for that, don't you think?"

"You had it rough," said Strange, "like a whole lot of kids. I'm not gonna deny you that. But you made your own bed, too."

"I did. Can't say I'm ashamed of it, either." Oliver closed his eyes slowly, then opened them again. "Will you work for me?"

"Have your lawyers call my office," said Strange.

Strange signaled the guard. He left Oliver sitting at the table in chains.

❐

"How *y'all feel?*"
"*Fired up!*"
"*How y'all feel?*"
"*Fired up!*"
"*Breakdown.*"
"*Whoo!*"
"*Breakdown.*"
"*Whoo!*"
"*Breakdown.*"
"*Whoo!*"

The Petworth Panthers had formed a circle beside the Roosevelt field. Prince and Dante Morris were in the center of the circle, leading the Pee Wees in calisthenics. Strange and Blue and Dennis Arrington stood together in conference nearby, going over the roster and positions. Lamar and Lionel tossed a football to each other on the sky blue track.

In the stands, Janine sat with the usual small but vocal group of parents and guardians. Among them were the parents and guardians rooting for the opposing team, the Anacostia Royals.

Arrington noticed a white man and white woman walking slowly across the field, the woman's arm through the man's, where two refs stood conferring at the fifty-yard line. Arrington nudged Strange, who looked across the field and smiled.

"Terry," said Strange, shaking Quinn's hand as he arrived. "Sue."

"Hey, Derek," said Sue Tracy, pulling an errant strand of blond away from her face.

"Runnin' a little late, aren't you?" said Strange.

"Had a meeting with my attorney," said Quinn. His cheek was bandaged. His jaw line was streaked yellow, the bruise there nearly faded away.

"They're not gonna drop the charge?" said Strange.

"Assault with intent," said Quinn, nodding. "They got to charge me with something, right?"

"Well," said Strange, a light in his eyes, "wasn't like Wilson came to your apartment and kicked *your* ass."

"Right," said Quinn. "But with Stella's testimony, he's gonna do some time."

"Soon as they take those straws out his nose and rewire his jaw."

"It'll keep him off the stroll for a while, anyway. As for me, my lawyer says, I get sentenced at all, it'll be suspended."

"The authorities don't want no one mistaking you for a hero."

"I'm no hero," said Quinn. "I got a temper on me, is all."

"You think so?" said Strange. He nodded to Quinn's cheek. "Still need that bandage, huh?"

"All these scars, I look like Frankenstein." Quinn grinned, looking ten years older than Strange had ever seen him look before. "I don't want to scare the kids."

"Bring it in!" said Blue, and the teams ended their six-inches drill and jogged over to their coaches, where they took a knee.

"Glad you could make it," said Arrington, looking Quinn over as they met the boys.

"I'm like you," said Quinn. "I wouldn't miss it."

"Just doing God's work," said Arrington, and he shook Quinn's hand.

Quinn and Blue went over positions and told the boys what they expected of them. Arrington led them in a prayer, and Strange stepped in to give them a short talk as Dante, Prince, and Rico, the designated captains, went out to the center of the field.

"Protect your brother," said Strange. "Protect your brother."

The game began, and from the start the contest was fierce. Many times when one of the black teams from D.C. played a primarily white suburban team, the contest was over before the first whistle. White boys taught by their parents, indirectly or directly, to fear black boys sometimes gave up and lay down the moment they saw black players running onto the field. That fear of the unknown was the seed of racism itself.

But this was not the case here. Today there were two teams from the inner city, a Northwest-Southeast thing, kids battling not for trophies but for neighborhood pride. You could see it in the charging style of play, in the hard eyes of the defenders, the way it took three kids to bring one kid down. And you could hear it in the ramlike clash of the pads, echoing in the bowl of Roosevelt's field. By halftime, Strange knew that the game would be decided not by one big play, but by one fatal mistake. With the score tied in the fourth quarter, with the Petworth Panthers controlling the ball and threatening on their own twenty, that was exactly how it went down.

On one, Prince snapped the ball to Dante Morris, who handed off to Rico, a simple Thirty-two play, a halfback run to the two-hole. The Petworth linemen made their blocks and cleared an opening. But Rico positioned his hands wrong for the handoff and bobbled the ball as he tried to hit the hole. He ran past the ball, leaving it in the air, and the fumble was recovered by Anacostia. The play broke the Panthers' spirit. It took only six running plays for Anacostia to score a touchdown and win the game.

At the whistle, the boys formed a line at center field and congratulated their opponents. To their counterparts, the coaches did the same.

"Take a knee!" said Lydell Blue.

The boys formed a tight group, the parents and guardians, along with Lamar, Lionel, Janine, and Sue Tracy, standing nearby. Blue looked at Arrington, and at Quinn, visibly upset. Quinn chinned in the direction of Strange. Strange stepped up to address the boys.

He looked down into their faces. Turf was embedded in their cages, and some of their helmets were streaked with blue, the color of Anacostia's helmets. Dante was staring at the ground, Prince on one knee beside him. Rico was crying freely, looking away.

"All right," said Strange. "We lost. We lost this one game. But we didn't lose, not really. You don't have to be ashamed about anything, understand? Not a thing. Look at me, Rico. Son, *look* at me."

Rico's eyes met Strange's.

"You can hold your head up, young man. You made an error, and you think it cost us the game. But if it wasn't for your running out there, the courage and the skill you showed, we wouldn't have even been *in* this game. That goes for all a y'all."

Strange looked down at the boys, trying to look at each and every one of them, holding his gaze on them individually, before moving on.

"We had a tough season. In more ways than one, it was so tough. You lost one of your fellow warriors, a true brother. And still you went on. What I'm trying to tell you is, every so often, every day, you are going to lose. Nobody is going to give you anything out here, and you will be knocked down. But you got to stand back up again and keep moving forward. That's what life is. Picking yourself up and living to fight, and win, another day. And you have done that. You've shown me what kind of strong character you have, time and time again."

Strange looked over at Lionel. "You know, I never did have a son of my own. But I know what it is to love one like he was mine."

Strange's eyes caught Janine's as he returned his attention to the team kneeling before him.

"You *are* like my own."

Rico ran the back of his hand over his face. Dante held his chin up, and Prince managed a smile.

"I am so proud of you boys," said Strange.

❐

STRANGE left Prince, Lamar, and Janine sitting in his Cadillac, said good-bye to Blue and Arrington, and walked toward Quinn, who was beside Sue Tracy, leaning on his Chevelle. Leaves blew across Roosevelt's parking lot, pushed by a cool late-afternoon wind that had come in out of the north.

Strange greeted Tracy and kissed her on the cheek. "Sorry I didn't get to talk to you much today."

"You had your hands full," said Tracy.

"So," said Strange. "You gonna throw us any more work?"

"I had the impression," said Tracy, "you didn't want to get involved with this prostitution thing."

Strange looked at Quinn, back at Tracy. "Yeah, well, I had some personal issues I had to take care of with regards to that subject. I believe I've got it worked out."

"There's always work," said Tracy. "We did get Stella back to her home in Pittsburgh. We'll see how long that lasts."

"What about the one you snatched away from Wilson?" said Strange.

"Jennifer Marshall. She left home again, and she's missing. So far, she hasn't turned up."

"Gotta make you wonder sometimes, why you keep trying," said Strange.

"Like you told the kids," said Tracy. "Live to fight another day."

"We're getting a beer, Derek," said Quinn. "You and Janine want to join us?"

"Thank you," said Strange. "But I need to get up with her alone on something, you don't mind."

"Some other time."

Strange shook Quinn's hand. "It was a good season, Terry. Thanks for all your help."

"We did the best we could."

"I'll call you tomorrow. Looks like I'm picking up a big case, and I might need your help. You gonna be at the bookstore?"

"I'll be there," said Quinn.

They watched Strange cross the lot and climb into his Brougham.

"I told Karen, the first time we met him," said Tracy, "that he was gonna work out fine."

Quinn put his arms around Tracy, drew her in, and kissed her on the mouth. He held the kiss, then pulled back and touched her cheek.

"What was that for?" said Tracy.

"For being here," said Quinn. "For sticking around."

❏

AFTER dropping Prince and Lamar, Strange stopped by Buchanan, going into his house to pick up Greco while Janine waited in the car. They drove up to Missouri Avenue, turned left, and continued on to Military Road. Strange parked in a small lot on the eastern edge of Rock Creek Park.

Strange leashed Greco and the three of them walked onto the Valley Trail, up a rise along the creek. Strange held Janine's arm and told her about his meeting with Granville Oliver while Greco ran the woods through bars of light. They returned to the car as the weak November sun dropped behind the trees. Greco got onto his red pillow in the backseat and fell asleep.

Strange kept the power on in the car so they could listen to music. He played some seventies soul, and kept it low.

"You going to take the Oliver case?" said Janine.

"I am," said Strange.

"He represents most everything you're against."

"I know he does. But I owe him."

"For what he did with Potter and them?"

"Not just that. The way I see it, most all the problems we got out here, it's got to do with a few simple things. There's straight-up racism, ain't no gettin' around it, it goes back hundreds of years. And the straight line connected to that is poverty. Whatever you want to say about that, these are elements that have been out of our hands. But the last thing, taking responsibility for your own, this is something we have the power to do something about. I see it every day and I'm convinced. Kids living with these disadvantages already, they need parents, *two* parents, to guide them. Granville Oliver was a kid once, too."

Strange stared through the windshield at the darkening landscape. "What I'm saying is, Oliver, he came out of the gate three steps behind. His mother was a junkie. He never did know his father. And I had something to do with that, Janine."

"What are you talking about?"

"I knew the man," said Strange. "I killed his father, thirty-two years ago."

Strange told Janine about his life in the 1960s. He told her about his mother and father, and brother. He recounted his year as a uniformed cop on the streets of D.C., and the fires of April 1968. When he was done, gray had settled on the park.

Strange pushed a cassette tape into the deck. The first quiet notes of Al Green's "Simply Beautiful" came forward.

"Terry gave me this record," said Strange. "This here has got to be the prettiest song Al ever recorded."

"It's nice," said Janine, slipping her hand into Strange's.

"So anyway, that's my story."

"That's why you brought me here?"

"Well, there's this, too." Strange pulled a small green jewelry box from his leather and handed it to Janine. "Go on, take a look at it. It's for you."

Janine opened the box. A thin gold ring sat inside, a diamond in its center. At Strange's gesture, she removed the ring and tried it on.

"It was my mother's," said Strange. "Gonna be a little big for you, but we can fix that."

"You planning to ask me something, Derek?"

Strange turned to face her. "Please marry me, Janine. Lionel needs a father. And I need you."

Janine squeezed his hand, answering with her eyes. They kissed.

Strange kept her hand in his. They sat there quietly in the Cadillac, listening to the song. Strange thought of Janine and of her heart. He thought of Joe Wilder, who had fallen, and of all the kids who were still standing. Outside the windows of the car, the last leaves of autumn drifted down in the dusk.

Deep fall had come to the city. It was Strange's favorite time of year in D.C.

Reading Group Guide

HELL
TO
PAY

A Novel by

GEORGE P. PELECANOS

From a conversation
with George P. Pelecanos

Walker Lamond talks with the author of *Right As Rain*
for *Stop Smiling* magazine

*Basketball comes up a lot in your books, usually as a kind of respite from
the violence. What is it about the sport that appeals to you so much?*

It's a meritocracy, for one thing. It doesn't matter who your father
is. If you can't play, you can't play — you gotta sit on the sidelines
and watch. Everybody is on an equal footing. It doesn't matter
where you came from, what neighborhood or who your daddy is.

*Did you grow up looking for those pickup games like the characters in
your books?*

Yeah. We'd go into the city and try, whether it was Candy Cane
City or Hamilton Rec — just driving around with your boys and
seeing what's going on. There wasn't anything else to do. I mean,
you came over today and my kid is downstairs with his friend
playing video games. That wasn't there. There were three channels on TV — four if you count Channel 20, UHF. You weren't
going to sit around. So you played basketball. I'm not trying to be
like Jack Armstrong, the all-American boy, or something. We
were smoking herb, too, when we were playing, or you'd take a
break and somebody had beer or whatever.

Where were the baddest games in town?

On this side, Candy Cane City was pretty good. That's where it
got kind of serious and you played for push-ups. A lot of times

that was black against white. Your group would go in there and call winners. Nobody wanted to do push-ups in front of the other guys. That's pretty demoralizing.

Your books about Washington span from the thirties to the present. What do you think was D.C.'s golden era?

It depends on who you're talking to. You talk to people who can remember: If you talk to my mom, she'll tell you about the glory of Washington when people used to be down on F Street dressed up in overcoats and fedoras, looking at the Christmas displays in the windows at Woodies. At the same time you had Washington's Harlem on 7th Street, and those people were decked out to the nines. There was this idea from certain people that blacks were in their own world and doing better, which is not true. We had some really bad slums and alley dwellings here at the same time.

If you ask me, I'll say the seventies, because it was my time, it was my teenage years, and I just thought everything was so cool down in the city. And it was. Nobody will be able to convince me otherwise. You take all the emotion out of it, and I have to say that when I go down to Shaw now — what I still call Shaw — that's the dream realized. You see people of all colors and economic backgrounds interacting, living together. I have friends who call me when they're down there and they'll say, "Hey, man, this is the way it's supposed to be. We finally got here." So I think now is a golden era.

When you see the new Shaw, is part of you nervous that, for example, Ben's Chili Bowl is becoming just a tourist attraction? I mean, if crime leaves D.C., it's good for the city, but not great for a crime writer, right?

Yeah, but that's cool. I'm happy to be out of the business of D.C. crime fiction. I really am. I don't know where I'm going with this stuff anymore. When I see that Ben's is packed with people and it's not just black people anymore — it's tourists and everyone like that — the only thing I'm thinking is, "Man, there are a lot more jobs for people in this place, and owners Virginia and Ben and all those people are going to make more money, and they're going to pass it on to their employees."

Walker Lamond's conversation with George P. Pelecanos originally appeared in the issue of *Stop Smiling* dated November 21, 2008. The interview can be read in its entirety at www.stopsmilingonline.com. Reprinted with permission.

Question and topics for discussion

1. Why do you think Derek Strange feels that he's not "right" for Janine and her son, Lionel?

2. Why does Terry Quinn feel as if he has accomplished nothing, even after rescuing Jennifer?

3. When Jennifer runs away from home and returns to prostitution later in the novel, how does Quinn's position on taking runaways off the streets change?

4. What is the point Oliver is making when he says, "And it begets violence. Poor black kids see the same television commercials white boys and white girls see out in the suburbs. They're showed, all their young lives, all the things they should be striving to acquire. But how they gonna get these things, huh?"

5. Why does Derek Strange take up the investigation of Joe Wilder's death even though he knows that the police are working on it?

6. Is Strange's decision to go after Little and Garfield Potter motivated by retribution or justice?

7. Oliver spares Little and Potter's lives, despite their having taken his son's life away. Why does he let them walk?

8. Why doesn't Quinn want the police to be informed about what Stella had told him?

9. What does Derek Strange believe is the seed of racism? Do you agree with him?

10. What is Strange's solution to the racism that goes back so many years? What does *Hell to Pay* suggest about the individual as an agent of change?

About the author

George P. Pelecanos is the author of several highly praised and bestselling novels, including, most recently, *The Night Gardener*, *The Turnaround*, and *The Way Home*. He is also an independent-film producer, an essayist, and the recipient of numerous writing awards. He was a producer and an Emmy-nominated writer for *The Wire* and currently writes for the acclaimed HBO series *Treme*.

. . . and the next Derek Strange novel

Derek Strange returns in *Soul Circus*. Following is a brief excerpt from the novel's opening pages.

chapter

1

T HE chains binding Granville Oliver's wrists scraped the scarred surface of the table before him. Manacles also bound his ankles. Oliver's shoulders and chest filled out the orange jumpsuit he had worn for half a year. His eyes, almost golden when Strange had first met him, were now the color of creamed-up coffee, dull in the artificial light of the interview room of the D.C. Jail.

"Looks like you're keeping your physical self together," said Strange, seated on the other side of the table.

"Push-ups," said Oliver. "I try to do a few hundred every day."

"You still down in the Hole?"

"You mean Special Management. I don't know what's so special about it; ain't nothin' but a box. They let me out of it one hour for every forty-eight."

Strange and Oliver were surrounded by Plexiglas dividers in a space partitioned by cubicles. Nearby, public defenders and CJA attorneys conferred with their clients. The dividers served to mute, somewhat, the various conversations, leaving a low, steady mutter in the room. A thick-necked armed guard sat watching the activity from a chair behind a window in a darkened booth.

"It won't be long," said Strange. "They finished with the jury selection."

"Ives told me. They finally found a dozen D.C. residents weren't opposed to the death penalty, how'd they put it, *on principle.* Which means they found some white people gonna have no problem to sit up there and judge me."

"Four whites," said Strange.

"How you think they gonna find me, Strange? Guilty?"

Strange looked down and tapped his pen on the open folder lying on the table. He didn't care to take the conversation any further in that direction. He wasn't here to discuss what was or was not going to happen relative to the trial, and he was, by definition of his role as an investigator, uninterested in Oliver's guilt or innocence. It was true that he had a personal connection to this case, but from the start he had been determined to treat this as just another job.

"The prosecution's going to put Phillip Wood up there first," said Strange.

"Told you when I met you the very first time he was gonna be my Judas. Phil can't do no more maximum time. Last time he was inside, they took away his manhood. I mean they ass-raped him good. I knew that boy would flip." Oliver tried to smile. "Far as geography goes, though, we still close. They got him over there in the Snitch Hive, Strange. Me and Phil, we're like neighbors."

Wood had been Granville's top lieutenant. He had pled out in exchange for testimony against Oliver. Wood would get life, as he had admitted to being the triggerman in other murders; death had been taken off the table. He was housed in the Correctional Treatment Facility, a privately run unit holding informants and government witnesses in the backyard of the D.C. Jail.

"I've been gathering background for the cross," said Strange. "I was looking for you to lead me to one of Phillip's old girl-friends."

"Phil knew a lot of girls. The way he used to flash . . . even a bitch can get some pussy; ain't no trick to that. Phil used to drive this Turbo Z I had bought for him around to the high schools, 'specially over in Maryland, in PG? Drive by with that Kenwood sound system he had in there, playin' it loud. The girls used to run up to the car. They didn't even know who he was, and it didn't matter. It was obvious he had money, and what he did to get it. Girls just want to be up in there with the stars. It's *like* that, Strange."

"I'm looking for one girl in particular. She swore out a bru-tality complaint against Wood."

"The prosecution gave you that?"

"They don't have to give you charges, only convictions. I found it in his jacket down at the court. This particular charge, it was no-papered. Never went to trial."

"What's the girl's name?"

"Devra Stokes. Should be about twenty-two by now. She worked at the Paramount Beauty Salon on Good Hope Road."

Oliver grunted. "Sounds right. Phil did like to chill in those beauty parlors. Said that's where the girls were, so he wanted to be there, too. But I don't know her. We went through a lot of young girls. We were kickin' it with 'em, for the most part. But we were using them for other shit, too."

"What else would he have used a girl like Devra Stokes for?"

"Well, if she was old enough, and she didn't have no priors, we'd take her into Maryland or Virginia to buy a gun for us. Vir-ginia, if we needed it quick. We paid for it, but she'd sign the forty-four seventy-three. What they call the yellow form."

"You mean for a straw purchase."

"A straw gun, yeah. Course, not all time. You could rent a gun or get it from people we knew to get it from in the neighborhood. It's easy for a youngun to get a gun in the city. Easier than it is to buy a car. Shoot, you got to register a car."

Strange repeated the name: "Devra Stokes."

"Like I say, I don't recall. But look, she was workin' in a salon, chance is, she still doin' the same thing, maybe somewhere else, but in the area. Those girls move around, but not too far."

"Right."

"Phil's gonna say I killed my uncle, ain't that right?"

"I don't know what he's going to say, Granville."

Oliver and Strange stared at each other across the desk.

"You standin' tall, big man?" said Oliver.

Oliver was questioning Strange's loyalty. Strange answered by holding Oliver's gaze.

"I ain't no dreamer," said Oliver. "One way or the other, it's over for me. The business is done. Most of the boys I came up with, they're dead or doin' long time. One of the young ones I brought along got his own thing now, but he's cut things off with me. Word I get is, he still got himself lined up with Phil. Shoot, I hear they got two operations fighting over what I built as we sit here today."

"What's your point?"

"I feel like I'm already gone. They want to erase me, Strange. Make it so I don't exist no more. The same way they keep poor young black boys and girls out of the public's eyes today, the same way they did me when I was a kid. Warehousin' me and those like me down in the Section Eights. Now the government wants to bring me out and make an example out of me for a hot minute, then make me disappear again. And I'm a good candidate, too, ain't I? A strong young nigger with an attitude. They want to strap me to that table in Indiana and give me that needle and show people, that's what happens when you don't stay down where we done put you. That's what happens when you rise up. They want to do this to me bad. So bad that they'd fuck with someone who was trying to help me to stop it, hear?"

You left out the part about all the young black men you killed or had killed, thought Strange. And the part about you poisoning your own community with drugs, and ruining the lives of all the young people you recruited and the lives of their families. But there were some truths in what Granville Oliver was saying, too. Strange, following a personal policy, did not comment either way.

"So I was just wondering," said Oliver. "When they try to shake you down — and they will — are you gonna stand tall?"

"Don't insult me," said Strange. "And don't ever let me get the idea that you're threatening me. 'Cause I will walk. And you do not want me to do that."

Strange kept his voice even and his shoulders straight. He hoped his anger, and his fear, did not show on his face. Strange knew that even from in here, Oliver could have most anyone killed out on the street.

Oliver smiled, his face turning from hard to handsome. Like many who had attained his position, he was intelligent, despite his limited education, and could be a charming young man at will. When he relaxed his features, he favored his deceased father, a man Strange had known in the 1960s. Oliver had never known his father at all.

"I was just askin' a question, big man. I don't have many friends left, and I want to make sure that the ones I *do* have stay friends. We square, right?"

"We're square."

"Good. But, look here, don't come up in here empty-handed next time. I could use some smokes or somethin'."

"You know I can't be bringin' any contraband in here. They bar me from these meetings, it's gonna be a setback for what we're trying to accomplish."

"I hear you. How about some porno mags, though?"

"I'll see you next time."

Strange stood.

"One more thing," said Oliver.

"What is it?" said Strange.

"I was wonderin' how Robert Gray was doin'?"

"He's staying with his aunt."

"She ain't right."

"I know it. But it's the best I could do. I got him all pumped up about playing football for us this year. We're gonna start him in the camp this summer, comin' up."

"That's my little man right there. You're gonna see, that boy can jook. Check up on him, will you?"

"I get the time, I'll go by there today."

"Thank you."

"Stay strong, Granville."

Strange signaled the fat man in the booth and walked from the room.

❏

OUT in the air, on the 1900 block of D Street in Southeast, Derek Strange walked to his car. He dropped under the wheel of his work vehicle, a white-over-black '89 Caprice with a 350 square block under the hood, and rolled down the window. He had a while to kill before meeting Quinn back at the office, and he didn't want to face the ringing phone and the message slips spread out on his desk. He decided he would sit in his car and enjoy the quiet and the promise of a new day.

Strange poured a cup of coffee from the thermos he kept in his car. Coffee was okay for times like this, but he kept water in the thermos when he was doing a surveillance, because coffee went through him too quick. He only sipped the water when he knew he'd be in the car for a long stretch, and on those occasions he kept a cup in the car with a plastic lid on it, in which he could urinate as needed.

Strange tasted the coffee. Janine had brewed it for him that morning before he left the house. The woman could cook, and she could make some coffee, too.

Strange picked up the newspaper beside him on the bench, which he had snatched off the lawn outside Janine's house earlier that morning on his way to the car. He pulled the Metro section free and scanned the front page. The *Washington Post* was running yet another story today in a series documenting the ongoing progress of the Granville Oliver trial.

Oliver had allegedly been involved in a dozen murders, including the murder of his own uncle, while running the Oliver Mob, a large-scale, longtime drug business operating in the Southeast quadrant of the city. The Feds were seeking death for Oliver under the RICO act, despite the fact that the District's residents had overwhelmingly rejected the death penalty in a local referendum. The combination of racketeering and certain violent crimes allowed the government to exercise this option. The last execution in D.C. had been carried out in 1957.

The jury selection process had taken several months, as it had been difficult to find twelve local residents unopposed to capital punishment. During this time, Oliver's attorneys, from the firm of Ives and Colby, had employed Strange to gather evidence, data, and countertestimony for the defense.

Strange skipped the article, jumping inside Metro to page 3. His eyes went to a daily crime column unofficially known by longtime Washingtonians as "the Roundup," or the "Violent Negro Deaths." The first small headline read, "Teen Dies of Gunshot Wounds," and beneath it were two sentences: "An 18-year-old man found with multiple gunshot wounds in Southeast Washington died early yesterday at Prince George's County Hospital Center, police said. The unidentified man was found just after midnight in the courtyard area behind the Stoneridge apartments in the 300 block of Anacostia Road, and was pronounced dead at 1:03 A.M."

Two sentences, thought Strange. That's all a certain kind of kid in this town's gonna get to sum up his life. There would be more deaths, most likely retribution kills, related to this one.

Later, the murder gun might turn up somewhere down the food chain. Later, the crime might get "solved," pinned on the shooter by a snitch in a plea-out. Whatever happened, this would be the last the general public would hear about this young man, a passing mention to be filed away in a newspaper morgue, one brief paragraph without even a name attached to prove that he had existed. Another unidentified YBM, dead on the other side of the Anacostia River.

River, hell, thought Strange. The way it separates this city for real, might as well go ahead and call it a canyon.

Strange dropped the newspaper back on the bench seat. He turned the key in the ignition and pushed a Spinners tape into his deck. He pulled out of his spot and drove west. Just a few sips of coffee, and already he had to pee. Anyway, he couldn't sit here all day. It was time to go to work.

GO TO ONE MEETING AT THE PENTAGON, THOUGHT NICK FURY, *AND EVERYTHING TURNS TO CRAP.*

"Do we know anything about them?" he asked.

"We hope to by the time Mister Stark comes out of there," Hogan said over the secure communications connection. It was hard for Fury to hear him over the roar of the helicopter.

Fury suppressed a curse. Stark was a wunderkind when it came to technology, but he wasn't the guy they wanted fighting in close quarters—or for that matter, fighting at all.

Suddenly, a chill climbed Fury's spine. *What if the intruders are after Banner?*

In his savagely altered state, Banner had been a big gun for the Ultimates. Fury hated the idea of someone else having so destructive a weapon. Before he would allow that, he would see Banner put down. He didn't like the idea of killing someone who trusted him—someone who hadn't knowingly done anything wrong.

Of course, he reflected, *I might be jumping to conclusions. This might have nothing to do with Banner whatsoever.*

But over the years, Fury had developed a habit of anticipating the worst. It was one of the biggest reasons he was still alive.

THE ULTIMATES®

TOMORROW MEN

A novel by
Michael Jan Friedman

Based on the
Marvel Comic Book

POCKET STAR BOOKS
NEW YORK   LONDON   TORONTO   SYDNEY

An *Original* Publication of POCKET BOOKS

A Pocket Star Book published by
POCKET BOOKS, a division of Simon & Schuster, Inc.
1230 Avenue of the Americas, New York, NY 10020

This book is a work of fiction. Names, characters, places and
incidents are products of the author's imagination or are used
fictitiously. Any resemblance to actual events or locales or
persons, living or dead, is entirely coincidental.

ISBN-13: 978-1-4165-1065-9
ISBN-10:   1-4165-1065-6

This Pocket Star Books paperback edition September 2006

10 9 8 7 6 5 4 3 2 1

POCKET STAR BOOKS and colophon are registered
trademarks of Simon & Schuster, Inc.

Cover design by John Vairo, Jr.
Cover art by John Van Fleet

Manufactured in the United States of America

For information regarding special discounts for bulk purchases,
please contact Simon & Schuster Special Sales at 1-800-456-6798
or business@simonandschuster.com.

For Kalli

THE ULTIMATES®

TOMORROW MEN

TOMORROW, TONY STARK ECHOED INWARDLY.
He turned over beneath his bedcovers, unable to
find a comfortable position. *See you tomorrow, Tony.*

The words were etched into his brain, as
inescapable as one of those inane commercial jingles
that always lingered with him for days, imposing on
him its too-happy hype for a pine-scented air fresh-
ener. Or a frozen dinner. Or a new kind of bunion
remover.

I shouldn't talk, Stark mused. *My companies make all
those things.* But then, there was precious little in the
world his companies *didn't* make.

See you tomorrow, Tony . . .

He had heard that somewhere. *Recently,* he decided. *But where? And from whom?*

Then it came to him. He slid his hand along the silken surface of his sheet toward the other side of his bed. Unfortunately, there was no one there.

Annoyed, Stark swore beneath his breath. He could forgive himself for a lot of things, but being a bad host wasn't one of them.

Especially when his guest had been Terri Topasandra. Most men would have donated a kidney to get near the sexy, platinum-haired co-host of America's favorite morning talk show.

Her producer had arranged an interview with Stark, who was serving as corporate spokesman for Special Olympics, to talk about the upcoming games. The plan was for the two of them to meet for drinks so they could flesh out what they were going to say.

One thing led to another, which led to Stark's midtown penthouse, which led to his five-thousand-square-foot bedroom with its ornately carved Italian-marble columns and its staggering, one-way-glass view of New York City, which led to—

Nothing, apparently. Or at least nothing Stark could remember. *Shame on me.*

Unavoidably awake, the billionaire decided that he might as well open his eyes. But when he did, he found the pouting, bespectacled, slightly paunchy figure of his butler standing beside the bed.

"Wakey-wakey," said Jarvis, a note of sarcasm in

his voice that was no less cutting for its familiarity. Using the remote control in his hand, he turned up the lights.

"You hate me," Stark groaned, "don't you?"

"As nature hates a vacuum," said his butler. "Which reminds me—I need to refill your Scotch decanter. Someone left it as empty as the void between here and Mars."

"That would be me," Stark admitted.

"Do tell. I had a feeling it wasn't the young woman who accompanied you to Driscoll's on the Park last night. She didn't seem ample enough to drain a decanter all by herself."

Stark looked at him. "You wouldn't, by any chance, know what time Terri left?"

"I would say it was between two and two-fifteen," said Jarvis. "Fortunately, I was up watching reruns of *The Iron Chef*, so I was available to call her a cab."

Stark smiled ruefully. "Sorry about the inconvenience."

"If I may say so, sir, it is not me to whom you should be apologizing. The young lady looked rather disappointed when she left."

See you tomorrow, Tony . . .

"Do me a favor," said Stark. "Send her a bouquet of flowers. A big one."

"Of course," said Jarvis, with a roll of his eyes. "That will take care of everything."

Stark looked at him. "Meaning?"

"Meaning you have been drinking a great deal of late—even for *you*. To this point, your liver has made a heroic effort to keep you from poisoning yourself, but I doubt it will be inclined to do so indefinitely."

Stark closed his eyes again and managed a wistful smile. "No need to be worried about 'indefinitely,' Jarvis."

"Ah, yes," said the butler. "The tumor in your head. As if it were possible I had forgotten."

It was the tumor, untreatable and inoperable, that made Tony Stark work so hard—not only at business, but at life. And for him, drinking had become part of both endeavors. *A vicious circle if ever there was one.*

Funny, though—his head didn't hurt the way it used to when he got drunk. *A little compensation for the stranger in my skull?* he wondered, not for the first time. *Or have I finally killed too many nerve cells to know when I'm in pain?*

"By the way," said Jarvis, "you have another full slate of appointments today. Breakfast with the governor . . ."

"Of which state?" Stark asked.

"*This* one," said Jarvis. "Followed by the interview with Miss Topasandra, assuming she is still disposed to speak with you after the way you treated her. After that, a videoconference with General Fury and your engineering staff, golf at Shinnecock with Mister Rodriguez, and . . ."

"Roll that back for me," said Stark.

"Golf?" asked Jarvis.

"No. The Fury thing."

"Apparently, he wishes to discuss the improvements you are implementing in your armor. As you will recall, he requested that he be kept abreast of such developments."

Stark sighed. *The armor.* Some days he couldn't wait to get into it. Other days he couldn't wait to get out of it.

Today is one of the get-into days.

"Call Hogan," he said, "and tell him to get the new unit ready. I feel like taking her for a test drive."

Jarvis made a sound of disapproval. "Last time you did that, you missed breakfast entirely. Mister Gates was most perturbed, if his unfriendly takeover bid was any indication."

"Gates got over it," said Stark, pulling aside his bedclothes and swinging his legs out of bed. "And if it comes to that, the governor will too. Especially if he wants that Stark Dynamics plant to break ground in Schenectady next month."

"I'll phone the governor," said Jarvis, "and inform him that you'll be delayed. Also, that you recommend the eggs benedict for elected officials who have been stood up by rude, unthinking industrialists."

"Hey," said Stark, as he got up and padded across the tawny, lavishly grained wood of the floor to take a shower, "whose side are you on?"

"The side of Good, of course," said the butler.

The water in Stark's shower, which was as cold as he could make it, stung him into high alert. By the time he emerged from his spacious, white-tiled bathroom, toweled and dry, Jarvis had laid out a set of silk boxers, a lightweight tan suit, a contrasting dark blue shirt, and a pair of soft, imported loafers.

"By the way," said the butler, "it's been some time since you gave Happy Hogan a raise. You asked me to remind you about it. Also, it's been some time since you gave *me* a raise."

"I asked you to remind me about that as well?" Stark wondered as he dressed himself. "Or did you come up with that on your own?"

"On my own," Jarvis conceded readily enough. "Still, I would say it's worth the most careful consideration."

Stark chuckled. "You're lucky I don't turn you in for tax evasion, you old fraud. Or are you going to tell me you've been claiming those bonuses I give you every—"

Before he could finish his sentence, a brassy chime—like the banging of a distant gong—filled the room. All too aware of what it meant, the billionaire said, "Stark here," just loudly enough for his comm system to pick up.

"Mister Stark," said the Brooklyn-accented voice of Happy Hogan, "we've got trouble here in River City."

River City being Hogan's nickname for the Triskelion, the breathtaking, three-pronged facility built on a boomerang-shaped island in the upper bay of New York harbor. Stark had developed it to house his latest flier, a joint venture with the federal government.

The venture had already paid a whopping big dividend—if one could call the rescue of the human species from an extraterrestrial horde a *dividend*.

"Anyone else there?" asked Stark.

"For now," said Hogan, "just us chickens."

In other words, no "persons of mass destruction," as the government preferred to describe them. *Too bad,* Stark thought. He had discovered the value of having superpowered colleagues to make up for his suit's inconsistencies.

And his own.

Still, he said, "I'm on my way, Hap. And don't forget the olives."

"I'll cancel the governor," said Jarvis, making his way to the phone.

"Thanks," said the billionaire, leaving his street clothes on the bed and heading for one of the room's smaller closets—an intimate one containing a single suit, and not at all the kind Jarvis had laid out for him.

At a word, the zebrawood closet door slid into a pocket in the wall beside it, revealing a golden set of molded, metal-alloy body armor with a few apple-red highlights. And yet, with its immense capacity to store and direct electromagnetic energy, it was so much more than mere body armor.

It was, effectively, Iron Man. Or at least an earlier version of Iron Man, rendered obsolete months earlier by the development of more advanced models.

But in a pinch, it would do.

With Jarvis's help, Stark slid into the armor piece by piece: first the plastron, then the leg units, then the gauntlets, and last of all the headgear. It took him a moment to get used to breathing the suit's air supply, but no more than that.

After all, he was an accomplished scuba diver. Having to depend on a portable oxygen supply was nothing new to him.

Once Stark was certain everything was locked into place, he released the thick green lubricant that cushioned him from impacts and kept the suit's hard parts from rubbing against him. Then he moved to the set of transparent doors that led to his balcony, emerged from them into a windy blue Manhattan sky, and took a running jump.

As he cleared the balcony, he activated his propulsion system and shot through the air—all in one fluid motion. *But then,* he thought, *I've had a fair amount of practice at it.*

Dipping his left shoulder, he veered past the steel-and-glass skyscraper directly in front of him. Normally, he took a moment to wave to the secretaries inside it. *Perhaps more than a moment,* he allowed.

But not this time. *I'll give them two shows tomorrow,* Stark promised himself silently.

Suddenly, he hit a headwind and bounced up and down. Reaching for his palm controls with his middle finger, he slowed himself a little. Then he angled off on an ascent vector, finding an altitude where the wind wasn't quite so strong and oppositional.

Of course, the latest version of his armor would have sliced through headwinds twice as strong. But that suit was hanging in the Triskelion, where he had left it.

Funny, Stark thought. *Six months ago, this armor was cutting-edge. I felt as secure in it as I would in a Stark International corporate jet. Now I feel like a Ping-Pong ball in a wind tunnel.*

Not that he was averse to a little risk now and then. *It's not like I'm going to live forever.*

Steve Rogers shook his head slowly from side to side, and said, "I don't think I can do this."

"Sure you can," said Janet Pym, the willowy brunette sitting across the round, imitation-marble table from him. "You're Captain America. You can do anything."

He looked up at her. "Not this."

"Oh, come on," she said sweetly. "For me?"

Rogers looked down at his plate again and scowled at the offending item. "I don't think so."

Jan covered his hand with hers. It was slender but strong, like the rest of her, and cool to the touch. "Look," she said, "we've been through this before. Have I ever led you astray? Even once?"

"No," he conceded.

Though the newspapers would say otherwise, Rogers couldn't help thinking. They had called Jan an adulteress for being with him. But that was a separate subject, even more distasteful to him than the one at hand.

"When we went to Taste of Japan," Jan reminded him, "you thought you were going to barf. But by the end of the night, you were scarfing down sushi like there was no tomorrow."

"That was different," he said.

"Raw fish? What could be more daunting than raw fish?"

"I ate raw fish back in the service," he admitted. "It was part of survival training."

She looked surprised. "You never told me."

"It didn't seem like a good time to bring up the war."

In fact, it had been their first night out, when they weren't sure yet what they might mean to each other. Looking into the dark mysteries of her eyes, the war in Europe was the *last* thing he had wanted to think about.

Jan nodded. "Gotcha. But you're still not off the hook." With her free hand, she moved his plate a little closer to him. "One bite. That's all I'm asking."

Rogers forced himself to consider what she had ordered for him. "But for the love of God," he whispered, so the other diners in the restaurant wouldn't hear him, "pineapple on *pizza?*"

She smiled. "There's a first time for everything."

And in the last couple of weeks, she had introduced him to any number of firsts. *The first time I took a picture of someone with a telephone. The first time I hit a ball with an aluminum bat. The first time I made love to a married woman.*

He was still getting used to that last one. But it wasn't as if he had *planned* to get involved with Jan. *Fate threw us together,* he thought, echoing a line from a black-and-white movie whose name he couldn't remember.

One thing Rogers *didn't* feel was sympathy for Jan's estranged husband. Hank Pym was a louse. Any man who brutalized a woman didn't deserve her. *Period.*

People called him old-fashioned all the time, but standards of civilized behavior weren't supposed to change with the decade—or even the century. To his mind they still applied, though he had been asleep in an ice floe for sixty years.

"You're stalling until it gets cold," Jan said, mistaking Rogers's reverie for a tactic. "But it's not going to work. There's plenty more pineapple pizza where that came from."

He sighed. "I'm sure there is."

She wasn't going to relent until he gave it a shot. So before he could gag at what he was putting in his mouth, he picked up the slice and took a bite.

"There," said Jan, looking ever so pleased with herself. "Not so bad, right?"

Rogers didn't answer. He was too busy crunching pineapple chunks in his mouth and trying not to think about the other ingredients that came with them.

Suddenly, he felt a buzzing against his thigh. Reaching into his pocket, he pulled out the small, cell phone–like device Tony Stark had given him.

"What do they want?" asked Jan, who was no doubt feeling the buzzing as well.

Since the two of them had become an item, they had received a summons from the Triskelion maybe half a dozen times. Initially, Jan had reached for her comm device the same way Rogers had, only to have him beat her to the draw.

But then, his reflexes were considerably faster than those of a normal human being. *Part of the super-soldier package,* he reflected.

Holding the device to his ear, he said, "Rogers."

"It's Hogan," came the response. "We need you at the Triskelion on the double. Jan too," he added without a hint of irony, "if you happen to know where she is."

"I do," said Rogers, smiling wryly to himself. He gave Hogan the address of the building they were in. "Send Gottschalk. He's better at this than Valentino."

"Will do," Hogan said, and terminated the link.

Jan hadn't waited for the end of the exchange to put her sunglasses away and close up her bag. When Rogers got up from the table, she was right beside him.

Fortunately, they had paid for their food already. That was a habit they had gotten into after the first time they were precipitously called away.

Emerging from the restaurant, they came around the building and entered the alley beside it. Then Jan handed Rogers her bag and disappeared out of her clothes—or seemed to. In actuality, she had shrunk to the size of an insect, in which form she would ascend through the upper reaches of the alley until she reached the roofline.

Rogers had his own way of getting up there. Slinging Jan's bag over his shoulder, he leaped onto one of the alley's walls. Then, using a crack in one of the bricks for purchase, he propelled himself to a higher spot on the wall opposite.

By repeating the process over and over again, he made it to the roof seven stories above him in less than thirty seconds. A flight of stairs would have made the job easier, but it hadn't been an option.

Besides, anything was better than eating pineapple on his pizza.

A moment after Rogers swung himself onto the roof, Jan showed up full-sized as well, in a special expandable-and-contractible bodysuit Stark had designed for her. And a moment after that, they heard the distant but unmistakable hiss of helicopter blades.

Rogers looked back over his shoulder, in the direction of the harbor and the Triskelion. A small, sleek black-and-gray copter was heading for their rooftop, looming larger as it came. And unless his eyesight was going, it was Gottschalk at the controls.

Rogers was grateful. He didn't mind risking his life if that was what the situation called for, but he didn't want to lose it because he had drawn the wrong pilot.

Making his way east between rows of upward-thrusting office buildings, airborne Tony Stark caught sight of the East River. It glistened restlessly in the morning sunlight, a slice of green wedged between Manhattan and Roosevelt Island.

Away from the skyscrapers, he thought, *I'll make better time.* And if the urgency in Hogan's voice had been any indication, time was very much of the essence.

Rocketing past edifice after edifice, the street below him little more than a blur, Stark finally broke free of the skyline. This time he veered right and tracked the river, his optical filters darkening to compensate for the direct sunlight, the wind howling at the speed of his passage.

Up ahead, the elegant antique span of the Brooklyn Bridge stood guard over the lower reaches of the river. In a matter of seconds, Stark was sailing between its towers, watching the Upper Bay of New York Harbor spread out before him like a dream of emeralds.

Lower Manhattan vanished on his right, to be replaced by the more distant shore of New Jersey. On his left, Brooklyn fell away to reveal the Verrazano Bridge and Staten Island.

The chunks of rock called Ellis and Liberty loomed in front of him, Lady Liberty raising her torch with quiet confidence from the confines of the latter. And just beyond those historic pieces of public property, taking up every inch of a man-made island, lay the imposing, ultramodern structure known as the Triskelion.

Built by Stark Industries, thought the billionaire, *at a cost to the taxpayer of virtually nothing.* But then, it wasn't the first time he had treated Uncle Sam to a free lunch.

It was all part of the Stark legacy. When he was gone, he wanted people to say nice things about him. *That Tony Stark, what a guy. Too bad he had that time bomb in his head.*

And so on.

Aiming for the truncated cylinder in the Triskelion's center, he curled around it to approach the round asphalt disc of the helicopter pad. Cutting thrust at the last possible moment, he landed on both feet. Then, without breaking stride, he headed for the gray steel security door.

Happy Hogan was waiting for him alongside it. A strapping fellow with a head for details and the hands of a heavyweight boxer, Hogan was the supervisor of every important operation Stark Enterprises had ever undertaken. That made him the man in charge of not only the Triskelion, but also the Iron Man project.

"Good to see you," said Hogan, the wind snatching half his words.

"What's going on?" Stark asked.

He had forgotten how awkward it was to walk in this version of his armor. *Like wearing ski boots,* he thought. *Strictly heel to toe, no give in the instep.*

"We've got intruders," said Hogan, using a palm-sized remote control device to open the door.

Stark eyed his colleague through the optical filters of his mask. "You're kidding, right?"

"Wish I was," Hogan told him, and led the way inside.

2

INTRUDERS? STARK REPEATED TO HIMSELF AS he followed Hogan into the bowels of the Triskelion.

The Chitauri had infiltrated the place months earlier, but they were extraterrestrials with the ability to take on human forms. It was disconcerting to think that with all the Triskelion's security measures, the place could be invaded a second time.

"Any idea who they are?" Stark asked, as they negotiated the corridor that led to the facility's operations center. "Or what they're here for?"

Hogan shook his head. "None. Worse, we don't know how they got in. One minute, everything's fine. The next, my security screen is lighting up like a Christmas tree."

At the end of the corridor, an interior door slid aside for them. It revealed the Triskelion's expansive, high-ceilinged operations center, a blue-gray amphitheater with six ascending ranks of sleek black computer stations.

The place was crawling with SHIELD personnel in army-green uniforms, not to mention Stark's civilian-garbed security people. As he walked in, they all stopped what they were doing and looked up—and then returned to their respective tasks.

"I'd like to see these intruders," said the man in the high-tech armor, heading for the center's security monitor.

"Be my guest," said Hogan.

Stark stopped in front of the oversized monitor, which was vaguely concave, and peered at its screen. It showed him a well-illuminated section of gray corridor, though he couldn't have said on which level it was located.

The intruders, all five of them, were moving along the passage without the slightest appearance of caution. They were all tall and athletic-looking, wearing white jumpsuits with narrow green modules of indeterminate purpose deployed along the sleeves, thighs, and left side of the midsection. And they were all bald, including the lone female in the group.

"Watch this," said Hogan, punching a quick command into the keyboard beneath the monitor. "It's what happened to the first security detail I sent to meet them."

It was made up of six highly trained SHIELD personnel, all of whom Stark knew by name. In accordance with Triskelion security protocols, they had their weapons in hand when they confronted the intruders and asked them to surrender themselves.

The officers' advice fell on deaf ears. The intruders didn't even so much as break stride.

At that point, the security team had no choice but to use force. Leveling their weapons, they hammered the intruders with a barrage of hard-rubber projectiles.

But the bullets never seemed to reach their targets. Instead, they were deflected by what appeared to be invisible barriers.

"Impressive," said Stark. "Personal shields. And no flare at the point of impact."

"Also," Hogan reported soberly, "some impressive directed-energy ordnance."

As if on cue, the intruders unleashed a series of pale violet beams. Whenever one of them struck a security officer, it sent him or her flying backward.

In a matter of seconds, the security detail was sprawled on the floor, unconscious, and the intruders were stepping over them on their way along the corridor. Stark's jaw clenched.

"That kind of tech takes serious power," he said. He tapped his metal-alloy forefinger on the screen. "So where the hell is it coming from? You see any batteries on them?"

"I don't," said Hogan.

The billionaire's latest Iron Man armor used batteries no bigger than a cell phone, but they were absolute state-of-the-art, a Stark International exclusive. The intruders couldn't be packing anything smaller . . .

Could they?

Hogan punched in another command and the scene on the monitor changed. "The second detail," he said with obvious reluctance, "didn't last even as long as the first."

As before, the intruders remained unscathed in the face of the security team's barrage. Then they cut loose with an attack of their own, felling all obstacles in their path.

"Whoever these bastards are," said Hogan, "they're well equipped."

"That they are," said Stark. "Let's see how they fare against someone *better* equipped."

"We've gotten hold of Rogers and Jan. You want to wait for them?"

"They can join me when they get here."

"Roger that," said Hogan. He consulted the data scrawling across the bottom of the monitor in bright green characters. "They're in section eighteen now, trying to burn their way through the door. I'll insert you myself, if you like."

"I'd be honored," said the billionaire.

But he was already on the move, so he didn't know if Hogan had heard him. Making his way across the ops center, he went through a door perpendicular to the one he had come in and proceeded along the Triskelion's wide central corridor.

Seeing the boss was in a hurry, the security people stationed in the passage moved to either side for him. Normally, the place would have been full of engineers moving from office to office, but not after an intruder alert.

The engineers have all been evacuated, Stark thought. *And the administrative staff along with them.*

"I'm assuming you want to ambush these guys from behind," said Hogan.

"You must be a mind reader," said Stark.

"If there's one thing I know about you, it's that you have no qualms about blindsiding the opposition."

Stark glanced at him, feigning injury to his feelings. *"Ladies' Home Companion* called me 'the picture of chivalry' in their Big Spring Cleaning issue."

Hogan grunted. "Ask Victronix Technologies about your chivalry. You put them out of the computer chip business so fast their heads are *still* spinning."

"I had to protect my stockholders," said Stark. "Besides, the Victronix people were coming after us.

If I hadn't skewered *them,* they would have skewered *me.* And correct me if I'm wrong, but didn't I make sure all their employees had job interviews with my companies?"

"Sure," said Hogan, "split hairs."

A stranger would have deduced from their conversation that they weren't worried about the intruders in section eighteen. Nothing could have been further from the truth. Stark's banter with Hogan was his way of getting loose, like an athlete before a game—except he was stretching his mind instead of his muscles.

Less than three minutes after he left the ops center, Stark found himself standing in front of a metal ventilation grate. As he watched, Hogan pulled a miniature tool kit out of his pocket, removed a Phillips head screwdriver, and began working on one of the screws that held the grate in place.

Stark took a deep breath and let it out slowly. *Five of them,* he reminded himself. *So you've got to keep moving. And stay close to them, so they get in each other's way.*

At heart, he had always been more of a talker than a fighter. Even in grade school, he had been able to worm his way out of confrontations with a handful of well-chosen remarks.

But the intruders weren't interested in talking, if their encounters with his security people were any indication. *So we go to Plan B,* he thought, checking the readout on the inside of his wrist to make sure he was getting his full download.

Which he *was*.

Stark's armor had its own energy supply for routine applications. But special situations called for amplifications of its power, and these were relayed to him from hidden sources through one of several Stark International satellites.

Hogan finished removing the last of the screws holding the grate in place. Then he pulled it away from the wall, exposing an aluminum passage that connected with other aluminum passages in a network that ran the length and breadth of the Triskelion.

These would, with the assistance of Stark's tracking system, lead him to the intruders.

"You ready?" asked Hogan.

"Never more so," said the billionaire. Then he activated his propulsion system and plunged into the passage.

Go to one meeting at the Pentagon, thought Nick Fury, *and everything turns to crap.*

"Do we know anything about them?" he asked.

"Not yet, General," Hogan said over the secure communications connection. It was hard for Fury to hear him over the roar of the helicopter carrying him back north. "But we hope to by the time Mister Stark comes out of there."

Fury suppressed a curse. Stark was a wunderkind when it came to technology, but he wasn't the guy they wanted fighting in close quarters—or for that matter, fighting at all.

That armor of his had worked fine in the aerial battle against the Chitauri, where Stark had room to maneuver. But within the confines of the Triskelion, it was as likely to do harm as good.

Which brought to mind the guy Fury would have preferred under those circumstances. "Any word from Rogers?"

"He's on his way," said Hogan. "Mrs. Pym, too."

Personally, Fury thought it was fine that those two were playing house, considering what they had been through lately. They both needed someone to lean on, so why not each other?

But there was the team to think about. The Ultimates were still a publicly financed operation, at least in part, and folks in the Bible Belt weren't going to take kindly to their heroes breaking one of the Ten Commandments.

Make that two, Fury thought, correcting himself, *if you include Thou shalt not kill.*

But it wasn't Rogers or Jan who had broken that commandment. It was the guy in the transparent holding unit deep in the heart of the Triskelion—the guy who would stay there no matter what threats might manifest themselves.

Suddenly, a chill climbed Fury's spine. *What if the intruders are after Banner?*

They would have to have known about him first, and that assumed a lot. But they had penetrated the Triskelion without leaving any evidence of their entry, which Fury would have called impossible until a little while ago. To pull off that kind of stunt, they must have had access to top-secret information. It wasn't that much of a stretch to imagine that they had data on Banner as well.

In his savagely altered state, Banner had been a big gun for the Ultimates in their battle against the alien Chitauri. Hell, he had saved the whole damned day. Fury hated the idea of someone else having so destructive a weapon.

Before he would allow that, he would see Banner put down.

He didn't like the idea of killing someone who trusted him—someone who hadn't knowingly done anything wrong. *But it's a cruel world.* Sometimes people had to do things they weren't proud of. Hell, he had *already* done some of those things, hadn't he? So what was one more?

Of course, he reflected, *I might be jumping to conclusions. This might have nothing to do with Banner whatsoever.*

But over the years, Fury had developed a habit of anticipating the worst. It was one of the biggest reasons his bad, one-eyed self was still alive.

"Keep me posted," he told Hogan, speaking into the little grate in his phone. "And don't worry about the minutes, cowboy. I've got plenty of them."

As Stark rocketed his way through the Triskelion's ventilation system, propelled by the plasma emitters in his boot heels, he kept an eye on the tiny, convex monitor in his gauntlet. It showed him a black maze on a blue background, with a red star near the middle of the maze and a green one not far from it.

The red star was the location of the intruders, the green one his own location. And they were getting closer together by the second.

Negotiating one last bend in the system, Stark slid a metal panel over his gauntlet monitor and focused on the grate up ahead. Then he extended his fists and rammed through it.

And shot out into the corridor beyond, perhaps ten yards behind the unsuspecting intruders.

In the fraction of a second it took them to register Stark's presence, he wheeled and hit them with all the power at his disposal. The resulting electromagnetic pulse barrage, visible only as a distortion of light waves, was enough to send one of the intruders flying backward, head over heels.

But the quartet behind him remained standing, unperturbed by Stark's assault. *An automatic adaptation,* he had time to reflect. Then he saw them raise their arms and felt the sudden, devastating force of their counterattack.

It flung him back the way he came, caught in a seething, spitting confluence of violet energy beams. But before it could send him crashing into the door at the opposite end of the corridor, he managed to veer off—taking an angle rather than resisting the barrage directly—and come back for another pass.

The intruders were relentless, dogging him with their energy bursts. But Stark's armor was nothing if not fast, and it could turn on something considerably smaller than a dime. Making the most of its capabilities, he stayed a half step ahead of his adversaries' attentions.

However, he wasn't just reacting. All the while, he was setting up his next move, jockeying for a particular position. And when he got it, he didn't hesitate.

Spinning like a big power drill, Stark insinuated himself into his adversaries' midst. Then he crossed his arms over his chest and fired at the intruders on either side of him.

They jackknifed under the impact of his volley and hit the walls behind them. But Stark didn't stay to see if they lost consciousness. Instead, he darted down the corridor to gather himself for another pass.

As he came about, he saw the last two intruders standing in front of their fallen comrades, shielding them. But they weren't firing back. In fact, one of them was preventing the other from doing so.

"Please," he called to Stark, "this is a mistake. There's no need for hostilities."

"Really," Stark said beneath his breath.

"I know this is hard to believe," the intruder insisted, "but we're not your enemies."

Stark was tempted to laugh. "I get it. You broke into our building and leveled our security details because you're our *friends.*"

"Actually," said the intruder, "we didn't break into the Triskelion. At least, not in the sense you think we did. I trust you'll give us the opportunity to explain."

"You place a lot of trust in someone you've been pounding like there's no tomorrow."

"That's true," said the intruder, "I do. And I feel comfortable doing so. After all, you *are* Anthony Stark."

"Don't believe everything you've seen on television," the billionaire advised him.

"That won't be a problem," said the intruder, "since I've never seen a television in my life."

Stark looked at him askance.

The intruder turned his hands palm-up. "I really *would* like a chance to explain."

Just then, Stark heard a voice through his ear filter—the kind of voice Tinker Bell would have had, if J. M. Barrie had seen fit to give her some dialogue. "What's going on?" it asked.

Obviously, Jan had followed him in through the vent. And that meant Rogers would be by before long as well.

Stark didn't answer Jan's question directly. Instead, he contacted Hogan over his built-in comm system and said, "Hap, get me a conference room. My . . ."

Before he could finish, the door behind him seemed to implode. And before it had completely clattered to the ground, Steve Rogers was standing in the corridor.

He looked confused by what he saw. But then, he had heard someone broke into the Triskelion. He had expected Stark to be trading shots with them, not negotiating with them.

The billionaire held up his hand for Rogers's benefit. Then he continued his message to Hogan: "As I was saying, my *friends* and I need to talk."

By the time Fury arrived at the Triskelion's helipad, he saw that Stark had already freshened up and changed his clothes, and was waiting with his hands in his expensively tailored pockets.

Walking across the asphalt surface, the wind from the bay whipping at him, the general tried to get a read on the billionaire's expression. Thanks to Happy Hogan, Fury knew what had transpired up to the point when the intruders surrendered to Iron Man.

What he didn't know was what they said after Stark got them in the conference room.

But as Fury joined Stark at the security door, the latter didn't look especially worried. *A good sign*.

"How was your trip?" Stark inquired, ever the charming host.

"Bumpier than the Cyclone at Coney Island. I understand we've got some unexpected guests."

"Just a handful."

"By the way, Money Man, in the future let's leave the interrogations to the experts."

"Sorry," said Stark. "Didn't mean to overstep my bounds."

"Where are your intruders now?"

"Three of them are in the infirmary. The other two are languishing in a detention cell."

Fury scowled. "How many guards in the infirmary?"

"A half dozen, not including Rogers. But I don't think the intruders will be causing any more trouble. They've voluntarily turned over their weapons and they're contrite about using them in the first place."

"Is that what they said?"

"More or less."

"That's funny. They break into our house and take out two security teams without blinking, and suddenly they're contrite. What made them see the error of their ways?"

"*Me,*" said the billionaire.

"Baloney," said Fury, who knew a lie when he heard one. "There's more to it than that."

"They said their encounters with the security teams were unfortunate. They were just trying to defend themselves."

Fury stopped in his tracks. "Correct me if I'm wrong, but weren't *they* the ones who broke into *our* place?"

"Clearly," said Stark. "But they claim it wasn't to do any damage. They just wanted to talk with someone in charge."

"Really? Well, *you're* someone in charge—and they did their best to take you out."

"Because they didn't recognize me," said Stark. "They expected me to show up in a different Iron Man unit."

Fury didn't get it. The suit Stark had worn that morning was primitive in terms of its technology, but closely resembled the more recent models.

He said so.

"Actually," Stark explained, "they expected me to show up in a suit of black armor, made of a nanite-based material I haven't invented yet."

Fury felt as if he had stumbled into an episode of *The Twilight Zone.* "If it's not a lot of trouble, would you mind telling me what the hell you're talking about?"

"I don't mind at all," said Stark. And he told the general what the intruders had told *him.*

It took a few moments for Fury to absorb the information. "Well," he said, *"there's* something you don't hear every day."

"So you see," said Betty Ross, public relations liaison for the government's high-profile Ultimates project, "it's not at all a matter of whom I like. It's the boss's decision that determines which operatives get to go public."

As she spoke, she watched platinum-haired Pietro Maximoff take three quick strides on the ice, leap into the air, execute a perfect spin, and then land with the grace of a professional skater.

Betty wasn't the only one who noticed, either. Every female skater in the place had been ogling Pietro and his movie-star good looks since he walked through the door.

Pietro's sister Wanda, who had gotten the nickname the Scarlet Witch from her SHIELD coworkers for good reason, pouted impatiently at Betty from the rail that separated the ice from the surrounding surface. With her formfitting red skating suit, she had attracted considerable attention from the males in the rink.

"And it was General Fury's decision to expose Natasha and Clint to public scrutiny," she said, "but not me or Pietro."

"That's right," said Betty, checking her wristwatch. "But really, I wouldn't take it personally.

From a public relations standpoint, it's perfectly understandable."

"Then why don't I understand it?" Wanda asked.

Betty frowned. She had gone over the answer twice already. But for the hell of it, she would try one more time.

"As I told you," she said, "you've got three strikes against you. First, you're a foreigner."

Wanda dismissed the notion with a wave of her hand. "Anna Kournikova is a foreigner. I saw her on television just this morning in a shampoo commercial."

So that's what this is about, Betty thought. *Fricking commercial endorsements. What happened to "I'm offering my services in exchange for the release of political prisoners?"*

"Anna Kournikova isn't a mutant," Betty noted. *At least as far as we know.* "You and your brother were card-carrying members of the Mutant Brotherhood, for godsakes. And even if you weren't, you don't have the kind of persona Americans like."

In the background, Pietro executed another midair spin and then glided out of it. But then, he was capable of making so many minute adjustments in such a short amount of time, there were few sports he couldn't master.

"What's wrong with my persona?" Wanda demanded.

Where do I begin? Betty asked herself. "Not a thing, if you're going for cold and haughty. But in this country, we like our public figures just the slightest bit approachable."

"But I'm beautiful," Wanda pointed out.

The public relations woman couldn't argue that. Wanda's features, like her brother's, looked as if they had been chiseled from some smooth, expensive stone.

"In this case," said Betty, "I'm afraid beautiful's not enough."

"Nonsense," Wanda retorted. "Beautiful is *always* enough. General Fury is just peeved that I won't sleep with him."

That got Betty's attention. The last thing the Ultimates program needed was a sexual discrimination suit. "Did the general *ask* you to sleep with him?"

Wanda shrugged her slender shoulders. "Not in so many words. But a woman knows."

Sure she does. "Listen, girlfriend, I've got a press conference downtown at eleven-thirty. We'll talk another time."

Wanda looked at her, undoubtedly as dissatisfied as she was before. "Fine," she said. "Go to your press conference."

Like I need your permission, Betty thought. "Thanks," she said, and headed for the door.

But halfway there, she realized her bra straps had broken. *Both of them.* And at the damnedest time, considering she was supposed to greet a room full of reporters in just a few minutes.

She swore to herself. *I hate when this happens.*

Then she remembered with whom she had been talking, and the expression on Wanda's face, and it occurred to her the bra straps might not be an accident.

Casting a glance back over her shoulder, she saw Wanda was still standing by the rail. And she looked like the cat that had swallowed the canary.

They're right to call her a witch, Betty thought. *Or something that rhymes with it.*

As she emerged from the rink onto the street, she did her best to ignore her undergarment problem and focus on getting a taxi. However, she hadn't quite made it to the intersection before her cell phone went off.

Fishing it out of her skirt pocket, she snapped it open and said, "Ross here."

"It's Fury," came the response. "Send someone else to the press conference. I need to speak with you."

Betty was surprised. "What about?"

"The future," the general told her.

3

SITTING AT THE SLEEK BLACK TABLE IN THE
Triskelion's main conference room, Stark used one
of its built-in computer terminals to go over the
security-cam images of his encounter with the
intruders.

All in all, he reflected, *I didn't do that badly.* His
approach through the ventilation system caught his
adversaries off-guard, as he had intended. And his spinning entry into their midst had worked like a charm as
well.

However, the last two intruders had been given an
open shot at him as he finished his pass. That they
chose not to take advantage of it didn't excuse his

error, or assure him that another enemy would be as generous.

Got to watch that, Stark told himself.

Next time, he would do something unpredictable, like pull up sharply and loop around. *If that's even possible under a ten-foot ceiling.*

He was considering his other options when the door slid open and Natasha Romanov appeared on the threshold. As usual, she was wearing an all-black ensemble, one of the reasons she had been given the code name Black Widow.

The other was how many enemies she was said to have dispatched in her career as a Russian spy. Fortunately, she worked for the Ultimates these days.

"May I come in?" she asked.

With her auburn hair, her exotic features, and her slender, supple body, Natasha was difficult to deny. *Not only now,* Stark couldn't help thinking, *but that other time as well.*

"Of course," he said.

She pulled out the chair next to him and sat down. "Anything new on the intruder front?"

"Not yet. We're waiting for test results."

"You think they're mutants?"

"They seem to have materialized out of thin air. We have to check out every possibility."

"Then you don't believe their story?"

"For now," he said, "I'm approaching it with an open mind."

Natasha nodded. "That's probably the best approach."

Stark had a feeling she hadn't come just for an update on the intruders. A moment later, she confirmed it for him.

"Listen," she said, "you know that moment of . . . camaraderie we shared in the men's room, just before our battle with the Chitauri?"

He remembered it both fondly and in great detail. "I suppose camaraderie would be one way to describe it."

"I just hope you weren't thinking it was a portent of things to come. People do things in stressful circumstances they would never do otherwise. Not that I regret it for a minute."

Stark found himself smiling at the novelty of the situation. "Hang on a second. Are you telling me you just want to be friends?"

"Not really," said Natasha. "I feel uncomfortable working alongside friends. Comrades is more what I had in mind."

He looked at her. "Comrades . . . ?"

"I mean," she said, "it couldn't have been a meaningful liaison for you either. Not when you have so many attractive women at your beck and call."

Actually, Stark had gotten more satisfaction from his brief encounter with Natasha than from entire weekends with other women. But his life had been so crammed full of stockholder meetings and test flights and power lunches, there hadn't been time for him to contemplate an encore.

His sex life over the last few weeks had been rife with Terri Topasandras—utterly unplanned events, barely considered before or after. The way he lived, that was all he could handle.

Besides, Stark couldn't forget the growth lodged in his brain. It made anything even approaching an ongoing relationship problematical at best.

"Unfortunately," Stark said, "they're not as attractive as you make them out to be. And most of them are rather shallow. But the more I think about it, the more I agree with you—people who work together shouldn't get involved. What happened before the battle was . . . a pregame warm-up, nothing more."

"Then you understand," she said, obviously pleased with him.

"Absolutely," he told her.

"Good," said Natasha, getting up from her chair. "I'm glad we had this conversation. It's made me feel better."

And with that, she left. A few moments later, the room was as silent as before she arrived.

Stark should have felt better as well, having dodged yet another threat to his bachelorhood. But he didn't. He felt irritated.

Why is that? he wondered.

• • •

Henry Pym had always loved to immerse himself in the world beneath his microscope.

He didn't *get* people sometimes—why they did certain things, whom they embraced as friends. Sometimes he didn't even get *himself*. Those were the occasions when he did things he came to regret, things that made him feel mean and stupid.

Mean was bad. Pym knew that from growing up with a father who took a belt to him every chance he got. But stupid was even worse. There was nothing he hated more than someone speaking down to him, giving him less than the respect he felt he deserved.

Hell, he had developed a method of shrinking people to the size of insects, and another that made them as big as houses. And the helmet he had designed allowed him to direct the activities of ants. If those accomplishments didn't translate into respect, he didn't know what the hell would.

Still, there were those who insisted on belittling him. Saying, for instance, that Bruce Banner was a superior geneticist.

Well, Pym thought, *Banner's penned up in a damned holding unit down in the basement, and I'm the one they brought in to analyze the blood samples they took from the intruders. So in the final analysis, who's the more successful scientist?*

Just then, he heard the door slide open. *Gotta go,* he thought, pulling himself out of the microscopic world with something like physical pain. When he finally looked up from his microscope, he saw Nick Fury standing there.

The general looked like a man with ground glass in his underwear. "What's the verdict?" he asked without preamble.

"Well," said Pym, "I can safely and unequivocally say these people are human."

It was a concern because the Chitauri had possessed the ability to make themselves *look* human. These intruders, on the other hand, were the genuine articles.

"Diseases?" Fury asked.

"None that are still alive," said Pym. "But they've got an interesting collection of dead ones. I found pieces of critters in their blood that would make your hair stand on end. I mean," he added in recognition of the general's shaved head, "if you had any."

"These critters," said the general, "you've seen them before? Or at least read about them?"

"Some. Others I've *never* seen."

"Any idea where they came from?"

Pym shrugged. "They could be designer viruses. The kinds of things a terrorist organization might have developed. If that's so, we'd better start working on a vaccine now, because they'll make the Ebola strain look like heat rash."

"How do you suppose these people got exposed to such viruses?"

"Hard to say. Maybe they were guinea pigs—the ones who managed to survive. Or maybe they lived in a part of the world that has an unusual number of exotic microorganisms."

"Which one do you think it is?"

Pym shook his head. "Neither. But you talked to these people, right? Did anything they said provide a clue?"

Fury didn't respond for a while. When he finally spoke, it was in a more contemplative voice.

"Is it possible," he asked, "in your professional opinion, that these viruses are from an era two centuries from now?"

The scientist chuckled at the absurdity of the suggestion. "What do you mean?"

"I didn't tell you," said Fury, "because I didn't want to influence your analysis, but the intruders have told Stark they're from two hundred years in the future."

At some point, the scientist realized his mouth was hanging open. He closed it. "Time travel?"

It was probably just a story the intruders had concocted. But if there was even the least bit of truth to it . . .

"Thanks," said Fury. "Stick around. I may need you for something else."

As he left the room, Pym's mind was aflutter with the possibilities. *Time travel* . . .

• • •

Tony Stark wasn't happy.

He had things to think about. Important things, like the Tomorrow Men, as Fury called them, not to mention business decisions that would significantly impact the economies of a half dozen Asian and Latin American countries.

But instead, as he stared out the window of his office at the Triskelion, he was thinking about Natasha Romanov.

The arch of her back. The tilt of her chin. Things he had barely noticed before, which he suddenly couldn't get out of his mind.

It was that line she had given him: *Comrades is more what I had in mind.*

No one had ever said that to him. *No one.* And now that someone had, he couldn't accept it.

Stark had been obsessed most of his life with one thing or another. That was how he had gotten to be who he was. But obsession with a woman . . . that was an entirely new experience for him.

And he didn't like it.

As he thought that, he saw a reflection in the re-inforced glass of his office window—in addition to his own. Turning, he saw he wasn't alone in the room anymore.

The new arrival was tall and rawboned, with a mane of long, yellow hair and a beard to match. The kind of guy who would have stood out in a crowd even if he hadn't been wearing a sleeveless, black leather jumpsuit with a quartet of round, silvery energy nodes distributed across his chest, or a broad metal belt of the kind one saw in a wrestling ring.

Then there was the weapon in his hand—a long-handled job made of some bright, shiny metal, half axe and half mallet, that would have looked impressive in a museum collection. And as formidable as it appeared, it was even more so. After all, it could unleash the power of a lightning storm.

Which made its owner formidable too. Something out of this world, to hear him tell it.

Thor, thought Stark. *The god of thunder*—though the billionaire still wasn't certain he believed it.

"Where have you been?" he asked his colleague.

It came out funny, as if he were implying that Thor should have been present to deal with the intruders the day before. But he wasn't implying that at all.

Thor and Rogers and Stark himself were volunteers. It was only the duty each of them felt to his fellow human beings—and, of course, to his teammates—that kept him coming back to the Triskelion.

So Stark wasn't posing the question to elicit an excuse. He asked only because the answer was always so entertaining.

"Muspelheim," said Thor. "The Realm of Fire. To show Surtur he can't cross the Nine Worlds with impunity."

"Surtur . . . ?" said the billionaire.

"Lord of the Fire Giants. Also known as Flint-Spark, Smoke Maker, Flesh Scorcher, and Burner of Forests."

Don't invite him to the same party as Smokey the Bear, Stark thought. But what he said was, "Oh, *that* Surtur."

Thor smiled at him, flashing a row of flawless white teeth. "Having fun at my expense, are we?"

"Naturally," said the billionaire. "What are friends for?"

Thor chuckled into his beard. From the beginning, he had warmed to the casual tone Stark took with him, and his matter-of-fact approach to Thor's unusual attributes and opinions. But then, Stark had Oprah's private number on his cell phone. He was a rather difficult man to impress.

"So what's going on here?" asked Thor. "When I returned to Midgard, I had a message that we had been invaded."

Midgard, Stark had come to understand, was the planet Earth—as opposed to the other eight worlds in the cosmology offered by Scandinavian legend. "In retrospect," he said, "'invaded' seems a little overdramatic. But we do have visitors. From the future, if they can be taken at their word."

Thor's brow knit. "The future?"

"Hard to believe," said Stark, "I know." *Even for a man who claims to be a thunder god, apparently.* "But you may find it less so once you've met them."

"Then you believe them?"

Stark shrugged. "Let's just say I'm reserving judgment."

"What are they doing here?" Thor asked.

"That," said the billionaire, "is still a matter of conjecture. They wanted to wait until we were all present before they revealed their purpose here—or should I say *now.*"

"Then what are we waiting for?"

Just the gentleman who laid the smackdown on the Burner of Forests. "Absolutely nothing," said Stark.

If there were an award for couch potatoes, Bruce Banner would have been a world-class contender.

He didn't think much anymore about Warshovsky and Crespo, the afternoon-shift guards patrolling the security chamber in which his holding unit was situated. They had become like wallpaper. Unless they spoke to him, they were just *there*.

But television? That was a different story entirely.

Unfortunately, the scientist didn't have access to *all* television. He could only watch those channels that weren't likely to get him excited—that wouldn't get his volatile biochemistry in a boil and turn him into a murdering behemoth again.

Like the rerun of *The Brady Bunch* he was watching at the moment. Nothing much to get excited about there—except, of course, that the little kids were getting the short end of the stick.

Banner had been an only child, but he couldn't help sympathizing with Cindy and Bobby. They meant well. But somehow, they always wound up taking the blame. In fact—

With an effort, he stopped himself.

Listen to me, Banner thought miserably. *Is this what I've been reduced to?*

He was like those housewives who sat and watched soap operas all day, waiting to see if Anne-Marie's baby belonged to Lance or his half-brother Jeremy. Except when the soaps were over, those housewives could drag their fannies over to the mall.

Banner had to stay home. *Forever,* as far as he could tell.

Pressing one of the two green studs on his remote, he left Bobby and Cindy to their own devices and switched to the History Channel. *You can always depend on the History Channel.*

He found himself watching black-and-white footage of Adolf Hitler that appeared to have been taken from a newsreel. The little dictator was ranting in front of rank after rank of German soldiers, inspiring them to go out and conquer the world.

The narrator—a veteran actor whose name Banner couldn't remember—was saying that France had fallen and the British were on their heels. And while some thought the United States would remain unscathed by the Axis, others were more realistic.

So even before the Japanese attack on Pearl

Harbor, Franklin Roosevelt authorized a secret program to design a superlative fighting man. *A super-soldier*.

The scene on the television switched to an unassuming redbrick building in New Jersey, now boarded up and surrounded with barbed-wire fencing. It was there, according to the narrator—whose name Banner *still* couldn't remember—that a group of biospecialists got together and laid out the super-soldier blueprint.

Though the program was expected to eventually produce an entire regiment, it never fulfilled that promise. Instead, it wound up creating but a single superb specimen whom the public came to know as Captain America.

At first, people thought he was a figurehead, meant to inspire American troops. But those who fought alongside him came back with stories of prodigious strength and unbelievable agility and something approaching outright invulnerability.

They were only slight exaggerations.

But in the spring of 1945, in the midst of a strike against a German military base in Iceland, Captain America was lost in combat—and presumed dead. Given the fact that he was the only success to come out of the super-soldier program, it didn't seem likely the world would see his ilk again.

Except to Bruce Banner.

He was certain that the formula that created Captain America could be duplicated. And the government, dealing with terrorists now instead of Nazis, was willing to back the chance that he was right.

Suddenly, Banner found himself with a mess of funding. He had never been so pumped in his life. But creating a super-soldier turned out to be harder than it looked.

Banner had always been first in his class, all through college and then grad school. He had always been the smartest person he knew. It shouldn't have been so difficult to accomplish something someone else had accomplished sixty years earlier.

Granted, his predecessors were intelligent people, maybe the best the world had to offer at the time. But they were working with primitive computers, without the twenty-first century's understanding of cell biology.

For godsakes, he thought, *back in the forties they hadn't come up with a vaccine for polio yet.* How advanced could the super-soldier brain trust have been?

Still, Banner had foundered. Every approach he tried led him to a dead end. His grant money was running out and he hadn't produced a damned thing to show for it.

Then, just when he thought he was completely screwed, he received his first set of promising results. He was onto something—he was sure of it. Unfortunately, there was no time to refine his formula, no time to test his hypotheses.

No time to arrange for human subjects. So instead of exposing someone else to his procedure, as those other scientists had done, Bruce had the temerity to test it on himself.

Big mistake.

The formula he developed made him big and strong, all right. *Even bigger and stronger than Captain America.* But it also made a rampaging monster out of him.

A *hulk,* as it were.

His mind reduced to that of a madman, he tore up Chelsea Piers on the west side of Manhattan. That incident earned him the scrutiny of a cadre of doctors, charged with monitoring his blood three times a day for what they called "Hulk cells."

It was a short time later, in one of life's all-time greatest ironies, that the world's original super-soldier—a guy named Steve Rogers—was fished out of an ice floe in the Arctic Ocean by a team of flabbergasted marine biologists.

Suddenly, Captain America was back. "And in light of recent events," said the TV narrator, whose name continued to elude Banner, "we couldn't be happier about it."

At the time, Banner was happy about it too. After all, he would enjoy access to Rogers's blood. He could analyze it with the help of a high-powered microscope and get some insights into Captain America's miraculous metabolism.

But it didn't work out the way he had hoped. Even with the blood samples, he couldn't duplicate the super-soldier formula. Disappointed and frustrated by his failure, he cracked a little.

That was when he did something stupid, something he wished like hell he hadn't even thought of. Mixing the blood of the resurrected Captain America with the serum that had made Banner the Hulk, he rolled up his sleeve and injected it all into his vein.

By the time the Ultimates corralled him and forced him to revert to his original form, he had killed people. *Hundreds* of them. He had brought buildings crashing down—buildings that still had human beings in them. He tried not to think of that on a daily basis, but it was always lurking in the back of his mind.

Like the Hulk himself.

Unfortunately, it wasn't just in Banner's mind that the creature survived. It was in his cells as well, because his Hulk intrabodies had bonded with his DNA. *Permanently.*

So, despite the cocktail of medications he was taking, he could turn into the Hulk at the drop of an adrenalin surge. Which meant that he would never be allowed to leave his holding unit.

He had screwed up, and it seemed likely he would pay for his mistake every day for the rest of his life.

As he thought that, the door to the security chamber slid aside. It didn't make a sound loud enough for

Banner to hear through his transparent barrier. But thanks to the change in his guards' behavior, he was aware of it all the same.

"Ten-shun!" said Warshovsky.

"At ease, Lieutenant," said a voice Banner recognized.

Its owner crossed the space between the door and the transparent wall of the holding unit, his stride as purposeful and assured as always. When he reached the barrier, he placed his hand on it.

Just as he always does. Banner knew the man too well.

Nick Fury was the American general serving as the head of SHIELD, which meant he was in charge of the Triskelion. *And therefore,* Banner added, *in charge of* me.

People who met Fury for the first time always commented on his resemblance to Samuel L. Jackson, the actor. Banner didn't see it. He thought Fury looked like a biology professor he had known back at New York University.

Except, of course, for the black eye patch he wore, covering up what was reportedly an empty socket as well as most of the scar tissue around it. Fury had never told Banner how he lost the eye, but the scientist had dreamed up an interesting scenario or two.

In his holding unit, he had time to come up with such strange tales. *Lots of it.*

Getting up from his easy chair, Banner padded across his floor on bare feet. He didn't feel compelled to wear shoes or socks anymore, any concern with formality long since discarded.

"Banner," said Fury. "How are you?"

"As well as can be expected," said the scientist.

The general seldom came to visit him. Banner wondered why he had done so this time.

"I'm guessing you need my input on something."

"Actually," said Fury, "we do." He briefed Banner on the situation. "I'll see to it you're patched in on a closed circuit. Two-way, so you can interact with the intruders."

Banner nodded, causing his glasses to slide down his nose. He pushed them back up again. "I'll be happy to help."

"I appreciate it," said Fury.

Then he turned smartly, the way military people were trained to turn, and left the room.

Banner appreciated the fact that the general hadn't lingered. It would only have underlined the uncomfortable distinction between them. The scientist, after all, was a man in a cage, and Fury was the fellow whose orders had put him there.

Not that the general was a bad man. *He just has some tough decisions to make,* Banner allowed.

And one of them, apparently, was what to do with the intruders in the green and white suits.

• • •

Steve Rogers looked around the black briefing room table at the other components of the government's highly publicized Ultimates team. With the exception of Thor, whose physique and long-handled hammer set him well apart from the man on the street, no one there looked like he was capable of foiling a house burglary, much less a full-scale extraterrestrial invasion.

Stark was surprisingly unimposing outside his armor, which was difficult for him to wear for more than a couple of hours at a time. Jan was a resourceful woman with unusual abilities, but she was too slim and feminine to scare anyone. And Rogers himself, while more muscular than the average Joe, gave no indication of the considerable power he could bring to bear.

Probably the least impressive person in attendance was Bruce Banner, and he wasn't even there in the flesh. He was only monitoring the meeting through a wireless comm link from his holding unit in the heart of the Triskelion.

The man who had once been in charge of Fury's super-soldier program was reduced to little more than a prisoner, thanks to the murderous rampage he had gone on as the Hulk. And the general had no plans to release Banner any time soon, considering he could cut another swath of destruction at the drop of a hat.

But Banner was still a genius, by all accounts, and

Fury had wanted to hear the guy's take on the Tomorrow Men. And Banner had been happy to oblige, considering he didn't have a whole lot else to do.

Banner's situation made Rogers understand how close he had come to being transformed into a monster himself. If the scientists who had built him up into a super-soldier had adopted Banner's approach instead of their own, Rogers too might have lived out his life in a high-security cage.

But he hadn't thought about that back in the forties. All he had known was that his country required a hero, and that he was in a position to give it what it needed. *Possible side effects?* No one had mentioned any.

Was that because the scientists back then were naïve? Rogers wondered. *Or just too sharp to make the mistake Banner made?*

Just then, the door opened and General Fury came in. And he wasn't alone.

As Rogers watched, the so-called Tomorrow Men filed into the room. They were all wearing the same green-on-white uniform, all sporting billiard-ball haircuts.

Which are considered fashionable these days, he reminded himself. *Stop living in the past, old-timer.*

Taking the chairs left for them, which were all on the same side of the briefing table, the Tomorrow Men sat down. One of them, who was swarthier than the others, seemed to stare at Rogers.

"Something wrong?" Rogers asked him.

"No," said the Tomorrow Man, in a surprisingly melodic voice, "not at all. It's just that I never expected to meet you in the flesh."

The woman—whose head was shaven as clean as those of her comrades—smiled with what seemed like unmitigated delight. "You're Steve Rogers."

"Mister Rogers," said another of the Tomorrow Men, a fellow with a long face and a deeply cleft chin, "it's a pleasure to meet you." And his companions echoed the sentiment.

"You know me?" Rogers asked.

"Of course," said the man with the long face. "Everyone knows the exploits of Steve Rogers."

Rogers was surprised. After all, Captain America was the celebrity. Steve Rogers was just the guy who tagged along with him.

The dark-skinned man smiled at him. "Are you surprised your civilian name is known in our time?"

"Frankly," said Rogers, "I'm surprised it was known in *this* time."

"For those of you who haven't had the pleasure," said Stark, "allow me to make introductions."

He went on to identify the intruders one by one. The man with the long face was Weyland—their leader, apparently. The woman, an athletic-looking specimen with big, blue eyes, was Haggerty. The dark-skinned fellow was Chadaputra. The fourth Tomorrow Man, a sober-looking Asian, was Matsubayashi. The fifth, a brawny individual with a spray of freckles across his wide, flat nose, was Kosar.

Five of them, Rogers thought, *because temporal transit is rough, and they didn't know how many of them would survive it.* Or so the intruders had said.

"We've come a long way," said Weyland. "We appreciate the opportunity to speak with you."

"We know it's difficult for you to accept the fact that we're from the future," said Haggerty. "However, we came prepared to dispel your doubts."

"How?" asked Thor.

"By providing personal details no one else is likely to know," said Chadaputra. "For instance, the name of your family's pet dog. Garm, wasn't it?"

Thor chuckled. "So it was."

"He lived to the ripe old age of seventeen before he succumbed to a hip dysplasia problem. His death came the same weekend as that of your mother."

Thor's smile faded. "Correct again."

"It was in your memoirs," said Chadaputra, "the ones you'll write more than thirty years from now." He turned to Fury. "Growing up in Brooklyn, your best friend was Isadore Cohen. His family operated an establishment known as a candy store."

Fury didn't confirm it. However, he also didn't deny it.

"On Saturday nights," said Chadaputra, "between the ages of eight and twelve, you and Isadore would assemble Sunday editions of *The New York Times* for customers to purchase the following morning."

The general remained silent. His only response was the twitching of a muscle in his jaw.

"That," said Chadaputra, "was in *your* memoirs." He looked at the image of Banner on the screen in front of him. "You, Doctor, have two extra nipples protruding from your abdomen, several centimeters below the traditional pair. While they appear to be nothing more than moles, they were mentioned prominently in a study of—"

"We get the *idea,*" said Banner, cutting him off.

"You sound offended," said Weyland, obviously concerned. "I assure you, Doctor, that wasn't our intention. As you're a scientist, we thought you would—"

"Right," Banner interjected. "Let's move on."

"Actually," said Fury, "I think we've heard enough. What we need to know," he told Weyland, "is why you're here."

The Tomorrow Man frowned. "I know this will sound bizarre to you, General." He looked around the table at the Ultimates. "To all of you. But we've come to change the past."

4

"THE PAST . . . ?" FURY ECHOED, BEATING Stark to the punch.

"*Our* past," Chadaputra elaborated. "What you would call the present."

"And you want to change it . . . why?" Jan wondered.

"If I'm too specific," said Weyland, "I'll jeopardize the integrity of the timeline. But I can tell you this: In the next two hundred and thirty years, civilization will devolve. Nations will vanish, to be replaced by regional dictatorships. Large portions of the world will become lawless, recognizing allegiance to no government at all. Wars will become commonplace and infinitely more brutal than you have known them to be. Slavery, torture, mass execution . . . there will be no end to the misery."

Sounds inviting, Stark thought.

"All the evils you have buried or are attempting to bury in the twenty-first century will claw their way to the surface again—all because of a single organization, which has managed thus far to remain undetected as it recruits its personnel and builds its bases and stockpiles its armaments. If left unmolested, it will go on preparing just a little while longer. Then it will strike everywhere at once, and no one on Earth will be able to stand against it.

"Its name," said Weyland, "is Tiber."

"Never heard of it," said Stark.

"Me either," Jan chimed in.

Fury shifted in his chair. "I have."

Surprised, Stark looked at his colleague—and he wasn't the only one. "Holding out on us, General?"

Fury spread his hands. "All we had was a name and scattered reports, held together by the same modus operandi. Humanitarian food caravans disappearing into thin air. Drug trafficking operations that would be there one day and gone the next. Raids on precious-metal repositories that left dozens dead in their wakes.

"All because of Tiber. We're sure of that. But we haven't been able to identify any of their members or track them to their hideouts. A couple of locations have been suggested, but nothing concrete. Just the occasional rumor."

"Tiber is more than a rumor," said Weyland.

"What do they want?" asked Stark.

"World domination," said Weyland.

Thor smiled. "Spooky."

"With all due respect," said Weyland, "it would be a mistake not to take Tiber seriously. In this case, world domination isn't a madman's fantasy. It's a realistic objective."

"Which is realized only briefly," said Chadaputra, "but paves the way for the world to come."

"So," said Rogers, summing it up, "if Tiber isn't crippled in our time, they'll end up ruining the world in yours."

Weyland nodded. "Which is why it's so important to us to clean out their nests."

"When you put it that way . . ." said Jan.

"Tiber," Thor said thoughtfully. "As in 'Tiber River'?"

Chadaputra turned to him. "A logical conclusion, but an incorrect one. Apparently, the organization's founder was an individual named Tiber. He first turned up in a monastery in France during the Middle Ages—the fourteenth century, to be precise."

"A monk?" asked Rogers.

"He was studying to become one," said Chadaputra. "However, before he took his vows, he experienced a change of heart. Rejecting the notion that the world had been created by a supreme being, he slaughtered every last member of the religious order that inhabited the monastery, claimed the place for his own, and drew to him an army from the dregs of the medieval landscape."

"I never read this in any history book," said Banner, his skepticism evident on the monitor screens in front of them.

Weyland smiled politely. "By now, Doctor, you must know that not every piece of valuable information is recorded for posterity. I imagine you've heard that history is written by the victors. In certain instances, those victors have found it useful to remain absent from the accounts of their victories.

"That was what happened in Tiber's case. With the help of his army, he secured a large part of central France and ruled it sternly. But it wasn't enough to satisfy him. With success came ambition, and he was intelligent enough to set his sights higher than others might have.

"His only impediment was a rare blood disease, which his physicians said would make him infirm before his time and ultimately shorten his lifespan. However, it would be years before it had any visible effect on him.

"Tiber wasn't discouraged by the news. He was already forty-six years old, and most men of his primitive era were dead by that age anyway. If anything, he was inspired by his limitation, determined to show that he could transcend it—that, despite everything, he could seize the greatest prize imaginable."

"And what was that?" asked Stark.

"The world in its entirety," said Haggerty. "Every last clod and stone of it. But he had profited from his study of earlier conquerors like Alexander and Julius Caesar. He knew there was no army large enough to take and hold so vast an empire. Eventually, his forces would be spread too thin to put down rebellions, which were certain to crop up from time to time.

"To have any real hope of conquering the world, Tiber needed more political power, and more wealth, and more shrewd, educated men like himself. But it would take time to amass all three, and time was Tiber's enemy.

"In the end, he did something we believe to be unprecedented in the history of our species—he created a scheme for world domination that would span hundreds of years, the culmination of which he would never live to see. But when it finally came to fruition, those who benefited from it would speak the name Tiber in awe and gratitude, and those ground underfoot by it would curse him as no one had ever been cursed before."

"Lovely," said Jan.

"And impressive," said Thor. "For a mortal, of course."

To plan something that wouldn't take place until

the next millennium? To leave a legacy so ambitious, so powerful, that it would outlive its creator by several centuries?

Stark found it impressive as well.

"What do you want us to do?" he asked.

"Unfortunately," said Weyland, "we can't address Tiber in this era—not directly. And even if we could, there are only five of us. We don't have the resources you do."

In Stark's view, the Tomorrow Men had *plenty* of resources. His neck was still stiff from getting bludgeoned with one of them. But he refrained from bringing that up.

Weyland leaned forward in his chair. "We need you to destroy Tiber—utterly. And we have obtained information that can assist you in that effort."

"Including," Fury said hopefully, "the locations out of which they operate?"

It was a logical assumption. But Weyland shook his head. "Unfortunately, we don't know everything about your era. And when it comes to Tiber, we know very little."

Thor looked at him askance. "No offense, but I find that difficult to believe. You know intimate details of my life, and those of my colleagues. You knew enough about the layout of the Triskelion to appear safely inside her."

"And," said Rogers, picking up the thread, "you know about the fourth-century monk who founded the organization. So why wouldn't you know where its operations were?"

Stark had to admit it was a valid question.

Weyland sighed. "What you did, even in your personal lives, was eventually public knowledge. The layout of this facility was public—in fact, there are remnants of it still standing in my time. But the location of Tiber's nests remained a secret, to the final dying breath of its last adherent.

"The regimes that rule the world in my era might have exhausted their resources to find these places. However, there was no reason for them to do so. As long as Tiber was no longer a threat to them, they couldn't have cared less what secrets were contained in some hollow, predator-infested mountain."

"But," said Jan, a note of irony in her voice, "you'd like *us* to destroy Tiber."

"We would," Weyland confirmed. "And since we believe this was a critical time in the perfection of Tiber's security systems, we would like you to do it as quickly as possible."

Well, Stark thought, *at least he's not shy about it.*

"We'll need some time to absorb this," Fury advised the Tomorrow Men. "In the meantime, I'll see to it that you're escorted back to your accommodations."

Weyland looked as though he would have preferred a more immediate response. But he said, "Thank you."

With a tap of a stud built into the underside of the table, the general summoned a couple of guards. Seeing them enter the room, the intruders got up from their seats and filed out.

Leaving Stark and the other Ultimates to kick around what they had heard.

Clint Barton, three-time Olympic gold medalist, stood at the edge of the Triskelion's black asphalt helipad and fit a red-fletched arrow to his titanium-alloy bow. All his arrows had red fletching—a warning to his enemies.

Barton's target, a cone-shaped, open-framework green buoy, was rocking gently in the frothy chop of the Upper Bay. A seagull was sitting on top of it, training a hungry eye on the waves.

Barton's magnifying goggles could have showed him the texture of the skin on the gull's feet if he had needed them to. As it was, they gave him a nice, clear picture of the bell dangling in the middle of the open cone.

It was nearly a quarter mile away, with a variable crosswind of what he estimated was five to fifteen miles an hour. *Piece of cake,* Barton told himself.

Lifting his bow, he took aim at the bell and pulled back on the thin, flexible cable that served him as a bowstring. Then, allowing for wind, the effect of gravity, and the rhythm of the waves, he released the shaft.

A moment later, the bell rang out clear and true. Barton could barely hear it, but he didn't have to. The goggles had shown him the arrow striking its target.

"Any idea what's going on with these Tomorrow Men?" Wanda asked.

She was standing behind Barton, leaning against the wall with her arms folded across her chest. *Looking seductive,* he thought. But then, she *always* looked seductive.

Not that he would ever consider making a move on her. For one thing, he had a loving girlfriend and a couple of great kids, and he knew better than to do anything that might mess that up. For another thing, he had a rule against mixing work with play. And for a third, Wanda was at heart just a tease, too wrapped up in her brother to get involved with anyone else.

In fact, it was only lately that he saw them apart occasionally. Most of the time, they were like Siamese twins—and very bizarre Siamese twins at that.

"Fury and the others are talking to them now," he said.

"They never tell me or Pietro *anything,*" said Wanda. "It's as if we're not even part of the team."

"Of course you are," said the archer. "You're the part that gets dirty. The part that goes into dark, smelly places and rubs up against the cockroaches."

"What a delightful image," said Wanda, making no effort to conceal her revulsion, "but what does it have to do with our being snubbed by General Fury?"

"If you were in the business of trusting people with your secrets," said Barton, "would you trust them to those most likely to be captured and tortured?"

Silence. Obviously, Wanda had seen his point.

"Hell," he continued, "I told them I don't *want* to know what's going on. Then I won't have to worry about giving anything up."

"You're being facetious, of course."

"Not at all," Barton said.

Removing a second shaft from the quiver strapped to his thigh, he knocked it and took aim again. Drew back on his string. Made minute adjustments. Let the arrow fly.

Again, the bell pealed plaintively across the waters of the bay. Barton slipped another arrow from his quiver.

"Then you don't mind being left out of things?" Wanda asked.

"Meetings aren't my idea of a good time."

As far as the archer was concerned, there would be plenty of big brains in the room saying plenty of big-brain type things. They wouldn't miss his two cents' worth of junior college insights.

"Doesn't anything bother you?" Wanda demanded,

obviously hoping he would confide in her that something *did*.

Barton smiled to himself as he snugged the arrow against his string. "Not a thing."

"I don't believe you," said Wanda, a hint of pique in her voice. "I think you're having a joke at my expense."

The wind was kicking up more than before, so the archer aimed a little to his right. Then he pulled back until the fletching was tickling his ear, and fired.

Like the other shafts, this one shot across the water, headed unerringly for the buoy. Barton watched it with a degree of satisfaction, anticipating the inevitable convergence of arrowhead and moving target.

Until it missed.

Not by more than an inch or two. But to him, it might as well have been a city block.

"I *never* miss," he mumbled to himself, an unfamiliar heat creeping into his cheeks.

It wasn't a brag—it was a well-known fact. Geese flew south for the winter. Water froze at thirty-two degrees Fahrenheit. And "Hawkeye" Barton hit his marks.

As he came to grips with his failure, he saw Wanda turn and touch the door control. That was when it hit him.

"Hey," Barton called after her, "that was *you!*"

"Excuse me?" she said, as the door opened.

"You made me miss!"

Wanda shrugged. "You think so?"

Barton scowled at her. "Damned right I do."

"All right," she said, rolling her eyes, "if it makes you feel better, go ahead."

Then Wanda entered the building and left him standing there by himself.

Barton swore beneath his breath. It was *her*, all right. And he would prove it.

Freeing another arrow from his quiver, he knocked it and got the bell in his sights again. Then he pulled back, allowed for a respite in the wind, and let go.

The shaft rang the bell as surely as the first two.

He grunted. *"Freakin' witch."*

Suddenly, he heard a voice in his ear: "Actually, it was *me* who made you miss."

Whirling, Barton managed to catch a glimpse of a dark gray blur retreating across the expanse of the helipad. *Pietro,* he thought, with an air of resignation.

If it wasn't one of them, it was the other.

In the absence of the Tomorrow Men, Fury scanned the faces of the Ultimates, looking for a preview of what they thought.

"So?" he asked finally.

"If Tiber's as bad as the general suggests," said Stark, "we've got to pounce on this."

"I agree," said Banner.

"Then you believe these people are really from the future?" asked Jan.

"I don't know," said Banner. "Time travel is a little out of my league."

"Mine too," said Rogers, "unless it's the kind that involves being placed on ice."

"Actually," said Stark, "*I* know a bit about this subject."

"How so?" asked Banner from his video screen.

"Some years ago," said Stark, "a guy came to me with plans for a time-travel device. Wanted me to back him. I didn't take him seriously until my research guys told me time travel was possible. In fact, scientists had already made it happen in a particle accelerator, using quarks as guinea pigs."

"Quarks?" said Thor.

"A subatomic particle," Banner explained.

Fury jerked a thumb over his shoulder, indicating the Tomorrow Men. "Those guys aren't subatomic particles."

Stark smiled. "So I noticed. And when we calculated how much power we would need to transport a person into the past—even to a point only a couple of minutes earlier than his departure—it was more than the sun generates in a decade. But the real problem wasn't power. It was causality."

"Causality . . . ?" Fury echoed.

"Also known as the Grandfather Paradox," said Stark.

Banner picked up the thread, eager as the kid in third grade who couldn't keep his hand down. "Say you traveled back in time and met your own maternal grandfather. If you wanted to—or even if you *didn't* want to—you could keep him from meeting your grandmother, which would prevent your mother from being born, which would in turn prevent *you* from being born. So if you never existed in the first place, how could you ever have gone back in time?"

"You're making my head hurt," said Rogers.

"What you're saying," said Jan, "is you would be screwing up time somehow?"

"It gets worse," said Banner. "The laws of physics only work when cause precedes effect. If you go back in time and change things, effects are divorced from their causes. It's not just time going out the window—it's Natural Law."

"Not necessarily," said Thor. He leaned forward, resting his powerful arms on the table. "Isn't your action in the past a cause as well?"

Banner frowned. "Yes, in a manner of speaking. But an effect can't have two causes—only one. The universe has to work the same way all the time. A law can only be a law if it's infallible."

Thor looked sympathetic. "Not even Odin is infallible."

Fury was skeptical about the whole Odin-and-Asgard thing, and had been all along. Obviously, Thor was an individual who boasted some crazy-ass supernatural abilities. But a lot of people thought his talk about gods and demons was delusional, and the general was tempted to agree with them.

"So time travel is inadvisable," he interjected, getting the discussion back on track, "because you might prevent yourself from existing—maybe even put a dent in the way things work. I get all that. But you're saying it's *possible*, right?"

"That's my understanding," said Stark.

"Then it's also possible that our friends are telling the truth? That they came from the future, for godsakes?" Fury scowled. "I'm having a hard time getting on board with that."

"Because it's insane," said Rogers.

"Says the man who slept in an iceberg for sixty years." Stark looked around the table. "My researchers told me time travel would require huge stores of power. But two hundred years in the future, they may be capable of harnessing such power—by tapping into energy sources we've yet to consider."

Thor shook his head. "I'm not satisfied these people are what they say they are."

"Me either," said Jan.

The general scanned their faces, sparing Banner's video image a glance as well. "And the rest of you?"

Banner pushed his glasses up his nose with a fore-finger. "I don't think we have enough to go on."

"I agree," said Stark. "We need more information."

Rogers drummed his fingers on the table. "I can't imagine their telling us anything that will make a difference. Still, I suppose we should keep an open mind."

Stark turned to Fury. "What do *you* think?"

The general sat back in his chair. "I think I need to have another talk with the Tomorrow Men."

5

As Jan stood at the transparent wall of the Triskelion's state-of-the-art gym, she remarked on how much she loved to watch her boyfriend work out.

For a big guy, he was so quick, so agile, so fluid. *One would never know he's pushing eighty-five.*

Certainly not as he swung bare-chested around the horizontal bar, all six-foot-two of him fully extended, his expression relaxed, even serene. Then again, he was comfortable on the high bar. It was one of the things that hadn't changed much since 1945.

But even with Steve's display of athleticism to

distract her, Jan couldn't help thinking about the Tomorrow Men, and the direction of the conversation after Fury left the conference room. For her part, she had continued to express the doubts she'd had all along. But Thor was more skeptical by half.

"With all due respect to Doctor Banner," he had said, *"the fact that he has a couple of extra nipples is something any of us could have found out—if we were motivated to do so."*

"Wouldn't there be medical records?" Steve had asked. *"Something in Banner's scholastic file?"*

The scientist had looked as if he were in pain, though Jan didn't think anyone else noticed.

"And military documents," Steve had continued. *"Extra nipples might even be cause for a deferment."*

"No offense, Doctor," Stark had chimed in.

"None taken," Banner had responded, though that clearly wasn't the case.

Jan was just relieved the Tomorrow Men hadn't gone into the details of *her* life.

People were invariably surprised when they found out she was the Wasp. They seemed to expect someone tougher, someone who could play linebacker for the Jets if no one looked too closely.

Not a slim Asian woman who would rather wear a lab coat than track shoes, and whose experience in combat, until recently, had been limited to self-defense lessons at the Y.

Yes. They were surprised, all right.

But how much *more* surprised would they have been if they knew the truth—that she wasn't a human being at all, strictly speaking? That she was a mutant, a member of a species as different from homo sapiens as homo sapiens was from the Neanderthal?

On the outside, she looked human enough. *Thank God*. But on the inside, she was all screwed up. She had organs normal people didn't have, proclivities that would have made her an outcast if everyone knew about them.

The Wasp . . . it wasn't just a handle she had picked because her boyfriend could shrink her to insect size, or because she had invented a device that emitted a kind of sting. It was what she *was*, what she had *always* been, before Hank's shrinking process ever came close to being a reality.

When she went to bed at night she felt a powerful attraction to light, even if it was only the glow of a digital clock. When she got up in the morning she found clutches of tiny eggs in the bedclothes.

Her need for sweets could be irresistible, often leaving her lightheaded with hunger. Unlike other people, she wasn't repelled by the thought of eating flies. And without realizing it, she would sometimes find herself chewing on pencils.

No, not just chewing. That would be almost normal. She would manipulate the wood in her mouth, mix it with her saliva, and turn it into some kind of paper.

Like a wasp.

It had always scared her that she was so different. It had torn her up inside, keeping her from making friends lest they find out the truth about her.

Finally, after all those years of desperately pretending to be like other people, she hooked up with a group in which *everyone* was different. Thor, depending on whether one believed him or not, was either a madman or a Scandinavian god. Stark was a fanatic, in a social and economic stratum all by himself. Steve was the larger-than-life product of a government super-soldier program. Banner could turn into a damned monster if he wasn't careful.

It should have been easy for Jan to lose herself in such a crew. *To fit in.* But she was still scared, because habits like hers could make even a god lose his lunch.

Contrary to what was apparently popular belief, Steve Rogers didn't like to exercise.

He never had, going all the way back to the days he had spent as a 128-pound weakling, before the super-soldier program got hold of him. And then, after he was transformed into Captain America, he didn't *have* to exercise.

All those changes in Rogers's musculature were products of the treatments they had given him. He hadn't earned any part of them in the gym. They had just *happened*.

But there were instances, however rare, when he did work out—times when he found comfort in mindless physical repetition. *Like now,* he thought as he executed loop after fully extended loop around the horizontal bar.

And it was because of the Tomorrow Men.

After all, Rogers had been thrust into the harsh glare of the twenty-first century with a lot of catching up to do. And he was doing it—he was making the adjustment. But every so often, he caught himself wishing he was still living in 1945.

Back then, people had gotten their news from the daily paper and their entertainment from the radio. The phone company—and there was only one—had needed only seven digits to distinguish each of its customers' numbers. And far from thinking about cloning or nuclear power or the Internet, people were marveling at the fact that stockings could be made of synthetic fibers.

It nettled him to think so many of his favorite things and people had been swept away in the rush of time. Like the blueberry pie at the Horn & Hardart automats. And the big band sound. And most of the guys alongside whom he had fought Hitler's blitzkrieg.

All ghosts. All irrevocably, irretrievably gone.

But even more unsettling to him were the things and people he had missed entirely. Hula-Hoops. *The Honeymooners.* Jackson Pollock. Drive-in movie theaters. Mickey Mantle. The Berlin Wall. Martin Luther King. The World Trade Center. Disco.

He wasn't sure he would have appreciated it all, but he wished he had been given the chance. It was—for him, at least—as if a big hunk of history had simply never happened.

And Jan wonders why I like to keep to myself so much. It wasn't because he couldn't cope with the wonders of the twenty-first century. It was because he was still coming to grips with all the decades that came before it.

Now the Tomorrow Men were giving him another era to contend with, another endpoint without anything connected to it. Despite his physiological superiority, despite the air of confidence people imputed to him, it was almost more than he could handle.

Executing one last loop around the bar, Rogers tucked his knees into his chest and carried out a quadruple somersault before he planted his feet on the floor—his heels together, his arms extended, his weight balanced within a hundredth of an ounce.

This I can do, he thought.

It was only then that he realized he had attracted a gallery of gawking SHIELD personnel—Jan among them. Smiling a little to acknowledge her, he went over to the towel he had laid on the floor beside the apparatus and wiped his face with it.

Not that he needed it. He had barely broken a sweat.

For just a moment, Rogers felt unreal. As if he weren't part of the twenty-first century or any other. As if he were a phantom made up of people's expectations, drifting through time.

And it scared him a little.

But he was Captain America, damn it. He would get through it.

As Fury approached the chamber where the Tomorrow Men had been sequestered, he was pleased to note the vigilance of the half-dozen SHIELD guards posted outside the door.

"Sir," said Nakamura, the man in charge of the detail.

"I'd like a word with our friends in there," said the general.

"Of course, sir," said Nakamura. "And the password?"

Fury was the one who issued the new ones every morning. He always had to resist using "Swordfish."

"Gabriel Jones," he said, citing his parents' favorite jazz musician, who had recently celebrated his eightieth birthday in a Westchester nursing home.

Nakamura nodded. "Thank you, sir."

Before the Ultimates' confrontation with the

Chitauri a few weeks earlier, Fury wouldn't have believed such security measures necessary. After all, Nakamura was standing right there, looking at his superior face to face.

Nothing like having your headquarters invaded by shapeshifters to make you a little paranoid, the general thought.

"Would you like us to accompany you inside?" Nakamura asked.

Fury shook his head. "That won't be necessary."

"As you wish, sir," said Nakamura.

He turned and tapped a six-digit code into a touch-sensitive screen imbedded in the wall. A moment later, the door to the Tomorrow Men's cell slid aside.

"Go ahead, sir," said Nakamura.

As Fury walked in, he saw the Tomorrow Men's eyes move in his direction. They searched his face.

"General," said Weyland, standing up to greet Fury. "Your discussion lasted quite some time."

"Not really," said Fury. "I just wanted to mull everything over before I came to see you."

"And?" said the Tomorrow Man.

"We need more proof."

Weyland frowned. "We believed we had *given* you proof."

"The personal details you mentioned—Thor's dog and such—would be difficult to dig up these days, but not impossible. If you're really from the

future, you must know something about us even *we*
don't know—at least, not yet."

Weyland appeared to weigh the suggestion. "A logical approach, I'll grant you—except anything we tell
you will change the timeline in some way. It will
encourage you to take a certain action or adopt a certain attitude, or else back off from certain actions or
attitudes. And in doing so, you'll invite a temporal
disaster."

Fury saw the problem. "You have a better idea?"

"I don't," said Weyland. "Which perturbs me,
because we should have foreseen this possibility.
Knowing what we knew of you, we just assumed that
you would trust us."

"Which, frankly, doesn't help your case."

"I understand," said Weyland. "But what have you
got to lose by going after Tiber?"

"That depends on how nefarious you are."

"You know the kinds of crimes Tiber has committed. I would think you'd jump at the chance to stop
them."

"If I knew for sure we would be doing that. For all
I know, we'd be walking into a trap."

"Why would we want to trap you?"

"You tell *me*," said Fury.

"So you won't go out on a limb?" asked Weyland.
"Even if it means you would be saving your world?"

"Even then."

"But isn't that your organization's reason for

being? So it can address threats to the security of your nation and others?"

"It is," the general conceded. "But first we've got to qualify our sources. In this case, we haven't been able to do that."

Weyland frowned. "I'll have to give this some thought."

"Keep in mind," said Fury, "we're not looking for something we can find in the *Post.*"

"A paper periodical," said the Tomorrow Man. "The reference isn't lost on me."

"Good," said Fury.

The ball, as the saying went, was in Weyland's court.

"In my *brain?*" Rogers echoed.

"Yes," said Chadaputra.

They were all back in the conference room, the Ultimates on one side of the table and the Tomorrow Men on the other. And Rogers couldn't believe what he had just heard.

He cast a glance in Fury's direction. "It's a joke, right?"

"I don't blame you for being skeptical," said Chadaputra. "Were our positions reversed, I'm sure I would feel the same way."

"You see," said Weyland, "the scientists in the super-soldier program had never created anything— that is, any*one* like you before. They didn't know what to expect. There were so many changes taking place in your body, especially at the genetic level . . . there was no telling how they might affect your mind."

"You need look no further than Doctor Banner to appreciate the validity of their concern," said Haggerty.

Banner frowned on their video screens, but he didn't say anything in response.

"You might have become prone to fits of anger," Weyland continued. "Or paranoia. Or bouts of resentment. Or all of the above."

"Or," said Kosar, "you might simply have decided you preferred national socialism to democracy."

Rogers felt a spurt of disgust. "Impossible."

"It didn't happen," said Kosar, "but it *might* have. And if you did align yourself with the Axis cause, you would have represented a more formidable threat to the Allies than Adolf Hitler."

"So the super-soldier scientists installed a failsafe," said Chadaputra, "a way to neutralize you if you went astray. They had to protect their country, after all. It was the prudent thing to do."

"I don't buy it," Fury interjected. "When we found Cap floating in the Arctic, our best people scanned him six ways to Sunday. If there had been a device floating around in his brain, they would have identified it."

"It's not easily identified," said Weyland. "If it

were, it would have been useless, considering the advanced level of technology the Germans had at their disposal."

Thanks to the Chitauri, Rogers added inwardly. He couldn't help wondering how much more quickly the Allies would have won the war if the Germans hadn't had extraterrestrials on their side.

"We can debate this until *our* century," said Matsubayashi. He glanced at his colleagues. "Perhaps we should just show our hosts what we're talking about."

"How?" asked the general, saving Rogers the trouble.

"You have a state-of-the-art emergency medical facility here on the premises," said Chadaputra. "In my era, I'm an expert in the field of medical technology as well as an accomplished surgeon. With a little work, I can upgrade your equipment—enable it to show us what we need to see."

"And if you find it?" asked Rogers.

"I can remove it," said Chadaputra, "if that's your wish. Or I can leave it where it is. But first, let us identify the device."

"What's involved in *that*?" asked Jan, her concern touchingly evident in her voice.

"The procedure is no more dangerous or invasive than magnetic resonance imaging," Haggerty assured her. "And it takes just a few moments."

Fury looked at Rogers. "You're the only one here who can give them the okay, Cap."

The super-soldier scowled. "I should have my head examined for even considering it," he said. "But you've aroused my curiosity, so what the hell. Let's do it."

6

As **Henry Pym** sat by himself in the Triskelion's ridiculously comfortable north-wing lounge and watched Steve Rogers's surgery on a high-definition television screen, part of him wanted the patient to die on the operating table.

He was ashamed of the fact, but he couldn't deny it. He hated Rogers and everything about him. He hated the way Rogers had tracked him down and confronted him with his beating of Jan, and then given him a taste of his own medicine.

As if he were my damned father, Pym thought bitterly, *taking his belt to me.*

Then, to literally add insult to injury, Rogers had

taken Pym's place as Jan's lover. It was written up daily in the tabloids, the talk of all the celebrity TV shows. And every time Pym saw it, he felt a knife twisting in his guts.

So Pym had good reason to hate Steve Rogers, good reason to want the red, white and blue son of a bitch dead. Not that it was going to happen. Not that he *wanted* it to happen, really.

And yet, there was that part of him that *did*.

"Did you get it?" Nick Fury asked.

"See for yourself," said Chadaputra, indicating the microscope he had been using when Fury walked in.

The general crossed the laboratory, which he still thought of as Banner's, and took a look through the microscope's eyepiece. It showed him something that looked like a boomerang, except it was bone-white and couldn't be seen by the naked eye.

Smaller than a fingernail clipping, Fury thought. And yet it had the ability to kill a man.

Even a man like Steve Rogers.

"There aren't any others," he asked, "are there?"

Chadaputra shook his head. "We checked, just to be certain. I assure you, General, this was the only one."

Well, Fury thought, *that's a relief.* The idea of a fail-safe mechanism in Captain America's brain was almost as disturbing to him as a mechanism in his own. *Come to think of it, maybe it wouldn't be a bad idea to scan me too . . .*

"When can I speak to him?" he asked the Tomorrow Man.

Chadaputra shrugged. "Any time you want. Captain Rogers was awake throughout the operation."

Tony Stark smiled at his swiftly recuperating teammate. "You look like you could jump out of bed and take on the entire Swedish bikini team."

Rogers watched a nurse check his pulse. "I've never heard of that team," he said without a hint of irony in his voice, "but taking it on sounds kind of . . . um, dull and unfulfilling."

"You'd *better* say that," Jan remarked from the opposite side of the bed, "or our friend the nurse here is going to be the *only* one holding your hand."

The nurse, a chunky blond woman, wrinkled her nose at Stark. "I know you're the boss here," she said, "but it's a little unusual to bring alcoholic beverages into a patient's room."

"Just making certain I've got no germs," said Stark, sloshing his martini around in its glass. "They don't thrive in an alcohol-rich environment, you know."

"You're bad," said Jan.

"But if the smell of a martini offends you," Stark told the nurse, "I'll be happy to escort it out of the room." He winked at Rogers. "Anyway, it's time I took care of a few things. See you when they let you out."

Which would be in only a few hours, thanks to Chadaputra's skill with a laser beam and Rogers's uncanny healing abilities. *Incredible,* Stark reflected as he let himself out of the infirmary.

It was difficult to keep from imagining what *else* the Tomorrow Man might accomplish with his advanced surgical know-how. If he could remove a microscopic sliver from Rogers's brain, would it be any more difficult to take out a tumor—one considered inoperable by the doctors of the twenty-first century?

An interesting question, Stark thought.

But it wasn't the feasibility of the procedure that would determine Chadaputra's willingness to go ahead with it. The important thing, from the perspective of the Tomorrow Men, would be the repercussions of Stark's death.

If the growth in his brain never killed him, how would the timeline be changed? Radically—or barely at all? Would the future take shape in a new and even more frightening way? Or, as in the case of Rogers's surgery, would Stark's leave nary a blip?

It was something he hadn't dared to think about

since he received the verdict about his tumor. The possibility of living a normal life, free from the sword of Damocles hovering over his head . . . the prospect of marrying, having a family, growing old . . .

But the Tomorrow Men are aware of my problem, he thought. *They must be. Hell, they know how many god-forsaken nipples Banner has. They have to know about the growth that killed one of the wealthiest men on planet Earth.*

And they haven't offered to do anything about it.

Which suggested that they had analyzed his impact on the timeline, and concluded that saving his life would cause too much havoc. *So the tumor stays,* Stark told himself. *And you may as well forget about lying on that bed with your friend the nurse taking your pulse.*

Because it isn't going to happen.

"Tony?" someone said.

Someone feminine. But the way he gadded about, that didn't narrow it down much. Turning, he saw it was Natasha.

"You're coming from seeing Rogers?" she asked.

He nodded. "Yes."

"How is he?"

"Well enough to take on the Hulk again, if he had to. In fact, the Hulk's entire extended family."

Natasha smiled at the quip. And she kept smiling long after the effect should have worn off.

"Something on your mind?" he asked.

"I just wanted to compliment you," she said. "So many men say they can place a liaison in perspective, and then find they're just fooling themselves. In reality, they're pining away."

"But not me," he said.

"Not you," she agreed. "Then again, you've had a lot more experience than most men. You have an advantage in that respect."

"Thanks," he said. *I think*.

"Seeing how you've handled the situation," she said, "it increases my respect for you as a man. And as a teammate."

He nodded. "I'm glad."

"Well," Natasha said, "see you," and continued past him into the infirmary.

Stark stood there a moment longer, thinking about what had just happened. Then, shaking his head, he went to see Fury.

After all, the Tomorrow Men had given the Ultimates the proof they requested—and in doing so, put themselves in what had to be a whole new light.

Henry Pym was surprised when Fury summoned him to the conference room to serve as "another informed opinion." But no more surprised than the other Ultimates, if their expressions on seeing him were any indication.

Pulling out a chair, the scientist admired the renovation of the room since the last meeting he had attended there. *Before I tortured my wife half to death,* he thought bitterly. *Before Rogers found me half-drunk and took out his frustrations on me.*

As a member of the team, Jan was sitting there in the room, diagonally across the table from him. *As far away as possible,* he thought. Not that he blamed her.

She was the only one who wouldn't look at him. And for her sake, he did his best not to look at her.

Fury scanned the faces around the table and asked, "Who's convinced?"

"I am," said Banner on his little video screen. "For godsakes, they knew something was in Rogers's *head.*"

"You know," Thor said, "they could have gotten that sort of information in the here and now. Say, by tracking down one of the scientists who worked on the super-soldier project. Or his son. Or his former mistress."

"Unlikely," said Banner.

"Is it *more* likely," asked Jan, "that these guys are visitors from the far, hazy future?"

"What I mean," said Banner, "is that everyone even remotely associated with the super-soldier program has been accounted for. General Fury knows that better than anybody."

"The general also thought he knew about

Rogers's brain," said Thor. "But as it turns out, he was wrong there too."

"So we're back to square one?" asked Banner.

Fury shrugged. "Maybe square one and a half. Personally, I have a hard time believing the future *exists,* if you know what I mean."

"You mean because it hasn't happened yet," said Stark.

Fury nodded. "So how can you be *from* it?"

"Sounds logical," said Stark, "if your vantage point is the present—that is, the early twenty-first century. But someone in the past might say *we* haven't happened yet. And to someone in the future, we're ancient history."

"That may be," said the general, "but this is the time I'm experiencing now, and this is the time I'm sworn to defend, so this is the time I'm damned well going to use as a reference point."

"Pretty parochial," said Banner, "if you ask me. Especially considering the time we call the present is becoming the past even as we speak."

"Don't give me that gobbledy-gook," said Fury. He glanced at Stark. *"Either* of you. As far as I'm concerned, we might as well be talking about Oz, or Never Never Land, or—"

"Or Asgard?" Thor suggested.

"No offense," said the general, "but I find *that* pretty hard to accept too."

"But you're not asking us to go charging after

some secret organization," Jan told Thor. "So it really doesn't matter *where* you're from."

Thor chuckled in his beard. "Remind me not to ask you folks for help against the armies of Jotunheim."

"So what do we do now?" asked Banner. "Ask the Tomorrow Men for more proof?"

"We trust them," said Stark.

Everybody turned to him. "Despite our concerns?" asked Jan.

"Despite everything," said the billionaire. "At the risk of making a really bad pun, time is of the essence. Especially if Tiber is in the process of making its fortresses more difficult to penetrate, as Weyland suggested. If we wait too long, we may regret it."

"According to the Tomorrow Men," said Thor.

"Who," Stark maintained, "have given us ample evidence that they're on the level."

"*Circumstantial* evidence," Jan reminded him.

"Which," said the billionaire, "is the only kind they have. They didn't make the trip here to win a court case, remember. They made it to save their world—and ours."

"Look at it *this* way," said Banner. "We haven't seen anything that conclusively proves they're telling the truth. But we also haven't seen a shred of evidence to the contrary. Not even a . . . I don't know. What's smaller than a shred?"

"Never mind," said Fury. "We get the idea."

"Then you'll investigate their claims?" Stark asked.

Or do I have to do it on my own? The industrialist didn't say it, but it was implicit in the way he asked the question.

To that point, Pym hadn't contributed a damned thing to the conversation. He had sat there like a dummy, listening to everyone else.

Waiting for his chance. And now it was here.

They had reached a critical juncture. There was a decision in the offing, and Pym had an opportunity to influence it one way or the other.

He wanted desperately to do so. But he couldn't think of anything to say that hadn't already been said.

Fury stroked his chin for a moment. Then he said, "All right. We'll go so far as to check them out."

As everyone rose from the table, the general cast a glance in Pym's direction. A glance of disappointment, it seemed.

Fury was probably regretting his decision to bring Pym to the meeting—which was about the worst result the scientist could have hoped for.

Stark watched Weyland's expression become one of relief as he absorbed what Fury had to say to him.

"You won't regret this decision," said the Tomorrow Man.

"I hope you're right," the general told him.

Their voices echoed a little in the conference room, where it was just the three of them. But then, with the Ultimates' position set in stone, Fury hadn't seen the need to entertain another "mob scene," as he had put it.

"However, it won't be easy to obtain the information we need," Weyland advised them. "As I told you, our intelligence on Tiber is pretty spotty."

"Exactly what have you got?" Stark asked.

"Just a single lead, unfortunately. It concerns a high-ranking member of Tiber. In his public life, he was a security executive for a powerful industrial conglomerate headquartered in what you call the United States."

Stark was glad Rogers wasn't in the room. He wouldn't have taken positively to the reminder that the nation he was named after wasn't going to survive forever.

"The guy's name?" asked Fury.

Weyland frowned. "We don't know it. Only his position and the entity for which he worked."

"And which entity was it?" asked Stark.

The Tomorrow Man told him.

Stark smiled. Then he took out his cell phone and advised Morgan, his pilot, to get the Stark International jet ready.

"Where to, sir?" asked Morgan.

"The south of France," said Stark.

"Hell of a time for a vacation," said Fury.

"It'll be a working vacation," Stark assured him.

7

STARK FOUND MILES JOSEPH MORTIMER ON A
sun-drenched balcony jutting from the red-clay hills
of the French Riviera.

Mortimer was a heavyset fellow with a ruddy
complexion and thinning red hair, who could have
used a hat in all that bright sunshine but for some
reason eschewed one. Against the startling blue of
the heavens, he looked like a boiled lobster.

"Tony," he said. "It's been a while, hasn't it?"

"It certainly has," said Stark, moving to meet
Mortimer and shake his hand.

Miles Mortimer was one of the richest men in the
world, and one of the shrewdest as well—despite the

country-boy façade he affected. But Stark was richer. *And smarter*.

Beyond the rail of the balcony, he could see a cascade of chalk-colored houses spilling down to the shrugging surface of the Mediterranean. But he couldn't see the town's black sand beach. It was hidden from him by the hills.

Twenty years earlier, before Stark filed his first microtechnology patent, he had spent the night in a beat-up sleeping bag on that beach. He remembered grumbling to himself about how hard the rocks were beneath him.

As he regarded Mortimer, those days seemed far away.

Mortimer clapped him on the shoulder. "Can I get you something to drink?"

"I thought you'd never ask. Martini, two olives."

"Good for you," said Mortimer. "I see another blue cocktail, I'm going to barf."

Using a walkie-talkie lying on a nearby table, Mortimer ordered his guest a drink. As they waited for it, he produced a cigar and asked, "Mind if I light up?"

Stark shrugged. "Not in the least."

In point of fact, he found tobacco smoke repugnant, but he had gotten good at disguising the fact. Even in the twenty-first century, it was often necessary to make deals in smoke-filled rooms.

"So how the hell are you?" Mortimer asked, puffing on the cigar and throwing the match over the rail of the balcony.

"Never better," said Stark. "You?"

"I've got wicked high blood pressure, my cholesterol's verging on two-eighty, and I'm popping six different kinds of medication." He coughed once, then took another puff. "How the hell do you *think* I am? I'll be lucky to see sixty."

Stark would never see *forty*. Still, he maintained his careless appearance as a white-garbed servant brought his drink out on a silver tray. "I trust the oil business is treating you right?"

"Losing my shirt," said Mortimer as he watched Stark take custody of his drink. "Another day, another button. They don't build wells the way they used to."

"And the radio stations?"

"Worst idea I ever had. The damned things hemorrhage money left and right. Want to buy them? They'd go nicely with those TV markets you picked up."

"Yes," said Stark, "I'm sure the FCC would appreciate that. Then I could buy a chain of newspapers and a cable system, and really make their day."

Mortimer chuckled bitterly. "Stiff-necked bastards. Why can't they leave us honest businessmen alone? Isn't it hard enough to make a buck these days?"

As it happened, Mortimer made a buck every

three point one seconds. *But,* Stark thought, *who am I to quibble?* "Devilishly hard," he said sympathetically. "And by the way, while we're on the subject of corporate philanthropy . . ."

Mortimer looked at him askance. "Is *that* the subject we were on?"

Stark smiled. "I imagine you've heard about my little venture into health care."

"I believe I have," said Mortimer. "Uptown Presbyterian, isn't it? Nice little pickup, from what I understand."

"I've made worse deals," said Stark. "But to be honest, it wasn't an investment. Not in the financial sense of the word."

"You mean there's another sense?"

"That area needed a real hospital," said Stark, "with adequate staffing and state-of-the-art equipment. Now it's got one. But it could use a children's wing."

"You're breaking my heart," said Mortimer, blowing smoke rings into the air.

The man was famous for his refusal to give money to charity, and Stark knew it. What's more, Mortimer *knew* he knew it. But Stark persisted anyway, in a manner Mortimer could appreciate.

"Too bad about that campaign scandal," said Stark, wincing as if it had happened to him instead. "The media always blows those things out of proportion."

"Tell me about it," said Mortimer, warming to the subject. "Everybody and his mother slips money to those Senate hoohahs—on the golf course, in the men's room, even in the church parking lot. How is it *I'm* the one who gets caught?"

Of course, there were heads of corporations who *didn't* make illegal campaign contributions, Stark among them. But he refrained from bringing that up.

"It's like I'm a leper all of a sudden," said Mortimer. "Took me years to convince old man Fujimoto to joint-venture a line of hybrid vehicles. Now he says he wants nothing to do with me. Says he's worked too hard to get a piece of the American market to take a guilt-by-association hit."

"The truth," said Stark, "is I wouldn't touch you either."

Mortimer made a sound of disgust.

"On the other hand," Stark added coyly, "there's a way to change the public's perception."

"Hey," said his host, "don't you think I'm paying my public relations people to do that? Lot of good they're doing me. You know what those monkeys get an hour?"

Stark didn't answer. He just looked up and swept his hand slowly across the sky, as if he were reading words off a celestial billboard. "I can see it now. The Miles Joseph Mortimer Children's Wing of Uptown Presbyterian Hospital. Has a nice rhythm to it, don't you think? And it'll make people forget about your little indiscretion."

Mortimer's eyes narrowed above his cigar. Then he took the thing out of his mouth and laughed out loud. "Leave it to Tony Stark to make a philanthropist out of an old skinflint like me."

"It's a gift I have," said Stark.

"You think I can get my name done in neon? Might as well get my money's worth."

"Sure," said Stark, "why not?"

But Uptown Presbyterian wasn't the only reason he had made the trip. *Far from it.*

Stark walked out to the rail, looked out over the sea, and sipped his martini. "I understand you have a new head of security. Worked for Papadopoulos at one time, if it's the fellow I'm thinking of."

"He's the one," Mortimer confirmed. "Miercoles. Why? You planning on trying to steal him away?"

Stark glanced at him. "First chance I get."

Mortimer laughed, coughed, and laughed some more. "You kill me, Stark, you know that?"

Stark shrugged. "Another gift."

"Anyway," said Mortimer, "you wouldn't like Miercoles. He's a little more heavy-handed than the guys you're used to. A little quicker to go for the jugular."

"Oh?" said Stark.

"Some of the businesses I'm in, you need that. But then, we've all got a few skeletons in our closet. Another martini?"

Stark polished off the remainder of the first one. "Actually, I've got to run. It's been a pleasure, Miles."

"Hey," said Mortimer, "the pleasure was all mine."

Jan was uncomfortably self-conscious about the click of her heels as she crossed the expansive slate floor of the Triskelion's mess hall.

Actually, the place was anything but a "mess." The limited-edition watercolors gracing the walls, the cherry wood chairs and tables, and the bronze light fixtures descending from a majestic cathedral ceiling created an atmosphere more in line with a five-star restaurant than a military cafeteria.

She had never seen the place so empty. But then, the lunchtime crowd had come and gone, and the only diners were the Tomorrow Men. A half-dozen armed guards stood along the walls, trying to be watchful without being obtrusive.

As Jan approached Weyland and his comrades, they stopped eating and turned to her. She waved away the need for it.

"Nothing official," she told them. "I just wanted to speak with Mister Weyland for a moment." She turned to him. "In private, if you don't mind."

It wasn't that she was going to say anything the others didn't already know, if they were telling the truth about being from the future. She just felt awkward discussing her personal life in front of a group.

"No problem at all," said Weyland.

Wiping his mouth with his green cloth napkin, which matched the chair cushions, he got to his feet. Then he allowed Jan to escort him to the windows, where she wouldn't have to worry about the guards overhearing their conversation.

"Listen," she said, standing in front of an unobstructed view of the Statue of Liberty, "I'm still not one hundred percent certain you're from the future. But if you are, I . . ."

Jan found it hard to say, even in private. She didn't know this man, after all. And this was something she hadn't ever discussed with anyone except her husband.

Oh hell, she thought, *just spit it out.*

"If you *are,*" she continued, "you must know about me. What I am. How I do the things I do."

"I know you're a mutant," Weyland said with shocking matter-of-factness, "if that's what you mean."

Damn it, Jan thought, *they really* are *from the future.* "Do you also know what people think of mutants these days?"

"They don't trust them," he said, "partly because they're different, partly because of the public actions of certain individuals."

Jan nodded. "With that in mind, I'd appreciate it if you kept what you know about me to yourself."

"There's no need to worry," Weyland told her.

"We're careful to avoid anything that might introduce unintended complications to the timeline. And if the public discovered you were a mutant, unintended complications would surely follow."

"Actually," said Jan, "I'm not just talking about the public. I don't want any of my teammates to know either."

He considered the request. Then he said, "Agreed. They won't find out from me or any of my colleagues."

But they may find out from someone else, Jan thought. *Is that what you're telling me, Tomorrow Man?*

She hoped not. It was tough enough being Captain America's girlfriend. Being Captain America's *mutant* girlfriend might be more than she could handle.

Then something else occurred to her—something bigger than her own small life. "There are mutants in *your* time, right?"

Weyland just looked at her.

"Sorry," she said, feeling stupid. "I forgot—the timeline."

"No," said the Tomorrow Man, his voice full of sympathy, "I'm the one who's sorry."

Jan wondered what he meant. Was he sorry that he couldn't comment, because of his concern for the timeline, or sorry about what would happen to mutantkind by the time his era rolled around?

She hoped she would never find out.

• • •

Thor leaned forward on his park bench and tossed a piece of bread to the pigeons amassed in front of him.

Eagerly, they converged on it, but only one pigeon managed to pick up the morsel in his beak. Then he hurried away with it while the others chased after him.

Thor grunted. *Greedy little creatures. No different from the bastions of corporate America.*

Each one gobbled up *what* he could *when* he could, and the hell with everyone else. As long as his ego was bloated with a diet of success, nothing else mattered.

Including the generations that came after such men, which would have to deal with their air pollution and water pollution, and their depletion of non-renewable resources. But why worry about people who hadn't been born yet? Where was the fun in that?

Stark, surprisingly, was an exception to the rule. Thor wouldn't have thought so a couple of months earlier, before Fury recruited him into the Ultimates. But the better he got to know the man behind Stark International, the more he came to respect him.

That was one of the reasons Thor stayed with the group, though it was enmeshed in America's chauvinistic military-industrial complex. He trusted Stark to pursue a nonpartisan agenda, its only objective the good of humanity.

And that was why Thor was sitting in Brooklyn Heights, a hammer's throw from the Triskelion, when he could have been drinking honey-beer with his Aesir brethren. Stark had asked him to stay, in case something came up regarding the so-called Tomorrow Men.

Reaching into his paper bag, he tore off another piece of the loaf inside it and flung it over the heads of the pigeons. As before, they scampered mindlessly in pursuit of it.

There were no pigeons in Asgard, the stronghold of the gods. *Only seabirds,* he thought, *rising and diving in an eternal cycle.* And they had too much respect for themselves to go running after crumbs.

Closing his eyes, he transported himself—but not by accessing the god-road. The only power he used was his ability to remember, to see at that moment what he yearned to see above all else.

Asgard . . .

The light that bathed her every morning, igniting the snow on the highest peaks. The wind that touched off showers of red and gold leaves, freeing tender buds to grow in their places. The irresistible music of harp and voice, heard wherever the bone-white streets converged into a square.

The dark clouds that gathered every night, always foreshadowing rain but never bursting. The silver lightnings that stung them, cackling like hags.

And the halls that pushed against the heavens . . . such splendor, such majesty. Even the thought of them took Thor's breath away. Sky-blue Himminbjorg, the loftiest of them, so Heimdall could watch for Asgard's enemies. Breidablikk, Baldur's palace, her walls yellow like the sun. Odin's beloved Gladsheim, a fortress painted crimson for blood and black for night.

In their hearths roared mighty fires. In their orchards hung apples so crisp and pungent his mouth watered at the thought of them. On the slopes beside them ran frosty, white waterfalls, full of melting snow from the heights.

If Thor's friends saw her just once, they would love her as he did. He was certain of it.

Their eyes would sting trying to take in her beauty. Their throats would close with a longing they didn't know they had. Their hearts would soar like birds and die and soar again.

But they never gave themselves the chance.

It wasn't as if Thor hadn't offered to take them with him, either individually or en masse. It would be as simple a feat to transport his comrades to Odin's feast-hall as to dispatch them to a bus station in Jersey City.

But time and again, they had declined his invitations. After all, in their eyes he wasn't a god at all—he was a man, and one with a history of mental instability. What if in his madness he transported them to the airless reaches of sublunar space? Or the bottom of the ocean? Or someplace so hellish men didn't even have a name for it?

They liked the idea of his fighting alongside them, for there was no disputing his effectiveness on the battlefield. Some of them even valued his company. But when it came to exploring the wonders of the Nine Worlds, they would—as Tony Stark had put it—"take a rain check."

It was a pity. They were passing up a chance to see what only gods had seen. However, he wouldn't try to change their minds. As Odin had pointed out more than once, mortals couldn't simply be given wisdom; they had had to seize it on their own.

Like children, he thought, tearing off another piece of bread for the pigeons. But then, compared to the Aesir, human beings *were* children. And though they liked playing at being gods, they had a lot to learn.

Happy Hogan stood outside the Triskelion's gym and watched the Tomorrow Men work out the kinks.

They hadn't complained once about being confined in their cells. But Weyland had requested that, if their confinement was going to continue for any length of time, they be allowed to exercise now and then.

Despite the obvious need to keep the intruders under wraps, the general didn't like holding people prisoner. Apparently, he had been a prisoner himself once. In the end, he okayed the idea.

And Hogan had come down to watch. And to ask a question, if it wasn't too big a hassle.

Funny, he thought. The Tomorrow Men looked so athletic, he had expected them to take to the gym's weight-training machines like ducks to water. But they hadn't. In fact, they looked awkward on them, as if they had never seen such equipment before.

In the future, Hogan thought, *they probably don't have weight-training machines.* Especially in the kind of future the Tomorrow Men had described.

Matsubayashi was the first of them to take a break. He sat down against the far wall of the facility and rested the back of his hairless head on it, his eyes closed as if he were asleep.

Hogan didn't want to disturb the guy. But at the same time, he knew he might not get another chance to talk with him.

Fortunately, he had top clearance in the Triskelion. So when he entered the gym and walked across it, none of the SHIELD officers standing by the walls did more than glance at him.

As he approached Matsubayashi, the Tomorrow Man opened his eyes. "Good morning," said Hogan. "I'm—"

"Harold Hogan," said Matsubayashi, "director of special projects for Anthony Stark."

Hogan looked at him. "You know me?"

"Of course," said the Tomorrow Man. "You're an important figure in the history of Stark International."

Hogan liked the sound of that. With all he did for the boss, it was nice to know he would eventually get some recognition.

"Listen," he said, "I've got a question for you. And before you object, it's got absolutely nothing to do with the future. Just the here and now."

"What is it?" asked Matsubayashi.

"It's about Thor. I mean . . . he says he's a thunder god. Not just a guy women think is a god, or one who plays ball like a god, but a real, honest-to-goodness god."

The Tomorrow Man nodded. "I think I see. You want me to tell you if he's what he says he is."

"I sure as hell do," said Hogan.

"Have you asked Thor this question?"

"Not personally, but I know what he'd say. He's told everyone who'll listen that he's Odin's son, visiting Earth to return it to its ancient purity—or something like that."

Matsubayashi smiled. "You present me with a dilemma, Mister Hogan."

"How so?"

"What if someone asked me something about you? Say, about your degree from the Massachusetts Institute of Technology?"

Hogan felt a rush of blood to his face. He had never quite gotten that degree—had, in fact, fallen a couple of courses short because of a fistfight with a professor.

Never mind that the guy was a letch. Never mind that he had been all over Tilda Washington, a girl too timid and studious to say anything about it.

Hogan had told the bastard to lay off Tilda, and it had come to blows right there in the guy's office. And whom was the school going to believe—some wet-nosed undergrad or the chair of MIT's award-winning physics department?

So Hogan had gotten thrown out of school. And when he tried to finish up those courses some-where else, it always came down to the reason he left MIT.

Changing tacks, he started applying for jobs, but that didn't go any better. Nobody wanted a kid who had *almost* gotten his degree. By the time he got to Stark, whose company was a lot smaller and looser at the time, he had decided he was just going to lie.

It worked. Hogan got the job. And though it occurred to him sometimes that he should tell Tony Stark what he had done, it became harder and harder to admit it.

After all, the boss trusted him as he trusted no one else. How could Hogan tell him he had lied to him all those years ago?

"That's different," he told the Tomorrow Man. "That's personal."

Matsubayashi shrugged. "Maybe Thor's truth is personal too."

Hogan allowed the possibility. "I guess I'll withdraw the question. Not that you would have told me anyway."

"Insofar as the answer might have affected the way you act toward Thor, and therefore had an impact on future events . . ." Matsubayashi's voice trailed off meaningfully.

"Yeah," said Hogan, "that's what I thought."

"So," said Fury, leaning forward in his chair to greet his guest, "what was your little tête-à-tête in the mess hall about?"

Sitting down on the other side of the general's desk, Jan shrugged. "I wanted to know something about the future. Something personal. Weyland told me he couldn't say."

"He didn't want to screw up the timeline."

"Not even for me. I'm insulted."

Fury was tempted to ask what Jan's personal question was about, but decided to leave it alone. From the beginning, she had been as loyal and levelheaded as anyone on the team. The way he saw it, she had some leeway coming to her.

"Listen," he said, "I've got an assignment for you." He told her what it was. "And before you object, I already know you're not the undercover type. But you can shrink to the size of an insect, and none of our undercover people can do that."

Jan frowned. "What I *can't* do is get around very quickly. Flying for even the length of a city block can be a monumental effort when I'm that size."

"I know," said Fury. "We've got someone else covering that leg of the race."

As far as Pietro Maximoff knew, he was the fastest man on the face of the Earth—which was what made the assignment at hand so very ironic.

If you were setting out to torture such a man, he thought as he sat drinking coffee by candlelight in front of the best hotel in Geneva, *if you were doing your best to drive him over the edge . . . what better course could you pursue than to make him wait for hours on end?*

In fact, that was what he was doing: waiting. Just as he had waited the day before, from morning until late at night, and the day before that as well. *And for what?*

To keep an eye on Antonio Miercoles. So when the security chief made contact with his comrades in Tiber, Pietro would be there to witness it—and if he were fortunate, put the Ultimates a little closer to finding a Tiber base.

Once Tony Stark identified Miercoles as the Tiberite cited by the Tomorrow Men, it became possible for Fury's people to monitor the fellow's travel plans. And though Miercoles traveled a great deal in his legitimate line of work, this particular trip had the earmarks of something else.

After all, Miles Mortimer's companies, widespread as they were, didn't do any business in Geneva.

With Pietro's inhuman speed, he was uniquely suited to both staying out of sight and staying close, so it became his job to keep track of Miercoles. And at the outset, the assignment had sounded simple enough. But what if Miercoles didn't contact his cronies for a week? Or an entire month?

Then I will go irretrievably insane, he thought. *And Wanda will be left with a vegetable for a companion.*

Not that it would be the first time, he thought with a smile. Back when he and his sister were small, she had taken a sweet potato from the cupboard and dressed it up as if it were a doll.

But is a sweet potato a vegetable? the mutant asked himself. *I can never remember.*

What he *did* remember, and all too well, was the way Wanda's eyes shone with tears when a dog got hold of her doll and tore it to bits. And he remembered as well the heat in her cheeks when he attempted to console her, and the mewling noise she made as she tried to stifle her little-girl sobs.

As distasteful as his mission was to him, it was made even more so by the absence of his sister. Ever since the two of them were little, they had relied on each other for emotional support, to a degree most people didn't understand.

The hell with them, Pietro thought.

People were just jealous. They envied him and Wanda their closeness—though if he had lacked a soulmate in life, someone with whom to share his joys and sorrows, he might have been jealous too.

And where are you now? he asked his sister silently. *In some cold, dismal corner of the Triskelion, watching the rain sluice down a windowpane? Or walking the streets of Soho through clouds of sewer steam, wishing you had someone to show an especially delicate objet d'art in the window of an old antique shop?*

He was still pondering the question when the revolving door of the hotel across the square began to spin. A moment later, black-bearded Miercoles emerged from it, a black raincoat draped over his shoulders, his eyes alert beneath thick, dark brows.

He looked about the square, paying no particular attention to Pietro. Then he shrugged on his coat, ran his fingers through his brush of dark hair, and proceeded down the street to his left.

Pietro waited until Miercoles was out of sight before he laid some coins down for the waitress and offered pursuit—not so quickly that anyone would suspect him of being *homo superior,* yet quickly enough to close the gap before Miercoles got too far.

But when the mutant turned the corner onto another cobble-stoned square, he found it was empty—except for some ornate black streetlights, each with a nimbus of fog around its lamp. Miercoles was nowhere in sight.

Pietro felt the heat of frustration rise in his cheeks. *It can't be,* he thought. *I just saw him.* Swearing softly, he began combing the narrow streets that fed off the square.

Had anyone been present to witness his search, all they would have seen was a black streak—black being the color of both his slacks and his jacket. Such a witness would have been startled, but would never have suspected that the streak was even vaguely manlike.

Miercoles might have given some other operative the slip. However, at Pietro's accelerated rate of speed, he would be able to find the Tiberite eventually. He was certain of it.

Until the minutes passed, one after the other, and he failed to catch even a glimpse of the bearded man. Gradually, Pietro reached the inescapable conclusion that Miercoles had eluded him.

More than likely, he thought, *he entered a building as soon as I lost sight of him—either because that was his destination or because he realized he was under surveillance.*

Either way, Miercoles was gone. And along with him, the possibility of finding Tiber.

Fury won't be happy, he thought.

Then, as if there were a God and he was inclined to answer the unspoken prayers of doubting mutants, Pietro caught a glimpse of someone who *might* have been Miercoles.

He was far away, emerging from a doorway that opened on a hilly, poorly lit street. But his hair and garb were dark enough to match the security chief's description.

Yes, thought Pietro, *it's him.* He was sure of it.

Determined not to lose the bastard a second time, he pelted down the street as fast as he could. However, he was careful to keep to the shadows so his speed would go unnoticed.

Finally, the street ended and he came to a bridge that crossed the Rhone. It was then that he realized Miercoles had given him the slip again.

Where in hell did he go now? Pietro demanded of himself.

"Turn around," someone behind him said in a deep, distinctly Spanish-accented voice. "But do it slowly, or it's the last thing you'll *ever* do."

Pietro turned and saw that the threat had come from Miercoles. The short, ugly gun in the Tiberite's hand was pointed directly at the mutant's face.

Miercoles grinned triumphantly in his beard. "You thought I didn't see you?"

Pietro didn't move. He couldn't, lest he give away the secret of his superhuman speed.

"Well," said Miercoles, "you were wrong. Now tell me who you are and what you're up to."

Pietro just stood there.

"You're working for that damned Hesselbach," said the bearded man. "Isn't that right?"

Still Pietro remained silent.

Miercoles tilted his head to the side, as if to get a better look at his adversary. "It takes courage to remain silent when someone's got a gun pointed at you. Unfortunately, courage won't keep you alive. Now I'll ask you one last time—are you working for Hesselbach?"

The mutant didn't respond.

Miercoles made a sound of deep-seated disgust. Then he pulled the trigger of his gun.

What happened next was tricky, even for someone as fast as Pietro. It wasn't just a matter of dodging a bullet at close range, which was difficult enough. He also had to make it close enough for Miercoles to think he was dead.

As it happened, the mutant miscalculated ever so slightly. But it was enough for the bullet to scrape the front of his jacket as he tossed his head back and plunged over the iron railing.

Crap, he thought.

Pietro had purchased the jacket only a few days earlier, and had looked forward to showing it to his sister. Now it would be ruined—not only by the bullet, but by the bath he was about to take.

A moment later, he hit the rushing water of the Rhone with a splash, and allowed himself to be carried by the current. *But not for long,* he assured himself.

Perhaps a hundred feet downriver, he broke the surface. By then, Miercoles had put his gun away and was walking briskly from the scene of the apparent crime.

Too quick for the security chief to see, Pietro grabbed hold of the railing and pulled himself up over it. Then he darted into a pool of shadow and waited for Miercoles to turn the corner.

Having learned his lesson, Pietro wouldn't wait long before pursuing his "killer." He would follow in a few seconds, using his speed to remain a blur.

One thing, at least, would be in his favor: Miercoles wouldn't feel the need to be quite as vigilant now that he believed his pursuer had been neutralized.

Pietro just hoped his cell phone hadn't gotten ruined in the river. Because when the security chief led him to his destination, he needed to be able to make a call.

8

PIETRO HAD BEEN STANDING ON THE DARKENED
rooftop for nearly half an hour before he heard a
tiny, high-pitched noise in his ear—one that
wouldn't have sounded like a voice at all except for
the fact that he was expecting it.

"It's about time," he whispered.

"Screw you too," came the response. "You think
everybody moves as fast as you do?"

Pietro made a derisive sound. "Believe me, that is
one illusion under which I have never labored."

He pointed past the edge of the roof to a truck,
which was parked in front of the warehouse across

the street. There were two men sitting in the front of it, and its engine was idling.

"Miercoles?" she asked.

"Gone," Pietro told her. "But they didn't start loading the truck until he had been in the warehouse for a couple of hours. I don't know what they're waiting for, but my guess is they'll leave as soon as they get it."

"Gotcha," said the tiny voice.

"By the way," he said, "how is my sister?"

"She's well," said Jan. "Call her. She said something about a restaurant in Riverdale the two of you like."

Pietro smiled to himself, remembering the last time he and Wanda had visited the place. *How we scandalized the waiter!*

"Yes," he said, "I know the establishment."

But there would be time for reminiscences later. For now, he had a truck to keep an eye on.

As if on cue, two other men came out of the warehouse with a long crate in their hands. It looked heavy.

"That could be it," he said.

In fact, it was. The men carrying the crate loaded it onto the truck, pulled its metal gate down, and locked it into place. Then one of them rapped twice on the gate.

"You had best get going," Pietro told his colleague.

But Jan was gone already. Or at least, he didn't hear her say anything in return.

"Good luck," he breathed as the truck pulled away from the curb and went rumbling down the street.

Tony Stark entered the Triskelion's virtual-reality room even though the red light was on in the corridor outside, signifying that the facility was in use.

He found Natasha sitting in one of three semi-enclosed training modules, her black-garbed figure tinted red in the lurid illumination from the emergency lighting strips. Though most of her body was still, her hands were moving at a frenetic pace, each of her sensor-equipped forefingers pulling an imaginary trigger several times a second.

Stark had no way of knowing how she was doing. That information was only available through the black plastic visor she was wearing, which tracked her progress through a sea of randomly generated adversaries via a bright green graphic in its upper right corner.

Like a video game, he thought, except it had grim implications. After all, Natasha had to stay sharp for those times when she encountered the real thing.

Leaning close to her, Stark ever so gently pulled away one of the black plastic muffs covering her ears. Then he said, "I'm disappointed in you."

Natasha stopped firing and removed her visor. Then she looked up at him and said, "Welcome back. And why is it, exactly, that you're disappointed in me?"

"This playing-hard-to-get approach you've adopted. I've decided it lacks the ring of authenticity."

She swiveled in her chair and smiled at him. "I'm not playing hard to get at all. I simply don't want to pursue any long-term relationships, with you or anyone else."

"Of course not," Stark said patronizingly.

"And," Natasha continued, "it's a bit conceited of you to think I'd make an exception for you. No, scratch that—*more* than a bit."

"It might be," he agreed reasonably enough, "if you really weren't after me. But you are."

"Listen," she said, "I've been trained to manipulate people's feelings—men's, in particular. I've been taught how to set a trap for them and lure them in. If I were after you, as you put it, don't you think I'd have gotten you by now?"

Stark shrugged. "The best traps often take the longest."

Natasha rolled her eyes. "There is none so blind as he who will not see."

"I've got an optical tracking system that can pick out an undersized jackrabbit from a height of thirty-five thousand feet. I can see just fine, thanks."

"Maybe you need to work on an olfactory

enhancement," she said, "so you can wake up and smell the coffee."

It was a good comeback. He had to give her credit for that. "My olfactory equipment works quite well," he told her, "and what I'm smelling isn't coffee."

Natasha chuckled. "Clever, but wholly inaccurate. I am not, in any sense, after you."

Stark chuckled. "Right." He indicated the visor. "Good hunting, by the way."

Then he left the room, feeling better than he had in days.

Hank Pym was grateful Fury had given him the chance to say goodbye to the only people in the Triskelion who really mattered to him.

"Well," he said to the Tomorrow Men, as a couple of SHIELD guards looked on, "it's been nice meeting you."

Weyland looked at him. "Are we going somewhere?"

"Actually," said Pym, "*I* am. I was only called in on a temporary basis, to take a look at your blood and so on."

"I see," said Weyland.

But he couldn't have *foreseen* it. Pym had only been called on because of the Tomorrow Men, so his return to the Triskelion wouldn't have been part of any recorded history.

"I imagine people have been asking you questions," he said. "About their futures, I mean."

"Some have," Weyland conceded.

"I have to admit," said Hank, "there are things I'd like to know as well. Like who's going to win the Kentucky Derby."

That got a smile out of the Tomorrow Men.

"I could be a rich man if I knew *that,*" said Pym. He chuckled to himself. "But I'd be taking advantage. You've got to be careful about how you affect the timeline."

"That's true," said Weyland.

"If I could ask one question," the scientist continued carefully, "it wouldn't be about getting rich. It wouldn't be about me at all. It would be about Jan."

"Your wife," said the Tomorrow Man.

"That's right," said Pym.

Weyland didn't say anything in response. However, he could hardly have missed the whisper of pain in the scientist's voice.

"I wouldn't try to change anything," Pym noted. "I doubt I could do anything about it anyway. I would just want to know if she's going to go on hating me forever."

"I wish I could tell you," said Weyland. "But the timeline—"

"Is sacred. I know. I just thought—" Pym stopped himself, gathering what was left of his dignity. "Anyway, that would be the question I'd ask. If I had the chance."

Weyland nodded. "I understand." But he didn't provide any answers.

"Well," said Pym, "nice talking with you."

"The same," said the Tomorrow Man.

"Damn," said Fury, peering over Hogan's shoulder at the monitor and its vicious-looking swirl of blood-red graphics.

"Just what I was thinking," said Hogan.

"How far away is it?" Stark asked, his voice taut with concern.

Hogan, who was seated at a keyboard, tapped in a command. A moment later, Fury could see an irregular green outline. The crimson swirls, magnified now, were encroaching on the edge of it.

"Not far enough," Stark concluded.

"Why did they wait so long to contact us?" the general asked.

"The storm wasn't supposed be that strong," Hogan said, "or that fast, and it wasn't supposed to move in that direction. Then, suddenly, it was on top of them."

Fury shook his head. "It's thousands of miles from here. We'll never get there in—"

Suddenly something occurred to him. Judging from the look in Stark's eyes, the idea had dawned on him as well.

"Thor," said the billionaire.

"Damned right," said Fury. He leaned over, punched the stud that gave him access to the intercom system, and barked: "Thor!"

"I'm here," came the response. "In the southeast lounge. Is there something I . . ." But he never got any further, because Fury's declaration cut his question in half.

"Back in Arizona," said the general, "when we were fighting the Chitauri, you transported their doomsday bomb to another plane of existence."

"Nastrond," said Thor. "It's a desert, though—"

"Tell me later," said Fury, interrupting again. "What I need to know now is . . . can you transport people as well? Say, to some other part of the world?"

"Of course. I just need to know where they're going."

"As in point it out on a map?" asked the general. "Show you a picture? What do you need to pull this off?"

"What's the problem?" Thor asked.

"Apparently," said Fury, "there's a hurricane bearing down on an island off the coast of Venezuela. It's called Calibaña—population four hundred and sixty, including children. And if we don't hurry, there'll be nothing left of them."

"A globe would be best," said Thor, now that the general had explained his sense of urgency, "but a map will do. If you've got the team in mind, get it together."

"I do," said Fury, moving toward the door, "and I will. As for a map, there's a big one on the screen in the ops center."

"Perfect," said Thor. "I'll meet you there."

Fury turned to Hogan. "I'll need Rogers. And Romanov. And Barton." He would have added Wanda and Pietro to the list, except they had to remain out of the public eye.

As for Stark, he was already on his way out of the room, headed for the chamber where he kept his "work clothes."

Thor had no sooner set foot in the central market plaza of Calibaña than he felt the lash of wind-driven rain on his face.

In the sky, ponderous, smoke-gray clouds raced like a herd of wild, shaggy horses. Lightning scrawled a blinding white rune on the world. Thunder bawled like a hunger-crazed bear.

Thor was the god of the storm, the son of Odin All-Father. He lived for this weather. But as he looked around at his comrades, he doubted they would have said the same.

Stark looked as stolid as ever in his high-tech armor, but Romanov and Barton couldn't help cringing in the face of such elemental fury. Even

Rogers, whom science had annointed with powers rivaling those of Thor's brethren, felt compelled to take shelter beneath his shield.

Their mission was a far less complicated one than Fury had initially imagined. The island's last call for help, once SHIELD tracked it down, said that its entire population of nearly five hundred people would take shelter in the sturdiest edifices available to them—the handful of small hotels built by a wealthy speculator to accommodate a tourist trade that had never materialized.

Thor could see people cowering in the nearest of the hotels, the Spindrifter, their faces pressed against the glass doors of its lobby. "Start with *them*," he told Barton.

"Gotcha," said the archer, lowering his head and taking off across the plaza.

Thor dispatched Rogers and Romanov to the left of the Spindrifter, where they would find two other hotels nestled along the beach. At the same time, Stark took off in the direction of the Tradewinds, a fancier place built on a bluff a mile in the opposite direction.

The plan was to bring the inhabitants back to the plaza, one group after another. Then the son of Odin would whisk them to a refugee camp Fury was setting up in central Florida.

It would have been better if Thor could snap his

fingers and transport every living soul off Calibaña, regardless of how many of them there were and where they had chosen to hide. But even he couldn't do that.

He was, after all, a god and not a magician.

9

As Stark caught sight of the Tradewinds, a pink, horseshoe-shaped complex set atop a picturesque green bluff, he hoped there wasn't anyone inside it.

Unlike the other hotels on the island, this one wasn't recessed into the jungle. It stood exposed and unprotected, which allowed it, in better weather, to offer a spectacular and unobstructed view of the Calibañan sunrise.

But now, that unmitigated exposure left it open to the full wrath of the storm. Froth-laced waves from the dark, churned-up ocean came crashing against the Tradewinds' stucco walls unimpeded. And according to the latest weather reports, the situation was going to get worse before it got better.

Which was why Stark hoped to heaven the place was empty. If there were people inside, it would take a while for him to carry them to the market plaza. And at this rate, the hotel wasn't likely to last a whole lot longer.

Slicing through the elements, he approached the Tradewinds' colorful mosaic patio. It had lost not only all its furniture but the doors that led into the building as well, leaving the restaurant within open to the storm.

Without slowing down, Stark plunged through the open doorway into a gaily decorated dining room, which he crossed in a fraction of a second. Then he negotiated a couple of turns and came out in the hotel's pastel-colored, seashell-shaped lobby.

So far he hadn't spotted a soul. However, he hadn't gotten a look at the guest rooms yet. And until he did, he couldn't cross the place off his list.

Stark had stayed in too many hotels not to have a sense of how they were designed. There were elevators with stairwells beside them on either side of the lobby. Picking one of the stairwells, he spiraled up its shaft until he reached the second floor.

The corridor there boasted about a dozen doors. One by one, he battered them down with carefully controlled blasts of electromagnetic energy. And in each case, the room beyond appeared empty.

On the third floor, the story was the same. Twelve rooms, no one inside any of them. That led Stark to the fourth floor, and the fifth, with the same results.

However, there was still the other side of the hotel, accessible from the alternate stairwell. Using minimum thrust in his descent, he returned to the ground floor and crossed the lobby.

Seen through a rounded glass wall, the storm was building rapidly in intensity, bending a decorative grouping of towering palm trees until they were almost parallel to the ground. Before long, they would tear loose of their moorings and go crashing into the jungle.

Hurry, Stark told himself.

This time, when he reached the second floor, he saw the first door on his left was ajar. Pushing it open the rest of the way, he looked beyond it into the guest room.

It looked empty, like all the others. Inhabited recently, judging by the way the bedcovers had been pulled and crumpled, but apparently inhabited no longer.

He was about to go on to the next room when he heard something—a whimper, as if from an animal. *Or a child,* he thought. And it had come from the vicinity of the room's only closet.

Walking over to it, he opened it—and exposed a quartet of youngsters, none more than ten years old.

They were cowering in the corner of the closet, wide-eyed with apprehension.

"Don't worry," Stark said as reassuringly as he could. "Help has arrived."

But they didn't greet him the way he had expected. They began screaming, as if he were a bigger threat to them than the storm ravaging their island.

Stark held up his metal-gloved hands. "It's all right," he told the kids. "Really."

Thanks to the armor's state-of-the-art audio tech, he sounded as if he were speaking in a natural voice. But it didn't seem to calm the children one iota.

I must look pretty frightening, he realized.

In designing his armor, he hadn't given any thought to how it would appear to children. If he had had an audience in mind, it had been the army of secretaries he saw when he wove his way among the spires of Manhattan.

Unfortunately, he couldn't please everyone. *But it won't hurt to get a few focus groups going, especially with kids in mind. Maybe there's some tweak I can make . . .*

Suddenly, the thought was interrupted by a crash. *A window,* thought Stark. *Something went through it— maybe part of a tree.* At least he hoped that's what it was.

"Come on," he pleaded with the kids, "come out of there and I'll take you somewhere safe."

They didn't budge. But then, their parents had no

doubt warned them about talking to strangers, and there wasn't anybody quite as strange as a man in a metal suit.

So Stark wasn't going to talk the kids into cooperating. That left him only one other option.

Reaching into the closet, he scooped up two of the children in his metal arms and walked out of the room with them kicking and pounding at him. Once out in the hall, he blew out a window with an energy pulse, then flew through the opening.

Instantly, he was buffeted by a fierce, sideways blast of wind. But he didn't let it stop him. Holding the kids to him as tightly as he could without hurting them, he headed for the rendezvous point.

Thor watched the red, gray, and yellow figure of Iron Man vanish into the embrace of the storm as Stark returned to the hotel room where he had discovered the children.

The thunder god looked down at the two of them, huddled against him in the hissing, spitting rain. *Scared and miserable,* he thought. *But not for long.*

Thor hadn't counted the people he sent from storm-wracked Calibaña to Fury's refugee camp in Florida. He just knew there had been a lot of them. A hundred, perhaps, if he had to guess.

But there were a great many more somewhere on the island. And time wasn't being kind to them.

The clouds around the island were galloping faster

than ever, the winds keening more loudly, the lightning flashing more brightly. By the time the storm was done with the place, there wouldn't be much left of it.

Just then, another bunch of Calibañans came bustling across the plaza, clutching their offspring and the few small belongings they could carry. They looked at Thor with trepidation, knowing from the instructions of whoever had rousted them— Romanov or Barton—that the bearded man was to be their savior.

But they couldn't know in what manner. After all, he didn't have a boat for them, or a plane, and even if he had possessed such a thing, it would have been unwise to trust it in such weather.

Beckoning, Thor got the natives to gather around him, joining the children Stark had delivered to him. Then he raised his hammer to the heavens and brought down a shrieking bolt of lightning.

But it wasn't the kind that would reduce a man to a shriveled husk, though whoever saw it from a distance might think so. It was the kind that only a thunder god could summon, the kind that would open a god-road to a different place.

One that wasn't so far away, by Thor's standards. *Not nearly as far as Vanaheim or Niflheim, or one of the other worlds*.

Looking around him, he saw that the Calibañans were gone. And since their transit would have been instantaneous, they would be wondering how they had come to appear in another place.

Though I would be surprised, he reflected, *if they were inclined to complain about it.* Especially after they realized some of their friends had preceded them there.

In the meantime, another group had appeared at the edge of the plaza—a small one this time. *Only five,* Thor decided, as he peered at them through the rain cascading into his eyes.

Then he realized they weren't Calibañans. They were wearing uniforms—a white and green variety he had seen not too long ago, back at the Triskelion.

On the Tomorrow Men.

Thor told himself that his eyes were playing tricks on him. But the longer he stared at the approaching figures, the more certain he was that they were the intruders.

"What in Odin's name are you doing here?" he demanded, the wind snatching his words as soon as he barked them.

"We've come to help," Weyland yelled back over the roaring voice of the storm, rain streaming across his face and into his eyes. "Just as you have."

If Thor had trusted them more, he might not have thought twice about accepting their presence there. As it was, he felt compelled to keep an eye on them.

After all, the Ultimates were vulnerable in the midst of such chaos and confusion. And if anything unfortunate happened to one of them, it would be easy to blame it on the storm.

"What can we do?" asked Weyland.

Thor was tempted to tell him to return to the Triskelion, and his companions along with him. However, he didn't think any of them would listen. *And truth be told,* he admitted silently, *we can use the assistance.*

Thor pointed his hammer at one of the hotels they hadn't checked yet, which lay further down the shoreline. "It's called the Beachcomber. Check each room. There's no telling who may be hiding inside them."

The Tomorrow Men didn't say anything in response. They just took off in the direction Thor had indicated, looking eager to follow his instructions.

The son of Odin hoped that's *all* they would do.

This time, Stark didn't bother entering the front door of the Tradewinds. He flew through the window he had destroyed and swerved into the room.

The kids were in the closet, right where he had left him. *Thank God.* But the fact he had taken their friends away certainly wasn't making them any happier to see him.

When this is over, he thought, *I'll take them out for ice cream. As much as they can eat. Flavors they've never heard of.*

And he would leave the armor at home.

But first Stark had to get them out of there. Grabbing them up as he had grabbed the other kids, he headed for the door. The kids were kicking him, trying to wriggle free, but the armor kept Stark from feeling anything.

Using the shattered window for an exit again, he emerged into a cauldron of wind. It was even worse than before, hammering at him, trying to push him off his course.

With the help of his thrusters, Stark resisted it. The Tradewinds fell away beneath him as he rose above the level of the treetops, looking for a glimpse of the plaza where Thor was waiting for him.

Then he saw it—the open square, surrounded by a jumble of white buildings. He couldn't see Thor yet through the slashing rain, but he expected to rectify that deficit in the next minute or so.

Until a more powerful blast than all the others drove him sideways, forcing him off course as if he were caught in the grip of a giant hand. He swung his feet to the left to right himself, but the wind was too strong. It flipped him over and sent him careening in the direction of the treetops.

Just in time, Stark pulled out of his dive and shot upward again. But he was caught in another monstrous gust, as unrelenting as the first. And as he fought to maintain his heading, his body twisting to keep his heels pointed in the right direction, he felt one of the kids slip out of his grasp.

Before he knew it, the kid was flying away from him, as if he had a propulsion system of his own. Flying so fast through the sheeting rain that he would be out of sight in a matter of moments.

No! Stark thought, horrified as he had never been horrified by anything in his life.

Maintaining his hold on the other child, he boosted his propulsion setting a full notch and shot forward. But one heel-thruster seemed to hit a touch harder than the other one, causing him to veer to his right—and suddenly, though he had lost sight of his objective for less than a second, the boy was nowhere in sight.

Stark's stomach muscles clenched in panic. *He's going to die,* he thought. *He's going to die because of* me.

Then he got hold of himself, forced himself to think. He had a few seconds, probably, before the kid was killed in one of several ways, all of them too grisly to contemplate.

Speeding up some more wouldn't help him accomplish anything. And it might kill the kid who was still tucked under his arm.

Then it came to him.

Touching a stud just behind his mask, he activated his armor's infrared-vision function. Instantly, he was looking at an entirely different tableau, marked not by reflected light but by the amount of heat everything gave off.

And the boy was giving off more heat in that howling mess than anything else.

He showed up in the mask's eye slits as a vaguely human-shaped red blotch, spinning like a trapeze artist at the height of his signature stunt. Making a beeline for the kid, Stark saw the blotch getting steadily bigger.

But there was something behind it, something that gave off a very faint heat signature of its own. *Something big enough to be a hotel,* he thought grimly.

He didn't know which one, but it didn't matter. If he didn't move quickly, it would be a deathtrap.

Knowing his timing had to be perfect, Stark maintained his speed until he caught up to the kid. Reaching out, he clamped his fingers around the boy's ankle. Then he shot straight up, the front of his plastron grazing the stucco surface, until he could arch his back and loop away from it.

Gotcha! he thought.

Even more firmly than before, he held the kid to him. Held *both* kids. And this time he got closer to the ground, even if it meant weaving through the jungle.

It took longer that way, and Stark wasn't always sure he was going in the right direction. At one point, he was certain he had doubled back toward the Tradewinds.

Then a line of white buildings loomed through the slanting rain. Relieved, he entered their welcoming embrace—and a moment later, reached the plaza where Thor was waiting, half-drowned but still standing his ground.

Natasha had combed through the last section of the shuddering, glass-littered Beach Tree hotel, and was heading for the next storm-wracked building along the coast, when she caught sight of someone who didn't look the least bit like a native.

The person was running along the beach, just beyond the edge of the jungle. It was a woman, though her head was shaven. And she was wearing the green and white garb of the Tomorrow Men.

Haggerty? Natasha asked herself.

It didn't seem possible. However, the Tomorrow Men had already accomplished the impossible, if their story could be believed. And escaping the Triskelion couldn't have been any more difficult than sneaking into it.

So the question wasn't whether it could be Haggerty springing along the beach. It was what she was *doing* there.

Natasha's first priority was the evacuation. That wasn't going to change. But she was also going to see if she couldn't figure out what the Tomorrow Woman was doing on Calibaña.

Stark was taking off again into the teeth of the hurricane, headed for the last of the shoreline hotels, when he heard his name called over his comm system.

It was Natasha's voice, and it was full of urgency.

"What is it?" he asked, hoping she could hear him better than he could hear himself.

"I'm at the Terraces," she snapped, "landward side! I need your help!"

Stark changed direction, slicing through sheets of pounding rain as if they weren't there. It took him twenty-five seconds to reach the Terraces, and another two to find Natasha.

She was kneeling amid a field of debris—the remains of a wall that had been ripped off the hotel's steel skeleton, exposing a honeycomb of guest rooms. There was someone lying beside her, half covered with chunks of heavy masonry.

One of the Tomorrow Men, Stark thought, his heart pounding.

Landing next to Natasha, he lifted the wall fragments and hurled them away. But the damage had been done. The figure in white and green lay there pale and unmoving. And with the debris gone, Stark could see who it was.

Haggerty. Her features were slack and there was blood trickling from the corner of her mouth.

What's she doing here? Stark wondered.

Then he remembered Thor trying to tell him something as he dropped off the second pair of kids.

But the storm had been too loud for him to make out the words.

They must have been a warning: *Haggerty's here.* And maybe the other Tomorrow Men as well.

Natasha tried to give the woman mouth-to-mouth, probably not for the first time, but it didn't take a doctor to see it was too late. Haggerty was gone, her ribs cracked, her insides pulped by the impact of the falling wall.

Stark cursed to himself. Then, as gently as he could, he tried to pull Natasha off Haggerty's lifeless body.

"We've got to go," he said.

Natasha pushed his gauntleted hand away and kept at her resuscitation attempt. But after another few seconds, Stark tugged at her again. And this time, she relented.

"Crap," she breathed over her still-active comm link.

Crap is right, he thought.

Stark didn't know how Haggerty had escaped her confinement in the Triskelion, or how she had traversed thousands of miles to get to Calibaña. But her objective seemed obvious enough: to help with the evacuation.

She could have remained in a safe place and let the Ultimates carry out their rescue operation. It wasn't her job or that of her comrades to get involved. But she had gone out of her way to lend a hand, in the process putting her life on the line.

And she had paid the price.

"Take her," said Natasha. "I've got one hotel left."

Part of Stark wanted to tell her it was too dangerous, but it wasn't his place to do so. She was an Ultimate. She had the right to make her own decisions.

As gently as if Haggerty were still alive, Stark picked her up in his arms. Her head lolled and she flopped like a fish, her back broken. Shifting his grip on her so he could secure her to him a little better, he rode the winds back to the plaza.

He wasn't going to abandon Haggerty there on Calibaña—not after what she had done. As long as he had a say in it, she would leave the island the same way as the rest of them.

10

"ALL RIGHT," SAID FURY, GLARING AT THE FOUR grim-looking Tomorrow Men seated at the briefing room table, "I want someone to explain a few things to me. First, how you got to Calibaña without any visible means of transportation. Second, how your meddling in a high-profile event like a hurricane evacuation isn't going to be a problem for your precious timeline. And third, what I'm supposed to say to the news media who got pictures of you appearing and disappearing."

Weyland looked appalled. "Pictures . . . ?"

"You're damned right," said the general. "One of the networks obtained satellite images of the rescue effort, which wound up on TV screens all over the world. They caught you materializing on the island, obviously without any help from Thor, and then dematerializing when the evac was over.

"Nice publicity for the Ultimates, except it begs a question: who are those guys in the green and white suits, and why haven't we heard anything about them before?" He leaned back in his chair. "So who's going to give me some answers?"

Fury wasn't the only one waiting for them. Stark, Thor, and Rogers, seated around the table as well, were every bit as eager for an explanation.

"I will," Weyland said dutifully. "We traveled to Calibaña and back by means of teleportation devices implanted in our nervous systems. A number of our people have them. It's the method we've developed for staying a step ahead of the tyrants."

"And you didn't see fit to tell us about these devices?" Fury asked.

Weyland looked at him. "To be perfectly honest, General, we needed a way to address the Tiber problem if you couldn't—or wouldn't."

"If you had that in mind all along," said Thor, "why bother enlisting our assistance at all?"

"Because," said Weyland, "the likelihood of our being able to stop Tiber by ourselves is so slim, it's statistically insignificant. That option was only to be considered as a last resort."

"I see," said Fury. "And all this business about

maintaining the integrity of the timeline . . . why did it go out the window when it came to Calibaña?"

Weyland frowned. "Every abuse of the timeline has repercussions. Our coming here was such an abuse, despite our care in keeping it an exceptionally minor one. But it too will have repercussions, and one of them was to keep Janet Pym from participating in the rescue."

"Jan?" said Rogers, making a face.

"How was she going to contribute?" asked Stark. "Her specialties are shrinking and flying around—neither of which is much of an asset in high winds. All she would have succeeded in doing is becoming another casualty."

"I'm not at liberty to give you the details," said Weyland, "but we were trying to minimize the impact of her absence. So rather than damaging the timeline, we were trying to preserve it."

"At the cost of Haggerty's life," said Chadaputra, a hint of recrimination in his voice.

Weyland turned to him. "There was no way we could have foreseen that."

Chadaputra shook his head. "She was too eager. You said so yourself."

"She was also better qualified than anyone else. I had no choice but to include her on the team."

It was the first time Fury had heard two of the Tomorrow Men disagree on something. To that point, it was as if they'd been speaking with one voice—usually Weyland's.

"Hang on a second," said Rogers. "Maybe I'm being a numbskull, but you folks can travel in time. If Haggerty wasn't supposed to be part of this timeline anyway, can't you just go back to the moment before she died and do something about it?"

"It's possible," Weyland conceded, "but wholly inadvisable. If we were to go back and influence the same sequence of events a second time, the risk of damage to the timeline would be compounded exponentially—and the results would be unpredictable."

"So you might save Haggerty," Stark suggested, "but at the cost of civilization."

"Perhaps," said Kosar, "or more realistically, at the cost of the hundreds of lives we saved on Calibaña. It's impossible to say."

"There's another problem," said Chadaputra, "in that the timeline has limitations. Our research tells us that it can withstand a certain amount of alteration at any given juncture. But an attempt to rewrite that juncture a second time . . ." He shrugged.

"What would happen?" asked Rogers.

"It would be like a videotape," said Stark, "that's used over and over again. Eventually, it's going to lose its ability to support a recording."

Weyland nodded. "An apt analogy."

"Wait a second," said Rogers, his brow furrowing. "Are you saying that part of the timeline would be *erased?*"

"In a manner of speaking," said Chadaputra. "Imagine a section of it simply dropping out, leaving a gap between the event before it and the event after it."

"So what happened in that spot never *happened?* It's just *gone?*" asked Fury.

Rogers sighed. "What," he asked, "does that mean in practical terms?"

"We don't know," said Kosar. "There's no precedent for us to go by. But it's clear that it wouldn't be a good thing, either for that point in the timeline or for any other."

There was silence around the table as they absorbed the remark. But it didn't lessen their frustration or their sense of loss.

"Then she's gone," said Thor.

Weyland looked tired, beaten. "I'm afraid so."

Chadaputra turned to Stark. "Haggerty's body?"

"Will be cremated," said the industrialist, "as you suggested."

"When this is all over," said Rogers, "I'd like to see to it that Haggerty is honored somehow."

"That would be much appreciated," said Weyland. "But keep in mind that if we're successful in destroying Tiber, our era will be altered—perhaps to the point where Haggerty and the rest of us will never be born."

Rogers swore to himself. "Now you're *really* giving me a headache. If she's not born in the future, how can she come back with you to the past? And if she doesn't come back with you to the past—"

"How can she alter the future?" asked Fury. "I'd like to know that myself."

"I know it defies common sense," said Chadaputra. "But *much* about time travel does that. All I can tell you, without going into an elaborate lecture about temporal mechanics, is that common sense isn't always applicable."

"Doesn't seem right," said Rogers.

The Tomorrow Man turned to him. "Not to any of us."

Fury eyed Weyland. "As far as your teleportation devices, we can't surgically remove them. But I want your word you won't use them again, under any circumstances—or all bets are off."

Weyland looked at his colleagues, then nodded. "Agreed."

Fury glanced at Nakamura. "You can take them back to their cells now."

"Aye, sir," said the guard.

Fury watched the Tomorrow Men file out. Only after they were gone and the door was closed did he say, "I'm *really* getting to hate this timeline business."

"I'll wager *they* hate it more than you do," said Stark. "You heard what they said—if they're successful, it'll be as if they never existed. What's dying next to that?"

Fury considered it. *To have never been alive . . .*

"Man," said Rogers, scanning the faces of his comrades. "Every mission I went on in World War II was potentially a suicide mission. But it wasn't a forget-I-ever-existed mission."

Bruce Banner gazed through the transparent wall of his prison at the most beautiful woman in the world—in his opinion, anyway.

But then, Betty Ross wasn't just the Ultimates' public relations director. She was also the woman to whom Banner had been engaged until a year or so earlier, when she dyed her hair pink and suggested they take a break from each other.

A break that now seemed permanent.

Unfortunately, Betty wasn't Banner's only problem these days. But sometimes, it felt bigger than his others.

"It's a nightmare," she said. "A bona fide, grade A, ass-kicking nightmare with all the trimmings."

"Why a nightmare?" he asked, genuinely concerned.

Betty frowned. "Imagine hearing that a posse of mysterious strangers has arrived from the future to drop in on your favorite government-funded superteam. And not only that, they've come to screw with the timeline, which happens to be the only timeline you've got—the one where you're going to retire to south Florida on your biotech-powered Roth IRA."

Banner's IRA had accumulated more than twenty thousand dollars. Not that he would ever get a chance to spend any of it.

"Bad enough," said Betty, "but at least no one's going to see these Tomorrow Men. They're a secret and there's no reason to believe they won't stay that way. Then you pop into Starbucks for your venti half-caf mocha latte-to-go and you see on the TV they've got propped up in the corner that the Tomorrow Men are helping your superteam with a nine-one-one on some Aruba-wannabe."

Is there really such a thing as a half-caf mocha latte? Banner found himself wondering. But what he said was, "It would raise some questions, I guess."

"Damned right it would raise some questions," said Betty. "And do we like questions?"

Banner had two choices. "No?"

"Not at all. So we need to come up with answers before people start distrusting the Ultimates. And they'd better be the *right* answers, or we'll be holding a bake sale to pay the electric bill."

He tried to picture Betty baking a cake. *It would be easier to picture Thor on the pro golf tour.*

"So what are you going to do?" he asked.

Betty bit her lip. "I'm thinking."

Banner liked it when she got that look on her face—the one where she pressed her lips together and the skin made a little knot between her eyebrows. He found it sexy.

"We can't claim they're from another planet," she said, thinking out loud. "Not after that business with the Chitauri. And we can't say they're part of our development program, because then we'll have to explain their disappearance when they leave."

"Right," said Banner, just trying to be supportive.

"All right," Betty said finally, "I've got it. Forty years ago, a bunch of disgruntled scientific geniuses established a hidden colony in the frozen wastes of the Arctic. The Tomorrow Men are their kids, empowered with technologies developed by our best minds working in total seclusion. They're bound to be different from anyone we've ever seen before."

Banner made a face. "The Arctic?"

"Sure," said Betty. "Where else would you go if you wanted the world to forget you?"

A heavily guarded cubicle here in the Triskelion, he thought. But what he said was, "That's not the point. There's no electricity in the Arctic, no factories, no access to raw materials. How could these disgruntled scientists have done any work?"

Betty sighed. "Use your imagination. They brought in generators and . . . I don't know, manu-facturing facilities."

"How?" Banner asked. "By pack mule?"

Even before he got the last word out, he realized he had made a mistake. When Betty was making up a story for the press, she didn't like anything to get in her way. *Like reality, for instance.*

It was just an inconvenience to her. And anyone who insisted on it was an inconvenience as well.

She looked at her watch, as she always did when she had endured enough of him. "Jeez, where's the time go? I've got about half a million calls to—"

"Betty," he said, cutting her off in his haste to make amends, "I didn't mean to say that. I'm just—"

"Trying to help," she said, "I know. And don't think I'm not appreciative. Stay out of trouble, okay?"

And she was on her way, her cell phone already pressed to her ear. A moment later, the doors opened for her.

"—so lonely," Banner finished.

Then the doors closed again and Betty was gone, and he was left with yet another regret.

11

JAN HAD ONCE DRIVEN CROSS-COUNTRY WITH
a girlfriend from college, a rogue spring in her passenger's seat biting into her butt and making the trip
seem longer than it actually was. It was nothing
compared to the trip she had taken in the back of
the Tiberites' truck.

But then, her cross-country jaunt had lasted only
a few days, and the truck journey had already taken
twice that long. And in the car, she had been able to
sleep undisturbed, while in the truck she was forced
to sleep with one eye open.

Not that anyone was going to notice Jan when she
was wasp-sized. But it took concentration for her to

maintain that stature, so she didn't go small the whole time. She resorted to that option only when confronted with the prospect of customs inspections or the Tiberites' own annoyingly frequent cargo checks.

Which was why she couldn't let herself fall asleep entirely. The last thing she wanted was for someone to pull open the truck's rear gate and find a normal-sized sleeping beauty.

Yeah, right, Jan mused, huddling in a convenient pile of dirty blankets against the steadily increasing cold. *Sleeping beauty. That's definitely me.*

Next time she went on a trip like this one, she was going to bring her makeup case. Then she wouldn't look like hell when she came out on the other end.

Speaking of which . . . the truck had been moving slowly for hours now, jostling her left and right as if making its way over rough terrain. And the air she was breathing seemed not only markedly colder, but also markedly thinner.

Jan had a feeling that they would reach their destination soon. And when they did, she needed to be ready.

Steve Rogers felt a hand on his shoulder. Looking up, he saw that it belonged to Thor.

"I didn't hear you come in," Rogers said. As far as he had known, he was alone in the lounge.

Thor smiled sympathetically. "Captain America

didn't hear a metal door open and close? He must have been pretty distracted by something. The welfare of his lady friend, perhaps?"

Rogers shrugged. "This is new for me, you know?"

"What is?" asked Thor, taking a seat on the couch across from his colleague's.

"Back in the forties, when I went overseas to fight the Nazis, I always felt bad for my fiancé. She had to wait back home, never knowing how I was or what was happening to me."

Thor's brow bunched a little. "Right. And now *you're* the one sitting home and worrying."

"Exactly," said Rogers.

"Not an easy thing," said Thor, "is it? But I have faith in Jan. She's tougher than she looks."

Rogers agreed. But it didn't help him worry any less.

When Jan felt the truck full of armaments come to a stop, she knew it was time for her to shrink again.

By the time the gate rumbled open, she was insect-sized, hidden among the mess of blankets that had been keeping her warm. But even with the blankets to shield her, the blast of frigid, snow-dusted air from the outside stung her like a slap in the face.

Looking past the grubby, unshaven Tiberite whose turn it was to check the cargo, Jan saw a spectacular vista of blinding-white peaks. They looked like a crown of diamonds shining in the sun.

Not much farther now, she decided.

She would have dearly loved to remain in the truck, where she was protected from the worst of the freezing temperatures. However, it would have been rude to hog all the fun for herself. She wanted to share it with her friends.

As soon as Jan was sure the Tiberite was looking the other way, she flew past him—and immediately regretted it. The wind outside the truck was like a swarm of tiny knives, cutting mercilessly through her bodysuit into her flesh.

It was also harder for her to fly—significantly so. She had to pump twice as many times, it seemed, to cover the same distance.

Thin air will do that, she thought.

But Jan didn't have the option of returning to her shelter. It wasn't enough that she was, at long last, on the verge of finding the Tiberites' hideout. She also had to let her teammates know where it was.

Where *she* was.

Otherwise, she would find herself all alone in a very bad place. Even worse, Tiber would be allowed to proceed with its security upgrades unimpeded.

Fortunately, Stark had given her a trio of minia-turized, one-way comm devices. Each one was capable of transmitting a continuous signal to the nearest Stark International satellite, no matter the intervening weather conditions.

Of course, if the damned thing went on the blink, it wouldn't be the first machine ever to do so. That was why Stark had equipped her with three of the suckers.

Taking one of them out of her belt pouch, she kissed it for luck. Then she swooped down beside the truck's rear left tire, activated the device, and laid it down in the snow.

A moment later, the Tiberite hauled the gate closed and joined his comrades in the cab of the truck. Then the vehicle took off at a crawl, its former stowaway clinging to the side of it.

Somewhere in orbit above the Earth, Tony Stark's satellite was relaying a message to the Triskelion, telling the Ultimates to get ready. Their pal the Wasp, like Gretel in the fairy tale, had dropped the first of her breadcrumbs.

Rogers fidgeted a little as he sat across the desk from Fury. "Tell me you've got good news, General."

"As a matter of fact," Fury replied, "I do. We've got a signal from Jan. That means she's getting close."

Rogers breathed a sigh of relief. "When do we leave?"

"O nine hundred. I'll be alerting the others in the next few minutes."

"Got it," said Rogers, pushing out his seat and getting up.

"By the way," said Fury, "my guys are really juiced about this. Taking part in a covert op with Captain America . . . it's the kind of thing they can tell their grandchildren."

Rogers remembered the enthusiasm with which men had followed him into battle in World War II. Some things never changed.

"I'll try to bring them all home," he told Fury.

"I know you will," said the general.

Jan—and the truck she was using for cover against the frigid, bone-chilling wind—had been approaching a particular snow-covered slope for some time when a hole opened in it.

Except it was too geometrically perfect to call it a hole. *A door, then,* she thought. *A door in the side of a damned mountain.*

It was big enough to admit a truck, though only barely, which meant she and her ride would be trundling into the Tiberite facility in the next couple of minutes.

By then, Jan had strategically dropped two of her homing devices. Taking out the third one, she activated it and let it fall into the snow beside the truck. Then, keeping her jaw clenched so her teeth wouldn't chatter, she endured the cold just a little longer.

Unfortunately, her task wasn't over yet. A big part of it was still to come.

As Jan had expected, the truck wasn't allowed to enter the door in the mountain without a security check. A half-dozen armed men in red snow-jackets issued forth and stopped the vehicle.

First, one of them—a dark-skinned man with a goatee—spoke briefly to the Tiberites in the cab. Then he had them open the back of the truck so he could see its cargo for himself.

After a few minutes, the bearded man seemed satisfied. Pulling the gate down himself, he waved for the truck to proceed.

As Jan rode the vehicle through the doorway, she marveled at the size of the facility rising up on every side of her. Tiber appeared to have hollowed out the entire mountain, turning it into an immense atrium with at least a dozen safety-railed levels connected by stairwells as well as transparent elevators.

From a wasp's point of view, it was even more gigantic, more impressive. But she didn't have time to gawk.

Launching herself off the truck, Jan set off in search of the facility's communications center—knowing she had no more than an hour to reach it before Fury's task force arrived.

• • •

As Hogan watched his boss don his armor in the Triskelion's Iron-Tech launch hangar, he was proud of what he saw. *Damned* proud.

And not just of the technology that went into the metal components. He was even happier to be associated with the very human component at the heart of them all.

Someone else might have cursed his fate and the god that inflicted it on him, or bowed under the crushing weight of it. Not Tony Stark. Not even for a second.

Of course, he didn't love the idea that he had an invader in his head, or that it would kill him some day. It wasn't fun knowing any given season might be his last. But even with that cross to bear, he had said more than once that he wouldn't change places with anyone in the world.

Because for him, it would have been a far greater tragedy never to have been Tony Stark in the first place—never to have built something huge and powerful and influential out of an idea and a knack for inspiring the confidence of investors.

That was the best part of who the man was. It wasn't having his pick of Hollywood's soft-skinned starlets, or living in circumstances so insanely luxurious that most people couldn't even have imagined them, or enjoying the respect and admiration of everyone he met.

Though those weren't bad things either.

The best part was having a say in how the world went—as a billionaire, as a business intellect unlike any other on the planet, and as a guy who could move mountains if the technology in his armor felt like cooperating.

At the moment, Stark and the latest version of his Iron Man project were headed for a remote part of the Caucasus Mountains. It was to those coordinates that their satellite had traced Jan Pym's signal, so it was there that Fury's task force would strike.

But first, it had to come together. And because this had to be a clandestine mission, it would be staged on one of SHIELD's gargantuan heli-carriers, concealed from prying eyes by a layer of clouds several miles thick.

As Stark locked his helmet into place, he turned to Hogan and waved. *See you shortly,* he seemed to say, *and make sure the vodka's chilled the way I like it.*

Hogan waved back. Then he watched his boss activate his thrusters, rise from his launchpad, and ascend through the aperture in the hangar's ceiling.

Only when he had risen out of sight did the aperture close again. With a sigh, Hogan headed for the exit and the Triskelion's main building, where he would keep tabs on the Tiber mission from his console in operations.

And hope nothing went awry.

• • •

Move it, Jan exhorted herself.

Pounding her wings as hard as she could, she raced the closing security door. For a moment, it wasn't clear whether she would make it or not. Then, by the merest of margins, she slipped past it.

I'm in, she thought.

It hadn't taken Jan that long to find the Tiber facility's communications center. After all, its door was labeled in red block letters bigger than she was.

More nettlesome had been the problem of getting inside. She didn't have the strength to depress the square green stud beside the door—not at wasp size—and she couldn't get big for fear of being seen. So she had been forced to wait for a Tiberite to walk in or out.

The communications center, as it turned out, wasn't a popular place. But eventually, a thin, hollow-cheeked man had come down the corridor and pushed the stud, and walked inside.

Which gave Jan the opportunity she needed. *Thank God.*

Rising toward the ceiling, where she was less likely to be noticed, she took a look around. She was in a windowless, low-ceilinged room that housed a series of sleek black control panels arranged in a horseshoe shape.

Only one of the panels, in the center of the horseshoe, was occupied. The guy behind it had a paunch and a badly receding hairline, but his forearms were bigger than Jan's waist when she was normal-sized.

Flitting out toward the center of the room, she snuck a look over his shoulder. It seemed he was scrolling through a log of recent communications.

But not sending, Jan thought. *That's good. Don't want to cut him off in the middle of a message.*

Slowly, she descended behind him, trying not to draw his attention. Then again, he was so intent on his screen that he probably wouldn't have noticed a *parade* of wasps.

But he would notice her soon.

When Jan reached the level of the guy's ear, she zapped it with her sting as hard as she could. Suddenly the guy was on his feet, slapping at the offending appendage—and probably wondering, somewhere beyond his pain, how a stinging insect had made it into the mountain.

But by then, she was no longer in the vicinity of his ear. She was under his chin, stinging him in the jaw. And when his hand went to that spot, she came around and needled him in the back of the neck.

Cursing out loud, the guy flailed at her—to no avail. Though he was pushing a considerable amount of air around, she had eluded better flailers in her day.

Finally, Jan had him just where she wanted him. Diving, she zapped him through his sock. When he brought his foot up, leaving himself standing only on the other, she rose again and launched a lightning series of attacks to the face—forcing her adversary to trip over his chair and smash his head on the console behind him.

It didn't quite knock him unconscious. But it dazed him enough for her to grow to full height and deliver a kick to his jaw. His eyes rolling back in his head, he dropped to the floor.

Leaving Jan the fox in the proverbial henhouse.

It felt good to relax her concentration, to be normal-sized again. And it felt even better to lock the door to the communications center from the inside.

After all, it wasn't just *this* Tiber stronghold they wanted to scour out. It was *all* of them. And to do that, they would have to keep the others from finding out the fate of this one.

Hence the communications blackout Jan had just instituted. And when the raid was over, Stark's men would install a program to send a series of dummy messages to the rest of the network.

Of course, they had to take *this* place before they could worry about any of the others.

Jan wished she could give her teammates a hand. However, she had to make certain her friend with the paunch didn't wake and try to send out a distress call.

Pulling out a chair, she sat down and waited for the task force to arrive.

12

"READY?" THOR ASKED.

Fury nodded. "Whenever you are."

Thor glanced at Stark, whose Iron Man armor looked resplendent in the brassy, high-altitude sunlight. Then he turned to Rogers, who was adorned with the red, white, and blue of Captain America.

Both of them were symbols of everything Thor had come to distrust in the world. And yet, he felt good about going into battle with them, considering the characters of the men behind the masks.

Then there were the other Ultimates—Black Widow and Hawkeye, Quicksilver and the Scarlet Witch. Though the first two weren't covert operatives any longer, all four of them were used to working quickly and efficiently in hostile environments.

Last of all, the son of Odin scanned the faces of the fourteen khaki-uniformed SHIELD operatives whom Fury had hand-picked for this mission. They looked focused, prepared to go into action at a moment's notice.

Though if all goes well, Thor reflected, *they'll have a bit more preparation time than that.*

No one seemed the least bit discomfited by the fact that they were standing on the deck of a heli-carrier some thirty thousand feet above the Caucasus Mountains. Which was strange, considering most mortals get jittery on their garage roofs.

On the other hand, none of the heli-carriers had ever lost anyone overboard—or so Fury insisted.

The plan was for Thor to transport himself into Tiber's hideout, then bring the rest of them down with him. Except for Stark, who would descend on his own power to watch for Tiberites who managed to escape the mountain.

Despite the difficulty everyone seemed to have with Thor's godhood, they had gotten comfortable with his godlike abilities in no time. In fact, they seemed to take them all for granted.

But Thor himself didn't take them for granted. He couldn't imagine himself *ever* doing that.

Especially since he hadn't always been aware of his identity, much less the extent of his abilities. Oh, he knew even as an adolescent that there was something different about him, that he had been chosen to do great things. He just didn't know by whom, or what those great things might be.

It's all right, he remembered telling himself at the time, his heart full of youthful optimism. *It will all be revealed soon enough.*

But as the years passed, he came no closer to the truth of his existence than he had before. He eventually fell into a career as a nurse, working in one institution or another—but not because that was what he wanted from life. It was just that he had to eat, and it seemed nobler to help people than to take part in the myriad business schemes that injured them.

It wasn't until three weeks short of his thirtieth birthday that Odin plucked him from Midgard, in spirit if not in body, and brought him to Mimir's Well. It was there, beneath towering oaks and circling eagles, that the All-Father had received his wisdom from the inky-black waters. It was there that Thor received wisdom as well.

Kneeling beside the well, with his father standing at his side, he had cupped his hands and dipped them into the water, and drank. With each sip, he felt as if a veil were being drawn away from a face.

And the face was *his.*

Suddenly, he knew who and what he was, and why the knowledge had been kept from him all that time. Odin had made a mortal of Thor and set his feet on the earth of Midgard so he could see things as mortals saw them, and understand better how to make the world of men pure again.

Humanity was abusing its world in every way possible, stumbling slowly but inevitably toward the brink of destruction. Someone had to wind the horn of warning before it was too late, and Thor was the one who had been chosen.

When he returned to Midgard, seeing his mission clearly for the first time, eighteen months had passed. His body had spent that time languishing in an asylum for the insane, where he had been placed by the Norwegian authorities. *An easy mistake,* he thought, considering his mind had been on another world.

But it was back. And with mind and body aligned, he was no longer the man he had been. He was Thor, son of Odin All-Father, wielder of heaven's lightning. He could perform feats of unimaginable strength and endurance, and traverse the Nine Worlds with but a thought.

So really, it was no trouble at all to transport himself to the heart of the Tiberite installation, where no one could reasonably have expected an invader to appear without warning.

"See you down there," he told his comrades.

A moment later, he found himself in a storage room deep in the bowels of the mountain. It was big enough to contain the task force and remote enough for them to be able to spread out from that spot before the Tiberites knew what was happening.

Perfect, he thought.

As lightnings played around his hammer, he drew the rest of the force down there with him.

Steve Rogers looked around and made certain his teammates and Fury's men had materialized alongside him in the storage room. Then he headed for the door, touched the pressure-sensitive control that sent it sliding open, and moved out into the corridor.

There was a single Tiberite out there. Seeing Rogers in his Captain America uniform, he froze for a moment.

Nothing like the element of surprise, Rogers thought.

Before the fellow could yell for help or try to get away, the red, white, and blue shield of Captain America caught him in the temple and sent him sprawling. Rogers didn't have to check to see if the Tiberite was still conscious. He just caught the returning shield, stepped over his victim, and continued down the corridor.

Fortunately, Thor's thus-far-inexplicable teleportation ability involved some measure of insight into his destination. As a result, he had been able to give them a crude sense of the facility's layout while they were still on the heli-carrier.

So Rogers knew he would find a stairwell at the

end of the corridor, and where it led, and approximately how long it would take to get there. It was invaluable information.

However, Thor wouldn't be joining them on their little foray. Having deposited them all in the lion's den, he was going to join Stark outside.

Rogers didn't mind. The last thing he wanted on a mission like this one was a guy whose hammer could demolish structural supports and discharge high-voltage electricity.

The idea, after all, was to incapacitate the Tiberites, not to bring the mountain crashing down on top of them.

When Rogers reached the door to the stairwell, he opened it and led the way inside. Then he took the stairs two at a time, expecting those behind him to do the same.

The first level he came to gave access to the kitchen and the mess hall. He passed them up, wondering for just a fraction of a second if they had ever served pineapple pizza.

No, he thought. *Don't think of her. That'll come later.*

Early in his World War II career, he had blundered into a hail of bullets because he was thinking of his fiancée instead of his work. He had vowed never to make that mistake a second time.

The level above the mess was the one Rogers wanted. With a glance back over his shoulder to make sure everyone was in synch, he depressed the control that governed the door.

As it opened, he went into action.

The space Rogers entered was immense, even bigger than he had expected. And there were as many as a hundred and fifty Tiberites inside it, gathered here and there around the computer workstations that lined the walls, discussing events in the world outside their mountain.

Perhaps two dozen of them were standing by the entrance, wearing red snow jackets and cradling rifles. The rest carried sidearms in shoulder holsters.

Pulling his shield back, Rogers flung it into one cluster of Tiberites. Then, without waiting to see the result, he took down two other men with a crossbody block.

He had seen what followed so many times that he could break it down into bite-size chunks. First, the fraction of a moment in which his enemies caught sight of him. Then the one in which they raised their weapons, followed by the one in which they aimed, and finally the one in which they fired.

Hauling in his shield as it returned to him, Rogers crouched behind it to deflect the angry barrage. Then he charged a knot of adversaries, bowling them over like tightly packed dominoes.

Using his momentum, he planted his hand on someone's shoulder and vaulted over the pack—just in time to face another one. Going low, he swept the feet of one out from under one man, jabbed a second with the edge of his shield, and turned sideways to avoid the weapons fire of the third.

Before he could aim again, Rogers laid him out with a right cross. Then he nailed someone in the belly with a side-kick and clanged someone else in the face with his shield.

And for a single, bizarre moment, Rogers was certain he was fighting the Nazis again.

After all, he had fought so many of them—in the streets of nameless French towns and in sprawling Gothic castles, in well-scrubbed underground research facilities and on sinister midnight supply trains. He had fought them with his fists and with his shield, every way and everywhere one could fight them, until all the raids and all the rescues blurred into one screaming, blood-flecked madness.

But that was in a different world.

In the one he lived in now, there was an objective to be met, a battle to be won. And he would be damned if he was going to let anyone keep him from winning it.

Seeing Captain America go in one direction, Natasha Romanov went in the other.

She found her first target still drawing the handgun from his shoulder holster. Planting her heel in his face, she snapped his head back. Then she whirled and took him down with a harder kick to the base of his skull.

Naturally, that drew the attention of his comrades. But Natasha flattened herself as they fired, allowing the bullets to pass over her head. And before they could adjust, she was somersaulting through the air, automatic weapons sliding into her hands from the feeders beneath her sleeves.

Before she hit the floor, she had taken out all four of them. Not with killing shots, just disabling ones. After all, Fury wouldn't be happy without people to interrogate.

Then she flicked her wrists and slid the guns back into her sleeves. For one thing, she didn't want to hit any SHIELD operatives with friendly fire. For another, she only used firearms when she really needed to.

Natasha much preferred the satisfaction she got from hand-to-hand combat. The challenge of reading an opponent, adjusting to his intentions—and executing just the right move to take him down.

Nor was she concerned about getting hurt, or even killed. That was for amateurs.

Because there was a rhythm to these things, a slashing, leaping, cutting, rolling rhythm. And once she was in it, immersed in it and absorbed by it, she knew she wouldn't be touched. Not by an enemy's hand, not by a knife, not even by a bullet.

She might as well have been invulnerable.

•   •   •

People always remarked on Clint Barton's accuracy. It was what had gotten him the nickname "Hawk-eye."

But he wasn't just the most accurate marksman in the world. He was also the quickest.

Barton didn't know why he could fire a half-dozen arrows faster than a gunman could unload the same number of bullets. He just could. Which was why Fury had never suggested he switch to a more conventional choice of weapon.

Sometimes, it was up to him to take out a roomful of bad guys all by himself. This wasn't one of those times. With all the help he had, he didn't need to go on the offensive. He could concentrate on protecting the other members of the task force.

Not Rogers or Natasha—they didn't need protection. But the other SHIELD operatives, despite their training, were only human. They couldn't see an enemy drawing a bead on them from across the room.

Which was where Barton came in.

Knocking an arrow, he took aim and fired at the perpetrator of just such a sneak attack—a man in a red jacket trying to put a hole through one of Fury's people. Before he could pull his trigger, he was sent spinning with an arrow in his shoulder.

Catching sight of a gunman with an equally promising line of fire, Barton released another shaft.

It not only pierced the gunman's hand, but nailed it to the back of one of his colleagues.

Two for the price of one, the archer thought.

Then he whirled and put another arrow through a Tiberite standing behind him. Looking amazed, the man dropped his gun, clutched the part of the shaft protruding from his middle, and crumpled to the floor.

Because I deserve a little protection too, Barton reflected, as he loaded up again and looked for another shot.

By the time Thor transported himself into the frigid air above the mountain, Iron Man was already dueling with a couple of small, airborne attack craft.

They weren't the first ones Stark and his armor had confronted, judging by the fiery, smoking wreck in the valley below. And they wouldn't be the last, for several more were issuing from an egress in the side of the mountain.

The craft were extremely maneuverable and extremely fast—more so than anything Thor had seen before. And they seemed to have firepower to spare.

He was glad he had shown up when he did. Left alone, Stark might have been overwhelmed by the squadron. His power, after all, was the power of mortals.

And Thor's was something more than that.

As the aircraft recognized they had a second foe, a trio of them came after him and opened fire. But he was fast too. With an exertion of will, he skyrocketed out of harm's way.

Then it was Thor's turn to attack.

Swinging Mjolnir in the direction of the farthest flier, he released a blue-white bolt. As it skewered its target, the craft became a smoking, plummeting wreck. Its pilot ejected himself just before his vehicle collided with the side of a mountain and erupted into flames.

The SHIELD people would see to the pilot's apprehension, now that he was deprived of his craft. Thor's business was with the fliers still in the air.

Forging ahead through wisps of cloud, he took aim at another craft. Again, his lightning tore through the heavens. Again, it ripped a flier off its course and sent it plunging back to Earth.

Thor was so intent on it, he didn't notice the adversary behind him until it was almost too late. But at the last moment, he caught sight of something out of the corner of his eye.

Twisting in midair, he avoided a collision—but only by the merest margin imaginable. He was so close to the flier, he could feel the air displaced by its passage, and glimpse the expression on the face of its pilot.

There was no fear in it, no sign that the fellow was the least bit intimidated. But there *was* curiosity, and understandably so. How often did one find oneself in combat against a god?

Thor almost felt sorry for the fellow. *Almost*.

Still, he speared the craft with Mjolnir's fury, tearing a wing off and sending it spiraling groundward. He watched it just long enough to see the pilot spring himself from the wreckage. Then he turned and set his sights on another target.

13

FURY WHISTLED AS HE WALKED THROUGH THE
cavernous facility his task force had just secured.

Pretty impressive, he thought.

But then, Tiber had had more than ten centuries
to hollow out this hiding place. Given that long a
span, it could have done the job with a spoon.

At the moment, the only Tiberites in evidence
were the ones being slipped into body bags by
SHIELD's cleanup crew. Thor had already moved
the living ones, nearly a hundred of them, to the
heli-carrier for transport back home.

The general's interrogation teams would be

putting in overtime. Of course, most of the Tiber people would keep their mouths shut, knowing the worst SHIELD could do was give them to the governments against whom they had committed crimes.

But a few would talk, knowing how some of those governments treated criminals. And a few were all they needed to round out the electronic data SHIELD would be mining.

"Sir?" said a familiar voice.

Fury turned in response and saw Jasper Sitwell approaching him. It was a good thing, since Sitwell was the SHIELD agent in charge of mop-up.

He looked like he was fresh out of Harvard Law, with his white teeth, his rimless glasses, and his power haircut. But he was as down-and-dirty as any grunt when he had to be.

"What's our communications status?" the general asked.

"Secure," said Sitwell. "The Wasp saw to that."

Fury nodded. "Outstanding. And Dugan?"

"We found him in a corridor on level ten. It seems he ran into some Tiberites trying to make use of an exit we hadn't accounted for. Took a few bullets, I'm afraid, but none that will keep him from running another marathon."

"Good to hear," said Fury.

Then something else occurred to him. "Aren't the Bobbsy twins down here somewhere?" He had seen

Thor, Jan, Rogers, Stark, Natasha, and Barton on the heli-carrier, but not Pietro or Wanda.

Sitwell jerked a thumb over his shoulder. "Over there, sir."

Fury followed the gesture to the far side of the room, where he saw a couple of figures, one male and one female, dressed in the black outfits favored by covert ops. They were standing off to the side as usual, part of the team and yet apart from it.

Pietro's arm was wrapped around his sister's shoulders as if he wanted to shelter her from every evil in the world. Or maybe it wasn't shelter he wanted to give her—Fury was never sure.

He was just glad he didn't have a sister who looked like Wanda. *Life is complicated enough,* he reflected.

Because it was his job, the general went over to speak with the mutants. They watched him with an unmistakable wariness in their eyes. Of course, there were those who hated and feared their kind, so maybe they were justified in looking at him that way—even if he himself wasn't guilty of those emotions.

"Let me guess," he said. "You were in here fighting the whole time, right?"

"Where else would we be?" asked Wanda.

"And had we not been here," Pietro chimed in, "how would you have survived the packs of ravening attack dogs? Especially the third one, with all the Dobermans?"

Attack dogs? "I didn't hear anything about any attack dogs," Fury told him.

"Of course you didn't," Pietro replied, a quirk of amusement pulling at the corner of his mouth.

The general grunted. *Why do I even ask?*

Then he realized that Pietro was wearing a leather jacket over his bodysuit. The suit and the jacket were the same color—black—so the general hadn't noticed the change right away.

"Where did you get the threads?" he asked Pietro.

The mutant shrugged. "From an old friend."

Fury would require a more thorough explanation later. At the moment, he had the inside of a mountain to check out.

It wasn't until the third day after SHIELD's takeover of the Tiber facility that Jan managed to cut her hot-shower regimen from three a day, alternating with heavy doses of Steve Rogers, to only one.

She had just finished taking that shower and was visiting the Triskelion's southeast lounge to catch the evening news when she glimpsed someone dozing on one of the couches. *Hogan,* she realized, recognizing the wingtip shoes he favored.

Loathe to wake him up, Jan started back the way she had come in. Then she heard Hogan's voice.

"It's all right," he told her. "I'm not asleep. It's just my eyes that are tired."

Looking back over her shoulder, she saw that he was sitting up. "Still working on the Tiber data?" she asked.

"Not anymore," said Hogan, suppressing a yawn. "We're finished."

"Already?" said Jan.

She was hardly an expert on computer operations. But it seemed to her that a cult as old and widely distributed as Tiber would have had more information to sift through than the Pentagon.

"Not *completely* finished," he amended. "We could have spent weeks on the encrypted files alone—and eventually we will, because it looks like there's information there on all kinds of illegal activities, not just the ones in which Tiber was involved directly. Assassinations, sabotage, drug-running, you name it. But for now, we've got what we need."

"You mean with regard to their other hideouts."

"Damned right. One of them is discussed in great detail. It was just completed recently, and there was a bunch of talk about how and when certain building materials were going to arrive."

"So we've got . . . what?" Jan asked. "One more target?"

"So far," Hogan told her. "But we also captured the transmission logs. If we can do that at a second location, we can—"

"Triangulate," said Jan, whose father had been an oceanographer before he met her mom, "and flag every receiver on the Tiber map. But not until we've taken down another hideout."

"In a nutshell," said Hogan, "yes."

"Where *is* this second location?" she wondered.

"In the Andes. Twenty-eight degrees latitude, seventy-six degrees longitude, just under eleven thousand feet of elevation. The good news is it's not as cold as the place in the Caucasus. The bad news is it's pretty damned close."

"You're talking to a woman who spent six days in an unheated truck," said Jan. "I'm ready for the weather."

Hogan looked sympathetic. "That's good to hear. From what I understand, you're leaving the day after tomorrow."

Stark knew full well he didn't *have* to visit the captured Tiber facility. With all the accumulated SHIELD brainpower there, another cook would only spoil the broth.

But he wasn't going there to get involved in the process of data extraction and analysis. He just wanted to see what the place looked like at his leisure.

It was a piece of history, after all—and secret history at that. A peephole into a subculture that had survived undetected for seven hundred years, despicable though it might be.

Like an archeological excavation, the industrialist

mused as he soared over a breathtaking maze of pris-
tine white mountains, *but without the shovels.*

It wasn't as if he was needed anywhere else that
day. He had no business meetings, no charity events.
Besides, he wanted to see how his new armor handled
a long flight.

So far, Stark thought as he came in sight of Tiber's
mountain, *it's handled it quite well.*

There hadn't been anything even suggestive of a
malfunction. Even his normally cranky structural
integrity field—a force matrix generated between the
inner and outer layers of his armor—was working
like a charm.

Stark was about to open a communications link
when he realized the facility's front door was open.
How's that for hospitality? he asked himself, though he
wondered if a little more caution might not have
been in order.

Not that a lot of planes or other vehicles were
likely to brave these mountains. But one never knew.

I'll have to talk to Sitwell about that, he thought, as he
swooped through the man-made opening.

There was a truck inside, the one in which Jan had
snuck into the place. *But no SHIELD people,* Stark
observed. Or rather, none that he could see.

Stark ascended through the atrium, looking for
one of the two dozen agents assigned to the place.
But he couldn't find anyone.

How odd, he thought.

Then, with the help of his auditory enhancements, Stark heard something behind him. The click of something on the floor, near the entrance.

Relieved that he wasn't alone, he used his thrusters to whirl in midair. But it wasn't one of Fury's SHIELD personnel he found himself confronting.

It was a Tomorrow Man, in the white and green jumpsuit Stark had come to associate with his kind.

Had that been the only surprise Stark was compelled to absorb, it would have been enough to send his mind reeling in search of answers. But in the same moment, it occurred to him that this was a Tomorrow Man he had never seen before.

The fellow was thin to the point of scrawniness, with a wild, red goatee, so there was no mistaking him for the others. Almost too late, Stark saw the Tomorrow Man's hand go up.

Stark had seen that gesture before, back in the Triskelion, when he got his first glimpse of the intruders. He knew what it meant, and he didn't want to feel its impact a second time.

With a spurt of thruster power, he managed to dodge the ensuing energy blast. Then he fired back, only to find himself frustrated by the same kind of force field Weyland had used.

A second time, the Tomorrow Man attacked him with a beam of destructive force. And a second time,

Stark made him miss. But he was clearly at a disadvantage.

Then he heard another click on the floor and realized there was someone in back of him. Twisting in midair, he saved himself from the full brunt of the blast that followed.

He saw another Tomorrow Man he had never seen before—a stocky specimen with dark skin and light eyes. And there were two others right behind him.

Think, Stark demanded of himself.

Whatever had happened to Fury's people, the Tomorrow Men had something to do with it. Or maybe it was some other group from the future, in some way opposed to Weyland's. Either way, Stark had to get word back to the Triskelion.

Unfortunately, it wouldn't be easy to get out of there with the Tomorrow Men standing in his way. So he chose a different path—one that took him up to the twelfth and highest level of the atrium.

Caving in a metal door with his pulse emitters, he surmounted the safety rail and invaded a room that had served as living quarters for the Tiberites. It was empty at the moment, which was a good thing, since it would take him a few seconds to bludgeon a hole in its foot-thick rear wall.

What lay beyond it, according to the layouts they had drawn of the place, was the hangar for the one-man aircraft he and Thor had put out of business. If

Stark was lucky, he wouldn't encounter any resistance there as he tried to make his exit.

Who knows? he thought, pounding at the wall with the power of his metal fists. *Maybe they left the back door as wide open as the front one.*

As the pulverized cement fell away, Stark got his first glimpse of the hangar. Indeed, it looked unoccupied, though he was certain it wouldn't remain that way for long.

But there was something about it that felt wrong. A result of the lighting, perhaps? Or maybe a malfunction in his armor's sensory hardware?

He was still trying to figure it out when he felt something ram him in the small of his back, smashing him face first into a part of the wall that was still intact. Turning, he saw a Tomorrow Man standing in the open doorway, his palm raised for another shot.

Throwing himself out of the way, Stark saw the violet beam strike the wall instead, putting the finishing touches on his escape hole. Unhesitatingly, he flew through it.

And saw what was wrong—*very* wrong—in the hangar.

Part of the left-hand wall was gone. In its place stood a swirling depth of black energy that seemed to offer access to something, though Stark couldn't begin to guess *what*.

As he hovered there, enthralled by the sight of the energy maelstrom, his pursuer took another shot at him. It drove him into the far wall, just above the hangar doors.

Snap out of it, Stark told himself, angry about his lapse.

He looked around for a control panel that would open the doors, which looked too thick to pound through in the short time allotted to him. A moment later, that became no time at all, as a half-dozen Tomorrow Men swarmed into the hangar.

Stark swore under his breath. *Now what?*

Spreading out, the Tomorrow Men fired their beams at him from all angles, forcing him into one evasive maneuver after another. And none of it was getting him any closer to leaving the place.

Then he miscalculated—badly—and two energy bolts hit him at once, sending him pinwheeling wildly in a direction he hadn't intended, stunned despite the protection his armor afforded him.

Before Stark could pull out of it, a third beam hammered him from behind, making him spin even faster. Too late, he saw the black whirlpool looming, threatening to engulf him.

For a moment, he felt cold such as he had never felt before. Then his mind drained away into the darkness.

14

FURY WAS GOING OVER PLANS FOR THE ANDES
mission for the third and final time when he heard a
knock on his door and saw Happy Hogan enter the
room.

Normally, Hogan was the cheerful sort, the guy
one could always count on to lighten things up. But
at the moment, he looked as if he had lost his best
friend.

"We may have a problem," he said.

"What is it?" Fury asked.

"We haven't been able to raise Mister Stark since
he left for the Caucasus facility. And that was nine
hours ago."

More than enough time for him to get there, the general reflected.

"We need to contact the facility," said Hogan. "And I don't have the authority to . . ."

"Say no more," Fury told him.

Swiveling in his seat, he punched a command into his keyboard, opening a text channel to Tiber One. Then he sent a message asking if anyone there had heard from Stark lately.

In little more than a minute, he got his answer: *Negative.*

"I was afraid of that," said Hogan, his tone flat and grim.

"Let's not jump to conclusions," said Fury.

But he was concerned as well. After all, it wasn't like Stark to go incommunicado. Of course, there was another way to locate him, to which only the general had access.

Logging out of his link to Tiber One, he tapped in another command. This one connected him with a tiny black box in the Iron Man armor, the same kind that planes carried. It was planted there so they could find Stark's remains if he ever went down.

But there was no response from the black box. *Strange,* thought Fury. *That box is supposed to be able to withstand almost anything.* And yet it was as silent as Stark himself.

Fury didn't know if that was good news or bad.

• • •

"What's going on?" Banner asked his guards.

He was always the last to know anything going on in the Triskelion. *The downside of living in a goldfish bowl.*

"It's Mister Stark," said Warshovsky, looking none too happy about the news. "He's gone missing."

"Missing . . . ?" Banner echoed.

"Eleven hours now," said Crespo. "There's a device in his armor that's supposed to let us know where he is, even if he went down somewhere. But there's no response from it."

Not good, thought Banner, understanding the implications.

"Everybody's pretty broken up about it," said Warshovsky. "He was a good guy."

Banner thought so too. He found it hard to believe that someone who had battled the Chitauri and survived could have just disappeared. But it was possible, wasn't it?

He remembered Stark complaining about the vagaries of his armor's various leading-edge technologies. There was always some small thing going wrong with them, it seemed.

Maybe this time it was a big thing, the scientist allowed.

Natasha was standing in the north lounge, staring out the window at the wind-stippled water and the crowded tip of lower Manhattan, when she heard someone approaching.

It was Clint. She could tell by a half-dozen cues, not to mention his reflection in the window glass. Silently, solemnly, he came to stand beside her.

Finally, he spoke up. "I always figured it would be one of *us*. Not one of the headliners. And especially not *him*."

Natasha had figured the same thing. Stark was a survivor, a man who could have taught cats to land on their feet. It was hard to believe he was dead. *Very* hard.

"I know how you felt about him," said Clint. "So if you . . ."

"Need a shoulder to cry on?" She shook her head. "You know me better than that."

He remained beside her a moment longer. Then he said, "I've got to get home. I promised the kids I would tuck them in."

"See you," she told him. And heard his footsteps as he departed.

Natasha made a sound of disgust deep in her throat. Clint was right, of course. She *had* cared for Stark.

She wasn't sure when she had realized that. Not in the men's room before the battle against the Chitauri—that really *had* been an impulse born of pre-battle jitters, his even more than hers. *Later, then?*

Yes. In the aftermath of the battle for Earth, when Rogers was addressing the troops, making them feel good about having repelled an alien invasion.

Stark was standing off to the side, inscrutable behind his metal mask, his arms folded across his thick metal chest. He looked like power incarnate—as long as one didn't look too closely.

But Natasha knew the man inside the metal shell, and knew how different he was from his suit of armor. How fallible.

How human.

And that was the thing she came to love about him. Not the technology-powered air of invincibility. Not the force he could exert on the world, or the heights to which he could rise above it.

But the frailty of the man within the metal casing.

He wasn't a juggernaut like Rogers or Thor, or the aliens they were fighting. He was just a guy with an idea and the stubborn courage to see it through. *Or the stupidity.* Either way, she found it incredibly sexy.

But Natasha couldn't tell him so. He was so determined to be the bon vivant, the man about town, that he would have shied from her attentions like a deer downwind of a timber wolf.

So she played hard to get, as he eventually surmised. And little by little, she drew him to her, luring him into her web. But then, back in the Soviet Union, her superiors had nicknamed her the Black Widow for good reason.

With a little more time, Natasha would have

caught Stark for good. She was certain of it. But time had run out on them.

Stark wasn't sure how long he had listened to the bird cries, thinking them part of an especially persistent and disturbing nightmare, before he opened his eyes and peered through the optical filters in his mask.

Only then did he see where he was—in the charred, half-ruined shell of what had once been a brick building, its windows reduced to short, jagged shards of glass, its floor littered with piles of rubble and unidentifiable debris.

What the hell . . . ? he thought.

The last thing he remembered was spinning through the air of the Tiberites' hangar, propelled by the beams of the Tomorrow Men. *No—there was something else.*

The black whirlpool-thing. A feeling of extreme cold as he became immersed in it, as if all the heat had been leeched out of him. A sense that the world was fading around him.

And now, Stark thought, *here I am. Wherever that may be.*

The bird cries were getting louder, closer. Then he realized they weren't bird cries at all. They were shouts torn from human throats, albeit in an accent he had never heard before.

And they were vibrating with urgency.

Out of curiosity as much as self-preservation, the industrialist got to his feet and approached one of the shattered windows. *Now we'll see what's out there,* he thought.

Just in time to see something explode in his face.

Instinctively, he dropped to his knees—but it was too late. He had already been bludgeoned with chunks of brick and masonry, enough to kill him were it not for the protection afforded him by his armor.

Only in the aftermath of the explosion did Stark realize what had happened. The right side of the window frame had been sent flying at him by a blast of violet energy.

The same kind the Tomorrow Men use.

The incident made him more cautious. If someone out there was in league with the people who had fired at him, he didn't want to make himself too easy a target.

Raising his head, he peered out through the remains of the window. And as no one greeted him with a face full of shattered brick this time, he had a moment to survey the situation three or four stories below him.

Apparently, he was in the midst of a firefight—one sprawling across a bizarre grid of overgrown ruins and what looked like streets except for the greenery flooding through them.

The combatants on his right were distinguished

by dark blue uniforms and a certain amount of discipline. Clearly they were the aggressors, slowly but certainly gaining ground as they followed their energy barrages with short, controlled advances.

The group on his left was made up of what looked like civilians, lacking uniforms as well as organization. They were armed with energy weapons as well. But they repeatedly had to pull back, quite clearly getting the worst of the exchange.

Naturally, Stark's heart went out to the latter faction—an impulse he was forced to question. In his companies' dealings with undeveloped nations, he had encountered enough noble dictators and unprincipled "freedom fighters" to know appearances could be deceiving.

The one thing he could be absolutely sure of, based on the evidence before him, was that he was no longer in the world to which he had been born. That reality didn't *have* energy weapons, except for the few the Tomorrow Men had brought with them.

But the world of the future *did*.

It was a difficult conclusion for Stark to embrace—more difficult, somehow, than the notion that human beings could travel from the future to the twenty-first century.

The Tomorrow Men, after all, were people like anyone else. They were dressed differently, equipped differently, but they were people all the same. It was the implications they brought with them that were hard to accept—especially for people like Fury, who had been trained to think in concrete terms.

Stark hadn't had any trouble with the concept of visitors from the future. Having been immersed in theory all his life, he was able to deal with that.

But to be ensconced in that future time, to see and feel and hear it firsthand—that was an infinitely more bizarre experience than simply meeting the Tomorrow Men. It was the difference between having cocktails with Jacques Cousteau and being abandoned at the bottom of the ocean.

If it was the black maelstrom that had sent him there, it was some kind of time-travel device, one the Tomorrow Men had gone to great lengths to install in the mountain. But what did they need it for? What were they planning on doing with it?

Lots of questions, he thought. *No answers.*

As Stark followed the battle, the uniformed force continued to push the civilians back. Apparently, the former had the superior weaponry, their violet blasts longer-ranged and significantly more destructive than those of their adversaries.

Nonetheless, there were pockets in which the civilians held their ground. One of them was in the weed-choked street directly beneath Stark, where both sides were using piles of debris for cover and firing across a span of perhaps fifty yards.

He winced as one of the uniformed men was skewered with a violet energy beam, the force of which sent him hurtling backward. But for the most part, the battle was a stalemate.

Suddenly, a woman emerged from the hollowed-out structure opposite Stark's, right in the middle of the fight. And as she fled from the uniformed men, she seemed to waddle rather than run.

Then Stark saw why the woman looked so awkward. She had a child clutched to her chest—a toddler, it seemed to him, though he was hardly an expert on children.

The tiny life in the woman's arms didn't seem to deter the uniformed combatants in the least. They continued to fire their energy bolts, missing the woman only because she stumbled and fell providently behind a grassy mound.

That was all Stark needed to see.

No matter what enmities existed between these people, no matter what had driven them to fight in the first place, there was no excuse for shooting at children. *And no excuse for me to sit here and watch it happen.*

Taking a running jump, he launched himself through the battered window. And as he went horizontal, he activated the thrusters in the heels of his metal boots.

Suddenly, he was free of the building, soaring over the battle. It unfolded beneath him like a map, exposing parts of it he hadn't seen from his vantage point.

It was even bigger than he had thought, stretching

a quarter mile in front of him and almost that far behind, all the way to a body of water he didn't recognize. Then he saw something in the water, and it registered with him after all.

How could it *not?* The immense statue of Lady Liberty was half-submerged, but there was no mistaking her torch. It jutted out of the harbor toward Stark at a sad but defiant angle, telling him—as difficult as it was to believe—that he was in New York City. Or rather, what had been New York City once upon a time.

But there were no longer any skyscrapers crowding the southernmost tip of Manhattan. No Brooklyn Bridge. No Empire State Building. They had all been leveled, either by violence or neglect or both.

All this Stark observed in a fraction of a second. Then he was swooping toward the woman with the child in her arms, who had started running again.

Scooping her up, he carried her straight back over the ranks of her fellow civilians. When he got to a place where he saw other women and children, all of them retreating as quickly as they could, he set his charges down.

The woman shouted something to him that sounded like "Thank you." But he couldn't really tell, because he was already rocketing back in the other direction, heading for the front lines.

When Stark caught sight of the uniformed troops in the distance, he activated his pulse generators.

Then, just as soon as he was close enough, he made a statement.

It didn't rely on words, but it was eloquent all the same. *And memorable,* he hoped, as he watched a handful of aggressors fall under the impact of his pulse attack.

Their comrades weren't so intimidated that they didn't fire back. But by the time they got Stark in their sights he was somewhere else, his armor's propulsion system keeping him a step ahead of their energy bursts.

A second time, he raked the aggressors with his pulse emitters. And a second time, a bunch of them fell like wheat under a sharp and well-swung scythe.

As before, they returned fire, their energy beams crisscrossing around him as thick as bees. But he found a path through them, however tortuous, and wheeled for another pass.

By then, someone in charge had decided to change tactics. Stark could tell because the uniformed figures were pulling back, abandoning the fight—and their own casualties—for the moment.

Stark was glad to see it. *Nice to deal with someone who has some sense,* he reflected.

Then he saw an eruption of orange light from far away—as if a tiny sun had somehow come catapulting over the horizon. But it wasn't far away for long. It bore down on him with frightening speed, coming for him faster than his mind could register.

Stark twisted sideways and applied thrust, hoping to elude the ball of fire. But he couldn't avoid it altogether.

With a terrible roar, it dealt him a glancing blow—one that nonetheless came close to ripping his head off. He found himself hurtling end over end, unable to tell in what direction.

Come on, he told himself, refusing to give in to the vertigo threatening to claim him. *Pull it together.*

That was when Stark saw the ground rushing up at him and veered to avoid it. Continuing in the same direction, he gained altitude until his head cleared, and then surveyed the battlefield.

The aggressors were forging ahead again to the detriment of the civilians. And there was another fireball growing on the horizon, no doubt with Stark's name on it.

But he wasn't going to wait for it to find him. With a touch of the thruster control in his gauntlet, he sent himself plummeting back to Earth again.

Inches from the ground, he pulled out of his dive—right in the midst of the surprised blue suits. And the fireball, rather than pursuing him, passed harmlessly overhead.

So as long as he remained among the aggressors, he was safe. *From the fireball, at least.* The uniformed men themselves were spread out enough to get a shot in.

Which was why he had to keep moving, zigzagging unpredictably. And at the same time, try to do some damage.

The longer he kept the aggressors busy, the more time the civilians would have to retreat. That is, if they chose to do so, as he fervently hoped they would.

It was also possible they would see the enemy was distracted and rally for a counterattack. And if they did that, there would be little he could do to stop them.

But the civilians continued to draw back. And for his part, he continued to weave among the aggressors, sending bone-jarring pulse-impacts through their ranks.

When they fired their energy blasts at him, they hit each other if they hit anything at all. Every few seconds another uniformed figure fell, either by Stark's hand or that of a comrade.

After a while, the aggressors began to yield ground again, unable to cope with the man in the metal suit. But he didn't let up. Not until his adversaries were running from him full tilt, squeezing off only a token shot now and then to keep him off their tails.

Stark thought he might see another fireball at that point. But he didn't. It appeared both he and the sea of civilians were safe in that regard.

Three cheers for perseverance, he thought. *Or as Jarvis would have put it, being too stupid to know when you're overmatched.*

Rocketing skyward, Stark strove for another bird's-eye view of the battlefield. After all, the confrontation he had broken up was just one among many.

But on every parallel strip of green, a similar retreat was taking place. Whoever was in charge of the uniformed men seemed to have recalled them all at once, much to Stark's relief.

After all, his power wasn't unlimited. Back in his own time, he could have called for a boost via a Stark satellite. In this era, he had to rely strictly on his batteries.

All right, he thought, *now what?*

He needed to get his bearings, to gain some understanding of this world so he could formulate his next move. And he didn't expect to get any help from the blue suits—even if he could get them to halt their retreat long enough to talk to them.

That left him but one alternative. Looping around into a slow descent, Stark headed for the mass of civilians.

They pointed to him as he approached them, their eyes fixed on him. Not just those he had seen exchanging energy fire with the enemy, but older people and children as well.

Stark smiled to himself behind his mask. This was the sort of image he'd dreamed about when he first began working on his armor. People pointing up at him in admiration and gratitude. A little icing on the cake of his legacy.

As he came closer to the civilians, they appeared to clear a space for him. Again, it was as he had pictured it, back in the days when he was brainstorming the Iron Man technology in an icebox of an abandoned Tibetan monastery.

Gradually cutting power to the thrusters in his boots, Stark eased himself to the ground. Then he waited for a reaction.

A round of applause would have been nice. Or a cheer, like the one he had received at the company picnic the year before. Or just a thank-you, like the one the woman had given him earlier.

But he heard nothing of the sort. Instead, a couple of civilians pointed their weapons in his direction.

Stark held his hands up to show he meant them no harm. It was an empty gesture, considering his arsenal was built into his armor, but there was no way these people could have known that.

A woman with a shock of short, dark hair came forward, an energy rifle cradled in her arms. She would have been pretty except for the jagged scar that ran from her forehead to her jaw.

"That's close enough," she told him in the sharp, choppy accent he had heard earlier.

"Easy," he said, turning on the boardroom charm. "I'm the one who helped you, remember?"

"I know what you did," the woman said. "I just don't know who did it. Or *why*."

"Simple," Stark told her. "I don't like bullies."

She grunted. "Says the man who won't show us his face."

Can you wreck the timeline by tampering with the future? he wondered. *Or only with the past?* It was an interesting question. *After all, isn't this the past from the perspective of someone years from now?*

If he took his mask off and someone recognized him, he might place the timeline in jeopardy. And even if his opinion of the Tomorrow Men had changed, it still made sense not to screw around with the temporal status quo.

Then again, Stark doubted these people would know Tony Stark from Elvis Presley, especially if the armor hadn't tipped them off already. They didn't look like they had access to a whole lot of historical data.

Besides, he wasn't a big enough fish to have made his mark in a history book. He was just a businessman, a quirky little footnote, no matter how hard he tried to make himself more than that.

Unfastening the locks on either side of his mask, Stark took the thing off. It felt good to feel the air on his skin, and to breathe freely again. Despite the ruins around him, the air was remarkably fresh and sweet smelling.

Which is what happens, he mused, *when you eliminate all the heavy industry in the area.*

Seeing Stark without his mask, the woman studied his face—so intently, in fact, that he wondered if he had made a mistake after all. Then she made a gesture of dismissal.

"Put it back on, if you want. But stay where we can see you. Baker will want to talk with you."

"Baker," Stark repeated.

"That's right," the woman said. Slinging her energy rifle over her shoulder, she turned her back on him and started picking her way through the crowd.

Stark just stood there for a moment, the object of much scrutiny as people passed him on their way up the street. But no one said anything to him, gratefully or otherwise.

It made him wonder if he had picked the right side after all.

15

STARK DECIDED HE WOULDN'T WAIT FOR BAKER to find him. Instead, he would find Baker.

It turned out not to be as easy as he thought. When he asked for help from the flow of humanity around him, a number of people shrank from him. Others said a few words, none of them specific enough to be helpful.

Finally, one half-lame old man stopped to talk with him, defying the whispered advice of those with him. "I know Baker," he said hoarsely. "You stay right here. I'll get him."

Then someone said, "No need. He's already *here.*"

Stark followed the speaker's gaze and searched

the crowd for someone who looked to be in charge. But no one presented himself, at least not right away.

Then a tall man with a long, silver-gray ponytail appeared and moved to confront Stark. He had a look in his eyes that said he wasn't an easy mark.

"You're the stranger," he observed wryly.

"At your service," said Stark.

The man with the ponytail looked him over—first his face and then his armor. "People say you flew through the air like a bird. And blasted the Scaredy Men with some kind of invisible beams."

Scaredy Men? *Interesting name for them.*

Stark nodded. "Something like that."

The man's eyes narrowed. "So who are you? *What* are you?"

Stark didn't think it would be a good idea to tell him. He had already taken a chance by showing his face. Invoking the name of Tony Stark might be pushing his luck too far.

"You mean," he said, "you've never seen a guy in a suit of armor before?"

Baker scowled. "I asked you a question."

"And I can't give you an answer. I hope you'll respect that."

"Or what? You'll turn your weapons on *me?*"

"I'll do nothing of the sort," said Stark. "Whoever those uniformed people were, they were firing on a child. I won't countenance that."

"You don't know who they are?" asked the man with the ponytail, looking skeptical.

"I'm not from around here," Stark pointed out, "as you've no doubt surmised."

"He talks all fancy-shmancy," said the woman with the scar, moving up beside Baker. "Like the rats."

"The rats?" asked Stark.

"You don't know them either?" Baker asked.

"I'm afraid not," said Stark.

"He's lying," said the woman.

"No," said Baker, "I don't think so." He turned back to Stark. "The rats are the people in the Enclave—the ones with all the food. Enough to support a private army."

Stark looked at him. "So those people firing at you were mercenaries? Hired guns?"

"Hired *scum*," said the woman. "No different from us except for the fact they've sold out."

"Working for the Enclave," said Baker, "they get food, shelter, clothing. All the things we're missing."

"Except for self-respect," said the woman.

"Why were they after you?" Stark asked.

Baker chuckled. "The rats control a network of privileged places along the lines of the Enclave. They dole out tech information to these places and in return they get supply caravans.

"We've got the brass to believe those supplies should be ours, so we go after them. Sometimes we get them, sometimes we don't. Either way, the rats send the Scaredy Men after us, to make us think twice about doing it again."

"This time," said the woman with the scar, "we got most of the supplies. So they whipped us pretty hard." Her mouth twisted in a parody of a smile. "Or anyway, they tried to."

"So now what?" Baker asked Stark. "Now that you got your history lesson, you planning on going back where you came from?"

"Eventually," Stark replied hopefully. "But not yet. First I'd like to learn more about this Enclave."

"Digger can tell him anything he wants to know," said the woman.

Baker nodded, eyeing his armored benefactor all the while. "That's right, Torricelli. I guess he can."

"Can I speak to him?" asked Stark.

Baker shook his head. "Not a chance in hell. Digger doesn't talk to strangers. He hardly talks to friends."

"I'd like to give it a shot anyway," said Stark.

The man with the ponytail laughed humorlessly. "Yeah, I'll just *bet* you would."

"So," said Stark, "you're not going to tell me where to find him?"

Baker considered him. "We'll talk some more later. That is, if you're still around."

Stark couldn't imagine where else he would go.

●　●　●

Natasha Romanov wasn't especially surprised by what she found on Allegheny Street.

It wasn't the worst residential block she had ever seen, but it certainly wasn't the best. Though the empty plastic containers along the curb indicated a garbage collection just that morning, the place smelled like some of it had been left behind.

Mmm . . . fragrant, Natasha thought.

Each door on the block had a set of brass numerals nailed to it. She walked along, reading them to herself, until she reached the one she was looking for. *Twenty-three.* Or rather it would have been, if the three hadn't lost its top nail and swung upside down.

Walking up three brick steps, she noticed that the mailbox was full. But it was too early for the mail carrier to have shown up already, so it must have been the mail from the day before.

Maybe he's away, Natasha thought.

She sure as hell hoped not. She didn't know where else to turn.

Natasha couldn't find a doorbell, so she rapped on the door with her knuckles. *No response.* But she hadn't come all that way to walk away empty-handed.

She lifted her hand to knock again. But before she could connect, she heard a shuffling sound behind the door. A moment later, it was replaced by a metallic creaking, as of tumblers sliding in a lock that desperately needed oil.

Then the door swung inward, revealing a bleary-eyed, stubble-chinned Henry Pym.

He was wearing jeans, a loose-fitting sweatshirt, and a pair of mismatched socks, all of which looked thoroughly slept in. Most people wouldn't have noticed the disparity between the socks, but Russian spies were trained to notice everything.

"Miss Romanov," said Pym, obviously surprised to see her.

She was about to say, "Call me Natasha." But under the circumstances, she thought better of it.

After all, Pym was a bachelor these days, and she had shown up at his apartment unannounced, and she didn't want him to jump to the wrong conclusion. Especially since she considered him something of a slimeball after what he did to his wife.

"Doctor Pym," Natasha responded, keeping it professional. "Mind if I come in?"

"Not at all," he told her, stepping aside and gesturing for her to enter. "Just don't mind the mess."

It was a mess, all right. There were boxes of stuff everywhere. Manila folders. Compact disks. Science magazines. Photo albums. Also an elaborate terrain of soda cans, empty and half-full bags of chips, fast-food containers, bills, aspirin bottles, video cassettes, and newspaper clippings.

Much of it was covered with dust. So whatever was there had been there for a *while*.

But then, people's living conditions often mirrored their frame of mind. And after Pym's fall from grace at the Triskelion, his frame of mind had to be a dismal one.

Natasha walked past her host and sat down on the couch, next to a stack of *National Geographic*s that had the decency to topple the other way. Running his fingers through his thick, unkempt shock of dirty-blond hair, Pym deposited himself on an overstuffed chair.

Then he said, "So what brings you out this way?"

"I have a problem," she said, "one that's beyond my skill to address. But I have a feeling it's not beyond yours."

"What is it?" he asked, leaning forward in his chair.

"First off, you need to know that Tony Stark has disappeared. He was on his way to the Tiber place in the Caucasus when he went incommunicado and the black box in his armor stopped transmitting."

"That's terrible," said Pym.

"But if I'm right," Natasha continued, "it wasn't an accident that he disappeared. It's the work of the Tomorrow Men."

The scientist looked at her. "What makes you say that?"

"I've always found solace in food," she said. "I know you wouldn't think that to look at me, but it's true. So as I came to grips with our friend's disappearance, it was inevitable that I would wind up in the mess hall.

"It happened that the Tomorrow Men were there too, along with their guards. Seeing me, Weyland took the opportunity to express his condolences about Stark. I nodded or something, too lost in my thoughts to put much effort into a response.

"But thanks to one of the reflective strips in the back of a booth, I was able to watch Weyland return to his table. As he sat down, unaware that I could see him, he exchanged a look with Chadaputra.

"I was a spy, as you know. I'm trained to decipher people's expressions. The look Weyland exchanged with Chadaputra wasn't one of sympathy. It was the kind people exchange when they're up to no good. When they're *concealing* something.

"Until that moment, it wouldn't have occurred to me to suspect the Tomorrow Men had a hand in Stark's disappearance. But now I'm certain of it."

"What could they have done?" Pym asked. "Haven't they been under lock and key?"

"They have been," she confirmed. "But they're from the future. Who knows what they can do? At the very least, I believe, they've tampered with the data we received from Stark's black box.

"Which is why I came to you," she told the scientist. "You're the communications expert. I'm hoping you can find the original data, or at least confirm the fact that it's been modified, without attracting the Tomorrow Men's attention."

Pym's brow furrowed. "Have you told Fury about this?"

She shook her head. "Neither him nor any of my other colleagues. If the Tomorrow Men can erase communications logs from their cell, they can eavesdrop on conversations. That's the other reason I'm here. They may be able to bug the Triskelion, but I doubt they can hear us talking here in Chicago."

"So what do you say?" Natasha asked.

Pym stared past her for a moment at something only he could see. Then he focused again and said, "I can help. But I don't have access to the Triskelion anymore."

"Leave that to me," said Natasha. "Back in my espionage days, I got into the White House as a cleaning woman—twice. I think I can get you into our little top-security country club."

The sun was on its way down before Baker's people stopped moving through the slots between the ruins, and set up camp beside a meandering creek.

Gathering wood, which seemed plentiful in the overgrown rubble if one knew where to look, they set up tripods and took out pots that were no larger than a big man's fist. Then they filled the pots with water from the creek, got their fires going, and threw in pieces of food they had been carrying.

Stew, Stark thought.

It had been a long time since he ate anything that went by that description. *Maybe since college.* But things were different back then. He was cooking for himself, trying to keep body and soul together until he could file his first patent.

Moving closer to one of the fires, he watched a woman with braided blond hair stir the contents of her pot with a stick. He doubted there was anything fancy in the mix. *Roots, wild scallions, nuts, that sort of thing.* Whatever she had been able to scavenge.

Still, Stark's stomach growled at the smell, reminding him how long it had been since he put anything in it. *Not even the olive from a martini,* he mused.

Back in his own time, it wasn't unusual for him to miss a meal because he was too busy. But he always knew that he would eat sometime soon, and eat well.

In this era, Stark didn't have the same luxury.

As if the woman had eyes in the back of her head, she turned and looked at him. She had a kind and not unattractive face, though it clearly wasn't a happy one.

"The stranger," she said, smiling a little. "The one who saved us from the Scaredy Men."

"Guilty as charged," Stark said.

"Care for some?" the woman asked him, gesturing to the pot with a red, calloused hand.

Surprised, he nodded. "In fact, I would. If there's enough to go around."

"There is," she assured him.

It felt awkward for Stark to sit down, his armor tightening around his middle and the backs of his knees. But then, he hadn't designed it with a whole lot of sitting in mind.

In any case, he settled onto a chunk of rock and placed his mask on the ground beside him. Then he watched his hostess dip into the stew with a charred iron ladle and deposit a dollop on a chipped ceramic plate.

"There you are," she said.

Now that Stark was able to get a look at the stuff, it didn't seem so appetizing after all. But he had to eat *something*. And besides, he didn't want to offend his benefactor.

"I'm grateful," he told her.

"Don't mention it," she said.

For a while, they sat there in companionable silence. Just eating. It was a novel experience for Stark, who was accustomed to always either entertaining at dinner or being entertained.

Abruptly, the woman spoke up. "My name's Patricia."

"Michael," he replied warmly, using his middle name. "A pleasure to meet you. And thanks again for being so charitable."

"You're lucky," the woman told him. "I don't always have enough to share. How is it?"

"Very good," he said, lying.

The woman tried to smile again, though she was clearly out of practice. "I'm glad you like it."

Again, silence. And under its influence, Stark realized how tired he was. It had been a long day.

A couple of centuries long.

"Does it get hot in there?" Patricia asked, lifting her chin to indicate his armor.

Stark shook his head. "Not really. It's got a temperature control system. If I didn't feel the breeze on my face, I wouldn't have any idea what the ambient temperature is."

"Where did you get something like that?"

"I made it," he said. "With a lot of help."

"Things must be different where you come from."

Stark nodded. "They are."

More silence. Like a soft, comfortable blanket.

"You're a good-looking man," Patricia observed.

It took Stark a moment to recover from the compliment. "It's the mask, my dear. Does wonders for my complexion."

"Where you come from," she asked, "is there anybody waiting for you to come back? A woman, I mean?"

He knew exactly what she meant. From force of habit, he was about to reply in the negative. Then he remembered . . .

"There is, actually."

A shadow of disappointment crossed Patricia's face. "She's a fortunate woman."

Well, he thought, *there* was *the incident in the men's room.* But he doubted that Natasha would call herself "fortunate" on the basis of that alone.

"Do *you* have . . . anyone?" he asked.

The woman shrugged. "I used to. Tom was his name. He got killed a year ago assaulting an Enclave caravan."

"I'm sorry," said Stark.

She nodded. "Me, too. But lots of us have lost our mates. That's just the way it is."

But not the way it's supposed to be, he reflected. *It's more than two hundred years in the future. You're supposed to be living in a paradise. A utopia.*

That was what all his work had been about. That was why he had rushed from meeting to meeting, never stopping to take a breath, because he didn't want to let a single moment go by unused.

So the future would be better. He looked around. *Not so it would be like* this.

"You all right?" Patricia asked.

"Yes," he said. "Why?"

"You just got this look in your eye . . . I don't know. Like you wanted to hit somebody or something."

Stark laughed. "Did I?"

He didn't get angry very often. *Maybe because I'm too full of booze,* he conceded.

But what he had seen of this century made him *very* angry—at the people who had crushed his dream, replacing it with their own. And at himself, for allowing it to happen.

"I get a little angry myself sometimes," said Patricia. "When I think about the Enclave and everything they've got in there, and how little we have out here."

Stark nodded. "It's a shame."

If he ever managed to return to his proper time, he would do his best to set things right. But in the meantime, he had to embrace the Enclave the way a drowning man might embrace a life preserver—because it was his only shot at getting home.

16

STARK HEARD A TAPPING SOUND. AND IT wouldn't stop.

Where the devil is it coming from? he asked himself. *Somewhere not too far away . . .*

Then he realized something was hitting him on the top of his helmet, which was locked onto his head again. Instinctively, he reached for the offending party—and closed the fingers of his gauntlet on it.

Twisting his head around, he eyed what he had caught. It was a boy, perhaps six or seven years old. And he had a flat piece of rubble in his hand.

"Leggo!" the kid growled, struggling to free himself.

Stark released him and he went scurrying away in a hurry. Obviously, the boy hadn't expected the man-shaped pile of metal he had discovered to wake up.

Propping himself up on an elbow, Stark looked around. Though he could see Patricia's pot hanging over a pile of dead ashes, the woman herself was nowhere to be seen.

But most everybody else in the encampment was either eating or preparing something to eat. It made him wish he were doing the same.

Where's Jarvis when I need him?

Unfortunately, his butler had been dead for centuries, along with every other soul Stark had ever met. It was a sobering thought, to say the least.

And speaking of sobering . . .

It felt funny not to have a martini in his hands, or at least to be able to look forward to one. But he doubted martinis were the beverage of choice among these people.

It wasn't the alcohol Stark missed, strangely enough. It was the distraction it afforded him, the opportunity to focus on something other than his medical problem.

He didn't want to be a sad, worried man waiting for the end. Whatever time he had left on Earth, he wanted to spend as well and as productively as he could . . . regardless of what era he spent it in.

Stark looked at the ragged mass of humanity

around him. If anyone needed an Iron Man, these people did.

He knew there was a rational reason the time portal had sent him to New York instead of someplace else—some simple trick of calibration. And he had never been what one might call a religious man. However, it certainly seemed Providence had plunked him down where he could do the most good.

If he didn't get back to his own time, and the odds were pretty good in that regard, this one certainly posed its share of challenges. Enough to keep him busy for a lifetime, whatever span of months and days that might represent.

Hell, he mused, savoring the irony, *my doctors said I wasn't assured of seeing tomorrow. And here I am a hundred thousand tomorrows later, still kicking.*

It was funny, in a grim way. Stark wished there was someone with whom he could share the joke.

As he thought that, he heard voices rise suddenly in anger. Turning in that direction, he saw a crowd standing around the corner of a ruined edifice.

A second time, the voices cut through the morning air. But Stark still couldn't make out what they were angry about.

His curiosity aroused, he moved across the encampment, careful not to step on anything or anyone. Finally, he reached the crowd and peered past it.

What he saw inside the ruins were Baker and five

other people, two of them women, sitting on loose chunks of masonry. They weren't shouting anymore, but they looked as if they might reprise that behavior at any moment.

With no breakfast appointments on his schedule, Stark removed his helmet and tucked it under his arm. Then he turned to the bony-faced man beside him and asked, "What's going on?"

"The council's talking with the people who live around here," came the answer.

"What about?" Stark wondered.

"When you enter someone else's territory, it's customary to meet with their leaders. Otherwise, it can get bloody."

So, Stark thought, *it's not just the Enclave Baker has to worry about. It's other groups like his own.*

But then, as he had seen, resources were rather scarce. If people weren't inclined to share *within* their group, they certainly weren't going to share with strangers.

"What do you think will happen?" Stark asked.

He had come to like Baker despite his curmudgeonly behavior, and Patricia as well. He had even begun to think of himself as a member of their community.

But the people who lived there weren't from the Enclave. They weren't tyrants. They were just looking out for themselves, which they had every right to do.

So if the situation *did* get bloody, Stark couldn't fight on his friends' behalf. The only thing he could do, in good conscience, was try to defuse hostilities.

He hoped Baker knew that.

"I don't know," said the bony-faced man. "But they've been talking for a long time. There must be some complications."

"What kind?" Stark asked.

"Every meeting is different," the man noted. "It could be anything."

Anything? Stark echoed inwardly. He wished he had the slightest idea what possibilities fell into that category.

Back in his own time, Stark had dickered with just about every kind of executive officer and dignitary there was, from Tokyo to Tierra del Fuego. But in every instance, he had known what to expect.

Part of that was the emphasis he placed on preparation. The other part was his knack for looking across the polished mahogany table of a company's boardroom and figuring out the other players' agendas.

But that was only possible because he knew what their agendas might be. They might, for instance, be willing to sell a company for less than market value in order to invest the capital in an opportunity elsewhere. They might be looking for a write-off to offset an unexpectedly healthy profit on their balance sheet. Or they might be asking too much for a property because they really didn't want to get rid of it in the first place.

This era, on the other hand, involved quids and pro quos he had probably never considered before. And until he could, he would feel like a fish out of water.

Suddenly, Baker shot to his feet, as did a couple of the men facing him. Then, with markedly less enthusiasm, the other men in the building stood up as well.

Faces turned dark with anger. Index fingers jabbed the air. Voices became snarls.

Is this absolutely necessary? Stark thought.

For a moment, it looked as if it would come to blows. Then the men confronting Baker spat on the floor and moved off. But it was clear they weren't happy about it.

Baker's side didn't look happy either. However, they let the others go without another word.

With the scrap over, Stark saw Baker and his compatriots leave the building. The crowd seemed to approve of what had transpired, judging by their comments.

Stark moved to join the man with the silver ponytail, who acknowledged him only with a glance. "It looked heated in there," Stark observed.

"They didn't like the idea of our being here. They're the kind that doesn't want to invite trouble, and they know we're the ones who've got the Enclave mad at us."

"So how did you resolve the situation?"

"They're moving. And we're staying."

Stark looked around. "Seems there would be plenty of room here for both of you."

"Seems that way," said Baker.

Something in his voice told Stark it wasn't *Baker's* reputation that had sent the locals packing. "They don't want to be associated with *me,* do they?"

The man with the ponytail shook his head. "In that armor, you're easy to spot. And there are other people in the employ of the Enclave besides those who wear those uniforms."

"Spies, you mean."

"All over," said Baker, his mouth twisting with contempt. "When we catch them, we kill them. But we don't often catch them."

Stark frowned. "What would happen if they told the Enclave about me?"

"I don't know. But if I were the locals, I wouldn't stick around to find out."

"I don't want anyone hurt on my account."

"Too late," said Baker. "They know you helped us. As far as they're concerned, that makes you one of us."

"And as far as *you're* concerned?"

Baker shrugged. "For all I know, you're one of those spies."

Stark chuckled. "Yes, *that's* likely. Nothing like a suit of armor to help one blend in with the crowd."

"Maybe not. But if you were going to gain our confidence, saving our hides would be a good way to do it. Then, after we've come to trust you, you could lead us into an Enclave trap."

"You've seen what my armor can do," said Stark. "If it had been my intention to incapacitate you, I wouldn't have resorted to the trap approach. I would simply have attempted it on my own."

"So, if you haven't done that," said Baker, "why don't I trust you? That's what you want to know, right?"

"That's correct."

"Because," said Baker, "the enemy has its own way of looking at things. I have enough trouble planning my own strategies. You want me to plan the Enclave's too?"

"You *know* what I want," Stark told him. "To speak with Digger."

"Tell me something. Why do you want to know about the Enclave so badly?"

"If I gave you an answer, you wouldn't believe it."

"Try me," said Baker.

Stark considered doing so—but only for a moment. In the end, the timeline was too serious a concern.

"I can't," he said finally. "But I assure you, it's not just me I'm looking out for. If I accomplish what I need to, your people will benefit as well."

"And I can trust you on that account?"

"You can," said Stark.

Baker laughed. "You really *aren't* from around here." He made a gesture with his arm that included everything around them. "Someone sells out to the Enclave every other day. That doesn't make for a whole lot of trust."

"You have to trust *somebody*," said Stark.

"I do. I trust people like Torricelli, who fight alongside me month in and month out." A glance. "Who do *you* trust?"

The question caught Stark off-guard. *Who indeed?*

"I have comrades," he said. "People who've proven their loyalty over the years." *Hogan, for instance. And Jarvis.*

"But no one you've met recently," Baker echoed.

"Actually," said Stark, thinking of Fury and the Ultimates, "I have a few *new* comrades. And I trust them as well."

"The same way you trust the old ones?"

Stark mulled it over for a moment. "Maybe not," he conceded. "But it's close."

"Then you're lucky," said Baker.

But he didn't tell Stark where to find Digger.

Bruce Banner didn't get it.

It wasn't that he minded seeing Henry Pym again. After all, when one was penned up in an airtight holding unit, any company was better than no company at all.

But if Pym was there to check Banner's blood work-ups, as he had indicated, what was he doing accessing communications logs? Banner could see through his transparent wall what his fellow scientist was looking at, and the graphic Pym had called up was definitely not a blood work-up.

Was it possible the guy had just made a mistake? Banner didn't think so. Pym had had his share of personal problems lately, but he was too bright a guy to be confusing two such different kinds of files.

So what was going on? *And should I say something to Pym about it?* Banner wondered. *Or maybe speak to Fury?*

After all, the general would want to know if something fishy was happening. And it wouldn't hurt to remind him how valuable Banner could be, considering his dependence on Fury's goodwill.

But there was another possibility. Pym might have been down there to help Fury, albeit in a low-profile kind of way. And if Banner attracted attention to the fact, it might tick Fury off.

Which would be a bad thing, Banner reflected. *A very bad thing.*

So in the end, he decided to keep his mouth shut and let Pym go about his business, no matter what it was. Because guys who lived in glass cages weren't just ill-advised to throw stones.

They were ill-advised to get involved in pretty much *anything.*

• • •

Stark heard a tapping and—tired as he was—smiled to himself. *The kid again,* he thought.

"All right," he said, without opening his eyes. "No need to keep knocking. I assure you, I'm still in here."

But the kid didn't stop.

"You do hear me, don't you?" Stark asked. "This armor's occupied."

And still the kid rapped on his helmet.

"And now it's getting a little tedious," said Stark, doing his best not to lose his patience with the boy.

But the youngster persisted. It sounded like a woodpecker had taken a liking to Stark's favorite brand of alloy.

By that time, Stark was a tad annoyed. Opening his eyes, he saw through his optical filters that it was still night. *Still dark enough for the stars to be visible in the sky.*

He wondered why the boy was up at this hour. Had he lain awake hoping to have a better chance at the armor, thinking Stark would remove it in order to sleep?

He began selecting the words he would use to make the kid leave him alone. It was hard enough being a stranger in a strange land without being a sleepy stranger as well.

Finally, his choice of phraseology firmly in mind, Stark rolled over to address the boy—and saw at a glance why the youngster had been so persistent.

A battalion of perhaps fifty uniformed guards was standing at the edge of Baker's camp, not a hundred yards from Stark's location. And they all had rifles in their hands.

No one else in the encampment seemed to have noticed the intruders. They were sleeping too deeply to notice *anything*.

Powering up his armor's tactical systems, Stark turned to the boy and whispered, "Come here." Then he tucked the child into a crevice formed by two large pieces of broken concrete, all the while keeping an eye on the—what had Baker called them?

Scaredy Men.

There were too many of them to take out all at once. But if he didn't get them in a single swoop, the ones he missed would slaughter Baker's people as they slept.

And sounding an alarm wouldn't help. By the time everyone realized what was happening, the soldiers would have skewered them all on their energy beams.

How in blazes did they get here without alerting Baker's sentries? Stark wondered.

Then he saw a handful of guards blink into existence beside the others, and he remembered—the Tomorrow Men had used personal teleportation devices to get to Calibaña. If these soldiers had the same technology working for them, they could have materialized anywhere they wanted without making a sound.

But why attack this way, when their modus operandi in the past had been to approach Baker's people on foot? What had happened to make them change their tactics?

As Stark supplied the answer, a chill climbed his spine. *It's because of me.*

The Enclave wasn't used to its guards getting their butts kicked. So it was steeping up its level of retaliation, showing Baker's people they couldn't do that without paying a price.

And maybe looking for the metal-encased idiot who had done most of the butt-kicking, to teach him a really *special* lesson. Though that was hardly Stark's first concern.

He bit his lip. Pietro would have been fast enough to get to the intruders and ruin their aim. Thor could have brought the lightning down on them with his hammer.

But what can I do? Stark asked himself.

The wind swept over him, flattening the weeds around him and stippling his armor with tiny pieces of crushed concrete. One of the guards got some of it in his eye, and used a knuckle to rub it.

But it wasn't enough to keep him from aiming his weapon at a sleeping figure. Or listening for the order that would have him release a gout of killing force.

Suddenly, Stark smiled to himself. *Unless . . .*

Using the controls in his right gauntlet, he turned up the power in his pulse-emitters to maximum. Then he aimed his palms at a pile of rubble just this side of the soldiers.

This had better work, Stark told himself—and unleashed a pair of blasts powerful enough to pulverize a city sidewalk.

A layer of rubble was instantly crushed into dust—a cloud of it that swept over the Scaredy Men, obscuring them from him. But at the same time, it hid Baker's people from the Scaredy Men.

Which was exactly what Stark had hoped it would do.

It also started the guards coughing, which woke up their targets. And once the rabble was awake, its instincts took over. Hands groped for rifles. Children scampered for cover.

With the attack exposed, Stark was able to put his efforts into striking back. It didn't matter that he couldn't see much of the guards. He could still fire into the dust cloud. As closely packed as his adversaries were, he seemed bound to hit someone.

With each high-powered pulse emission, he heard a grunt or a curse or a cry of pain—evidence that his attacks were doing some damage. *Keep it up,* he told himself.

Suddenly, a half-dozen violet energy beams erupted at Stark from the depths of the cloud. None of them hit him, but a couple came close.

Looks like they've zeroed in on me, he thought.

But that wasn't a bad thing. If they were firing at him, they weren't firing at anyone else.

Then it wasn't just Stark's pulse emissions that were harassing the guards. There were energy beams pounding them as well. Baker's people were letting them know how they felt about midnight raids.

Between the pulse emissions, the beams, and the strength of the wind, the dust cloud was ripped apart. But as the air cleared, it was still impossible to make out any of the guards.

And Stark knew why. They were gone. *All of them.* As if they had never been there in the first place.

Flying over the spot, he confirmed it. The only thing left of the Scaredy Men was the blood they had lost.

Baker's people were shaken by the experience. Men and women were cursing the Enclave at the tops of their lungs. Children were crying, wide-eyed with apprehension.

But it could have been worse. A *lot* worse.

17

"HEY, ARMOR MAN!" SOMEONE YELLED IN THE
darkness.

Stark turned and saw it was Baker calling to him,
moving through his sea of followers. And as usual,
Torricelli was at Baker's side, looking like she had
eaten something rancid.

"You seem to be in good health," Stark observed.
He glanced at Torricelli. "Both of you."

"It was you who kicked up that cloud of dust," the
man with the ponytail said, "wasn't it?"

"It was," said Stark.

Baker looked at him for a moment, as if he were

trying to see through the metal mask to the man behind it. "If not for you," he said, "we would've been dog meat."

"It's hard to argue with that," Stark conceded.

Baker glanced at Torricelli. "You see? I told you we were wrong about him."

The woman didn't say anything in response. She just made a sound of disgust and walked away.

Baker turned to Stark. "You should be honored. That's as close as she comes to complimenting anyone."

Stark chuckled in his mask. "If she's not careful, she's going to give me a swelled head."

Baker smiled a weary smile. "That's one danger we won't have to worry about."

"So," said Stark, taking advantage of the situation, "can I speak with Digger *now?*"

Baker eyed him. "Will you take off as soon as you do? And leave us to the mercy of the bastards in the Enclave?"

"Not right away," Stark told him. "But eventually. As I said, I'm not from around here."

Baker considered him for a moment. Then he said, "I'll tell you how to find Digger in the morning. I just hope for your sake he's in one of his more lucid moments. He drinks a bit."

Stark had to smile at the irony. "It's all right. I've been known to drink a bit myself."

* * *

Natasha had never been the patient sort.

In her work as a spy, she had often been forced to bide her time. But it had never been easy for her. And now, as she waited to hear from Henry Pym in her apartment in Greenwich Village, it was even harder.

Pym had said he would call her at five o'clock with a progress report. But it was five forty-five already, and Natasha still hadn't heard from him.

It was possible that he had become too engrossed in his work to realize what time it was. Having seen his apartment, she understood that the real world could be an inconvenience for him, an annoying and apparently irrelevant set of restrictions.

But it was also possible that he had run into trouble, either with Fury or with the Tomorrow Men. And the longer he snooped around in the Triskelion, the greater the likelihood such trouble would rear its head.

Finally, Natasha couldn't stand it anymore. She crossed the room and reached for the phone. But before she could wrap her fingers around it, it rang.

Picking it up, she said, "Hello?"

"It's Hank," said the voice on the other end.

He sounded even more tired than when he answered his door the day before. But then, he wasn't the type to let sleep get in the way of his work.

"Anything?" she asked.

"Looks like you were right," Pym told her. "Someone tampered with the data."

I knew it, Natasha thought. "Were you able to get any of it back?"

"Just bits and pieces. But in sufficient quantity to tell us what we need to know. From all indications, Stark was headed for the mountain, all right. And it appears he made it."

Then something happened to him after he got there. And in some way, the Tomorrow Men were responsible for it.

"You've been a huge help," Natasha told the scientist. "I can't thank you enough."

"There's one other thing," he said.

She looked at the phone. "Yes?"

"I know I'm not on the A team anymore, but I can still be a valuable guy in a fight. And from the look of things, you may be in a little over your head."

"It's kind of you to offer," said Natasha. "But where I'm going, I expect my talents will come in handier than yours."

"Suit yourself," said Pym. "If you change your mind, you know where to find me."

She got the feeling he wasn't just talking about fighting bad guys anymore. The observation made her skin crawl.

"I do," she said. "And thanks."

"Hey," said Pym, "what are mad scientists for?"

• • •

Tony Stark walked through an Upper East Side that looked nothing like the stately, soaring environs he knew so well.

There wasn't a single tall building left standing. Not even one. In their place stood hillock after shaggy green hillock, all of them at their cores just enormous piles of debris.

For some reason, the smaller buildings seemed to have had an easier time of it. But they too had suffered cracked façades and broken windows and missing doors.

Remarkably, a number of lampposts had survived, even if they looked different from the ones Stark had known—not simply utilitarian, but dark and sinuous like rearing serpents. The product, no doubt, of a more advanced era than his own. And many of those lampposts still bore the Gothic-style street signs that had been affixed to them.

In keeping with his surroundings, Stark didn't look the same either. He was wearing a long, hooded coat that Baker had given him, meant for a man much larger than he was. But then, it had to be big to conceal the contours of his armor.

Knowing how little Baker's people had, Stark would normally have felt badly about taking a coat from one of them. However, its previous owner didn't need it any longer, as he had perished in the first retaliatory strike on which Stark had intruded.

Besides, Stark reflected soberly, *the coat is being used for a good cause.*

He allowed himself one stop en route to his destination, at the intersection of Lenox and 112th Street. After all, Uptown Presbyterian had been located on Lenox between 112th and 113th.

But there was no evidence of it anymore. The medical center Stark had bought and renovated for the sake of the community was gone, replaced by a mountain of overgrown rubble.

He sighed. He had been so proud of that acquisition. He'd had such high hopes for it.

Especially the children's wing. He wondered if Miles Mortimer had ever put up the money they had talked about, and if he had ever gotten his big neon sign.

Stark hoped so. The hospital might be gone now, but it could have helped a great many people while it was standing. *Thousands of them. Maybe tens of thousands.*

They were long dead and buried, along with the New York City they had known. But while they were alive, they might have had something good to say about Uptown Presbyterian. Stark found some comfort in that thought.

As he was starting to attract stares, he moved on. Seven blocks later, he came to one of the intersections without a lamppost, so he had to depend on the landmarks described to him.

A corner with a section of caved-in sidewalk. A remarkably intact brick wall with the mural of a bountiful garden on it. A maple tree growing crookedly out of a sewer grate.

Go right here, he thought.

Unlike the other weed-choked streets he had seen, the one that stretched that way looked deserted. If there were people living in its frail, ramshackle buildings, they were doing a damned fine job of hiding themselves.

Still, he continued in that direction, in accordance with Baker's instructions. Finally, he came to a spot where a building's brick façade had cracked away, revealing the light-colored mortar beneath. Whether by accident or design, the exposed patch resembled a woman's high-heeled boot.

Turning to look across the street, Stark saw a door. It was one of the few on the block still intact, much less hanging straight on its hinges.

This is the place, he thought.

When he crossed the street and turned the door-knob, he discovered that the place was unlocked—just as he had been told it would be. Pushing the door open, he found himself in a rubble-strewn foyer. Beyond it were the flimsy remains of a wooden stairway, which led to a higher floor.

Stark didn't want that option, according to Baker. He wanted to go through the door behind the stair-way and find another stair, which he did. This set of steps was cruder but better preserved, and it led down instead of up.

Moments later, he found himself descending into a dimly lit basement. When he got to the bottom step, he looked around. The place was a jumble of plastic jugs and metal cans, some opened, some unopened. There were blankets as well, piled haphazardly against a wall, not far from an old, stained mattress.

Stark almost missed the basement's only occupant, mistaking him for another pile of blankets. A second look showed him a stringy-haired figure in a long, threadbare coat, with a stubbly chin and a strangely hollow look to his eyes.

He's blind, Stark realized.

"Digger?" he ventured.

"That's me," came the response, in a voice as threadbare as the coat. "And who the hell might you be?"

"Someone in need of information. Baker sent me."

"Don't know any Baker."

"He told me you'd say that."

Digger didn't voice any other objections. *Apparently,* Stark thought, *I've convinced him I'm all right.*

"I'm thirsty," Digger said suddenly.

Fortunately, Stark was prepared. He handed Digger the flask Baker had loaned him and said, "This ought to help."

The stuff in the flask was watered down. After all, Stark wanted Digger to be in control of his faculties for the duration of their conversation. Still, Digger seemed to be satisfied with the quality of his libation. Putting the flask to his lips, he poured its contents down his throat all at once.

Salud, Stark thought.

Wiping his mouth with his sleeve, Digger eyed his visitor—or at least seemed to. "There's something different about you. The scrape of your boots . . . *definitely* something different."

"I'm wearing armor," said Stark. Then he dragged out the line he had given the others: "I'm not from around here."

"I guess not," said Digger. "No one around here has an accent like that." A pause. "Where did you get the armor?"

"Where I come from," he said, "there's lots of it." *A half-dozen suits could qualify as "lots," I suppose.*

Digger looked like he would continue to inquire about the armor. Instead, he asked, "What do you want to know?"

Everything, Stark thought. "Tell me about the Enclave."

Digger shrugged. "There's not much to tell. They have everything. We have nothing. Sometimes we try to take what they have. They beat us up and try to take it back." He pointed to his eyes. "One time, they took these. Shot me square in the face with an energy gun. Could've been worse, though. Guys have died from shots like that one."

"I imagine so," said Stark.

Digger frowned. "That's it. Thanks for the drink." Flipping his visitor the flask, he leaned back into the shadows.

Stark had haggled with his share of tough negotiators. It seemed Digger was cut from the same cloth. "I was told you knew more about the Enclave than anyone. Is there something else you need to jog your memory?"

Digger grunted. "I'm still thirsty. But not for that watered-down swill in the flask. I'm thirsty the way you're thirsty. Thirsty for knowledge."

"You want to know about me before you discuss the Enclave. Is that it?"

"Very perceptive," said the blind man.

Stark bit his lip. He desperately wanted what Digger could give him. But he wouldn't screw up the timeline to get it.

"You see," said Digger, thinking out loud, "the only place I know of that could armor a man is the Enclave. But if you were one of their Scaredy Men, you wouldn't be asking about them—would you? So there must be another place like the Enclave somewhere. Maybe farther down the coast. The question is . . . what are you doing here? Checking out the competition, maybe in preparation for a little empire-building? Or did you come to help us against our oppressor?"

Before Stark could respond, Digger laughed. It

was an ugly sound, and it echoed in the confines of the basement.

"Right," said the blind man. "Like that'll happen."

"Look," said Stark, choosing his words carefully, "I didn't come to your part of the world with the intention of helping you. But now that I'm here, I will. All I ask is that you give me an understanding of the Enclave. But I can't tell you where I'm from or how I got here. I've sworn to keep my mouth shut in that regard, and I'm not a man who goes back on his word."

Digger tilted his head like a dog. "Even if it means you walk out of here no smarter than when you walked in?"

"Even then," said Stark.

"Then go," said the blind man.

Stark thought about staying and arguing his case. However, he had a feeling he wouldn't get anywhere. Besides, there had to be someone else who knew about the Enclave. *Somewhere.*

Turning, he headed for the stairs and the door at the top of it. But before he could reach it, Digger said, "Wait."

Stark looked back over his shoulder. "Yes?"

"You said you were going to help us. In what way?"

"That depends," said Stark, "on what I learn about the Enclave."

Digger hesitated for a moment. Then he said, "All right. Sit down."

Stark found a wooden crate. Again, he wished he had designed his armor with an eye to sitting.

"The Enclave," said Digger, "has been around for a long time. A hundred and fifty years, at least. It started out as a housing development for rich people—what they used to call a gated community back then—with a private security force.

"Then things fell apart in the world. Nobody knows exactly why or how. But while the rest of us fought over what little food was left, the bastards in the Enclave got everything they needed."

"So it's just housing inside the Enclave?"

Digger shook his head. "It was, in the beginning. Then they moved their technology inside as well, because it wasn't safe for them to keep it anywhere else. The rats generate their own power, store their own food, make most everything they need. What few things they can't make, they bring in from other places. And their Scaredy Men help them keep it for themselves."

"Who's in charge of the place?" Stark asked.

"Somebody named Stringfellow. Weirdest-looking guy I ever saw, but the people in the Enclave seemed to respect him. His lieutenant, the one who oversees the Scaredy Men, is Weyland. He's the one I'd—"

"Weyland," Stark repeated, interrupting Digger's description.

"Uh huh. You've heard of him?"

"You could say that."

It was starting to come together in Stark's brain. The Tomorrow Men hadn't lied when they said the world of the future was full of tyranny. They had only neglected to say they were part of it.

"Have you ever heard of the Enclave doing something crazy with its technology?" he asked Digger. "Say, trying to send people back and forth through time?"

The blind man looked surprised. "In fact, I have. But I thought it was a joke." His features screwed into a knot. "Sounds like you know more about the rats than you let on."

"Not really," said Stark. "Just that one thing."

"And why are you *interested* in that one thing?"

"Don't ask," said Stark, "and I won't have to lie to you."

Digger chuckled—something he obviously didn't do very often. "You've got me going now, armor man. Don't tell me you want to see the future. It's not likely to be any better than what we've got now. Who knows, it may be worse."

That was what Stark was fighting to prevent. "If you wanted to get into the Enclave," he said, "how would you go about it?"

"There's no easy way in," Digger warned him. "Whatever you tried, you'd probably be dead before long."

"But there must be one approach that's a little more promising than the others," Stark insisted.

Digger seemed to ponder the question. "Well," he said finally, "if I was willing to throw my life away on a fool's chance, there's one thing I'd be tempted to try." And he told Stark what it was.

Stark looked at him with even greater respect. "How would I go about getting such a device?"

His host made a sound of disgust. "You can get one right here. I've got a couple of them."

Remarkable, Stark thought. "If I may be so bold, how did you get your hands on them?"

Digger didn't answer right away, and Stark began to wonder if he had offended his informant. Then the blind man spoke up, a sharper edge to his voice.

"It may be," he said, "that I was a Scaredy Man myself for a while, before I came to my senses."

Then he leaned way over to his left, rummaged under some blankets, and came up with the thing his visitor needed. "Here it is," he said, holding it out in his hand.

"Thanks," Stark said as he accepted it.

"It'll only get you in," he said. "After that, you're on your own."

Stark nodded. "I understand."

"What about that help you were going to give us?" asked Digger. "I hope you were planning on doing that *before* you get yourself vaporized."

"Just slightly," said Stark.

"Don't forget."

"I've got a good memory," Stark assured the blind man.

It was true. He remembered the twenty-first century as if it were only yesterday.

18

IT WAS GETTING DARK BY THE TIME STARK found Baker in his people's encampment. As usual, Torricelli was with him.

Judging from her expression, he still wasn't high on her holiday list. "You again," she spat.

"Thank you," Stark told her, smiling his warmest smile. "It's nice to see you as well."

"Did Digger tell you what you wanted to know?"

"He did," said Stark. "But to get inside the Enclave, I'll need help—the kind only you can give me."

"What did you have in mind?" Baker asked.

"A distraction. And while you keep the Scaredy Men occupied, I'll sneak inside."

"Like hell," said Torricelli. "We're not going to get ourselves killed for a guy we don't even know."

"He helped us," said Baker.

"It was easy," she countered. "He's wearing that armor. If I was tucked into something like that, I'd go helping people too."

"If all goes according to plan," said Stark, "none of your people have to get hurt."

"*If*," she echoed.

Baker frowned. "You're asking a lot."

Stark nodded. "I know."

The man with the ponytail regarded him for what seemed like an eternity. Then he said, "We'll do what we can."

Torricelli unleashed a series of curses. "We're just gonna get ourselves killed."

"It'll happen eventually," Baker said. "Might as well make it count."

"Thank you," said Stark.

"Don't mention it," Baker told him. "We'll go round up the ones who can still fight."

"I'm truly sorry about this," said Natasha.

She jerked hard on the ends of the nylon rope she had used to tie up Morgan, the pilot of Tony Stark's corporate jet. But then, she wanted to make certain his bonds were secure.

Morgan swore at her, his eyes popping out, his face ruddy with anger. But his words were unintelligible thanks to the gag she had stuffed in his mouth.

Next, Natasha turned her attention to the maintenance crew, which consisted of three other men. Like Morgan, they were tied up and gagged. It hadn't been easy to incapacitate them without causing injury, but she had managed.

Finally, there were the two security guards whose job it was to watch the hangar. They didn't look thrilled to have been disarmed and trussed up like Christmas turkeys. It was all right. They would get over it.

Getting to her feet, Natasha surveyed her handiwork. She couldn't imagine any of her captives getting free. The only way that would happen would be if someone found them.

Which would take place in just about four hours, with the change of shifts. But by then, if all went according to plan, she would be in spitting distance of her destination.

Not that she intended to do any spitting. *Just flying.*

Fortunately, Natasha had piloted any number of aircraft—jets included—in her spying days. The only difference was that this one had silk sheets on the beds, a fifty thousand dollar sound system, and a refrigerator full of good Russian caviar.

She wished she could enjoy it. But the journey on which she was embarking was anything but a pleasure cruise.

• • •

The Enclave was an immense, high-walled gray fortress that angled halfway across the mouth of the Hudson River from the west side of Manhattan, resting on a peninsula that hadn't existed back in the twenty-first century. All in all, it must have boasted a good five square miles' worth of space.

Stark had taken up a position on the roof of a ruined building almost in the leviathan's shadow. Otherwise, Digger's device wouldn't have worked. And though the hulk of an ancient, half-crumbled water tower had offered him some concealment, he had to abandon it if he was going to get a move on.

Line of sight, Digger had said. And Stark wasn't about to diverge from that admonition.

Farther uptown, Baker and his people were retreating from the rats' forces, having attacked the base of the Enclave wall with their energy weapons—a futile gesture, as it would have taken them hours of concentrated fire to punch a hole in it. All they had accomplished was to draw out a swarm of Scaredy Men.

Which, of course, was exactly what Stark had needed them to do. According to Digger, none of the guards would be held back in such a maneuver. The place would temporarily be bereft of its entire garrison.

That still left the Enclave's towering walls to keep its occupants separate and apart from the outside world. And ordinarily, they would have been enough. But with a little luck, Stark would soon find himself inside them.

The first step was for him to remove his armor, even though the thought of doing so made him uneasy, to say the least.

It wasn't just the fact that it boasted such powerful weapons, or that it protected him from the weapons of others. It was also his only link with the twenty-first century, the only tangible evidence that he had really traveled across time, and that he wasn't just some lunatic who *thought* he had.

But there was no way around it. If Stark was going to penetrate the Enclave and have a chance of getting home, he was going to have to risk everything on a single roll of Digger's dice.

First, he took off his helmet and laid it on the ground beside him. Then he slipped off his gloves and his boots, and placed them beside his helmet. Next came his arm pieces, his legs pieces, and finally his apple-red plastron.

All of which left Stark standing there in his underwear, his skin covered with viscous green lubricant. Unfortunately, the armor wasn't meant to be worn for such a prolonged time, and the stuff had begun to congeal here and there.

A wind curled around him, making him shiver. With his armor on, he hadn't fully appreciated how chilly the mornings were.

So here I am, he thought, *freezing on a mountain of debris hundreds of years in the future . . . in my undergarments. Of all the situations in which I never expected to find myself . . .*

Kneeling, Stark took the fist-sized device Digger had bestowed upon him and placed it in the pile of Iron Man components, which maxed out the device's mass limit all by themselves. Then he tapped in the command Digger had given him. Its accuracy was confirmed when the unit's blue-on-black digital readout displayed precisely the set of numbers it was supposed to display.

But Digger hadn't used the device in years. What if it malfunctioned and sent the armor to the wrong place? Or failed to return after it had done its job?

Then I'm just slightly out of luck, Stark thought.

Taking a deep breath, he touched the stud on the device that activated it. Then he got up and stepped back, and counted the seconds to himself. *Ten. Nine. Eight. Seven . . .*

Stark felt an urge to deactivate the device, or to at least throw it away from his armor. But he resisted it. He had to get back to his proper time, after all, and this was the only shot he had of accomplishing that.

Three, he thought. *Two. One . . .*

Suddenly there was a flash of yellow-white light, bright enough to blind him for a moment. When he opened his eyes, the device and his armor were gone.

Digger didn't say anything about a flash, he thought, his heart sinking in his chest.

Had something gone wrong? Stark would know soon enough. *In a matter of seconds, in fact.*

Rubbing his arms to subdue the rising gooseflesh, he watched the spot where the armor had been. And waited. And grew uncomfortably aware of the time passing by.

Come on, he commanded the device, *make it back to me. Show me I wasn't nuts to trust the guy I got you from.*

But nothing happened. Laden with disappointment, Stark sat down on the weed-covered mound. *All right. I'm a complete and utter idiot. I just sent my armor who-knows-where.*

What could he do now? Try to scale the walls of the Enclave? Give the guards a good laugh?

Hey, Joe, there's a guy out there in his underwear. Wanna bet I can take him down in one shot?

Stark chuckled miserably. *Yes, that's right. You might as well laugh.* He had just consigned the twenty-first century to whatever the Tomorrow Men had in mind for it.

Nice work, he told himself.

It was at precisely that moment that he saw another flash. And as his eyes recovered from it, he realized Digger's device was sitting in front of him.

Damned right, he thought, feeling a delicious surge of pure joy. *I knew Digger would come through for me. Never doubted the old scalawag for a moment.*

But he would have to trust Digger a great deal now, even more than he had before. Because the next thing to be teleported wasn't a pile of armor. It was Stark himself.

He had seen the Enclave's guards vanish into thin air, and assumed they had come out all right on the other end. But he hadn't received any proof of it.

And the guards had been using what must have been well-maintained, state-of-the-art equipment. Not the cobwebbed antique Digger had bestowed upon him.

Stark wished he knew what his armor looked like when it was done teleporting. He wished he could assure himself that it was the way he had designed it, and not rearranged in some way.

Because if he entrusted himself to Digger's device, he didn't want to be rearranged. He wanted to come out exactly as he was, down to the last glib, devil-may-care molecule.

But there's no guarantee of that, is there?

Not any more than he was guaranteed to wake up the next day, the growth in his brain content to leave him alone a while longer. Or to survive the test flight of his next set of armor.

Life, lived properly, was a series of risks. *If I needed certainty,* Stark thought, *I would have become an accountant.*

Scooping up the device, the industrialist reset it

according to Digger's instructions. Then he touched
the stud again, activating its teleportation function.

As before, he endured a period of approximately
ten seconds while the device powered up. But he
didn't count down. He just waited and wondered
what being teleported would feel like.

What it would *look* like. *Sound* like.

It wasn't long before he got his answer.

"You look distracted," said Weyland, in the most
sympathetic voice he could manage.

Sitting behind the desk in his office, Fury
scowled. "Tony Stark wasn't just my partner here.
He was my friend."

The Tomorrow Man leaned forward in his chair
and nodded. "I understand, General. It wasn't easy
for us to accept Haggerty's loss either."

In fact, it wasn't. Nor had it been easy for him to
ask her to make the ultimate sacrifice. However,
Haggerty hadn't hesitated to do her duty. She knew
how important it was to gain the trust of everyone in
the Triskelion.

But then, Haggerty had been one of the mission's
biggest supporters from the beginning. She came
from a large family. She knew what it would mean to
them if the mission succeeded—what it would mean
to *everyone* in the Enclave.

"Unfortunately," said Weyland, "Mister Stark was
also a big part of your task force. I hope you're not

going to have to delay your action because of his absence."

Fury shook his head. "We can't afford to. Our communications guys can only pull the wool over Tiber's eyes for so long. Even without Stark, we should have enough firepower . . ."

"But?" said the Tomorrow Man, hearing the word in the way the general's voice trailed off.

"But I'd have preferred to see him *with* us."

Weyland, on the other hand, couldn't have been happier about Stark's blunder. It played right into the Tomorrow Men's hands, depriving the Ultimates of one of their big guns.

So when they walked into the Tiber facility in the Andes, and were surprised that the fanatics were ready for them this time, they would have one less titan on their side. If all went well, the trap would prove the Ultimates' undoing.

Even Thor's. But then, history had shown he could be destroyed. It would just take some ingenuity, which the Tiberites possessed in abundance.

Then Weyland and his brethren would use their teleportation capability to join their comrades in the Caucasus, and the entire Earth would feel their presence.

"Anyway," the general said, "I just wanted to bring you up to speed. And to thank you for your help in finding these fanatics."

"It's I who am grateful," Weyland told him. "You

and your colleagues have made it possible for my people to find themselves in a whole new world."

Inwardly, the Tomorrow Man chuckled at his little joke—because that was *precisely* what the Ultimates had done. And soon they would have reason to regret it.

To Stark's surprise, there was *nothing* to feel or see or hear when it came to being teleported by Digger's device. It was simply a matter of being in one place one moment and somewhere else the next.

Fortunately for Tony Stark, that somewhere else was right beside the armor he had removed a few minutes earlier. Happy to see it again, he didn't waste any time putting it back on.

He was glad he wouldn't have to endure any interruptions. But then, he had materialized in the guards' barracks—an austere-looking place with overhead lighting, two levels of beds, and a computer workstation at either end—and all its occupants were otherwise engaged at the moment, thanks to Baker.

Still, it wasn't easy donning the armor. Back in the Triskelion, Stark had always had a team of technicians to help him get the parts on and off. There, in the heart of the enemy's stronghold, he had no one to look to but himself.

The plastron was the hardest part. It was made up of two sections, one in front and one in back, and they had to snap together just so. It was a job for a contortionist, and with the rest of his armor in place he was hardly in a position to be flexible.

Bend, for godsakes.

Finally, the plastron fell into line. Slipping his mask on, Stark completed his ensemble. *There,* he thought, *that's better.*

A graphic appeared before his eyes, notifying him that he was low on tactical power. *That's okay,* he thought. *If all goes well, I won't need much.*

Moving to one of the computer workstations, he hacked into the Enclave's network, which wasn't a great deal more advanced than the one he used back at the Triskelion. Then he kept the promise he made to Baker and Digger.

His next step was a little trickier. If there was a working time-travel device in the Enclave, it had to be attached to a considerable power source—one that would give off an easily distinguishable energy signature.

Of course, there was no guarantee the power source was in operation at the moment, so Stark would need a little luck to find it. Activating the energy sensors in his armor, he searched for the requisite level of output.

Paydirt, he thought, discovering an enormous energy signature not more than a hundred yards away.

If Digger's layout of the Enclave was on the money, the power source was in another building.

However, it would be accessible from the barracks through an underground tunnel.

Stark hoped Digger knew what he was talking about. After all, this wasn't just an industrial compound—it was also a place where people lived. There were bound to be some of them walking around, visiting their neighbors, taking their kids to the playground.

He had no problem going at it with the guards—the Scaredy Men, as Baker's people called them. But no matter what the Enclave had done to those outside its walls, Stark didn't want to place its innocents in a destructive crossfire.

Come on, he thought, aware that Baker's diversion wouldn't last forever.

Proceeding on foot, he moved out of the barracks and into the hallway beyond them. And immediately ran into trouble.

A couple of guards were in the corridor, headed in Stark's direction. Their eyes widening, they stopped and raised their energy rifles to fire at him.

Stark had time to think: *Digger was wrong. Not all the Scaredy Men are fighting off the rabble.*

Activating his thrusters, he twisted to the left to avoid the guards' energy bursts. Then he fired back, hammering his adversaries with electromagnetic force.

It sent them reeling head over heels, their rifles scarring the walls of the corridor with their fire. By the time the guards stopped tumbling, they were unconscious.

Stark had no intention of examining them as he flew past, heading for the underground tunnel. Then something caught his eye, forcing him to land at the guards' side.

He was transfixed by it, as incapable of motion as if his brain had been severed from the rest of his body. Because the thing he was staring at wasn't supposed to be there.

Stark ran his metal-encased finger over it, knowing it as well as he knew his own likeness in the bathroom mirror. And why shouldn't he?

He had *designed* it. He had sat through long meetings with a corporate image company from the Netherlands and, in the end, thrown away all their ideas in favor of his own.

The two supercontinents, Laurasia and Gondwana, that had existed one hundred and fifty million years ago, rendered in dark green on a disc of light blue ocean. With a yellow star at four o'clock and another at ten o'clock. All surrounded by a band of black, like the eternal night of space, and then a larger band of royal blue with the company's name on it . . .

Stark International.

His company. And its logo was on the sleeve of an Enclave mercenary two hundred years after his death. It didn't make sense. And yet, it did.

The grimmest kind of sense.

The Enclave was made up of the wealthy and privileged. People like Stark and his executives. People who could have maintained their advantage over the rest of society if they played their cards right, no matter how bleak the future became.

My God, he thought, a chill climbing his spine.

He had left his mark on the future all right. But it wasn't the kind of mark he had intended.

And the *Scaredy* Men . . . they were *security* guards. Baker and his people had mangled the word with their twenty-third-century accent, but all they were describing were the successors to Stark's private safety and security force.

It made him that much more eager to get back to his rightful time. To do whatever he could to prevent what he had seen there from becoming a reality.

Tearing himself away from the Stark insignia, he propelled himself along the corridor until he came to a juncture and turned left. A few meters later, he went right again. If Digger's memory hadn't failed him, this was the tunnel that led to the next building.

At the pace Stark was maintaining, he was able to negotiate the concrete enclosure in a matter of seconds. But at the other end, he found his way blocked by a metal door.

Rather than use his pulse-emitters, he put his head down and rammed right through it. Beyond the doorway was a large, multistoried chamber with an immense, spider-shaped generator in the center of it.

Stark could feel its power drumming in the floor as he landed on it. The engineer in him wanted to stop and understand how the machine worked, but the rest of him knew he had no time.

The time-travel device couldn't be far away. After all, why generate all that power unless there was a demand for it? And what was more energy-consuming an application than a portal through time?

All I've got to do, thought Stark, *is find it.*

He was trying to decide where and how to look when he heard the ominous sound of company coming. Unfortunately, he didn't think it was the Welcome Wagon.

Obviously, Stark had been spotted. Maybe by a hidden camera, maybe by a sensor he had tripped when he nailed the guards in the corridor. In any case, his job had just gotten a lot tougher.

The one thing he could depend on was that the security men wouldn't be firing at maximum intensity. Not when he was so close to the power generator.

As Stark thought that, two small squads of security guards burst in on him—one through the doorway he had smashed open and another through an entrance on the opposite side of the chamber.

Directing a series of pulses at the first group, he saw a couple of them get knocked backward. But the others kept coming. And before he could address the problem, he felt an impact from behind.

By rights, Stark should barely have felt it. Instead, it was like a hammer smashing him in the ribs, knocking the wind out of him and making him see stars.

And he knew why. His armor's structural integrity field had fizzled out all of a sudden, letting him down as it had so many times in the testing stage.

Bad timing, he mused.

Rolling to avoid a second hit, Stark took aim at the guards behind him—and sent a pair of them crashing into a wall. But a moment later, an energy beam drove him to the floor. His head swam furiously, placing him on the verge of blacking out.

It doesn't matter, he promised himself. *They're not going to stop me.*

Somehow, Stark dragged himself back from the brink of unconsciousness and fired in the direction the blast had come from. The cry he heard told him he had lucked out and hit his target.

A beam from somewhere else missed him, glancing off the floor beside him. Raising his head, he caught sight of his last remaining adversary and took him out with a well-aimed pulse.

The chamber fell silent, except for the rhythmic drumming of the generator. Stark would have liked to lose himself in it, to regroup after the beating he took. However, he still had a mission to accomplish.

Getting his legs beneath him, he thrust himself off the floor.

Just in time to see two more guards rush in through the ruined doorway. Dazed as he was, Stark couldn't fire as quickly as they did.

He didn't know which one hit him, but the impact was like a kick in the face, throwing him into a wall. Spitting blood into his mask, he pushed the wall away.

Not when I'm so close, he thought.

As if from a great distance, Stark heard a sound like a series of exploding firecrackers. *Footfalls,* he realized. The sound of more guards pouring into the room, adding to the odds against him.

Gritting his teeth, he raised his arms and tried to fire off a pulse barrage. But his emitters wouldn't respond, their power supply finally depleted. Stark heard laughter.

Then he felt the one last blow—the one that sent him plummeting into the depths of oblivion.

JEDEDIAH STRINGFELLOW SCRUTINIZED THE gray and crimson suit of armor crumpled at his feet.

It was difficult to believe there was someone inside it. And even more difficult to believe that that person could be the one who invented the armor in the first place.

But then, Stringfellow and his colleagues had opened a can of worms when they sent their agents back to the twenty-first century to pave the way for their exodus. And this, it seemed, was one of the worms that had squirmed out of the can.

"Remarkable," he found himself saying.

Of course, it was possible that the armor had

come through the temporal barrier on its own, and that one of the rabble had donned it out of curiosity. Or that it had been preserved outside the Enclave, though that begged the question of where it could have gotten its batteries charged.

However, Stringfellow and his comrades had accounted for all the armor in existence. If a suit wasn't hanging in their museum, it had been destroyed a long time ago.

Nor would it have been possible for someone to operate the armor so skillfully unless he enjoyed a certain intimacy with it. And only one man had ever enjoyed that sort of intimacy.

A man who died hundreds of years ago. Or at least that was the way things had gone the first time. At this point, there was no telling what his fate would be.

"What should we do with him?" asked the ranking security guard in the room.

"First," said Stringfellow, "get him out of the armor. Then confine him to an empty apartment."

"Actually," said the guard, "we've already tried to get him out of the armor—without any luck."

Stringfellow eyed the man. "It's locked?"

"I guess you could say that."

"You're sure?"

The guard nodded. *"Damned* sure. He's in there to stay."

Stringfellow sighed. He knew as well as anyone in the Enclave that the armor had an automatic locking trigger, assuming its wearer chose to activate it. And apparently, he had.

Of course, the armor wasn't indestructible. They could blast away at it until they punched a hole in it. But that would prove fatal to the individual inside.

Then they wouldn't know under what circumstances he had managed to transport himself through time. And that information might prove essential to the success of their enterprise before it was over.

So destroying the armor wasn't an option. Stringfellow would have to find another way to get what he wanted.

Cursing the razor-edged chill in the air, Natasha wished she could have ditched Stark International's corporate jet a little closer to the Tiber facility.

However, the snow-choked mountains through which she was trudging in her fiber-filled whitesuit weren't as chock-full of viable landing sites as she would have liked. As it was, she had nearly cracked up in a long, narrow valley. It was only the abundance of soft, powdery snow that had saved her—as well as Stark's winged investment.

Certainly, he would forgive her if she found him alive. And if she didn't, the shape of his flying playpen would unquestionably be the least of his problems.

Besides, she had plenty of her own worries. The possibility, for instance, that whoever had taken over

Tiber's fortress had taken note of her landing. Or that Stark's pilot had been discovered sooner than she had anticipated, and was already complaining to Fury about her stealing the plane.

Which would prompt the general to send out an advisory alerting the Tiber facility, along with a hundred other SHIELD operations around the world, to Natasha's little indiscretion. *Hell,* she thought, *he might have done it* already.

Except SHIELD wasn't in control of the Tiber facility any longer. It couldn't be, or its people would have answered truthfully when Fury contacted them about Tony Stark.

Which meant Natasha would find a nice warm welcome waiting for her. Not that she hadn't been welcomed that way before, on one occasion or another, and lived to tell of it. But seldom had so much rested on her shoulders.

It wasn't just Stark whom Natasha was hoping to save. It was also all the SHIELD operatives the general had left in the mountain, who might or might not have survived the Tomorrow Men's attentions.

And she didn't dare ask Fury or any of her Ultimates colleagues for assistance. Not when it might give her away, and in the process cost those operatives their lives.

Only after Natasha had rescued whomever she could rescue would she contact the general and tell him everything she knew. Because at that point, the Tomorrow Men wouldn't have a bunch of hostages to use as leverage.

Natasha trudged on, watching her breath freeze on the air ahead of her. She knew it was a long shot she was betting on.

But as Virgil had so aptly noted two thousand years earlier, fortune favored the bold. No self-respecting spy had ever waited for her stars to be in complete alignment before she undertook a mission. One had to roll the dice sometimes, leap now and look afterward.

So that's what I'm doing, Natasha mused. *Taking a chance. Rolling the dice.*

She just hoped they didn't come up snake eyes.

The door to the room where Stark was standing under guard slid open again. Turning his head, he saw someone enter.

But it wasn't another silent, wary security man coming to confirm that his battery was depleted. It was someone in civilian clothes. *Someone with authority,* Stark decided. At least, that was the way the fellow carried himself.

He was platinum blond and clean-shaven, except for an equally platinum tuft of hair in the cleft of his chin, with high cheekbones and thick lips. Though he was on the thin side, he looked soft, as if he hadn't exercised in a good, long while.

If ever.

"My name," the man said, "is Stringfellow. Like most everyone here, I'm a big fan of your work, Mister Stark. But then, I owe everything I have, indeed everything I am, to Stark International and its legacy."

Don't rub it in, Stark thought.

"I regret," said Stringfellow, "that you haven't had a chance to see our community here. It's really quite Utopian by twenty-first-century standards. A haven for the arts, for pure research, for spiritual introspection . . ."

"Where," said Stark, "you devise ways to keep the rest of humanity in perpetual fear and misery."

Stringfellow smiled. "If you've met those of whom you speak, you know how little they have in common with real human beings. Unfortunately, we are increasingly besieged by them, and security personnel willing to lay down their lives are difficult to come by. The likelihood, I'm afraid, is that our sanctuary will be overrun someday and that we'll pay a price for maintaining it.

"Unless, of course, we can find a way to escape our plight. But where in the world could we go where we wouldn't be subject to hatred and violence? Nowhere. Which is why we felt compelled to seek a refuge *beyond* this world."

Stark made a sound of disgust. Why hadn't he seen it earlier? "You're going to escape to the past."

"Precisely," said Stringfellow. "Hence, our efforts to open a massive rift in time—one that is big and sturdy enough to accommodate several hundred of us transiting from our time to yours.

"My guess is you've already seen a manifestation of that rift—in the Tiber facility you were kind enough to secure for us. That facility was important in that we needed more power to effect the transit, and Tiber boasted that level of power."

"Why not just send a few people at a time?" Stark asked. "The way you did with the first group?"

"Because," said Stringfellow, "even that modest effort was more dangerous than we expected, nearly blowing up our power generator and the rest of the Enclave along with it. We didn't dare try it again unless we had a source on the other end sharing the burden."

And even then, thought Stark, *there's an element of unpredictability in the process.* Otherwise, he wouldn't have woken so far from the portal.

"You think the Ultimates will stand by," he asked, "and let you carry out your plan unopposed?"

"Weyland will make certain your intervention is an isolated event. And once we make the transit, we don't expect any trouble. Quite clearly, we have the knowledge of future events and the technological expertise to dominate your era, and we intend to use those tools to their fullest advantage."

"Haven't you forgotten the Grandfather Paradox? Altering the past will alter your future—maybe even to the point where your parents never meet each other."

"It's not a concern," said Stringfellow. "You see, our world is in a different branch of the timeline—a branch that diverged from yours just prior to the year two thousand. So we can do what we like in your branch and still keep our past intact."

That explains that, Stark thought.

"In the meantime," said Stringfellow, "I would like nothing better than to sit down and talk with you about the innovations you implemented back in the twentieth and twenty-first centuries, and perhaps come to a better understanding of your thinking. However, until we effect the transit, you present something of a threat to us—much more so than the gutter slugs who assault our supply caravans from time to time, forcing us to retaliate.

"I have two options. One is to hold you until you waste away and turn to rot. However, I would like to avoid the unpleasantness of scraping you out of there. Perhaps a better alternative would be to make things uncomfortable for you—so very uncomfortable that anyone in his right mind would beg me to relieve his pain."

"Anyone but me," said Stark.

"We both know," said Stringfellow, "that you'll eventually give in and come out of your armor. It can't end any other way. If I were you, I'd accept that conclusion sooner rather than later."

"Not a chance."

"Come now," said Stringfellow. "We have studied your behavior down to the last minute detail—not only what you have done to this point in your life, but what you will do in the future. In some ways, we know you better than you know yourself."

"You don't know *me*," Stark told him. "All you know is the Tony Stark who existed in your branch of the timeline. And that's a whole different deal, my friend."

Stringfellow considered him for a moment. Then he said, "At the very least, it will be an interesting experiment in human endurance. I hope you come to see it that way as well . . . eventually."

"Go to hell," said Stark.

His captor chuckled. "I knew you'd say that."

Then he left the room, leaving Stark to ponder what he had learned.

20

IT WAS FORTUNATE, STARK THOUGHT, THAT the automotive maintenance building in which he found himself wasn't occupied by one of the supply trucks the Enclave entertained from time to time.

Because if that were the case, Stringfellow would have been compelled to find another place to bind his captive's wrists and ankles with chains of dark gray composite and spread-eagle him upright a meter above the floor.

"Well," said the blond man, "here we are. And we've yet to see a sign that you're willing to cooperate."

"Imagine that," said Stark.

Stringfellow chuckled. "You'll be interested to know that your counterpart in our timeline was every bit as stubborn as you are. But then, he was never asked to endure what you're going to endure.

"My security people have set their rifles on their widest aperture, which will drastically reduce the impact of their beams but in equal portion increase their temperature. Naturally, that heat will be transferred to your armor.

"Though it has a built-in cooling system, I assure you—having seen the specs for even more advanced models—it will prove insufficient. Unless you indicate you've had a change of heart and wish to remove the armor, you'll bake to death."

"Sounds nasty," said Stark.

"Only you will know *how* nasty," said his captor.

He signaled the half-dozen guards positioned in front of and behind Stark, and the barrage began. The six beams bathed Stark in their violet light, making his armor seem to glow.

Inside his helmet, an advisory graphic appeared. It warned him that the ambient temperature was climbing rapidly, and also showed him its projected effect over time.

In two minutes, the temperature inside the suit would climb to ninety degrees Fahrenheit. In an additional forty-five seconds, it would reach one hundred degrees.

And so on.

But Stark didn't need the graphic to tell him what his future held.

He could already feel the heat building up in his armor, sending beads of sweat trickling down the sides of his face.

It didn't help that his structural integrity field was on the blink, but even that would only have saved him for so long. Eventually, the guards' energy beams would still have gotten to him.

As they're getting to me now, he thought.

He felt like a lobster broiling in its shell. The armor's oxygen supply was already like the air on the hottest, stillest, most oppressive day of summer, when one couldn't inhale hard enough or long enough. It made him wish he could take his mask off, if only for a moment, to draw a breath of cool, fresh air.

But Stark wasn't going to give in to the bastards. Not when so much depended on him. Not when he was the only hope of two eras in two different time-lines.

His graphic told him the temperature in his armor was approaching a hundred degrees, and showing no sign of stopping. *It's not the heat,* he found himself musing idiotically, *it's the humidity.*

And it was plenty humid in his metal-alloy shell, a result of the perspiration squeezing out of his every pore, bathing him in its salty brew. But it couldn't cool him off because there wasn't any air around him to facilitate evaporation.

One hundred and four, according to the graphic.

Stark licked his lips. He was abominably thirsty. And he felt himself getting lightheaded, as if he'd had a few too many, which would have been *several* too many for anyone else. His knees were getting weak, rubbery, even though there wasn't any weight forcing its burden on them.

All he had to do was say a word to free himself from his sweatbox—the word that would audio-trigger a mechanism in his mask and pop it forward. *Nothing more complicated than that.*

But he wouldn't do it.

"It must be getting sticky in there," said String-fellow, wincing as if in sympathy. "If it were me, I'd have thrown in the towel a long time ago."

One hundred and eight.

"There's a point of no return," said Stringfellow. "You know that, right? Once your core temperature reaches a hundred and five degrees, there won't be anything we can do for you. But you can't wait that long, because well before that you'll be too confused to know what's happening to you."

He was right. Stark was losing focus, getting nauseous, feeling his heart start to pound in his chest. He was well on his way to suffering heat stroke.

One hundred and twelve.

"Do yourself a favor," said Stringfellow, "and open your armor before it's too late. You've fought the good fight. There's no shame in yielding now."

One hundred and fifteen.

"Please," said his captor, looking disgusted. "This doesn't have to go any farther."

Stark didn't answer him, but he knew he was in trouble. He had stopped sweating, which wasn't at all a good sign, and it wouldn't be long before he lost consciousness.

One hundred and eighteen.

The heat was unbearable, Stark's armor an oven wringing the last drops of liquid out of him. But he hung in there, knowing his ordeal would be over in a few more seconds.

"You're insane," whispered Stringfellow.

Am I? Stark asked silently.

Bending his middle finger to touch the palm of his metal gauntlet, he reactivated his tactical systems. All through his armor, energy surged in dramatically increased amounts.

Flexing his newfound muscle, Stark pulled against the composite chain holding his right hand outstretched and tore himself free of it. Then, with a jerk of his left hand, he ripped apart the chain on the other side.

"What's going on?" Stringfellow demanded shrilly of his guards.

"I dunno!" barked the highest-ranking security man.

But Stark knew.

The conversion unit in his armor that accepted downloads of extra power from Stark International satellites could also accept power from other sources—like the armor's surface, which boasted a crude energy-collection net.

So while the security guards were doing their best to cook Stark alive, his armor was diverting part of what they were dishing out and directing it to his primary battery.

Obviously, the collection net was a feature Stark's counterpart in this timeline hadn't included in his Iron Man designs. Otherwise, Stringfellow would have realized he was playing into his captive's hands.

"Switch to impact!" the blond man cried, his voice cracking with urgency.

Even as they maintained their barrage, the guards narrowed their apertures. Their beams became needle-thin, devastatingly powerful streams of force.

But Stark was ready for them. Engaging his heel-thrusters, he snapped the chains holding his ankles. Then, snaking his way around the walls at high speed, he began taking potshots at the guards.

Three of them went skidding across the floor

before any of them even dealt him a glancing blow. And two more were put out of commission before they came close again.

That left Stringfellow and a single guard remaining. But really just the guard, because the blond man was already fleeing the maintenance facility.

Let him go, Stark told himself.

Executing an evasive maneuver, he avoided the last guard's beam. Then he released a series of pulses and sent the man cannonballing into a pile of chains.

Which left no one to stop Stark from doing what he had penetrated the Enclave to do—finding the time portal that would, if he were lucky, get him home.

Unfortunately, he still didn't know where to find it. However, as one of the guards was still conscious, he hoped to rectify that deficit in short order.

Grabbing the man by the front of his uniform shirt, Stark lowered his masked face until he was almost nose-to-nose with his adversary. Then he said, "Where's the time portal?"

The man might have denied any knowledge of it, or told Stark to go to hell. But he didn't. In fact, he seemed to take some perverse pleasure in answering the question.

"If you're lying," said Stark, doing his best impression of Nick Fury, "I'll be back."

"You kidding?" the man muttered. "I don't like

this place any better than you do. If I didn't have to eat . . ." His voice trailed off miserably.

Satisfied, Stark released the man and headed for what he hoped was the building housing the time portal.

Baker was still marveling at his luck at sunset, when he came in sight of his people's encampment.

Torricelli, who hated to admit that she was wrong, wouldn't say a word to him as she went to find her blanket and get some rest. But her silence was as big a concession as anything she might have uttered.

Despite her misgivings, their entire party of forty-five had returned unscathed from its skirmish with the Scaredy Men—their third in as many days. They were bruised and bone-tired, but not really any the worse for wear.

And to be truthful, it had done Baker's heart good to see all those Scaredy Men swarm frantically out of the Enclave like angry bees from a violated hive. Even now, he couldn't help smiling about it.

In fact, he thought, *we'll have to do it again sometime, just to see how mad it makes them.*

As word got around that the fighters had come home, people gathered around them to hear the stories that had come of their effort—tales of suspense and relief, fear and courage. Tales to astonish and to inspire outrage.

Patricia seemed more eager than anyone to hear what had happened. But then, it was no secret that she had taken a liking to the armored man.

"Did he make it?" she asked Baker.

Though Patricia was the one who had posed the question, the others clearly wanted to know as well. But he couldn't give them an answer.

"We gave him the distraction he wanted," said Baker. "Beyond that, I have no way of knowing."

And it was possible he would *never* know.

One thing was for certain, though. Without the stranger, they were way the hell back where they had started.

For years, his people had been going after the Enclave's caravans. At times, it seemed that they were making progress, that they were on the verge of breaking the bastards' supply lines. But in the end, the Enclave had always gotten what it wanted.

And why not? It had all the resources, all the firepower, all the technology. All Baker had were fragile bodies and cranky old weapons, and whatever power sources he could scrape together.

The man in the armor had changed that. He had given them the upper hand for once. He had given them a chance. But now that he was gone, their chance was gone as well.

Baker sighed.

I'm the elder, he thought, *the leader. Everyone trusts me to make the right decisions.* But he couldn't do the impossible.

He had had such high hopes when he launched his first angry raid on the rats' supplies. He had dreamed of a time when there was no Enclave, and everything it had was the property of his people.

Dreams are for fools, he told himself.

"Hey, Baker," someone said.

He glanced over his shoulder. It was Torricelli. She looked like she had something on her mind, but when *didn't* she look that way?

Pulling him aside, she said, "Take a look at this," and handed him a palm-sized personal access device.

Baker scanned its green-on-black display. It showed him a series of seven- and eight-digit codes.

"What are they?" he asked.

"I had no idea either," Torricelli said, "until I checked out the source of the transmission. The coordinates put it right in the middle of the Enclave."

Baker punched in a command and confirmed it. Then he looked at his comrade. "Someone's transmitting codes from the Enclave?"

"You think it could be *him?*" she asked.

He shook his head. It seemed crazy. "It's hard to imagine he had the time to set up a transmission."

"But if he did," Torricelli said, "what would he have sent us?"

Baker smiled to himself. Was it possible? "Defense

codes." The kind that would disable the locks on the Enclave's entrances.

She looked at him disbelievingly. "You're not serious."

"There's a way to find out," Baker told her. "But we can only try this once. After that, they'll change the codes."

Torricelli smiled. "If this works . . ."

We'll be free, he thought. But he didn't want to jinx their chances by saying it out loud.

What he said instead was, "Find Perez and Chung for me. Looks like we've got something to talk about."

The security guard hadn't lied.

Stark found the time portal in an otherwise empty building far from the heart of the Enclave, in the shadow of one of its dark gray walls. Nor were there any guards there to stop him from blasting his way through the door, though he was certain he would have the pleasure of their company in the next minute or so.

The portal looked like a smaller version of what he had seen in the Caucasus—a black whirlpool eagerly corkscrewing itself into the fabric of reality. It was insufficient, at this point, to send the population of the Enclave back to the twenty-first century of Stark's timeline.

But it had enough juice to transport the Tomorrow Men,

he thought, *so it should have enough to transport me as well.*

Stark wished he knew if the mechanism's targeted time and place had been reset for some reason. Or if some essential component had been temporarily removed from it. Or if transport required data he wasn't prepared to input.

As it was, he might emerge in the fifth century, watching Attila the Hun slaughter a phalanx of Roman centurions. Or in the eleventh, witnessing Leif Ericsson's historic arrival at the shore of Labrador. In either case, he would be stuck there, since there weren't any time portals to bring him back.

But those weren't the worst fates he could envision. He might wind up dead, ravaged by the stresses of temporal translocation, or a reconfigured amalgam of organic and inorganic materials, borrowing matter from both his body and the armor. The prospect made him want to retch just thinking about it.

Not that Stark was going to let any of those possibilities stand in his way.

He thought about all the people he cared about, from Happy Hogan to Jarvis to Fury, to Rogers and Thor and Jan. Then he thought about Natasha in particular.

It was worth the risk. No doubt about it.

If the twenty-first century was flooded with a

population of future-spawned tyrants, it wasn't going to be because Tony Stark took the coward's way out. *Here goes nothing,* he thought, and propelled himself into the dark spinning energies of the whirlpool.

21

NATASHA CLUNG TO THE SLOPE OVER THE main entrance to the Tiber facility, perched on a couple of pylons she had driven into the icy surface, and waited for a response from the people within.

Whoever they were.

She doubted she would have to wait long. The current occupants couldn't have had too many callers since they moved in. It was a cinch they would be coming out to see who rang the doorbell.

Or more accurately, set off a tiny plastic explosive on the relatively flat surface outside their door.

Just as Natasha had expected, a section of mountainside receded, permitting access to the inside of

the place. A moment later, three figures came out
with rifles in their arms.

Two men and a woman, dressed in white and
green. *Just like the Tomorrow Men.*

Natasha didn't know where the bastards had come
from, or why they were there. But it was clear to her
that they were responsible for Tony Stark's disappearance, not to mention that of the SHIELD
contingent Fury had left there.

Thor would have needed more information
before he started swinging his hammer. Even Fury
would have wanted a little more context. But
Natasha had been a spy. She was inclined to start
firing *before* she knew all the particulars.

The trio of Tomorrow Men scanned the slope
below and around then, but never thought to look
up. Exchanging glances, they shrugged and retreated
through the open doorway.

Natasha smiled tautly. *Works every time.*

She waited until the faux section of slope had
begun sliding back into place. Then she pulled her
automatic pistols from their holsters, dropped to the
frozen surface in front of the entrance, and put a
silent bullet in each of the three sentinels.

That left her free to enter the atrium, her feet
moving so fast they barely touched the floor.

When Natasha entered a hostile environment, she
normally had a sense of where she was going. This
wasn't one of those times. Her plan was simply to

stay alive until she found Stark and whoever else was being held captive.

Assuming, of course, that their captors hadn't killed them yet.

Unfortunately, Natasha hadn't made it halfway across the atrium before she attracted energy fire from other watchmen. Violet bursts came at her from two different directions. As it happened, both of them missed.

Tucking and rolling, she crossed her weapons and returned fire. One Tomorrow Man fell over the rail and plummeted six stories to his death. The other one just kept firing.

Self-adjusting force fields linked in a wireless network, Natasha thought as she headed for the enclosed stairwell. *Got to love it.*

She had reached the second floor before another adversary added her energy beam to the first one. Then a third beam joined the party, and a fourth.

Natasha fired back, but it was no use—not with the Tomorrow Men's force fields stopping her bullets. And as quickly as she was moving, their crossfire was closing in on her, making it impossible for her to linger on the second floor.

But if she abandoned it, she was placing herself in even greater danger. Because in the office windows across the atrium she could see the reflection of yet another enemy, standing a floor above her, waiting to skewer her if she went over the rail.

She went over it anyway.

After all, she was the Black Widow, the zenith of Soviet technology. There could have been a hundred of the buggers and they still wouldn't have caught her.

But as Natasha swung up to the floor above her, intending to confront her hidden adversary at close quarters, she found he was gone. It was then that her feeling of invincibility faded, leaving a sinking feeling in its place.

She had known the Tomorrow Men could teleport. Indeed, she had anticipated their doing so since the moment she set foot in the place.

But she had no idea they could do it that *quickly*.

Suddenly, their energy beams were coming at Natasha from a whole new set of angles. She tried to make the adjustment, contort her body so that they all missed.

She almost succeeded. However, one beam proved too difficult to elude.

It spun her around and sent her crashing into the wall behind her. Lurching away from it, she tried to clear her head, get her bearings. But before she could accomplish that, another beam hit her in the ribs.

It knocked all the wind out of her. Gasping for breath, she tried to find her enemies through tear-filled eyes. What she could identify, she fired at, for all the good it did her.

Before long, her clips were empty. And there were Tomorrow Men standing all around her, their rifles trained on her. At this range, they would kill her with a single burst.

"Well," said one of them in a familiar voice, "I can't tell you how sorry I am to see you here."

It was Weyland.

The other Tomorrow Men—Chadaputra, Matsubayashi, and Kosar—were standing on either side of him, armed like their comrades. Obviously, they had teleported themselves there from the Triskelion.

"No doubt," Natasha rasped, "I would be sorry too if someone stumbled on my plot to double-cross the Ultimates."

"Fortunately," Weyland continued, "your teammates are already on a SHIELD heli-carrier, well on their way to the Andes—where, since we have warned Tiber they're coming, they will walk into a trap. And Happy Hogan will be unable to advise them of our disappearance, as we've incapacitated all his communications equipment.

"Of course, we would have preferred to keep a low profile until after the Ultimates were destroyed. However, the difficulty you presented here made it necessary for us to leave the Triskelion prematurely."

"I'm a pest," said Natasha. "It's my nature."

"So I see," said Weyland.

"What about Tony Stark?"

"I wasn't the one who encountered him," said Weyland, "but he's no longer an issue for us."

"So you killed him?" The words were bitter in her mouth, but she had to know.

"No," said Weyland. "Nothing quite so final. But you're not likely to see him again."

"There's no one left to stop you," Natasha observed.

"That's our assessment as well," Weyland told her.

Before the words were out of his mouth, Natasha had slipped between two of the Tomorrow Men and was sprinting for the open door. Her side still hurt and her breath was ragged, but she knew she had to make the attempt.

What's more, she almost made it.

But before Natasha could reach the exit, an energy beam slammed her square in the middle of the back. The next thing she knew, she was lying face-up on the floor, a frigid wind stinging her face—and she was numb from the waist down.

"That was inadvisable," said Weyland, making his way toward her with his rifle in hand.

Get up, Natasha told herself.

Using her arms alone, she pushed herself off the floor.

"You're determined," the Tomorrow Man observed. "History didn't lie in that regard."

Get up, Natasha thought, *and shut his mouth for him.*

But it didn't look like she would get the chance,

because Weyland was already aiming his weapon at her.

The first thing Stark saw as he burst into the atrium of Tiber's stronghold was a knot of nine or ten Tomorrow Men, energy rifles in their hands. The second was a feminine figure lying on the floor in one of SHIELD's whitesuits.

Natasha, he thought, his heart climbing into his throat.

And hers wasn't the only face he recognized. Weyland was looking back at Stark, surprise and anger fighting for control of his features. Clearly, he hadn't expected the armored Ultimate to return after he had been flung into the future.

If you've killed her, Stark had time to promise, *you'll wish Baker's people had gotten hold of you instead.*

Then the Tomorrow Men were firing their bolts of violet energy at him. And Stark, whose batteries were still seething with power because of the barrage they had absorbed, returned their fire.

Two Tomorrow Men went hurtling backward, despite their personal shields. But his next two targets didn't go down so easily, merely staggering under the impact.

They're adjusting, Stark thought, *just as they did back in the Triskelion.*

Applying a sudden burst of thrust, he avoided the beams of the Tomorrow Men who were still standing. But it wasn't easy, since they were coming at him from so many different directions.

Back in the Triskelion, Stark had been able to incapacitate the Tomorrow Men at close range, shields or no shields. He had to try to do that again.

Zeroing in on the closest of his adversaries, he unleashed a series of electromagnetic pulses at the highest intensity he could muster. At first, they only jostled the Tomorrow Man, spoiling his aim. But as Stark got closer, he was able to pound the invader into the wall behind him.

Zagging sharply, he saw the beams that had followed him gouge the wall instead. Then he went after another Tomorrow Man, positioned on the same wall but higher up.

But as Stark soared to reach him, a blast caught him in the shoulder. Without his structural integrity field, it hurt him worse than it should have. Then another energy stream sent him spinning off course. And as he tried to make a correction, a third shot drove him into a rail.

Can't stop, Stark thought, narrowly avoiding a violet beam as he flew off the rail.

But he was still weak from the searing heat he had endured in the Enclave, not to mention all the hits he had absorbed along the way. And as much as he wanted to end the threat of the Tomorrow Men, he was outnumbered and outgunned.

Eventually, the bastards would neutralize him. It was just a matter of time.

Then something bizarre happened. The Tomorrow Man closest to him—the one he had intended to go after—began slapping his neck instead of firing his weapon.

Stark felt like laughing. But instead, he hit the invader with a pulse volley, sending him sprawling.

Looking back over his shoulder, he saw a red, white, and blue shield collapse a Tomorrow Man across the atrium. Then another fell victim to a dark blur. A third one sprouted an arrow. And a fourth appeared to slip, banging his head on the rail to stunning effect.

One of the two remaining Tomorrow Men fired at the owner of the shield. *Big mistake,* Stark thought.

At the same time, he saw Weyland reach for the teleportation control on the inside of his sleeve. Rocketing at him with all the speed in his plasma thrusters, Stark emitted a stream of pulses.

They jarred Weyland, but not enough to keep him from firing back. Raising his rifle, he took aim at his enemy—whereupon Stark executed the maneuver he *wished* he had executed back in the Triskelion.

Pulling up short, he bent backward into a loop— thereby eluding the energy beam with which Weyland meant to spear him. Then he completed the loop and came around for another pass.

Too slow to react, the Tomorrow Man went down under the force of Stark's tackle, losing his grip on his rifle. It clattered across the floor and stopped ten feet away from him.

Of course, there was a chance he had other weapons in his suit. So, still embroiled with Weyland, Stark hauled off and struck him—hard enough to knock him out. But the Tomorrow Man remained in control of his senses.

"You can't beat me," Weyland said, spitting blood at his adversary. "I've got the future on my side."

"I've got news for you," Stark told him, recalling the codes he had sent to Baker. "Your future is about to become history."

Then he hit Weyland again, snapping his head around, and this time the Tomorrow Man went limp.

He was still breathing, still alive. But he wasn't going to do any conquering in the near future.

Finally, Stark was able to take a look at Natasha. She was lying on the floor, still as death.

Please be all right, he thought.

Thor hovered in the frosty air of the unheated hangar, his breath snaking from his nostrils and freezing on his moustache, and got his first glimpse of what Stark had called a temporal portal.

It yawned in front of him, a black flower, a fountain of liquid ebony. And if he watched closely enough he could see it grow, albeit in tiny increments, its hold increasing on Midgard's reality with each passing moment.

Somewhere beneath it were the engines that had helped to create it, working to open a passage from Thor's time to that of the Tomorrow Men. But the machines were hidden below the floor. All Thor could see was the rising, spreading darkness.

He was reminded of Mimir's Well at the outskirts of frozen Jotunheim. It too was black as pitch, and offered those brave enough to pay the giant's price a glimpse of the shadowy yet-to-be.

Indeed, if he waited long enough, he would see the future—in the form of the tyrannical elite on whose behalf the Tomorrow Men had labored. They would come pouring into this world from their own, a flood of human poison, carrying with them the wizardry to dominate this era as they had dominated their own.

But Thor was a god. He too wielded power, the kind mortals found it difficult to wrap their brains around. In fact, prior to his epiphany in the insane asylum, he himself had been unable to accept the things he could do.

Or who he was.

He had that trouble no longer. He marshaled the lightning of heaven with ease and familiarity, and even a measure of affection.

It was his tool, just like Mjolnir. His birthright, established with his first mewling scream at the gray, shrugging skies. It was what he *did*.

And he did it *now,* absorbing electricity from the air around him as if he were one of Stark's batteries, and then unleashing it through his hammer in a paroxysm of blue fury.

It plunged into the dark blossom below him as he had seen the world-serpent plunge into the sea, invading the portal's deepest depths, forcing its light down the thing's immense maw. And there it strove with the energies that powered the time-gate, striking at them with the force of its splendor, stabbing at them with the unbridled savagery of the storm.

Like a living thing, the portal struck back, sending shoots of black energy up at the source of its torment. But they didn't reach far enough to touch the son of Odin, or to stop him.

So he stuck another blue-white dagger into its heart. And another. And grudgingly, the maelstrom began to succumb. It shriveled, collapsed in on itself, and finally blinked out of existence.

Leaving nothing in its wake, as if it had never been there at all. Thor was pleased.

This world belonged to the mortals of the twenty-first century. He wasn't going to let any so-called Tomorrow Men take it away from them.

Kneeling beside Natasha, Stark brushed her hair away from her face. Then he flipped back his mask and listened to her chest.

Her heart was beating. He could feel it, strong and determined.

Thank God. As if to reassure him, her lids fluttered open. Her eyes looked tired, unfocused, but as beautiful as ever as they took in the sight of him.

"What do you think you're doing?" she muttered.

"Saving your rear end," said Stark. "Weyland looked as if he was about to demolish it, and the rest of you along with it."

"Actually," said Natasha, her voice slow and sluggish, "I was luring him into a false sense of security." She tried to move and winced in pain. "Though I may have done too good a job of it."

"Something broken?"

"It would be easier to tell you what's still intact. At least I'm starting to feel my legs again." She looked past him at their teammates. "What the hell are *they* doing here?"

"When I got here, I contacted Fury, who was on a heli-carrier over the Andes. I told him not to go ahead with the mission, which was a trap—and also to send reinforcements."

Natasha stared at him for a moment. Then she said, "Thor teleported them here. Of course." Her brow pinched. "But where the hell were *you?*"

"In the future," said Stark, "remarkable as it sounds. I'll tell you all about it sometime."

"What about Sitwell and the others?"

"At least some of them are still alive—locked up

two levels down, if my aural sensors aren't deceiving me. I would have freed them, except I didn't want to tip the Tomorrow Men to my presence here."

Natasha looked up at him for a moment. Then, without warning, she pulled his face down to hers and kissed him.

"What happened to 'Let's be comrades?'" he asked.

"Who said *that?*"

"I believe it was you."

"It must have been one of your other women."

"Right now," Stark said, "I can't think of any other women," and kissed her again.

"What the hell . . . ?" someone said.

It was Barton. And the reason for his exclamation was clear.

Each of the Tomorrow Men was disappearing into his or her own small, swirling blackness. And there was nothing the Ultimates could do about it but watch.

Until, a moment later, the invaders were all gone.

Thor emerged into the atrium, joining his comrades. "Obviously," he said, "the Tomorrow Men didn't need a portal to retrieve so few."

"Obviously," Barton echoed, looking a little creeped out by the manner of his adversaries' disappearance.

"You think they'll try again?" Pietro asked.

"Of course," said Rogers. "What have they got to lose? All they have to do is approach us earlier in our timeline. And if they fail, they can do it again. And again."

"Until they get it right," Thor suggested.

Jan shook her head. "I don't think so. I think there was something optimum about the moment in which they came to us."

"She's right," said Stark, helping Natasha sit up. "Otherwise, why choose *our* branch of the timeline over all the others available to them?"

"Then maybe," said Jan, "their next move will be against another branch. The one that gives them their next best shot."

"In that case," said Rogers, "I hope whoever's watching over it is ready for them."

Epilogue

"YOU'RE KIDDING," SAID BANNER.

On the other side of the transparent barrier, Betty Ross shook her head. "You didn't hear it from me, but Fury wasn't happy with the way things went down in the Caucasus. He says we need more firepower, especially if Thor decides to leave us flat someday, which—considering Goldilocks's politics—could happen without a moment's notice."

The scientist was almost afraid to embrace the news. "So he needs more super-people. And he wants *me* to work on them."

"Also Hank Pym," said Betty. "In fact, he wants

you to work on them together. That's not a problem, is it?"

Banner wanted desperately to feel useful again. He would have worked alongside Hannibal Lechter.

"Not at all," he said.

"Good. Because Fury thinks he can get the money in the next couple of months. And he wants to see Pym gainfully employed, considering how helpful he was vis-à-vis the Tomorrow Men."

Banner understood. If not for Pym, Natasha would never have gone to the Caucasus and given Stark the help he needed to wreck the Tomorrow Men's plan.

He was more surprised about his own inclusion in the project. After all, he had been one of the first to trust the Tomorrow Men. But eventually, *everyone* had trusted them. And Banner had been smart enough to keep his mouth shut when he saw Pym pull up communications logs instead of blood analyses.

In any case, he wasn't going to look a gift horse in the mouth. Not when he got so few of them.

Betty tilted her head as if to appraise Banner from a different angle. "You know," she said, "I haven't seen that smile in quite a while. You know, the one where the corner of your mouth goes up."

He shrugged. "It's been a while since I had a *reason* to smile."

She regarded the scientist a moment longer. Then

she said, "I think you need a reason to smile more often . . . if you know what I mean."

Whereupon Betty did something she hadn't done in years. She *winked* at him—just before she glanced at her watch, mumbled something, and took off.

As Banner watched her leave, he thought, *Sometimes life doesn't suck so badly after all.*

Tony Stark opened his eyes.

He was in the bedroom of his penthouse, looking out at the towers of Manhattan. In the east, a spectacular dawn was breaking. It painted the windows of the skyscrapers with golden light, making them look as if they were on fire.

It's a beautiful city, the billionaire thought. He wanted it to stay that way, always.

Natasha squirmed beside him, laid her head in the hollow of his shoulder. "You awake?" she asked.

"No," he told her. "Still sleeping, apparently. And having the most remarkable dream."

"What about?"

"A night of fiery, unrelenting passion. The stuff of which legends are made."

She smiled. "Now I know why they call you Iron Man." She ran her fingers through the hair on his chest. "No doubt, you've heard that line before."

"Never from anyone as beautiful as you," he told her.

"Such a silver tongue. Should I believe it?"

"Without question."

She purred. "I like the sound of that."

Without warning, Natasha sat up and pulled one of the covers around her. Then she got out of bed, gave Stark a wink, and said, "I'll be right back."

Her bare feet made tiny slapping noises as she made her way across the floor. They ended in the vicinity of a place he knew all too well—his liquor alcove.

"Martini," she said, "right?"

He shook his head. "No thanks."

She looked at him as if he had grown another head. "Are you feeling all right?"

They had beaten the Tomorrow Men, foiled their scheme to hand over the present to the privileged elite of the future. They had turned away an invader nearly as powerful as the alien Chitauri.

It was over.

And then again, it *wasn't*.

"It's my fault," he told her.

"I beg your pardon?"

"The state of the future," he explained. "The poverty, the violence, the oppression. All on my head."

Natasha chuckled appreciatively. "You've got some ego, you know that? Maybe somebody else deserves some of the credit."

"I saw the Stark logo on the sleeves of those security men. It wasn't a coincidence."

"Wait a second," she said, returning to bed. "The Tomorrow Men came from a different timeline. They said as much. So that's not our future."

"If it could happen in their timeline," said Stark, "it could happen in ours as well."

"So what are you supposed to do about it? Or *not* do about it?"

"I don't know," he said, smiling bitterly. "And therein lies the problem."

She shook her head. "No, Tony. There's no problem. Because in this timeline, you've received a warning. You know what to expect. And with that knowledge under your belt, you can avoid whatever mistakes you might have made in that other timeline."

"But how will I know they're mistakes?" he asked. "What if I always do what I think is right, but inadvertently make the choice that gets us into trouble?"

"What if I die tomorrow?"

In their line of work, it was always a possibility. "I'd miss you," Stark told her in all sincerity.

"My *point,*" Natasha said, "is there are no guarantees in this world. All you can do is forge ahead and hope for the best."

"I can't do that," he said. "It's not in my nature."

"I know," she said, "I've seen the documentary. Tony Stark is a human dynamo. Tony Stark won't take no for an answer. Tony Stark gets things done when no one else can. And why is that, I ask you?

Why are you the first, second, and third richest men in the history of the universe?"

"Actually," he said, "I'm the—"

"Because," she said, refusing to be distracted, "you don't second-guess yourself. You do the right thing and you don't look back. And you know, the more I think about it, the more I wonder if in forging that bleak future you saw, Stark International might have avoided an even *bleaker* future."

He felt as if his feet had been knocked out from under him. *I hadn't considered that.*

"What if Weyland's world isn't the worst-case scenario? What if it would have been even more nightmarish except for the relentless vigilance of Tony Stark?"

He shook his head. "That doesn't mean I can sit back and let things happen."

"Then don't. Oversee every little detail—you're going to do that anyway. Just don't fret about it." She traced a line from his temple to his jaw with the tip of her finger. "You'll get worry lines."

He had to admit that she made sense. "What did I do to deserve you?" he asked.

"Maybe you haven't done it yet," she suggested. "Time is a funny thing, you know."

He looked into her eyes. "Really."

"I have it on good authority."

Stark kissed her. He had no choice. But even then, the future invaded his thoughts.

He saw Baker and Torricelli hunkered down in the overgrown, rubble-strewn streets, ducking blast after blast, fighting a war they couldn't hope to win. But *he* could.

Stark had always been concerned with his legacy, how he would be judged by generations to come. But he had reason now to be even *more* concerned. He needed to go at his job even harder, take it even more seriously, because it wasn't just a matter of how people remembered him anymore. It was bigger than that.

As big as any aspiration Man had ever had. Because as Stark had seen, all those aspirations could come to nothing.

So he would wake each day thinking of the future, and do everything in his power to steer it in the right direction. *Every day,* he vowed, *without fail.*

But he would start tomorrow.

Today, he reflected, drinking in the heady nearness of Natasha, *I've got other things on my mind.*

Acknowledgments

I remember being eight years old, holding the first issue of *The Avengers* in my hands (my reward for not kvetching too much about the tooth I'd just had pulled), and thinking *Hmm, what's this?* Like many Marvel comics of its day, its cover was irresistible—a confrontation between Loki, god of evil, and a cadre of solo protagonists who had come together as "Earth's Mightiest Super Heroes."

You could just feel the resolve, the animosity, the power about to be unleashed. But then, that cover was penciled by Jack "King" Kirby, whose work was so visceral it leaped off the page, grabbed you by the throat, and left marks for days afterward.

But the real attraction, in my preadolescent mind,

was the prospect of seeing Thor (my favorite Marvel character), Iron Man, the Hulk, Ant Man, and the Wasp all in the same comic—not only then, but for months to come. And who was better equipped to direct this production than Stan Lee, the most exciting writer/editor in comics, whose fertile imagination had birthed all these characters in the first place.

I could barely wrap my head around the possibilities.

Flash forward about forty years. I'm a lot more than eight years old, and by now—inspired by titles like *The Avengers*—I've written almost two hundred comics myself, so it takes a lot to impress me. But I'm holding the first issue of *The Ultimates* in my hands and thinking, *Hmm, what's this?*

Writer Mark Millar and pencil artist Bryan Hitch (with Andrew Currie on inks, madman Chris Eliopoulos on letters, and Paul Mounts on colors) had breathed new life into the *Avengers* concept, making it more sophisticated, more ambivalent, more realistic. Again, I could barely wrap my head around the possibilities.

Then my editor at Pocket Books, Margaret Clark, called me with an offer. She wanted me to write a novel based on *The Ultimates,* filling in the gap between volumes one and two. *Obviously,* I thought, *there is a God, and he's a comic fan.*

So let me thank Margaret, along with Marvel Creative Services for giving me this absolute plum of an assignment; Lee, Kirby, and *The Ultimates'* creative team for building such a great sandbox; artist Don Heck for designing the original Wasp, Hawkeye, and Black Widow characters; and Joe Simon for (along with Jack Kirby) creating the iconic Captain America back in the forties. Not to mention Bob Greenberger, who gave me my first comic scripting assignment ever.

I couldn't have done it without you guys. And now, with your indulgence, I'm going to say something I've always wanted to say: "Excelsior, True Believer!"

Whew. I hope that was as good for you as it was for me.

—MJF